Praise for
STROKE OF MIDNIGHT

"Drake's flair for mystery, blended with humor and passion, will delight readers . . . utterly enchanting."

—*RT Book Reviews*

"A compelling romance filled with intrigue."

—*Affaire de Coeur*

"Another wonderfully written novel by Olivia Drake."

—My Book Addiction

IF THE SLIPPER FITS

"Filled with romance, breathtaking passion, and a dash of mystery that will leave you wanting more."

—*Night Owl Reviews*

"A dash of danger and a dash of fairy tale in the form of a very special pair of shoes add to the romance plot, filling out *If the Slipper Fits* nicely." —*Romance Junkies*

"Cinderella knew it was all about the shoes, and so does master storyteller Drake as she kicks off the Cinderella Sisterhood with a tale filled with gothic overtones, sensuality, sprightly dialogue, emotion, an engaging cast, and a beautiful pair of perfectly fitting slippers."

—*RT Book Reviews* (4 stars)

"I was enchanted with this story as Olivia Drake took the residents of Castle Kevern *and* this reader on an emotional, delightful journey. A magical fairy tale deserving to be read and read again!"

—*Once Upon a Romance*

Praise for Olivia Drake's Heiress in London series

SCANDAL OF THE YEAR

"The final installment of the Crompton sisters' trilogy is as charming, sweet, humorous, and poignant as any of Drake's previous books. Marked by her fine storytelling and engaging characters, this volume stands alone, but fans familiar with the series will revel in the conclusion." —*RT Book Reviews* (5 stars)

"An intricate plot with roots far in the past. The threads of mendacity revealed in the previous books are strengthened, then revealed in their entirety as the story progresses, bringing the series to a satisfying conclusion filled with danger and, of course, romance."

—*Fresh Fiction*

NEVER TRUST A ROGUE

"Olivia Drake will keep readers coming back for more."

—*Publishers Weekly*

"Drake is a consummate storyteller who cleverly blends intrigue, suspense, and sensuality into a pulse-pounding mystery, à la Amanda Quick. Give yourself plenty of time to savor this fast-paced, non-stop delight of a book." —*RT Book Reviews* (Top Pick, 4½ stars)

SEDUCING THE HEIRESS

"This book has it all: a fabulous hero, a wonderful heroine, and sizzling passion. Read it and watch the sparks fly!"

—Christina Dodd

"Guaranteed to seduce readers everywhere. This book is something truly special, an unforgettable story filled with passion, intrigue, and sweep-you-away romance."

—Susan Wiggs

"This decadent Regency romance is carried along by a spunky heroine and sumptuous descriptions of upper-class life. . . . There's enough glitz to keep readers coming back."

—*Publishers Weekly*

"Drake entices readers [and] twists the traditional with an unconventional heroine and a bad-boy hero that readers will adore."

—*RT Book Reviews*

"Drake takes what could be a been-there, read-that story of a scheming scoundrel and a headstrong hoyden, and weaves a tale of wit, seduction, secrets, and sensuality that's as vibrant as it is refreshing."

—Michelle Buonfiglio's Romance: B(u)y the Book®

Also by Olivia Drake

The Cinderella Sisterhood series

Stroke of Midnight

If the Slipper Fits

Heiress in London series

Scandal of the Year

Never Trust a Rogue

Seducing the Heiress

Abducted by a Prince

OLIVIA DRAKE

St. Martin's Paperbacks

ABDUCTED BY A PRINCE

For information address St. Martin's Press, 175 Fifth Avenue, New York, NY 10010.

ISBN: 978-1-250-00210-5

Printed in the United States of America

St. Martin's Paperbacks edition / May 2014

St. Martin's Paperbacks are published by St. Martin's Press, 175 Fifth Avenue, New York, NY 10010.

10 9 8 7 6 5 4 3 2 1

Chapter 1

"This is a travesty," said Walt Stratham, Viscount Greaves. "I demand a rematch at once."

"We'll discuss the matter in private." Noting the curious glances from several club members in the corridor, Damien Burke ushered the irate man into his study and closed the door.

The spacious chamber featured a claw-footed desk on a Persian rug, the finest that money could buy. At this late hour, the tall windows showed pinpricks of light against the darkness of the city. The scent of leather bindings came from the bookcase behind the desk. On the opposite wall, a gently hissing fire warded off the February chill.

No expense had been spared on the décor. Damien had fought long and hard to acquire the trappings of the upper crust. While his fellow Eton graduates had inherited their wealth, he had started out with nothing. He had accrued his own fortune, first by his skill at gambling, and then by prudent investments in shipping, property, and this club.

With ruthless resolve, he had built Demon's Den into

the most fashionable gaming site in London. Here, gold flowed freely from the pockets of the aristocrats into his coffers. If the nobility barred him from their drawing rooms, then by God, he would make them pay for the privilege of occupying *his* establishment.

In particular, this man.

Ignoring the pair of chairs by the hearth, Damien strolled to the desk, took a brown leather pouch from his pocket, and tossed it onto the polished surface. The ivory counters inside made a satisfying clink.

The viscount glowered at the sack. No wonder. The sum of his losses represented a full five years' worth of his quarterly allowance from his father, the Earl of Pennington. The earl had a reputation as a harsh, miserly man. With the expense of launching a daughter into society in the coming season, Lord Pennington wouldn't be amenable to making loans to his profligate eldest son.

Walt faced a grim future hounded by creditors. Not even his status as heir to an earldom would save him. His only recourse would be to agree to the terms that Damien would present to him in a moment.

But first, Damien wanted to savor his victory.

He purposely took his time opening the sack. Walt had changed little since their school days; he still exuded the inborn superiority of the upper class. But now the hazel eyes beneath a thatch of ginger hair revealed a telltale trace of panic. Over the years Damien had taught himself to read the nuances of mannerisms that betrayed a man's thoughts. A slight tic or nervous gesture, a tapping of the fingers or the lifting of an eyebrow, all served as clues to the cards in his hands.

Damien had employed that talent tonight to reel in his prey. He had craved this moment for over fifteen years. However, unlike the hotheaded schoolboy he had once been, he kept his expression cool and his emotions disciplined.

He poured the little discs into a heap on the desk and began to stack them into neat piles. He didn't really need to add up the counters; he already knew the precise amount of his winnings. Rather, the action was designed to further fray Walt's nerves.

"It's time to settle your debt," Damien stated. "There's paper and pen for you to write a bank draft to me."

Walt made no move to avail himself of the quill and inkpot placed at the corner of the desk. He elevated his chin to a disdainful angle. "The devil you say! If you were a gentleman, you'd grant me the chance to win back my funds."

"I'm afraid that wasn't our agreement. It was winner take all."

"Only because I thought—"

"You thought I'd be an easy mark." *Just as I was at Eton.* Damien had been small for his age back then, alone in the world, a charity student among the hordes of privileged boys from the best families.

Walt nervously gripped the lapels of his forest-green coat. "This is your club. You must have rigged the game."

Damien gave him a caustic smile. Walt had always been quick to blame his own failings on others, particularly those he considered to be his social inferiors. He would never have dared to fling such an insulting accusation at a fellow gentleman. As much as Damien would have liked to avenge the slur with his fists, he knew that violence would be antithetical to his purpose.

"I allowed *you* to deal each hand," he said. "So if there was any cheating at all, it must have been done by *you*."

"What blather! You marked the cards somehow."

"And you inspected the deck before the game

commenced. Now, enough of your excuses." Damien nudged the paper and pen toward him. "Write the bank draft."

Walt shifted from one foot to the other. "There's no point," he said sullenly. "I haven't sufficient funds in my account."

They were making headway, at least, since he appeared to have abandoned his false accusation of cheating. He would soon realize that Damien had no interest in fleecing Walt.

At least not of his money.

Damien strolled to the chair behind the desk. "Ask your father for a loan, then."

"Absolutely not! He despises gambling."

"Indeed? Then it seems you're in quite the quandary."

Walt groped for the quill and jammed the sharpened tip into the silver inkpot. "I'll write you an IOU if I must," he said through gritted teeth. "That will have to suffice."

"No. I'm afraid it won't. Let me be perfectly clear. I will have my payment before the week is out."

"Blast you!" Walt tossed down the pen so that black ink spattered the paper. "If you intend for me to sign my soul over to some dodgy moneylender, think again!"

Damien seated himself in the desk chair and steepled his fingers beneath his chin. The time had come to get an answer to the question burning inside him. "Very well," he said. "Since you have no funds, I'll allow you to repay me in another way."

"How? Tell me."

The hint of desperate hope in the man's voice gratified Damien. "You have something of mine in your possession. If you return it, I'll forgive the entire debt."

Walt frowned. "Something of *yours*? Why, I've scarcely seen you since we left Eton over ten years ago."

"You stole it from me while we were at school. If you rack your brain, perhaps you'll recall the incident."

Damien certainly did. The memories of that long-ago time burned like a canker inside him. An impoverished orphan, he had been taunted and bullied by the other boys. Perhaps his situation wouldn't have been so dire had he hailed from a highborn family that had fallen on hard times. But his ancestry had been—and still was—an utter mystery.

A matronly woman he'd called Mimsy had raised him in a tiny flat in the London borough of Southwark. Mrs. Mims had taught him proper speech along with a rigorous slate of academic lessons. Perhaps that was why, even as a small boy, Damien sensed he was different. He didn't fit in with the scruffy, unschooled children who ran free in the neighborhood. At times, Mimsy hinted that his father had royal blood. She spun tales of princely heroes slaying dragons and told him that he, too, must always be brave. As he grew older, he began to ask questions about his absent parents. Mimsy would offer only a vague story that he'd been given to her for safekeeping.

If he probed too persistently, her face took on a worried look that soon silenced him. Not even to satisfy his curiosity would he distress Mimsy. She was all he had in the world.

One day, they boarded the mail coach to Windsor and visited Eton College, where he sat in a stuffy room and took a long examination with numerous written essays and pages of mathematics problems. Afterward, she consulted with one of the headmasters in an ivy-covered building while Damien waited on the stone steps outside, watching the older boys walk past in chattering groups. They looked posh and unapproachable in their formal garb, making him keenly aware of his own shabby attire. When Mimsy came out, she informed him that he had been accepted as a pupil at the boarding school. He protested vehemently at the notion of being left among strangers, but Mimsy was adamant.

Before leaving, she placed a delicate gold chain around his neck. From it dangled a small iron key which he was told to hide beneath his shirt. "I've been waiting for the right moment to give this to you, my little prince. When I took you in as a babe, it was tucked in your blankets."

The key fascinated Damien as he examined it closely. "Did it belong to my father?" he asked. "Where is the lock that it fits?"

"You'll learn everything someday. It's all written down in a letter. In the meanwhile, you must guard the key. Never, ever show it to anyone. You're to study hard and make me proud." After a tearful hug and the promise of holiday visits, Mimsy trudged out the school gate.

Never to return.

Just before Christmas, the headmaster informed Damien that Mrs. Mims had died from a sudden illness. The news was delivered coldly, without a care that Mimsy was the only mother Damien had ever known.

After lessons that day, he stole outside so that no one would witness his tears. It was bad enough to be taunted for being a charity pupil without adding "sniveling infant" to the list of his sins. He sat among the barren rhododendron bushes with his back to the wall of the cloisters. The wintry cold bit through his short coat, and eventually, his grief spent, he scrubbed his sleeve over his damp face.

Reaching into his stiff-collared shirt, he drew out the key and traced it with his fingertip. One end had three teeth, the other end a little brass crown stamped into the iron and surrounded by a design of curlicues.

With Mimsy gone, this key was the sole link to his past. But she had never explained its significance. Did the crown verify her claim that he had royal blood? Damien wanted to believe it. He wished with all his might that he was a prince with enough riches to draw envy from all the other boys. Perhaps the key opened the door to a treasure room in a castle somewhere.

Visions of gold crowns and heaps of glittering jewels filled his imagination. Then another thought absorbed him. Maybe his father, the king, was imprisoned there, waiting for his son to rescue him . . .

The scrape of footsteps yanked him out of the fantasy. Damien froze with the key clenched in his fingers.

Walt Stratham approached with two of his hulking cronies. From the moment of Damien's arrival, they had singled him out for their tormenting. "Hey," Walt called. "Is that a necklace you're wearing? You must be a girl in disguise."

While the other boys chortled, one of them imitating mincing feminine steps, Damien stuffed the key back inside his shirt. Too late.

Walt made a wild grab for the gold chain. "Give me that."

Damien sprang from the ground in a flurry of punching and kicking. Frantic to protect the precious key, he threw all of his puny strength into the fight. His fist connected with Walt's nose, sending him staggering backward, blood trickling down his face.

It was the perfect chance to flee, but a fury born of grief transformed Damien into a wild beast. He lunged at the other two boys. He managed a few quick strikes before the pair of them joined forces to overpower him. They threw him to the rocky ground and held his squirming form in place.

In the throes of raw rage, he forgot all caution,

shouting, "Let me go! I'm a prince! My father is a king, and he'll chop off your heads."

A moment of stunned silence reigned. Then derisive laughter burst from the trio of boys. "King?" one jeered. "You don't even have a father."

His nose bloody, Walt bared his teeth in a sneer. "You're a filthy bastard." He grabbed the key, snapping its gold chain. "Your sire must be the Devil. That's what we'll call you. The Demon Prince."

"Well, Burke? Speak up! Tell me what it is you want from me."

Walt's voice dragged Damien back to the present. He sat behind the desk in the private study at his club, facing his longtime nemesis. Viscount Greaves stood with his fists clenched at his sides. His irate hazel eyes betrayed his impatience to settle the gaming debt and be gone.

Apparently, Walt didn't remember the incident; it had been only one of their many clashes at Eton before Damien had grown big and strong enough to best any challenger.

"You took a key from me when I was a first-year," he said tightly. "You and two of your mates overpowered me behind the cloisters."

"Key?" Awareness dawned on Walt's face, followed by a narrowing of his eyes in a guarded expression. "You're saying you'd erase my losses in exchange for some long-lost trinket? You must be mad."

"Nevertheless, you'll bring it to me."

"Good God, man, that must have been fifteen years ago! You can't expect me to recall what happened to it. I likely tossed it into a rubbish bin."

"That isn't what you said back then. You used to

taunt me that you'd put the key where I'd never find it."

"So? Wherever it is, I've forgotten now."

As he spoke, Walt averted his gaze. His avoidance of a direct look was a clear indicator of deception.

Damien felt his gut tighten with absolute certainty. Walt was lying. He *did* know the location of the key.

"It would behoove you to remember, then," Damien said. "It's your only chance to have your gaming debt forgiven."

Walt's resentful gaze slid back. "Why do you want a damned key?" he asked. "Does it fit a strongbox somewhere? It wouldn't surprise me to learn that you were harboring stolen goods even back then."

Damien kept his face wiped clean of anger. "You *will* retrieve the key. I'll give you until tomorrow evening to bring it to me."

"It might take longer than that," Walt said, a crafty glint entering his eyes.

"Don't even think to trick me. I remember every detail of that key, and I'll know if it's a forgery." Damien paused for dramatic effect. "If you fail to fulfill your end of the bargain, you'll force me to find another means to collect your debt—a manner that won't be to your liking."

"What is that supposed to mean?"

Damien allowed a cold smile. "You have a sister about to make her debut. Innocent, sheltered girls are often susceptible to the charms of a dashing stranger."

The viscount's face paled so that his freckles stood out. "By God! You wouldn't dare go anywhere near Beatrice."

"Then do as I say. Bring me that key."

Walt's chest heaved beneath his forest-green coat,

his nostrils flaring. Abruptly, he slammed his fist onto the desk and rattled the neat stacks of gaming discs. "Bastard! You may don the trappings of a gentleman, but you'll always be an upstart from the gutter."

Pivoting on his well-shod heel, he threw open the door and stomped out of the study.

Bastard.

Damien surged up from the chair and stalked to the window to stare out into the night. That word never failed to cause a visceral twist inside him. His ancestry had always been a blank slate. Deep inside him burned the need to give substance to his background. To learn who he really was. Not just for his own sake, but for Lily's.

His chest tightened. His daughter was only six years of age, but someday she would ask him questions about her absent grandparents. She would want to know who they were, where they had come from, why they had abandoned him. Mimsy had mentioned a letter that explained everything, presumably from his parents, but he had never been given her effects after her death. Nor had he found the letter years later, when he'd gone back to his old neighborhood and sought to discover what had happened to her belongings. Without Mimsy, the only person who might have provided the answers, he had no clue to his past.

Except for that key.

The shuffle of footsteps sounded behind him. Reflected in the window glass, a short, bandy-legged servant stepped into the study. Light from the gas wall sconces glinted off a head as bald as a billiard ball. Finn MacNab had once been a man-of-all-work at Eton, and Damien's sole ally at the school. He and his wife were the only ones to whom Damien had confided his secrets.

At the moment, however, Damien had no desire for

company. Turning, he said curtly, "I trust you didn't have your ear to the door."

Finn bared his teeth in a grin. "Might have, though I couldna hear it all," he said in his thick Scottish brogue. "Did his lairdship recollect wha' happened t' the key?"

"He hemmed and hawed. But he knows, I'm certain of it."

"Then he'll bring it t' ye on the morrow?"

"He has little choice in the matter."

Finn waggled a bushy eyebrow. "Beggin' yer pardon, sir, but these high-and-mighty lairds do hold the upper hand over us mortals."

"Not this time." Damien paused, his resolve hardening in regard to the bold plan that he had formulated. "If he fails to comply, I'll abduct his sister. The key shall be her ransom."

Chapter 2

As the footman headed up the staircase in the entrance hall, Miss Eloise Stratham stood in the doorway of the antechamber and felt the weight of misconduct lying heavily on her shoulders. She shivered from the chill in the air and wished she hadn't surrendered her cloak to the servant. Why had she allowed herself to be talked into making this call?

She had been caught off guard, that was why. Without warning, her cousin had instructed the coachman to stop. There had been little time for Ellie to voice an argument against it.

The moment the footman vanished upstairs, she turned to address her younger cousin, who strolled around the elegant room, examining the objets d'art on display. "We shouldn't be here," Ellie hissed. "This is entirely too forward of you."

Lady Beatrice Stratham looked up from her inspection of an alabaster dish on a table. She might have been a princess in the pastel-blue gown with its lace trimming. With a wave of her kid-gloved hand, she said, "Not another dreary lecture, Ellie. We're here and that's that."

"But it's beyond the pale to call on a lady you've never met, let alone one who is a pillar of society. You're not even officially out of the schoolroom yet."

"Oh, pooh, I'll be making my debut in a matter of weeks." Beatrice went to a gilt-framed mirror to preen at her reflection. She removed her bonnet and dropped it on a table, then primped her strawberry-blond hair. "Speaking of which, I intend to secure the most brilliant match of the season. Lady Milford can help me accomplish that."

The zeal in her cousin's blue eyes spelled trouble for Ellie. Beatrice was far too headstrong for her own good. When she wanted something, she always found a devious means to achieve her desire. The girl had been a constant headache ever since Ellie had lost her parents and had come to live in the household of her uncle, the Earl of Pennington.

"If his lordship finds out about this visit, he'll be furious," Ellie warned. "You know what a stickler he is for propriety. Since you're only seventeen, he might very well decide to postpone your season for another year."

Beatrice loosed a trill of laughter. "Don't be silly, I can always persuade Papa. Besides, he's at White's, and he won't return home for hours." Clearly bored with the quarrel, she glided toward a pedestal in the corner. "I say, have you ever seen such an exquisite Chinese vase? Lady Milford has truly impeccable taste."

Ellie remained standing by one of the green marble pillars that flanked the doorway. She longed to stalk out of this house, climb back into the waiting brougham, and leave Beatrice to her own folly. Regrettably, she could do nothing of the sort. Uncle Basil was depending on her to see to the well-being of his motherless daughter.

Over the years Ellie had fallen into the role of governess to the younger two of her three cousins. Devoting herself to that task, along with doing errands for her grandmother, made her feel less of a burden on her uncle. She had always been acutely aware that the earl had been obliged to settle the debts of his younger brother, her late father. Consequently, Ellie had worked hard to repay her uncle with her labor. Now, with Cedric off at boarding school, she had only the mission of guiding Beatrice's launch into society.

Begging favors of the exalted Lady Milford was hardly an auspicious means to achieve that purpose. One mistake, one thoughtless comment, and the foolish girl might see herself ostracized. And Ellie feared that she herself would be held to blame.

Worse, if Beatrice's season were postponed, that would mean another year's delay to Ellie's plan for her own future. Nothing disheartened her more than the notion of being forever dependent on her uncle's charity. At the age of six-and-twenty, she yearned to claim her independence and pursue her secret dreams.

The footman descended the stairs, bypassed Ellie, and bowed to Beatrice. "Her ladyship will see you now. If you'll follow me."

So much for hoping that Lady Milford wouldn't be home to them.

Resigned, Ellie took the tail end of the procession up the staircase. The servant hadn't even glanced at her, but Ellie was accustomed to not being noticed in social situations. Her dowdy attire marked her as a woman of reduced circumstances. Anonymity suited her, for if no one paid her any heed, she was free to watch people's expressions and mannerisms, to store them in her memory for future reference.

No one had the slightest inkling how she used those observations. Nor would they anytime soon. Ellie had kept secret the project she toiled on late each night in the privacy of her bedchamber. The family would learn of it only at the appropriate moment.

After Beatrice's betrothal and wedding.

Reaching the top of the stairs, Ellie told herself to stop fretting. Perhaps this meeting might prove fruitful for Beatrice, after all. Lady Milford *did* have a reputation as a matchmaker, having discreetly arranged a number of successful marriages among the nobility.

Ellie strove to recall everything she'd heard about the woman. People spoke of Lady Milford with awe and admiration. A legendary beauty, she had the ear of the prime minister as well as the royal family. According to rumor, she had once been mistress to one of mad King George's many sons.

That scandalous tidbit tweaked Ellie's curiosity. Despite having a shocking past, the lady commanded respect in the highest circles. How had she managed to foil the gossips? Ellie didn't know, but one thing was certain. Lady Milford's life must have been far more exciting than Ellie's was at present.

They proceeded along a sumptuous corridor and into a sitting room decorated in pleasing pastel shades of rose and yellow. There, a woman sat reading in a gilt chair by the window. A ray of winter sunshine crowned her upswept black hair and illuminated the deep claret silk of her gown.

Ellie realized at once that hearsay hadn't prepared her for Lady Milford. There was an elusive, ageless quality to that smooth face and slim figure. Seeing those high cheekbones and arresting features made Ellie long for a pencil to capture that classic beauty on paper.

As the footman announced them, Lady Milford set down her book and rose to her feet. With feline grace, she came forward to greet them. A slight smile curved her lips, though her aristocratic bearing spoke more of impeccable manners than warm welcome.

She must be wondering why two strangers had come to interrupt her afternoon, Ellie knew in dismay. It was clear Lady Milford possessed a sophistication that Beatrice lacked. Such a woman wouldn't be easily cajoled by a girl barely out of the schoolroom.

Apparently feeling no such misgivings herself, Beatrice dipped a pretty curtsy. "My lady, what a *great* pleasure it is to meet you. I hope you don't find me too presumptuous in calling here."

"I confess, you have me intrigued," Lady Milford murmured. "Pray sit down, both of you, and warm yourselves on this chilly day."

She escorted them to the hearth, where a fire radiated heat beneath a mantel of carved white marble. As Beatrice seated herself in the center of a chaise, she narrowed her eyes at Ellie in a warning glance. Ellie recognized that look. Beatrice wanted her cousin to sit elsewhere. And to keep silent.

The girl's audacity irked Ellie. However, asserting her authority would cause a scene and turn this visit into certain disaster. Lips compressed, she took a chair by the wall where she could observe the proceedings. If Beatrice landed herself in hot water, Ellie had every intention of interfering.

"You must be Pennington's daughter," Lady Milford said to Beatrice, taking the seat opposite her. "I'd have known that shade of red-gold hair anywhere. May I say, it's quite beautiful and distinctive."

A twinge of envy stirred in Ellie. Though she, too, had a version of the famous Stratham hair, hers was more auburn than golden, with an unfortunate tendency to curl wildly in damp weather. In her younger days, she'd also wished for Beatrice's milky-pale complexion instead of the dusting of freckles across the bridge of her own nose.

Beatrice reached up to smooth a perfect lock. "I do hope it isn't a detriment. Some gentlemen don't care for redheads, and I confess to being quite determined to secure a betrothal in my first season."

Ellie groaned inwardly. At times Beatrice had no sense of subtlety. And it was clear from the astute gleam in Lady Milford's eyes that she had surmised the purpose of this visit.

"I see," Lady Milford murmured. "Well, that is a worthy goal for any young lady of rank."

"I'm pleased that you agree, my lady." In a pose of angelic sweetness, Beatrice folded her gloved hands in her lap. "Heaven knows, the coming weeks will be a whirlwind of preparation. There are dress fittings, dancing practice, deportment lessons. A girl cannot help but wonder if all the effort will result in victory . . . or defeat, with nary a proposal in sight."

"Rest assured, the gentlemen will flock to a lovely ingénue like you. I doubt you'll have any difficulty in attracting suitors."

Beatrice dipped her chin in feigned modesty. "Your ladyship is most kind. Yet I have it on good authority that quite a large number of girls will be making their debut this season. I fear I shall be only one face among many. That is why I thought to come here and beg *your* assistance."

Lady Milford raised a cool eyebrow. "Has your father been tightfisted with your marriage portion? Shall I have a word with Pennington?"

"Oh, no, my lady! That isn't it at *all*. In truth, I wouldn't wish for him even to know that I'm here . . ."

At that moment, a footman wheeled in a tea tray.

Thankfully, Beatrice had enough discretion to bide her tongue in the presence of a servant.

Rising, Lady Milford picked up the pot and filled three porcelain cups. Ellie came forward to save their hostess the trouble of bringing one to her. As she did so, she took the opportunity to study the woman.

Lady Milford was even more striking at close perusal. She had remarkable eyes, a deep violet rimmed by black lashes and showing only faint lines at the corners. There was a timeless quality to her fine bone structure that defied Ellie's ability to gauge her age.

Then she realized that Lady Milford was giving *her* a keen perusal, too, taking in the ill-fitting gray gown of kersey wool with its long sleeves and high neckline. Ellie refused to quail under the frank assessment. So what if she was a drab sparrow beside Beatrice's peacock beauty? There was no shame in being the poor relation.

"You are also a Stratham," Lady Milford said to Ellie. "Would I be correct in presuming you're the daughter of the earl's late brother?"

"Yes. Lady Beatrice and I are cousins." Noticing that Beatrice was frowning from the chaise, Ellie added, "If you'll excuse me, my lady."

Turning, she retreated to her solitary chair against the wall. It was best to avoid being drawn into conversation. Beatrice would become peevish if she wasn't the center of attention, and Ellie preferred not to face a fit of the pouts on the way home.

The hot cup warmed her chilly fingers. Savoring a sip, she watched as Lady Milford resumed her seat across from Beatrice.

"Now," Lady Milford said, "you were telling me that you hope to lead the other girls in the race to the altar. And *I* was saying that a girl as lovely as you are is certain to attract scores of suitors."

"Oh, but I don't need *scores.* If I may confess something, my lady?" Without waiting for an assent, Beatrice set down her teacup and leaned forward in a confiding pose. "There is one man in particular who intrigues me. Perhaps you know him. The Duke of Aylwin."

Ellie concealed a start of surprise. She hadn't realized that her cousin had settled on a prospective candidate for husband. Over the past few months, Beatrice and their grandmother had spent hours bandying the names of eligible bachelors, looking up possibilities in *Debrett's,* and assessing the soundness of each man's finances. Ellie found it all quite tedious. She had become adept at half-listening while her thoughts traveled their own course, usually dwelling on her secret project.

"Aylwin?" Lady Milford said musingly. "I was acquainted with his late father. However, the present duke isn't one for social gatherings. He keeps to himself, and I must caution you, he has shown little interest in marrying."

"So I've heard." Beatrice released a wistful sigh. "His Grace spends all of his time cooped up in Aylwin House, studying relics from ancient Egypt. It must be a very lonely life. I can't help but think that he needs a wife to keep him company."

Lady Milford looked amused as she took a sip of tea. "Girls are often drawn to mysterious gentlemen. It is in their romantic nature to presume the man must be pining for love. However, the reality seldom matches the daydream. In Aylwin's case, he's nearly twenty years your senior and a scholar with no use for frivolities. I would counsel you to set your sights on someone closer to your age."

"You may be right, my lady. But how will I ever know

for certain unless I actually *meet* the duke?" Beatrice pushed out her lower lip as she often did when wheedling a favor from her papa. "I shall have to spend the rest of my life wondering if I might have been the one girl that Aylwin could have loved. Is there no way at all for you to help me?"

Lady Milford shook her head. "I'm afraid not, my dear," she said in a firm but gentle voice. "My acquaintance with Aylwin is slight. I have no favor of friendship with which to persuade him to do anything."

"But what if . . . what if you were to give one of your exclusive parties? People clamor for an invitation to come here. If you were to host an event and invite both of us, then at least I would have the *chance* to charm him." Beatrice clasped her hands to her bosom. "Oh, please, my lady, don't refuse me, I beg of you. You're my only hope."

That, Ellie decided, was the last straw. Her cousin's behavior had grown worse than bold; it was downright disgraceful! What must Lady Milford think of the girl's impudence in making demands?

Ellie set down her teacup on a table and stepped quickly to the chaise. "We've disturbed her ladyship long enough, Beatrice. I believe we should go now."

Her cousin cast a disgruntled glance up at Ellie. "Not yet. Lady Milford and I are engaged in a very cozy chat."

Ellie turned her gaze to their hostess. "Pray accept our sincerest apologies, your ladyship. We've some errands to complete and I fear that if we tarry, we won't be home in time to dress for dinner."

"Errands?" Beatrice asked, her pert little nose wrinkling as she allowed Ellie to draw her to her feet. "Why, what do you mean?"

"I'll explain in the carriage. For now, we must take

our leave, so kindly say your good-byes to her ladyship."

While Beatrice grudgingly complied, Ellie couldn't help but notice that Lady Milford's gaze rested on her, rather than her cousin. Those dark slender brows formed a faintly quizzical expression as if she were pondering a topic that required thoughtful consideration.

Ellie blushed to think that *she* might be held to blame for Beatrice's misconduct. It was, after all, her responsibility as governess to teach her cousin proper behavior.

"Miss Stratham," Lady Milford murmured to Ellie, "if you might delay your departure for a moment, I have something that may be of use to you. Pray, wait here."

Ellie's lips parted in surprise as she watched Lady Milford glide out of the sitting room. Something of use to *her*? What could she mean?

In a rustle of petticoats, Beatrice minced into view and planted her hands on her hips. Her reddish-blond ringlets framed pretty features marred by a disgruntled expression. "Why did you have to spoil everything? I was just about to convince Lady Milford to help me. Instead, she wants to give *you* something."

"A pamphlet on manners, no doubt," Ellie said. "She must have concluded that I've neglected your education."

The more she considered it, the more likely the possibility seemed. How mortifying to be judged as deficient in her duties! But that was precisely the way the situation must have appeared to their hostess. And as humiliating as it might be, Ellie would have to gracefully accept the instruction book.

Beatrice's lower lip thrust out in a pout. "Do you mean to imply that I've misbehaved?"

"Well, let's see." Ellie ticked the points off on her

fingers. "You presumed upon Lady Milford's good nature to assist in your marriage scheme. You demanded that she expend time and money in hosting a party. You even dictated who should be on the guest list."

"It's a brilliant plan," Beatrice declared. "Pray tell, how else am I to become a duchess? There aren't any other eligible dukes!"

"Then turn your mind to a marquess or an earl. Besides, you should be more concerned with the character of a man, not his rank. Whomever you choose to wed, you'll be bound to him for the rest of your life."

"Oh, la! Perhaps a title matters little to a spinster without prospects. However, *I* intend to marry well and be the envy of all society."

A spinster without prospects. The careless description stirred an ache in Ellie's bosom. The sensation startled her, for long ago she had buried her girlish dreams of love and marriage, when she had faced the hard truth that few gentlemen were willing to wed an impoverished nobody. Instead, she had devoted herself to repaying her father's debts through serving the family in whatever capacity was required of her.

Yet she had no intention of enslaving herself forever. Not a living soul knew it, but Ellie had conceived a bold, enterprising plan to earn her own way in the world . . .

A movement drew her attention to the doorway of the sitting room. Lady Milford entered, carrying a blue velvet purse in her hands. Reaching into the bag, she drew forth an article that glinted in the wintry afternoon light streaming through the windows.

Ellie blinked in surprise. A shoe? It appeared to be a fine, heeled slipper made of garnet satin, frosted with tiny crystal beads and bearing a dainty, filigreed buckle.

Lady Milford brought out its match and placed both shoes into Ellie's hands. "This pair was an old favorite of mine from my younger years," she said. "I believe they may suit you, Miss Stratham."

Ellie's fingers closed automatically around the shoes. Having expected an etiquette manual, she could not have been more flabbergasted. Never in her life had she seen anything more beautiful—or more wildly impractical. "You're very kind, my lady, but . . . where would I wear such shoes? They're far too elegant for a governess."

"You'll be accompanying your cousin into society, I presume. Surely you'll need slippers for dancing at balls and parties."

"That may be true for most ladies," Ellie said. "However, I'm afraid my gowns are rather plain and I've nothing in my wardrobe to—"

"As my chaperone, Ellie won't be dancing," Beatrice interrupted. Her covetous gaze flitted to the slippers. "And my feet are daintier than hers. Which means that *I* am far more likely to wear the same size as you, my lady."

An enigmatic smile curved Lady Milford's lips. "Indeed? Then perhaps you should sit down. You shall each have the chance to see if they fit."

Chapter 3

Departing Lady Milford's town house a short while later, Ellie gripped the blue velvet pouch beneath her drab brown cloak. The bag held the dancing slippers that had pinched Beatrice's toes so much that the girl had exclaimed in discomfort and kicked them off at once.

Consequently, Ellie had at first declined to try on the shoes. But Lady Milford had insisted, and by some miracle, the slippers had fit Ellie to perfection. She still didn't understand why. Though she and her cousin shared the same proportions in gowns, Ellie could have sworn that she herself wore a full size larger in footwear.

That mystifying thought evaporated under the joy of cradling the gorgeous shoes against her bosom. From the moment she'd slid her stockinged feet into the garnet satin lining, a sense of buoyant pleasure had uplifted her. It had felt as if all of her troubles had floated away. She'd wanted to wear them home, though her practical side had swiftly overruled such foolishness.

And although she'd put the slippers back into the soft pouch for safekeeping, her gloved fingers continued to trace the slim shape and the bits of crystal beading. It had been a long time since she'd possessed anything so lovely—not since her papa had been alive. He'd often showered her with presents, though upon his death everything had been sold to help her uncle pay off the creditors.

Ellie didn't want to remember that now. Nor did she wish to heed the sullen expression on her cousin's face. In a peacock-blue cloak, her hands tucked into an ermine muff, Beatrice marched toward the black brougham with the gold Pennington crest emblazoned on the door.

That scowl foretold trouble. No doubt Ellie would be soundly chastised on the way home. Nevertheless, she didn't believe for an instant that her cousin's ill humor had anything to do with a pair of cast-off dancing slippers. After all, Beatrice owned a cupboard overflowing with fancy shoes.

No, the girl's sulkiness was rooted in the failure of her marriage scheme. Having been pampered all her life, Beatrice had expected to persuade Lady Milford to do her bidding. Now, Beatrice would have to be soothed and placated, and Ellie didn't look forward to the task.

A footman in forest-green livery sprang to open the door of the brougham. However, Beatrice didn't climb inside. Rather, she stopped so abruptly that Ellie nearly collided with her.

Beatrice peered down the town-house-lined street where a few carriages and drays rumbled over the cobblestones. As if transformed by the wave of a fairy godmother's wand, the petulant set of her mouth altered magically into a coquettish smile.

"Oh, splendid!" Beatrice pushed past Ellie, leaving a cloud of rose-water perfume in her wake. "Wait here, or you'll spoil everything."

Ellie turned to see a gentleman on a fine bay mare

cantering toward them. He looked like the consummate fashion plate in his double-breasted blue coat, a white muffler tucked at his throat. As he drew nearer, Ellie recognized his boyish features. He was the son of one of the Earl of Pennington's acquaintances.

The man reined in his mount, swept off his tall black hat, and bobbed his fair head in a nod. "Upon my word, is it truly Lady Beatrice Stratham? What a lovely surprise on such a cold winter's day."

Standing on the curbstone, Beatrice simpered up at him. "Why, Lord Roland. Are you out paying calls, too?"

"Quite. And a dreary prospect it was, until I saw you standing there like an angel descended from the heavens."

A girlish giggle escaped Beatrice. While they exchanged flirtatious pleasantries, Ellie remained by the open door of the brougham. The chill wind bit at her cheeks and poked icy fingers beneath her cloak. She wanted nothing more than to settle herself in the carriage and tuck a woolen blanket over her lap.

Unfortunately, duty required her to keep an eye on her cousin. A girl not yet launched into society oughtn't be seen flirting with a gentleman in public.

Yet surely a few minutes couldn't hurt, especially since this impromptu meeting appeared to have put Beatrice in a better frame of mind. With luck, she might forget about betrothing herself to a duke who was twice her age. The younger son of a marquess, Lord Roland was only three years her senior and a far more suitable marital prospect.

Watching them, Ellie let her mind wander to the meager contents of her wardrobe. She debated the necessity of buying fabric at the linen drapers to sew a new ball gown. Such a purchase would require dipping into her precious stash of coins. Yet she couldn't abide the notion of wearing the shoes with a cheap, outdated frock.

A pity Lady Milford hadn't realized the impracticality of the gift.

For a moment, Ellie wondered at her wisdom in taking charity from a mere acquaintance. Always before, it had pricked her pride to accept hand-me-downs, and those had been from her own family. Had it merely been the exquisite shoes that had tempted her so greatly? Perhaps, but there had also been a lack of condescension in Lady Milford's manner. She had exhibited a sincere desire to be helpful, and it would have been churlish of Ellie to refuse such a kindness.

The chirp of Beatrice's laugh floated on a gust of wind. She chattered animatedly while Lord Roland leaned down from his mount as if to hang on her every utterance. Luckily, no one of consequence was out for a stroll on this frigid afternoon. The few pedestrians trudging up and down the street appeared to be servants or workmen bundled up against the cold.

Only then did Ellie notice the man seated in an open phaeton a few doors away.

A pair of spirited grays stamped their hooves and blew clouds of mist into the chilly air. With a slight tug of the reins in his gloved hands, the stranger controlled the horses with ease. He was clad entirely in black, from the hat with a curled brim pulled low over his dark hair to the greatcoat that created the impression of a hulking beast. A scarf swathed the lower portion of his face, and she had the oddest impression that it was meant for disguise rather than warmth.

With curious intensity, he was staring at her cousin.

Ellie's skin prickled, but she attributed the shiver

to the weather. The man must be waiting for a neighbor, that was all. His interest in Beatrice was nothing more than idle curiosity.

Nevertheless, Ellie decided that her cousin had been conversing with Lord Roland long enough. Anyone could be peering out of the nearby windows. It took only a whisper of gossip to brand a girl an incorrigible flirt and to tarnish her reputation.

Thankfully, at that moment, Lord Roland tipped his hat and bade Beatrice good-bye. He continued on his way as she came prancing back to the brougham, her face rosy with pleasure. She and Ellie climbed inside and, as the vehicle rumbled through the streets of Mayfair, Beatrice launched into a soliloquy on Lord Roland's fine manners and how he'd begged her to save him a dance at her come-out ball.

Ellie relaxed, letting the girl babble while offering a comment now and then. How mercurial her cousin was, how easily distracted by a handsome face. Perhaps Lady Milford was right; once Beatrice came to enjoy the courtship of gentlemen closer to her in age, she would relinquish her scheme to marry a reclusive duke.

As the brougham slowed to a halt in front of Pennington House in Hanover Square, Ellie decided that she was quite happy to be a spinster on the shelf. Nothing interested her less than flirting with an array of gentlemen in the hopes of attracting a husband. She had a far better plan for her life than wedlock.

A footman opened the carriage door. Beatrice stepped out first, her peacock cloak swirling as she abruptly turned back. "Oh, drat! I've forgotten my muff. Ellie, do be a dear and bring it into the house."

The white ermine muff had tumbled onto the floor. As Ellie closed her fingers around its furry softness, a movement at the other window caught her attention.

A carriage was passing slowly in the street, a phaeton with a dark-clad gentleman perched on the high seat.

Ellie's eyes widened. Those swarthy, hard-edged features looked eerily familiar. His lower face was wrapped in a black muffler, and a hat with a curled brim shaded his green-gray eyes. He stared with keen intensity as Beatrice walked toward the house.

With a jolt, Ellie realized he was the same man who had been watching her cousin outside Lady Milford's town house.

Lady Milford had been watching, too.

The moment her visitors had departed, Clarissa had proceeded straight to the drawing room window at the front of the house. Through the lacy undercurtain, she gazed down at the street to see Lady Beatrice in her peacock-blue cloak shamelessly flirting with Lord Roland.

But Clarissa had no interest in the antics of that vain, spoiled girl. Her concern lay with the shabbily garbed woman standing forgotten by the brougham.

How appalling that Pennington had never bothered to launch his own niece. Miss Eloise Stratham was the orphaned daughter of his profligate younger brother, yet she'd apparently been given no debut, no dowry, and no opportunity to marry. Instead, it appeared she had been treated as the household drudge.

The injustice of it wrenched Lady Milford's heart. It transported her back to her own youth when she had been plain Clarissa Wren, living on the sufferance of her widowed stepmother and two stepsisters in a manor house in the wilds of Yorkshire. By some legal chicanery, the stepmother had managed to have her husband's first marriage declared invalid, thereby rendering Clarissa a bastard. The interlopers then had squandered her late father's wealth on fine clothing and jewels while Clarissa was given rags to wear. She had been expected to cook and clean and fulfill endless demands. In the moment of her darkest despair, when she had sunk down by the ashes of the kitchen hearth to weep for her beloved Papa, a knocking had sounded at the back door.

An ancient Gypsy woman stood outside, begging for food. Fearing the wrath of her stepmother, Clarissa very nearly turned away the vagabond. But she took pity on the woman and offered to share her own meager dinner. In return, the wrinkled crone gave her a pair of garnet slippers and a cryptic message that they would lead her to true love . . .

A faint smile on her lips, Clarissa reflected upon the grand journey that had brought her to this point. She had come to London, married the aging Earl of Milford, and gained status and wealth as his wife. Yet only in widowhood had Clarissa finally realized the Gypsy's prediction when she had fallen madly in love with one of the king's sons. Though circumstances had made it impossible for them to wed, she and her darling Prince Frederick had engaged in a discreet affair of the heart for many blissful years. Upon his death, Clarissa had found solace in helping worthy young women find their own chance at happiness.

Now, as she gazed down at the latest recipient of the shoes, she sensed that Miss Eloise Stratham was in sore need of love. Yet never before had Clarissa loaned out the slippers without having first selected a specific gentleman as a match . . .

At that precise moment, she noticed the open phaeton parked a short distance behind the Stratham brougham. The restless stamping of the horses caught her attention. The driver controlled the pair of grays with an almost imperceptible tug on the ribbons.

Garbed from head to toe in black, he appeared to be a gentleman. Yet how curious for him to be waiting in front of a vacant residence, the owners having gone to their country estate for the winter.

Odder still, he was staring at Lady Beatrice. Who was he?

The girl gave a farewell wave to Lord Roland, then minced back to rejoin Miss Eloise Stratham. Both women entered the brougham, and as the coachman started down the cobbled street, the driver of the phaeton snapped the reins and began to follow the brougham.

On impulse, Clarissa twitched the lace curtain aside and rapped hard on the windowpane. As he glanced up, she stepped swiftly back and out of sight. But that one instant had given her a clear view of unusual green-gray eyes set in a harshly masculine face.

Astonished recognition rooted her in place. Why on earth would *he* have an interest in Lady Beatrice? Was it merely a coincidence? Clarissa stood there for a time, wondering, considering, pondering. Then she walked to the fireplace and tugged the bell rope.

A few minutes later, a distinguished butler with cropped white hair entered the drawing room. He proceeded forward in a stately fashion and bowed, waiting for her to speak. That was one of the things she'd always liked about Hargrove. He didn't waste words—yet he had an encyclopedic knowledge of society.

"Do you know of a man named Damien Burke?" she asked.

Hargrove thought for a moment. "Yes, my lady. Mr. Burke was ousted from society seven years ago due to an unsavory affair. Now he operates a gaming establishment known as Demon's Den."

"I just now saw him following Lady Beatrice Stratham's brougham. I should like for you to find out all you can about his present activities. There is something puzzling going on, and I need to know what it is."

"At once, madam."

As he departed the drawing room, Clarissa knew that no further instructions were necessary. Hargrove had a network of trusted spies, and he would use them with the utmost discretion. She had only to wait—and to ponder the secret that she had kept for nearly thirty years.

Chapter 4

"Papa, I've been thinking." Seated beside her father at the dinner table, Beatrice trailed the tines of her fork through the mound of peas on her plate. "In only a few weeks, I'll be launched into society. It'll be the most important night of my life. Yet I fear that my come-out ball may be a trifle . . . lackluster."

Lord Pennington, who had been concentrating on his beefsteak, looked up with a frown. The purple veins across the bridge of his ruddy nose clashed with his graying russet hair. His fleshy appearance reminded Ellie of a painting of Henry VIII that she'd seen in a museum.

"Lackluster, you say?" the earl asked. "I assure you, daughter, the bills for this event may send the entire lot of us to the poorhouse!"

"Oh, Papa, don't be annoyed. It's just that I fear there is nothing to distinguish *my* party from so many others."

The girl's voice held a wheedling note, though her clear blue eyes and milky complexion created the appearance of radiant innocence. The other four family members at the dining table listened to the exchange with interest.

Across from Beatrice, Ellie's eldest cousin, Walt, Viscount Greaves, slouched in his chair, his hazel eyes glassy from numerous cups of wine. Lady Anne, the late countess's timid sister, was seated opposite Ellie. At the other end of the linen-draped table presided the earl's mother, the stout Countess of Pennington, grandmother to Ellie and her cousins.

"Why, my dear Beatrice," the countess said, her brown eyes like sunken currants in a massively wrinkled face. "I can't imagine what you should find lacking. Your father has spared no expense on your behalf. There shall be hothouse roses, the finest chef, the very best champagne."

Beatrice dipped her chin in girlish modesty. "I'm ever so grateful, Grandmamma. But *all* debutantes have roses and champagne. Don't you see? I will be nothing special. How am I to become the triumph of the season if I don't stand out in the crowd?"

Walt elevated his wine goblet in a salute to his sister. "Perhaps we could arrange for you to be transported into the ballroom on a gilded throne, Bea. *That* would certainly stir the gossips."

Beatrice screwed up her nose at him. "Oh, do be serious. You're only jealous because Papa never hosted a party in *your* honor."

"Gentlemen needn't be paraded like horses for sale at Tattersall's. Rather, we are the ones who choose which mare we wish to purchase."

"How dare you compare me to a horse! Papa, tell Walt not to be so rude."

Chewing a mouthful of meat, Lord Pennington directed a low rumble of disapproval at his son.

The countess tapped her fork on her plate. "Enough! It is unseemly for the two of you to squabble like children. And do sit up straight, Walter." As he sullenly obeyed, she went on in a crisp tone, "Now, Beatrice, perhaps you should tell us exactly what it is you have in mind for the ball."

"I wonder if we might adopt an exotic theme, Grandmamma. I was thinking of decorating the ballroom with an Egyptian motif."

"Egyptian!" Ellie blurted out. Recalling the reclusive Duke of Aylwin with his scholarly study of Egyptian artifacts, she had a sudden suspicion of her cousin's purpose.

Beatrice slid a sly glance at Ellie. "Yes, you know, palm trees and pyramids and the like. I shall have to do a bit of research on the topic and see what I can find out."

"You, conduct research?" Walt scoffed as he signaled the footman to pour another round of burgundy. "I doubt you could even find your way to the lending library."

"Actually, I intend to interview an authority, someone who can offer suggestions as to the décor," Beatrice said archly. "Perhaps there is a scholar at the British Museum. I'm sure Ellie can escort me there."

Ellie suspected the museum wasn't her cousin's true destination. Beatrice was intending to use this latest scheme as an excuse to brazen her way into the Duke of Aylwin's house. "It wouldn't be appropriate for you to question a stranger," Ellie said. "I shall procure a book on ancient Egypt and you may draw your inspiration from it."

"Oh, no!" Beatrice said quickly. "I should rather speak to a real person than bury my nose in dusty old pages."

"I must overrule you in this matter, my dear," their

grandmother said. "For once, Eloise is correct. A young lady ought not associate with unknown characters. Do tell her to consult the book, Basil."

The earl gave a crisp nod. "I'm sure she'll be good enough to mind your wishes, Mother." He glanced at Beatrice with her pouty lower lip, and his ruddy face softened. "Now, don't mope, sweetcakes. If it makes you happy, I shall allow you the funds to decorate the ballroom in whatever manner suits you. Even if it *is* this Egyptian claptrap."

"Thank you, Papa." Beatrice gave him a sunny smile, but the look she flashed at Ellie held a hint of spite. She dabbed her mouth with a white linen serviette. "By the by, speaking of associating with unknowns, Ellie and I paid a visit to Lady Milford today."

The perky announcement cast a pall of surprise over the dining table. The earl tossed down his fork, Walt arched a reddish eyebrow, and Lady Anne drew an audible breath. The quiet clink of china filled the silence as the footmen removed the plates in preparation for the dessert course.

"Lady Milford?" the countess asked, a frown making her wrinkles more pronounced. "But my dear, you've never been introduced to the woman. It is an extraordinary blunder for a young lady not yet out of the schoolroom to make such a call."

"Oh, Ellie thought it was a wise notion. After all, Lady Milford is a pillar of society and her approval would be a great boon to my debut."

Everyone turned to stare at Ellie. A flush traveled up her neck and into her face, making her feel overheated. It was clear from the reproachful looks that they blamed *her* for the social faux pas. It was also plain that it would be useless to protest her innocence. They would never heed her word over that of her cousin.

What a scheming little liar Beatrice was!

The countess scowled at Ellie. "I trust you've an explanation for this shocking lack of judgment. Encouraging Beatrice to impose upon a lady of such influence! I pray no irreparable damage has been done."

"I assure you, it was an uneventful visit," Ellie hastened to say. "In truth, her ladyship could not have been more gracious—"

"Yes, she even gave Ellie a handout," Beatrice broke in. "A pair of old, cast-off shoes that my dear cousin was quite happy to accept."

Beneath the tablecloth, Ellie fisted her fingers around her gray serge skirt. She wanted to slap the innocent smile off Beatrice's mouth. At the same time, she longed to slide under the table and escape the disapproval on the faces of her uncle and grandmother. Even Walt's expression held a smirking interest.

The countess huffed out a breath. "You took *charity* from such a personage as Lady Milford? Good heavens! What must she think of us?"

"This is indeed an outrage," the earl said grimly. His cheeks red, he leaned forward to pin Ellie with a glare. "The Strathams are not beggars! Did you give no thought as to how this would reflect upon your family? And after I've settled your father's substantial debts, taken you under my roof, and allowed you to live here on my sufferance!"

Ellie gritted her teeth. Now was not the time to point out that her free labor had more than compensated for the cost of food and shelter. "I'm sorry, Uncle. It won't happen again."

"I'm sure Ellie meant no harm," Lady Anne ventured in a quavering voice. "Why, it would have been rude for her to refuse such a gift."

Ellie gave her a quick smile of thanks. Lady Anne

was no blood relation, being from the other side of the family tree, yet at times it seemed the frail woman was her sole ally in the household. She was the only one who gave Ellie a bit of money on her birthday, the only one who expressed gratitude for the errands Ellie did for her, the only one who didn't treat her as a lowly servant.

The earl turned his ire on his sister-in-law. "This is no small matter, Anne. My niece is to accept aid only from myself. Otherwise, the gossips will whisper that I'm too tightfisted to provide for her."

Lady Anne flushed, her gaze dropping to the dish of raspberry sponge cake that a footman placed before her.

Ellie found it ironic that her uncle would fear to be branded according to his true nature. "Lady Milford won't spread gossip," she said to draw his attention away from Lady Anne. "I assure you, she merely thought that I might like to have the shoes since I'll be chaperoning Beatrice at various events."

Beatrice, who clearly had been enjoying the controversy she'd stirred, said, "That reminds me. We can't allow dear Ellie to go about society in dreary rags. I would donate some of my old gowns, but I fear they are too youthful for a woman of her years. Grandmamma, is there anything *you* can do to help out?"

"What a sweet girl to think of your cousin." The countess gave Beatrice a fond smile that vanished when she turned her attention to her eldest granddaughter. "Eloise, you're quick with a needle. You may have some of *my* old gowns to make over."

Ellie eyed the countess's doughy form encased in a vast swath of burnt-orange satin. Nothing could be less welcome than a donation from a wardrobe that contained the most nauseating hues Ellie had ever had the misfortune to see. "That won't be necessary," she said.

"I'm sure that I can manage to purchase a bolt or two of cloth."

"Nonsense. You can't possibly afford the finest materials. I will not have you looking ragtag, especially in light of your taking charity from Lady Milford."

Then why do you or my uncle not offer to purchase a few new gowns for me?

Ellie knew better than to voice that question. It had been established long ago that since her father's debts had been so excessive, she should expect no further outlay of funds from the family. She reminded herself that her escape from this household would come soon enough. Until then, she'd wear sackcloth and ashes if necessary. "Thank you, then. It is most generous of you, Grandmamma."

Her grandmother arched an eyebrow, shifting a myriad of facial wrinkles. "I trust you are sincere in your gratitude, Eloise. I do not care to think you a bad seed like your father."

Ellie's anger flared. She could tolerate being treated like a poor relation for the remainder of her time here. She could not, however, endure the countess's biting scorn for her second son. "Papa may have had his faults, but he loved me very much. He was an excellent father."

"Do not confer sainthood on such a wicked man," the countess retorted. "Theo left you alone while he went off to gamble, sometimes for days on end. That is hardly the mark of a devoted father."

"I was never alone," Ellie said defensively. "There was always a servant with me. I didn't mind Papa's absence so very much."

Her mother having died when Ellie was six, she had learned at a young age to keep herself occupied with solitary pursuits. There were always books to read and stories to imagine, fictional worlds in which to lose herself for hours on end . . .

"I say," Walt drawled, "perhaps we should leave Ellie her illusions. Surely there can be no harm in them."

Ellie turned to see her cousin swirling the dregs of wine in his goblet. He was staring at her in a way that made her skin crawl. At times, Walt made her uneasy, especially when he'd been drinking. On several occasions he'd caught her on the upper stairs or in a dark corridor, cornering her on some pretext while patting her hand or touching her waist in a too familiar fashion.

Was he taking her side now merely as a means of currying favor? So that she would allow his advances? She quailed at the thought.

"No harm?" Lord Pennington echoed on a note of disdain. "My brother squandered his inheritance, and Eloise mustn't pretend otherwise. *I* would never behave so irresponsibly, nor would you, Walter. It is unforgivable for a Stratham to gamble."

During his father's speech, Walt's smile went stiff. He cast a quick sidelong look at his father, then stared moodily into his wine goblet. The curious reaction caught Ellie's attention. She wondered if, unbeknownst to the earl, Walt had dabbled in the vice of wagering.

It wouldn't surprise her. Like many idle young gentlemen, Walt spent an inordinate amount of time at various clubs and entertainments. He surely would have been tempted into playing cards or dice.

No one else appeared to notice. Beatrice piped up with a question to the earl about which gentlemen engaged in wicked behaviors so that she might take care to avoid them. That sparked a lively conversation about the girl's marital prospects, and Ellie was relieved to have the attention turned away from herself while the family ate their dessert.

She barely tasted her raspberry sponge cake. Tonight had been one of those times when she didn't know if she could bear one more hour under her uncle's roof. Only a few more months, she reminded herself.

A few more months, and then she would be free.

The hall clock was chiming ten when Ellie finally escaped upstairs to the nursery. When she'd come to Pennington House at the age of fourteen, grief-stricken from her father's sudden death, she had been assigned a tiny bedchamber near the earl's two younger children so that she could comfort them during the night and assist in teaching them by day. Eventually, she had become their governess. She'd remained here even when Cedric had gone off to Eton and Beatrice had moved downstairs to a spacious bedroom near the other family members.

No such honor had been offered to Ellie.

The darkened schoolroom and the adjacent bedchambers were empty now. She was the only one left in the nursery wing, and the solitary arrangement suited her just fine. Here, she had the privacy to attend to her own project without interruption.

She settled down on her cot, her back against a thin pillow and the coverlet pulled up to the bosom of her cotton night rail. Her knees raised, she propped a sketchpad against her thighs as a makeshift desk. By the wavering light of a candle on the bedside table, she drew preliminary renditions of two new characters for her children's book.

The first was a grand personage that Ellie had decided would be named the Furry Godmother. She was a tabby, sleek and elegant, clad in a long flowing gown. Standing upright, the cat wore on her hind paws a pair of sparkly dancing slippers that eventually would be painted a rich garnet hue when Ellie did her final version in watercolors.

She wondered if anyone would recognize those wise eyes and feminine features as belonging to Lady Milford.

Ellie smiled, using a few deft pencil strokes to add a pair of dainty whiskers to the portrait. The air was chilly, the mattress lumpy, the light dim. But nothing could mar her enjoyment of creating another episode in her storybook.

In the scene that occupied her at present, the Furry Godmother held a magic wand in one paw and waved it at a large, man-sized rat that had crept into the bedchamber of the sleeping princess. The hulking rodent wore a black greatcoat and a hat with a curled brim.

For this second new character, Ellie had taken her inspiration from the stranger in the phaeton outside Lady Milford's house. There had been something vaguely sinister about the man—or at least her fancy had fixed upon that illusion. How much more fascinating it was to think him a scoundrel than to acknowledge the probable truth, that he was merely a gentleman who'd wanted to view the much anticipated beauty of Lady Beatrice Stratham ahead of her debut.

Nevertheless, Ellie had decided to transform him into this villainous rat. Her muse worked in mysterious ways, she reflected. The day had been exasperating, the family dinner tiresome, and she should have been too weary for anything but sleep. Yet her hand flew over the paper, her imagination energized by this new twist in the plot.

A thick stack of finished watercolors was concealed inside a chest at the foot of her narrow bed. She had been working on the manuscript for several years, whenever she could escape her endless household duties. Having set autumn as her goal to complete the project, Ellie had been laboring far into the night until her eyelids drooped and her cramped fingers could no longer grasp the pencil.

Now, if only she could find a publisher for her finished book.

A twinge of anxiety crept down her spine. She would have to persuade a man in a publishing office to typeset her story, print the pages, and bind them into a finished volume. What if he refused to pay her until it had been sold in bookstores? Worse, what if no one purchased it and all of her work was for naught?

She would never be able to afford a cozy cottage in the country where she could live free of obligations while creating her stories. Instead, she'd be stuck here at Pennington House as an unpaid servant for the rest of her life. The very thought made her shudder.

Ellie buried her doubts. She refused to let herself dwell on the possibility of failure. When Cedric and Beatrice had been younger, she had read many bedtime stories to them. There had been morality tales, nursery rhymes, the fables of Aesop. But none of those published books had been quite like her own secret illustrated adventure of a brave lost princess on a quest to find her way home, who befriends talking animals and fights fierce creatures like dragons and ogres and sea monsters.

And now, in the present chapter, a menacing rodent.

Ellie paused, tapping the end of her pencil on the sketchpad. What should she name him? Was Mr. Rat too banal?

A sudden knocking made her jump. Frowning, she looked toward the door of her tiny bedchamber. Having been immersed in her imaginary world, it took a moment to collect her thoughts.

Seldom did anyone venture up to the nursery after hours. Perhaps it was her grandmother's maid, delivering the heap of old ball gowns.

"Who's there?" she called.

"It's me. May I have a word?"

Ellie froze with her fingers clamped around the sketchpad. She knew that muffled, raspy voice. *Walt.*

She'd assumed her cousin had departed after dinner for his entertainments, as was his custom. Why on earth would he come up to the nursery so late? It had to be approaching midnight. She could only think he had some nefarious purpose in mind. And here she was, curled up in bed wearing only her nightclothes.

With her precious drawings scattered around her on the coverlet.

She raised her voice. "I'm sorry, Walt. I was sleeping. Go away and we'll talk in the morning."

"Nonsense, you're awake. I can see your candle shining under the door." Another imperious rapping rattled the hinges. "Come out at once. Or I'll enter without your permission."

Blast! Ellie knew he meant it. Three years her senior, the favored son and heir, Walt had always done exactly as he'd pleased.

"Oh, give me a moment, then," she said.

Ellie jumped out of bed and cringed as her bare feet met the icy planks of the floor. Swiftly she gathered up the papers and the sketchpad, ran to the chest, and stuffed her art paraphernalia beneath a black serge gown. On top lay the precious garnet slippers, the crystal beads sparkling in the candlelight. She closed the lid again and then grabbed a shabby green dressing gown from a hook on the wall, thrusting her arms into the sleeves and tying it securely at her waist.

Glancing around, she saw nothing that might be used

as a weapon save for the pewter candlestick. She picked it up and opened the door a crack to peer out.

Her cousin lounged against the wall of the corridor, an oil lamp in his hand. The freckles across his cheeks and nose gave him the look of an overgrown choirboy, but Ellie knew that to be deceptive. The rest of him fit the description of a dissipated gentleman in his cups. The top button of his waistcoat was undone over a belly already going to stoutness. His ginger hair was tousled, his cravat slightly askew, his hazel eyes more glazed than they'd been at dinner.

"What did you want?" she asked frigidly.

It was an unfortunate choice of words, for his gaze dipped straight to her bosom. Frowning, Ellie reached up to clutch her lapels together.

"I need t' talk t' you," he said, his words slightly slurred. "In your chamber."

He took a step forward and Ellie thrust up the lighted candle to hold him at bay. "No, Walt. Whatever you have to say can be spoken right here. It's ill-mannered of you to disturb me so late, anyway."

"You're such a scold, Ellie." He lifted a hand as if to caress her, but the chilly look on her face must have registered in his pickled brain, for he stopped short and ran his fingers through his own hair instead. "I've something t' tell you, that's all."

"Then speak and be done. I must be awake at dawn."

Walt's brow puckered as if he struggled to remember his purpose. A slurry of words rushed out of him. "I need you t' promise you'll watch Bea at all times. D'you hear me? Keep her at home, out of sight . . . at least for now till I tell you it's safe."

Ellie was taken aback. What would prompt Walt to issue such a peculiar warning? She could smell the liquor on his breath, and she was tempted to think he was confused in his intoxicated state. Yet he looked unusually serious. "I don't understand. Is this because we visited Lady Milford today? Did the earl instruct you to speak to me?"

"No . . . *yes.* Yes, my father said Bea's t' be punished for . . . for behaving badly. Going t' see someone she don't know. It's bad form."

Walt was lying. Ellie could see it in his manner. He'd first shaken his head in denial before nodding, a clue that he had amended his story in mid-thought and seized upon a handy explanation. So why would he want to confine Beatrice to home?

Perhaps excessive drink had turned him maudlin. Perhaps it had awakened a dormant chivalrous instinct in him to keep his sister from making any more foolish mistakes.

Or perhaps he had made it all up on the spot to give him an excuse to come up here and pester Ellie with his amorous advances.

As if to validate that last possibility, Walt crowded closer, a leer on his face. "Why're you scowling?" he said cajolingly. "I could make you happy, y' know. Just lemme show you . . ."

All of a sudden, his hand jerked up to paw her bosom. His fingers painfully pinched her nipple. At the same time, he attempted to kiss her and she averted her face, his foul breath hot against her cheek.

Disgusted, Ellie acted without thinking. She thrust up the candle between them and burned his wrist.

With a yowl, he jumped backward. He shook his arm wildly. "Ah! Vixen! Why'd you do that?"

"Get out of here, Walt. And don't *ever* come back."

Slamming the bedchamber door, Ellie turned the skeleton key in the lock. The memory of his loathsome touch made her feel ill. Her heart thudding, she listened with an ear to the wood panel until the sound of his departing footsteps could be heard.

Yet she didn't feel quite safe again until she'd taken the extra precaution of dragging the heavy chest in front of the door.

Chapter 5

The following morning, an unexpected visitor to Pennington House pushed Walt's reprehensible behavior to the back of Ellie's mind.

Having slept late, Beatrice was lolling against the pillows in her four-poster bed, sipping hot chocolate and paging through a fashion journal. Ellie was sitting by the window, taking advantage of the morning light as she mended a rip in the hem of a white chemise.

Beatrice set down her cup in its saucer. "I don't see why we can't go to Aylwin House today," she grumbled. "My ball is the perfect ruse for me to meet the duke and ask his advice on creating an Egyptian theme."

Ellie knew she had to put a firm halt to that scheme. "It's already settled. Your father prefers that you use a book for inspiration. We'll stop at the lending library on our way to the modiste this afternoon."

She felt a momentary unease at the notion of venturing out of the house with Beatrice. Had Walt been telling the truth about his sister being punished? Ellie wasn't sure, yet she hesitated to risk flouting Uncle Basil's wishes. The only way to resolve the matter was to speak directly to the earl. However, he had gone out just after breakfast and she could only hope that he would return home by luncheon—

The door flew open, startling Ellie into pricking herself with the needle. She sucked on her injured forefinger as the Countess of Pennington burst into the bedchamber. Her grandmother's stout bosom heaved beneath a mustard-yellow gown.

She clapped her hands. "Beatrice! You must make haste! Lady Milford is waiting to see you in the blue drawing room!"

"Lady Milford, *here*? To see *me*?" Beatrice threw aside her fashion periodical and hopped out of bed. "Are you quite sure, Grandmamma? Why, it's not even noon!"

"Of course I'm sure. Oh, my darling, you must have made a brilliant impression for her to return your call—and so swiftly!" Those massively wrinkled features took on a haughty frown as she turned her gaze to Ellie. "Eloise, fetch the pale green silk gown, and be quick about it! I shall expect Beatrice—and you—downstairs in a flash!"

As the older woman sailed out of the bedchamber, Ellie made haste into the dressing room to gather the suitable undergarments for her cousin. All the while, she reflected on the incredible news. Why on earth had Lady Milford come here? And why had their grandmother specifically ordered Ellie to accompany her cousin downstairs?

Beatrice had *not* made a brilliant impression on Lady Milford, Ellie knew. Her cousin's behavior had been shockingly forward. Had the woman come to offer advice to Beatrice in their grandmother's presence? Or worse, to reprimand Ellie for failing to teach the girl better manners?

She had no time to fret in the mad scramble to bedeck her cousin in stockings and corset, petticoats and gown. Ellie buttoned and combed and pinned as swiftly as possible. It didn't help matters that Beatrice fidgeted impatiently and snapped at her to hurry.

When at last Ellie followed her coiffed and perfumed cousin down the stairway, the countess was entertaining their guest by the drawing room fire. Lady Anne sat nearby, her lace-capped head bowed and her thin hands folded in her lap as if she hoped not to be noticed. Ellie could sympathize. In a lilac silk gown and with beautifully styled black hair, Lady Milford looked sophisticated enough to make lesser mortals quail.

Beatrice dipped a pretty curtsy while Ellie quietly slipped into a chair at the perimeter of the group. Like Lady Anne, she, too, had little desire to draw attention to herself. Yet she found herself on the edge of her seat, wondering what could possibly have prompted this visit.

After an exchange of pleasantries, Lady Milford lost no time in satisfying everyone's curiosity. She turned to Beatrice and said, "In light of our lovely chat yesterday, I have resolved to pay a call at Aylwin House this afternoon. If it's permissible to your grandmother, I thought perhaps *you* might wish to accompany me."

Beatrice clasped her hands to her bosom. "To be presented to His Grace, the duke? Oh! Oh, my! Please, Grandmamma, may I?"

The Countess of Pennington appeared beatific and quickly voiced her approval. Ellie sat in utter astonishment. Yesterday, Lady Milford had claimed only a slight acquaintance with the reclusive duke. She had rejected Beatrice's scheme to finagle an introduction to him. What had happened to change the woman's mind?

All of a sudden, Ellie realized that Lady Milford

was addressing her. "Miss Stratham, you undoubtedly keep abreast of your cousin's schedule. Are you certain that she has no prior engagements today?"

"She does have a fitting at the dressmaker's," Ellie said. "Though I'm sure the appointment can be postponed . . ."

"Appointments can be difficult to rearrange so near to the opening of the season," Lady Milford said smoothly. As she studied Ellie, her violet eyes held a hint of mystery. "Since you appear to wear the same size as Lady Beatrice, may I suggest that *you* go in her place?"

"My lady, what a delight it is to welcome you to my establishment."

As the voice came from behind her, Ellie was garbed in an elegant ball gown and facing a long mirror. An assistant had helped her into the costly frock upon her arrival. It was sewn of pale pink tulle over white satin with sleeves edged by Belgian lace. The skirt whispered with her every move, and she had been imagining herself as Princess Arianna at the end of her adventures, restored to the loving company of her long-lost parents. On a whim, Ellie had fashioned a bit of white gauze festooned with pink roses as a makeshift crown over her upswept hair.

She turned to see the stout proprietress bustling into the dressing room. The woman had a toadying smile on her face, though this was the first time Ellie had been the recipient of it. She felt a tickle of amusement at being mistaken for her cousin. Always before, she had been the dowdy chaperone sitting forgotten on a chair in the corner.

She flicked the swath of gauze off her head. "Good afternoon, Mrs. Peebles. I'm Miss Stratham, Lady Beatrice's cousin."

The obsequious manner vanished as the woman gave Ellie a critical stare. Her upper lip curled. "Oh! Of course, I should have known. Your hair is a slightly darker shade than your cousin's. But why is Lady Beatrice not here?"

"She had an unexpected conflict, so she sent me in her stead."

It had been the oddest thing, the way Lady Milford had appeared out of the blue to invite the girl to visit the Duke of Aylwin. Odder still, her ladyship had proposed that Ellie stand in for her cousin at this appointment. Lady Milford had even insisted that Ellie borrow a gown and the peacock-blue cloak from Beatrice, and had cleverly maneuvered their grandmother into agreeing that the Earl of Pennington's niece must be more fashionably garbed when she went out into public.

Ellie decided that Lady Milford had been well cast as the Furry Godmother in her storybook. Nevertheless, Ellie had her doubts about receiving anything other than hand-me-downs. Not even a magic wand could pry open her uncle's purse strings.

Mrs. Peebles straightened the lace on Ellie's sleeve. "Well! I shall make the final adjustment on a number of hems today. Will Lady Beatrice's shoes have a similar heel to yours?"

On Lady Milford's sage advice, Ellie was wearing the garnet dancing slippers. No shoe had ever felt so soft and comfortable, and she smiled to see the tiny crystal beads sparkle in the light of the lamps mounted on either side of the mirror. "Yes, I'm quite sure of it."

Mrs. Peebles knelt down on the floor and tugged at the hem. She held a number of straight pins in one corner of her mouth, but that didn't stop her from talking around them. "I cannot say that I knew you to be so close in proportion to Lady Beatrice. You appear to be exactly the same size, except for the bosom, of course."

Gazing at her reflection in the mirror, Ellie eyed the too tight bodice that squeezed her breasts to the point of nearly spilling over the low neckline. Embarrassed, she could think of no reply to the frank comment. She had always been uncomfortably aware of being more endowed in that one area in comparison to her cousin.

"'Tis a crime to wear shapeless gowns when you've such a pleasing figure," Mrs. Peebles went on. "A woman should draw attention to her best assets. Turn, please."

Ellie obliged, inching around so that the seamstress could reach another section of the hem. "I'm merely the chaperone. It's my cousin who is making her debut, after all."

"Bah. All women must keep up appearances. Begging your pardon, but how else will you attract a husband?"

Ellie cast a glance downward at the brown sausage curls on the proprietress's head. Evidently, Mrs. Peebles had overcome her initial snit and now desired a friendly chat. Ellie didn't mind a conversation, but she balked at confessing her private plans to a stranger. Most people couldn't fathom how a woman could be perfectly happy without a husband to clutter up her life with his demands.

Of course, most people also didn't have a head full of stories.

"I'm sure you're quite right," Ellie said tactfully. "Tell me, if I *were* to improve my appearance, what colors would you recommend?"

Mrs. Peebles squinted up at her. "Your features call for jewel tones. A deep bronze would bring out the red in your hair. As would an emerald green or a marine blue."

Just as Ellie hoped, the woman proceeded to regale her with advice on fabrics and trimmings, successfully averting a lecture on Ellie's marital prospects—or lack thereof. By the time she'd tried on a series of Beatrice's gowns and waited through all the hemming, Ellie and Mrs. Peebles were friends, and the woman offered to sell Ellie a swath of jade-green silk at a fraction of its cost.

Ellie gratefully accepted the brown-paper parcel. Though it would make a dent in her savings, the fabric would provide a welcome alternative to remaking one of the countess's ugly gowns. With warm thanks, she promised to return on the following day with her payment.

Unless, of course, a miracle happened and her uncle paid for it. But Ellie wouldn't hold her breath over *that*.

Upon emerging from the shop, she paused in surprise to see that dusk had fallen and only a few shoppers remained on Bond Street. The afternoon hours had passed so enjoyably that she had quite forgotten the time. A cold rain had begun to sprinkle, and she drew up the hood of the cloak that she'd borrowed from her cousin.

Grasping the parcel strings in one hand, Ellie started on the short walk to Hanover Square. She now regretted wearing Lady Milford's pretty slippers. Not because they hurt her feet—indeed, they felt like walking on air—but when she'd departed home early in the afternoon, there had been no sign of stormy weather. From the ominous look of these black clouds, she worried that a downpour could ruin the shoes.

Her head bent against the icy droplets, she hurried past shop windows that glowed yellow with lamplight. Home lay only a brisk ten-minute walk away. Nevertheless, it would have been pleasant to be ensconced inside one of the many passing carriages, wheels rattling and hoofs clopping, while she relaxed in warm luxury.

Had Beatrice returned to Pennington House? Ellie was anxious to discover how the visit had gone and if, after all, her cousin had managed to charm the Duke of Aylwin. Despite her silly naïveté, Beatrice was a beautiful girl, and even the most bookish of gentlemen would find it hard to resist adoring blue eyes and a fresh, lovely face.

Would Walt be at home, too?

Shuddering, Ellie recalled the scene from the previous night that she'd pushed from her mind all day. He had pawed her bosom in the most shockingly obscene manner. Should she tell her uncle? No, Walt would only deny it, and Uncle Basil wasn't likely to believe her word over that of his son. She would just have to be more careful to avoid Walt until she sold her book and could afford to move away . . .

At the end of the block, Ellie turned the corner and, in her haste, bumped into a maidservant coming from the other direction. The girl dropped her basket and apples spilled over the wet pavement.

"Oh!" Ellie exclaimed. "I'm ever so sorry." Immediately, she bent down to help the girl retrieve the fruit.

While reaching for an apple that had rolled into the street, she happened to notice a man stepping out of a black coach a short distance away. He was a hulking fellow in a greatcoat and a hat with a curled brim pulled low over his shadowy face.

Ellie froze in a crouch with her fingers curled around the apple. Was it just her imagination, or did he bear an uncanny resemblance to the stranger who'd been eyeing Beatrice the previous day?

As he glanced in Ellie's direction, her heart slammed in heavy strokes. Yes, it *was* him. She recognized those harshly chiseled features. Then he strode toward one of the lighted shops, opened the door, and disappeared inside.

Ellie shivered from a chill that had little to do with the frigid dampness of the weather. Rising, she handed over the last apple and gave a distracted smile in answer to the maidservant's stammered words of appreciation. Wanting only to be safely at home, Ellie rounded the corner and made haste down the deserted side street, the parcel strings digging into her cold, gloved fingers.

She didn't know what to make of the incident. Was it just a horrid coincidence that she'd encountered the same man again? And why had he looked at her so keenly? Of course, she was wearing her cousin's peacock-blue cloak, the same one Beatrice had worn to visit Lady Milford. Was it possible that he'd mistaken Ellie for Beatrice?

Ellie tried to convince herself that she was overdramatizing a perfectly ordinary situation. He had made no menacing gesture toward her. Perhaps, given her propensity for storytelling, it was only natural for her to conceive the worst.

Then, while going past a dark alley behind the shops, she glimpsed something out of the corner of her eye. A ripple of movement. A black form hurtling through the shadows.

Straight at her.

Ellie sucked in a breath to scream. Before the sound could escape her lips, he pounced. His hand smothered her mouth and cut off her air. As if she weighed no more than a rag doll, he yanked her off the side street and into the gloom of the alley.

The parcel dropped from her fingers. In a wild panic she struggled and kicked. But he subdued her with the iron grip of an ogre. He thrust her up against a wall and pressed a sharp-smelling cloth to her face.

Taking a choking breath, she tried to turn her head away from the sickly-sweet aroma. A wave of dizziness drained the strength from her limbs. And the world melted away into nothingness.

Chapter 6

Ellie had been cast adrift in a shipwreck.

She was floating in an endless black sea. The rhythmic motion of the water rocked her, and she could hear the muted crashing of waves. Voices reached her ears now and then, the words garbled, too indistinct for her to decipher their meaning. At those times she struggled against the suffocating heaviness of lethargy. She wanted desperately to call for help, but only moans croaked from her lips.

Then a spectral hand would press a cup to her mouth, impelling her to swallow a liquid. And she would drift back into the gloom of her watery grave.

At last there came a time when the shroud of darkness began to lift. She grew aware of a warm, soft surface beneath her body. No longer did the vibrations of the sea hold her captive. She knew it to be day because a diffused, lemony light penetrated her closed eyelids.

Again she heard voices. This time, she detected the deep baritone of a man. Two men, to be precise. As she strained to make sense of their mutterings, specific words pierced the veil of her torpor.

Lady . . . missing key . . . ransom . . . the earl . . .

One voice had a distinct Scottish brogue, and the other the cool, clipped tone of the upper class. Their conversation grew louder as if they had moved to stand right beside her. Gradually, entire sentences became clear to her, though she was too woozy to make sense of them.

"Such a wee, drab wren she is."

"I daresay you're right. She did look much prettier from a distance."

At that, Ellie managed to lift her heavy eyelids. For a moment she blinked against the light and her vision swam alarmingly. Then the dark blotches that loomed over her coalesced into one silhouette.

A black-haired man bent down close, staring at her.

His features had hard edges, as if a sculptor had chiseled them from a block of marble in a fit of artistic fervor without adding any refining touches. His cheekbones were high, his nose a straight blade, his jaw square. In contrast to the somewhat swarthy tint of his skin, he had the most stunning green-gray eyes, and she found herself wondering how to re-create that precise color with paints . . .

In the same instant, memory struck like a hammer blow. She knew him. He was the stranger she'd seen on the street. The man who had been staring at her cousin. The man who had rushed out of the alley to attack her.

Choked by terror, Ellie tried to raise her hands to thrust him away. But her arms were trapped beneath the quilt and she felt as weak as a newborn kitten. The realization that she was lying in a bed only increased her fright. She thrashed to free herself from the tangled weight of coverings.

"Get away!" She meant to shout, but her dry throat allowed only a rasp of sound. "Or I'll . . . I'll scream."

He obligingly straightened up and retreated, though

taking only a single backward step. His charcoal-gray coat and silver waistcoat bespoke expensive tailoring. Hands on his hips, he gazed down at her, his mouth twisted in a grimace. "Calm yourself, Lady Beatrice. I've no intention of harming you—so long as you cooperate."

Beatrice? His statement confused Ellie and she searched the fuzzy edges of her mind for an explanation. Had he meant to abduct her cousin, then? It would seem so. She had to make him understand his mistake.

But first, Ellie wanted to stand on her own two feet. She felt horribly vulnerable lying down without any means of defending herself. Gathering all of her strength, she hoisted herself up on her elbows. Then she had to stop, panting with effort, as fatigue sapped her strength.

Much to her surprise, a woman appeared at the bedside to lend assistance. The middle-aged maidservant had kind blue eyes in a careworn face and she clucked in sympathy at Ellie's plight. With her help, Ellie soon found herself sitting against a mound of pillows and taking a sip of water from a proffered cup. The dull pounding in her head made her slightly nauseous. She ignored it, too busy trying to assess the direness of her situation.

She sat in an antique, four-poster bed with a sagging canopy and dark green curtains to be drawn around at night to keep out the drafts. The room had curved stone walls, narrow window slits, and heavy, old-fashioned furnishings.

It looked like a prison cell for a noble hostage.

The maid scurried back to her place by the door, joining a grizzled, bald-pated man with bandy legs. He must have been the other male voice she'd heard, Ellie realized. The presence of the servants made her feel only marginally safer.

Her gaze returned to her abductor. As if hewn of marble, he hadn't moved. He remained standing beside the bed in that arrogant pose with his hands flanking his lean waist and his gaze intent on her. The hard slash of his mouth showed no sign of softening.

"I'm afraid you've made a terrible mistake," she said.

He had the audacity to chuckle. "I'm sure *you* believe so, my lady. Allow me to introduce myself. My name is Damien Burke. It's a pleasure to make your acquaintance."

Ellie fleetingly noted the absurdity of a formal introduction to her abductor as if they were guests in a London drawing room. Then her mind latched onto his name. *Damien Burke*. Where had she heard it before?

From out of the mists of memory came a scrap of gossip. Some six or seven years ago, she'd been helping the countess sort her embroidery threads when Walt had burst into their grandmother's boudoir. He'd been eager to relate the latest scandal, that one of his old classmates, a scoundrel by the name of Damien Burke, had been caught *in flagrante delicto* with an impoverished lady and had been drummed out of polite society.

So much for the Demon Prince, Walt had said almost gleefully. *Now he'll return to the gutter where he belongs.*

The countess had agreed. She'd declared Damien Burke to be the sort of rogue who put a shiver down the spine of any decent lady.

Now, staring up at his stony features, Ellie didn't feel a shiver. Instead, she felt a swell of anger that he'd had the nerve to kidnap an innocent lady for his own nefarious purposes. Demon Prince, indeed!

She gripped her fingers in her lap. "It *isn't* a pleasure to meet you, sir. Nor will *you* find it a pleasure when you realize that I'm not Lady Beatrice. I'm her cousin,

Miss Eloise Stratham. You have imprisoned the wrong person."

His mouth quirked slightly and he stared more keenly at her. "Quite clever, my lady. But surely you cannot ask me to believe you're that drab nun I've seen in your company from time to time. She must be at least twenty years your senior."

"Drab nun? Twenty *years*? I beg your pardon!"

"Besides, you were wearing the finest garments. Your shoes alone would have cost a year's wages for a servant."

Ellie parted her lips to explain that the clothes had been borrowed, when she suddenly looked down at herself, distracted by the startling realization that she no longer wore the gown and shoes. Her garb had been replaced by a fine lawn nightdress, and her feet felt bare beneath the blankets.

A flush suffused her from head to toe. Who had removed her clothing? This wicked man? Worse, had he taken advantage of her while she was unconscious?

Too scandalized to ask, she said stiffly, "Where are my things? And what did you do with my shoes?"

"You'll have them back, all in good time. In the meanwhile, Mrs. MacNab will see to your needs." A glint in his green-gray eyes, he added, "I'm sure you'll be comforted to know that *she* took care of you during our voyage here."

Ellie glanced at the kindly maidservant waiting by the door, then back at Damien Burke. "Voyage?"

"Yes, we were at sea for three days. It was necessary for me to take you far enough away from London so that no one could easily mount a rescue."

Ellie tried to grasp the astonishing news. Three days had passed? Dear God, he must have drugged her, perhaps with laudanum. That would explain her headache and the sense of sluggishness. And it also explained the dreamlike period when she'd felt the constant rocking of the sea and heard the rhythmic crashing of the waves. She had vague, disjointed memories of someone feeding her, helping her to the chamber pot. And at other times, voices talking . . .

A cold knot formed at the pit of her stomach. Heaven help her. She had been gone for *three days*. The family would have discovered her disappearance the first evening when she'd failed to return home from the modiste. They would have been searching for her all this time . . .

"Where am I?" she asked hoarsely. "Where have you taken me?"

"Never mind, my lady. It is of no consequence whatsoever. You're to relax and enjoy your stay here. Consider it a holiday."

Damien Burke strolled away from the bed, stopping near a massive stone fireplace where a blaze crackled on the hearth. He leaned his forearm on the mantel in a cavalier pose. He was a tall man, broad shouldered and muscular, and it was no wonder he'd managed to subdue her so easily.

What did he intend to do with her?

Ellie's mind shied away from speculating, and she struggled to contain her fear and outrage. "Enjoy my captivity? You must be mad."

"You'll be treated in the manner to which you're accustomed. I've provided you with every luxury, including two servants to wait upon your every wish."

"I am *not* Lady Beatrice," she repeated. "And I *wish* for you to acknowledge that. Since you've wrongfully abducted me, I demand to be released at once."

"I'm afraid that's impossible. I've no intention of letting you go—until your brother complies with my demand."

"Brother? I don't have a brother."

He grimly regarded her, his face taut in a slant of weak sunlight from the window. "Enough with this charade, Lady Beatrice. It's growing quite tiresome. You shall remain here until Walt delivers the ransom. I sent him a note to that effect before we left London."

Ransom.

Latching onto that word, Ellie felt a modicum of relief. Damien Burke's purpose was not to force her into his bed. Nor would he try to coerce her into marriage on the faulty belief that she was an heiress.

He merely wanted *money* in exchange for her return.

Then her heart sank again. Her fate rested in the hands of her weakling eldest cousin. Walt wouldn't be able to pay; he lived off a quarterly allowance and he often grumbled about the paltry sum. Would he speak on her behalf and ask for help from his father?

Ellie despaired to imagine the earl's reaction. If Uncle Basil was too miserly even to pay her a wage, how could she expect him to redeem her from the clutches of this scoundrel? Especially since her reputation would be in tatters after such a long absence . . .

"What is the amount of the ransom?" she asked. "Because I can assure you, Walt seldom has funds to spare. And if you think he'll seek money from his father, well, your scheme won't work. I'm *not* the earl's daughter, and he won't pay so much as tuppence for my release!"

Damien Burke narrowed his eyes to ratlike slits. His expression thunderous, he stalked to the bedside and stabbed his forefinger at her. "The ransom is *my* concern, not yours. All I expect from *you*, Lady Beatrice, is for you to comb your hair, eat your meals, and most of all, stop trying to bamboozle me!"

With that, he pivoted on his heel and stalked from the chamber, slamming the heavy oak door behind him.

The manservant and Mrs. MacNab, who had been waiting in the shadows, now held a whispered conversation. The fellow departed in his master's wake, while the woman bustled forward. "Poor wee lass," she crooned in a thick brogue. "The laird oughtna bluster like that. And ye sufferin' such a shock, bein' dragged from the bosom of yer family."

The laird. Ellie seized the clue. "Where am I? Is this . . . Scotland?"

Mrs. MacNab pursed her lips. "'Tisn't fer me t' say, milady, though I wouldna deny that, neither. Now, I ken ye'll be wantin' the privy."

She helped Ellie out of bed and guided her behind a screen before allowing her seclusion to complete her business. Ellie pondered the woman's words. Since they had traveled by ship, did that mean they were near the coast? Could they have gone as far as Edinburgh? Or were they closer to the English border?

She came out to find Mrs. MacNab bending over an opened drawer of a tallboy. "Please," Ellie asked, "what is the name of this place?"

The woman looked up warily. "'Tis a castle. I canna say more."

A castle?

Ellie glanced around the chamber and noted the circular stone walls. This must be a tower room. In spite of the grim circumstances, she felt a spark of interest. She'd seen drawings of such fortresses in books and had sketched them herself, guided by her imagination. But never had she had the occasion to actually visit a castle.

Eager to look outside, she pulled a wooden stool to the window slit. But to her disappointment, the opening was too high for her to see anything more than the fast-scudding clouds. From the direction of the light, it appeared to be late afternoon.

A knocking sounded and the manservant entered, toting a huge can of water in each hand. "Over here, Finn," said Mrs. MacNab, dragging a small copper tub over to the fireplace. He emptied the cans into it; then he bobbed his bald head in Ellie's direction and left again, shutting the door behind him.

She scowled at the wood panel. Damien Burke had assigned these two servants to her. Where had the Demon Prince gone? Perhaps he was scuttling through some dark passageway like the rat he resembled.

He hadn't seemed at all concerned that she might try to escape. Had he stationed guards throughout the castle? Or maybe he simply didn't consider a London debutante to be intrepid enough to sneak past Mrs. MacNab while her back was turned.

Ellie pondered that notion. She hadn't seen either servant use a key in the lock. She might never have a better chance than now, for the woman was looking into an open wardrobe, busy at some task.

Keeping an eye on the maidservant, Ellie tiptoed toward the door, her steps silent on the rug. Just as her fingers curled around the cold metal handle, however, Mrs. MacNab glanced over her shoulder, shook her mobcapped head, and clucked her tongue.

"Now where would ye be goin', hinny, in yer nightdress an' bare toes? There be a north wind blowin', an' ye'll catch yer death. Come, let old MacNab brush yer hair."

If the woman had screeched or threatened, Ellie would have flung open the door and run for dear life.

But that motherly manner made her face the folly of the impromptu plan. Where would she go, anyway? Out into the barren countryside wearing only a thin shift? It was February, and she would freeze to death.

Mrs. MacNab drew her over to a dressing table. "Sit ye down, lamb. I'll work out the snarls afore yer bath."

Ellie found herself ensconced on a cushioned stool. Gazing into the age-spotted mirror, she gave a start of surprise. No wonder the Demon Prince had so rudely ordered her to comb her hair. Instead of her usual neat topknot, a frightful bird's nest perched on her head. The damp sea air had created a mass of reddish-brown waves that hung down her neck. She had dark circles under her eyes and her cheeks were pale, making the sprinkling of freckles appear more prominent.

Mrs. MacNab picked up an ivory comb and began to gently separate the tangles. As Ellie used her fingers to work at another section, she felt irked and out of sorts. Never in her life had she met a more boorish rogue than Damien Burke. He might garb himself as a gentleman, but his manner was arrogant and rude. He had even called her—or rather, Beatrice's companion—a *drab nun.* To make matters worse, he had surmised her to be a full two decades older than Beatrice, although in reality only nine years separated the cousins in age.

Stung by his assessment, Ellie scowled at her reflection in the mirror. Did she really look all *that* unattractive? Apparently to him she did. And maybe she should be glad because it meant that she needn't worry about him making any unwanted advances.

There was something else he'd said, too, during the dreamlike state before she'd opened her eyes. *She did look much prettier from a distance.*

Ellie tugged hard at a knot in her hair. Stupid, shallow man! Of course, Beatrice was the beauty of the family. That was precisely why he should have believed Ellie's assertion about her identity. The evidence was right in front of him, yet he'd refused to acknowledge his own blunder in seizing the wrong woman.

He would be forced to accept the truth when the ransom failed to materialize. But that could be weeks, and Ellie had no desire to wait so long for enlightenment to penetrate his thick skull.

Finn delivered two more cans of hot water, and after he'd gone, Mrs. MacNab moved the screen by the fireplace so that Ellie could have privacy while she bathed. She sank into the steaming bath and the pleasure of it had a mellowing effect on her mood. Relaxing in spite of herself, she concentrated on scrubbing herself with a hunk of lilac-scented soap, rinsing her hair until it was squeaky clean.

When she finished, Mrs. MacNab handed her a linen towel and brought forth a gown of ruby silk with a narrow waist and slim long sleeves.

"That isn't mine," Ellie protested.

"The laird bade me purchase all yer necessities. Ye'll find plenty more o'er there." The woman nodded at the oversized wardrobe, where the open door revealed an array of fancy gowns.

Ellie balked at accepting anything provided by the Demon Prince. It was beyond the pale for a lady to wear clothing given to her by a strange man. But what other choice did she have?

She accepted Mrs. MacNab's help in dressing and then sat near the hearth to run a comb through her long, wet curls. When the woman departed to fetch supper, Ellie jumped up from her stool and examined every nook and cranny of her prison cell. There were copies of fashion periodicals, a deck of playing cards, needlework supplies, and several gothic novels of the sort read by ladies. Then she peeked out the door to see a winding stone staircase lit by a flickering torch in a wall bracket. The steps went around a curve and vanished.

The prospect of escape sorely tempted her. But now was not the time, for the Demon Prince might be prowling the corridors. She must wait until late in the night when everyone was asleep.

Damien Burke had planned well for her captivity. But little did he know, Ellie intended to outwit him.

Chapter 7

In the dead of night, Ellie crept out of the tower chamber. The icy chill in the stairwell made her grateful for the hooded cloak. The pair of boots she'd discovered in the wardrobe pinched her toes, though that was the least of her worries.

After finishing supper, she had intended to stay awake reading in bed. But an irresistible weariness had come over her and she had fallen asleep over her book, only to awaken a few minutes ago to find the room dark save for the glow of embers on the hearth.

The problem was, she now had no notion of the time. It might be midnight . . . or it might be near dawn. If the latter was the case, then she needed to hurry. It was imperative that she put as much distance as possible between herself and Damien Burke.

Descending the steep, curving steps in her long skirt was a slow process that required her full concentration. The torch in its wall bracket had long since guttered out and her only light came from the candlestick in her hand. Cold drafts of air swirled around her, so that she was forced to keep one gloved hand cupped around the flame.

Heaven help her if she lost her only source of illumination. She'd never find her way through the pitch-dark castle. She might become lost in the dungeons, never to be seen again until one day someone stumbled upon her skeleton . . .

Ellie pushed the fanciful thought out of her head. It wouldn't do to spin stories when she faced a series of genuine trials. First and foremost, avoiding the Demon Prince.

Over a supper of cheese, sausage, and fresh crusty bread, she had engaged Mrs. MacNab in conversation, asking questions while trying to make the inquest sound like mere, wide-eyed curiosity. Where was the kitchen? Were there stables? A gatehouse? Did anyone else live in the castle? Where did the laird stay?

By the time she finished her food, Ellie had gleaned a rough idea of the layout of the castle. It sounded fairly simple. She was in one of the towers that marked the four corners of the fortress. A stone keep stood in the center of the castle yard. Once she managed to find that yard, there should be enough moonlight for her to see the gatehouse.

Beyond that, she had no idea how the portcullis was opened, or if she would have to let down a drawbridge as well. But there must be a way out. She had to be as clever and resourceful as Princess Arianna in her storybook.

At the base of the tower, Ellie arrived at a closed door and tugged at the iron latch. When it refused to budge, her heart sank. Was *that* why no one had bothered to secure her chamber? Because this lower door kept her imprisoned?

All of her hopes were dashed in an instant. No! It couldn't be true. She wouldn't let herself be trapped in here.

In a fit of desperation, Ellie set down the candlestick on the floor and used both hands to wrestle with the latch. She couldn't see a keyhole in the gloom. Was the door bolted from the outside? Or was there a bar across it to hold her inside? If so, her plan was doomed.

Beneath her fumbling fingers, the latch abruptly lifted with a loud, scraping protest. She laughed in relief, the sound a hollow echo in the gloomy stairwell. Praise God, the fastener had only been stuck in place.

Then disaster hit. As she pushed at the heavy door, a rush of frigid air came through the opening and doused her candle.

At once, a stygian blackness enveloped her. Ellie stood quaking in her too tight boots. She was afraid to move, afraid to step out of the tower and into the unknown. Heaven only knew what lay waiting for her in the darkness ahead.

It might be the Demon Prince.

Swallowing hard, she considered making the trek back up the winding staircase to relight the wick at the glowing embers of the hearth. Alternatively, she could simply crawl back into the warm cocoon of her bed and go to sleep.

Would Princess Arianna be defeated by the loss of a tiny flame?

No. Ellie drew a deep, cold breath. She had come this far and she mustn't turn back now.

Abandoning the useless candle, she applied her shoulder to the heavy door and it fully opened to a loud creaking of hinges. Icy fingers of air clutched at her face. The breeze must be coming from somewhere ahead of her, perhaps an opening to the outdoors.

Encouraged, she ventured slowly into the dense darkness, her arms outstretched. On either side, her fingertips brushed the unyielding stone walls. Was she in a passageway? Apparently so, yet the place had the oppressiveness of a tomb.

Gradually, her eyes adjusted and she distinguished a faint paleness in the form of a large archway some distance ahead of her. As she moved in that direction, the cold gusts grew stronger, tugging at her cloak and chilling her to the bone.

Ellie arrived at the opening and cautiously peeked out. To her great relief, she could discern the crenellated walls of the castle outlined against the vast expanse of the night sky. There was no moon. Only a few stars were visible between the massive charcoal clouds. Yet that small trace of light had lifted the mask of her blindness.

She was gazing out at the courtyard. In the center, the tall square keep crouched like a menacing black giant. According to Mrs. MacNab, the monolithic structure was the den of the Demon Prince.

Of course, the maidservant had not described the building in quite so gothic a fashion. She had merely confided that the laird had his quarters there, and that Ellie was not to worry about him troubling her because he was a fine, upright man despite his gruff manner.

Fine, upright man, indeed! Ellie didn't believe that description for the snap of a finger. Only a villainous rat would abduct a lady and hold her for ransom.

Over the whistling of the wind, she could hear the rhythmic roar of the sea. So the castle was located on the coast, after all.

Before leaving the shelter of the doorway, she scanned the open courtyard, straining her eyes to spot any movement in the shadows. All lay still. Where was Damien

Burke? With any luck, he was sound asleep in his bed, secure in the unwise belief that a pampered debutante would never attempt to escape.

Well, perhaps Beatrice would have been too distraught and weepy to formulate a bold plan of action. *She* would have been aghast at the notion of abandoning her creature comforts and creeping through a cold, gloomy castle in the middle of the night.

But not Ellie.

The gatehouse loomed on the adjacent outer wall. She decided against taking a straight route across the courtyard, opting instead to follow the wall where the shadows would conceal her progress. She needed to be certain that Damien Burke or his henchman, Finn, weren't hiding nearby. As she hurried along, the wind yanked at her hair and she drew up the hood of her cloak, holding it tightly beneath her chin.

The prospect of foul weather daunted her. If a storm was brewing, she would have to find shelter quickly once she left the castle. Perhaps there was a village nearby where she could conceal herself in an outbuilding or, better yet, throw herself on the mercy of a kindhearted crofter.

Reaching the gate at last, Ellie found the portcullis firmly shut. The crashing of the waves sounded louder here, and through the iron grating she could see the faint glimmer of water in the distance.

She walked back and forth, studying the massive barrier, but could find no handle or latch with which to open it. Now what? There had to be a way for the gate to be drawn up. Was there some sort of mechanism in a nearby chamber?

Spying a door in the wall, Ellie opened it. Instead of a room, however, she was startled to see an extremely narrow passageway. At the far end lay a shadowy aperture. Hardly able to trust her senses, she scurried through the tunnel and in a moment found herself standing outside the castle walls.

Euphoria lifted her spirits. She started to whirl around in a jig. Then a sudden squall of wind nearly knocked her over, reminding her of the need to make haste before the weather worsened.

On the theory that any pursuer would expect her to follow the dirt track in front of the gate, she turned in the other direction. Rocks and boulders littered the slope and she had to proceed slowly in the darkness. But at least there was no moat, probably because the castle appeared to be perched on a cliff overlooking the sea.

Ellie stumbled a few times going down the steep hill. Her boots were stiff, and she could barely see her way. Fierce gusts off the water cut like knives through the layers of her clothing. She kept moving, conscious of the need to flee the area as swiftly as possible. She had a vague plan of following the coast for a bit before veering inland and doubling back to the road.

At last the way flattened and the going became easier. On her right, the crashing waves glimmered in the faint starlight, foaming over the rocks and pebbles on the beach. To her other side, the castle loomed on the bluff facing the churning sea.

The cold seeped into her bones, and Ellie hunched inside her cloak, trying to stay warm as she hurried along the rocky beach. She cheered herself by imagining how dumbfounded Damien Burke would be when her absence was discovered in the morning. The Demon Prince would rant and rave, furious that his dastardly plot had been foiled.

Of course, it would have been foiled anyway when the ransom money failed to arrive. And then what would he have done to her?

She didn't want to contemplate that scenario.

Shivering, Ellie picked her way over the stone-littered sand. Freezing droplets of salt spray spattered her cheeks. She hastened onward, driven by the need to put distance between herself and the castle.

But when she glanced back to gauge her progress, the fortress still towered over her. Frustrated, she increased her pace, tramping over pebbles and keeping to the shoreline. The wind forced her to keep her head down, lest her hood be blown off. Her boots squelched in the wet sand, her hem felt damp and dragging, and several times she nearly stumbled under the sudden buffeting of a squall.

After a long period of slogging onward, she noticed that just ahead of her, an enormous boulder loomed on her left. Beside it lay a dirt track which ended abruptly at the edge of the rocky beach. Looking to see where the path went, she stopped dead, unable to believe her eyes.

The track meandered up the steep slope to the portcullis of the castle. She was back where she'd started.

How was that even possible?

Ellie blinked the salt spray from her lashes, convinced she must be hallucinating. It seemed she'd walked for close to an hour. Had she somehow become disoriented in the dark?

No, that explanation made no sense, either. The coastline had been at her right the entire time. She was absolutely certain of it.

Just then, something moved from behind the boulder. The silhouette of a huge hulking beast reared against the night sky. Like a creature from the netherworld, it sprang straight at her.

Shock paralyzed Ellie. Her heart gave a mighty jolt. She screamed, but the wind swallowed up the sound and carried it away.

She started to run, but the monster was upon her. His massive paws latched onto her shoulders. In the same instant, she spied his familiar features through the dense darkness.

Damien Burke. The Demon Prince.

"There's a storm brewing," he shouted over the wind. "You chose a rough night for a stroll on the beach."

Aghast, Ellie could only stare up at him. Her initial terror mutated swiftly into relief and then into anger at the fright he'd caused her. She yanked herself free and stepped back, nearly coming off-balance when her heel hit a stone. "You! You're supposed to be asleep."

"I would have been had I not spotted you from the window, creeping through the castle yard. I must say, it's been rather cold waiting for you to complete the entire circuit."

"Circuit?"

"We're on an island, my lady. Surely by now you've figured that out." His mocking chuckle joined the crashing of the surf.

The news crushed Ellie. An island! No wonder she had never lost sight of the castle. No wonder he hadn't bothered to lock her door or station any guards. Her escape had been doomed from the start. She was as much a prisoner as if he'd thrown her in the dungeon.

And now, after all the ill-treatment she'd endured at his hands, he had the gall to *laugh* at her.

In a blind rage, she launched herself at him, hammering his hard chest with her fists. "Monster! Evil rat villain! I hate you! I'd kill you if I could!"

She kicked viciously at his shins, stubbing her own toes without a care. At the same time, she lashed out at his jaw and boxed his ears. He caught hold of her upper arms, but she managed to stretch up her fingers to claw at his eyes.

Uttering a muffled curse, he twisted Ellie around and pressed her bosom against the huge boulder. She found herself trapped in between the hunk of cold stone and his large, muscled frame.

His fingers shackled her wrists so that she could no longer punch. The weight of his thighs at the back of hers immobilized her legs. Still, she fought in a fury to throw him off, wriggling in vain, panting from the effort. He merely held on tightly and waited her out, until eventually, she recognized the futility of the struggle and went still.

As she regained her breath, an unwelcome awareness of him seeped into her. The wind whipped frigid droplets against her face, but she felt toasty warm with his massive form molded to her back. His spicy scent invaded the brininess of the air. Never in her life had she been so close to a man. It felt shocking . . . scandalous . . . and curiously exhilarating.

No, that was anxiety churning in the pit of her belly. Although he hadn't struck back at her, she didn't trust him an inch.

He bent closer, his breath warm against her ear. "Evil rat villain?"

Ellie bristled at the humor in his tone. "It's the perfect description of you. Or would you prefer that I called you the Demon Prince?"

A deep growl emanated from his chest. "Walt told you that name. When?"

"What does it matter? Now, remove your hands from me at once."

He did nothing of the sort. "First, I must have your assurance that you've recovered from your tantrum."

Her blood boiled again, and she tugged at his iron grip. "Tantrum? Did you expect me to be docile when you're holding me imprisoned? When you kept me drugged for three days?"

"I expect you to behave, my lady. Else I'll be forced to lock you in your chamber."

Ellie bit back a retort about his fiendish nature. It was more important to correct his misconception. "Stop addressing me as 'my lady.' I'm *not* Lady Beatrice. I'm Miss Stratham. Miss Ellie . . . Eloise Stratham."

"So we're back to that again."

"Yes, because it's the *truth.* Beatrice is my *cousin.*" In wretched frustration, Ellie turned her head, looking over her shoulder to glower at his harsh features through the gloom. "*She* has strawberry-blond hair while mine is auburn. *She* has blue eyes and mine are brown. *Her* skin is like cream, mine is freckled. And you yourself said that I'm not pretty. That's because my *cousin* is the beauty of the family—not me!"

The darkness shielded his expression. But Ellie could feel his hands tighten ever so slightly on her wrists. His entire body felt rigid with skepticism. Did he believe her? She couldn't tell.

Abruptly, his weight lifted as he stepped back. "Come along," he growled. "We'll talk inside, out of this gale."

With that, he started up the dirt path to the castle.

Left alone on the beach, Ellie stood shivering in the absence of his warmth. She resented being ordered to heel like a pet dog. Especially by a man who was a despicable, ill-mannered rat.

For a moment she contemplated hurling herself into the sea, drowning in the cold brackish depths just to spite him. But then she would never have the chance to finish writing her storybook. She would never know the joy of reuniting Princess Arianna with her long-lost royal parents. She would never have that cozy cottage in the country where she could be free to pursue her dreams.

Gritting her teeth, Ellie started up the rocky slope to the castle. She had a plan for her life, and Damien Burke mustn't be allowed to ruin it. Somehow, she had to convince him that he'd abducted the wrong woman.

Chapter 8

Had he abducted the wrong woman?

Wrestling with the door to the keep, Damien wanted to punch his fist through the wooden panel. Every latch in this godforsaken castle was corroded by the sea air. He gave the iron handle another mighty tug and it finally lifted with a loud, creaking protest.

Pausing in the open doorway, he glared back at the hooded figure marching toward him across the darkened castle yard. The storm was gaining strength, and she staggered several times under the force of the powerful gusts. But he resisted the impulse to go to her and offer his assistance. The little witch would only bite his head off.

Dammit, she had to be Lady Beatrice Stratham. He didn't want to believe he'd made such a catastrophic mistake. He had tracked Walt's sister for several days. He had waited for hours outside that damned modiste's shop. He had grabbed her unawares and then smuggled her aboard one of his ships, a fast schooner with a loyal crew that had deposited them at this island without questioning the presence of an unconscious woman in his arms.

Damien had congratulated himself for pulling off the perfect plan.

Except maybe it wasn't so perfect, after all. If what she said was true, then it was an unmitigated disaster.

When she'd awakened in the tower bedchamber the previous afternoon, he had shrugged off her protests as a feeble attempt to trick him. He had been cocky and contemptuous, certain that she was lying about her identity in order to secure her release. Granted, his captive had looked rather ordinary compared to the exquisite girl he'd watched from afar. But he'd attributed the discrepancy to the fact that he hadn't ever viewed her up close. Anyway, how could she possibly be that middle-aged companion in the dowdy, shapeless garb? The slenderness of her body surely disproved that possibility.

Yet a few moments ago, she had catalogued the physical differences between her and her cousin: the hair and eye color and complexion. And he had heard the unmistakable passion of truth ringing in her voice. *You yourself said that I'm not pretty. That's because my cousin is the beauty of the family—not me!*

Dread soured his gut. How in hell could he have made such a blunder? If this irksome female turned out to be Lady Beatrice's spinster cousin—and he feared it to be true—then his plan to retrieve the stolen key from Walt was in serious jeopardy.

She approached the doorway where Damien waited. Though her features were shrouded by darkness, her manner radiated disapproval. When he stepped back to let her into the keep, she flicked her skirts aside to keep from brushing against him.

He caught a whiff of lilacs amid the cold sea air. That same feminine fragrance had enticed his senses while he'd held her imprisoned against the boulder.

He cursed the rise of heat in his blood. No matter

who she was, it would be the height of idiocy to imagine himself in bed with her. He shouldn't think of how supple and energetic she'd felt while struggling in his arms. Nor should he recall how her rounded bottom had rubbed him in exactly the wrong place. His business with her had nothing to do with seduction.

To hammer that point home, Damien banged the door shut. They were standing in the gloomy great hall with its rusty shields and the ragged tapestries on the stone walls. The only illumination came from an oil lamp sitting on a table and the glimmer of embers on the hearth.

"Follow me," he snapped.

He tramped toward the massive fireplace and threw several logs onto the grate. Then he grabbed the poker to stir the glowing coals, using more vigor than was necessary. As tongues of flame began to lick at the wood, he turned around to find his prisoner lurking in the shadows while eyeing the iron implement in his hand.

Good God. Did she think he meant to use it on her?

Irritated, he propped the poker against the stones and then waved at a wooden bench near the hearth. "Sit down," he said curtly. "You must be frozen."

She remained standing. "Where is Mrs. MacNab?"

"Asleep, I'm sure. It's after midnight."

"I shouldn't be here alone with you."

"Considering this wild claim of yours, *Miss Stratham,* you'll forgive me if I expect you to answer my questions straightaway. Would you prefer to do so here—or in your bedchamber?"

She pursed her lips and then seated herself on the bench at the end closest to the fire. "It isn't a wild claim. It's time you accepted that Lady Beatrice is still in London."

As she stretched out her gloved hands to the flames, the hood of her leaf-green cloak fell back to reveal an untidy mass of wavy hair that glowed red in the firelight. Her complexion had been rather sallow when she'd awakened some hours ago, but now her cheeks were rosy from the cold. The faint scattering of freckles across the bridge of her nose lent her an innocent look at odds with her shrewish, outspoken nature.

Damien stalked to the rough-hewn oak table and uncorked a decanter, pouring a liberal splash of liquid into a pewter goblet. He had always prided himself on paying close attention to detail. His skill at reading nuances of expression had enabled him to amass a fortune as the owner of a highly successful gentlemen's club.

When it came to Lady Beatrice, however, circumstances had forced him to observe her from a distance. Did she have any freckles?

Calling up an image of her face, he conceded that her skin had appeared to be pure cream. He also was certain that her hair had been a paler strawberry blond beneath her bonnet. And given her classic English coloring, her eyes were surely blue.

Not at all like the disapproving brown eyes that watched him now.

The reality of his colossal error drenched him in a cold wave. The woman sitting in front of him truly *was* Miss Eloise Stratham. Ellie, she'd called herself. God! How had he ever mistaken this sharp-tongued spinster for a guileless, seventeen-year-old girl?

It was her apparel that had fooled him. Damien had barely given Lady Beatrice's companion a glance, never bothering to look past her frumpish attire. Now, he felt perversely angry that she had dared to transform herself.

Striding forward, he thrust the pewter goblet into

her hand. "If you're the companion, you were garbed as Lady Beatrice when you went to the dressmaker. Why were you pretending to be her?"

"I wasn't! She let me wear a gown and cloak of hers, that's all. It was Lady Milford's idea." Looking down, Miss Stratham frowned at the contents of the goblet as if it were hemlock. "What *is* this?"

"Brandy. And why the devil was Lady Milford telling you what to wear?"

Damien remembered the beautiful woman from the time he'd spent in society as a wild young buck. After a rocky start at Eton, he'd realized the advantage of cultivating a bond with a select group of his fellow pupils, the more reckless of the noblemen. By the time he'd left the boarding school, he had been invited to numerous upper-crust parties despite his lack of a pedigree. He'd had a knack for cards even back then, winning more than enough to pay for the trappings of a gentleman.

Although Lady Milford had associated with a loftier circle, their paths had crossed from time to time. She had been unfailingly polite, yet he'd had the sense that those shrewd violet eyes were watching him, judging him. In particular, there had been one encounter that still twisted like a knife in his gut. She had sought him out at a ball, drawing him aside to warn him against his reckless courtship of Veronica . . .

Damien crushed the memory. Now was not the time to reflect on past mistakes. Lady Milford might be a grand doyenne of society, but she was just another meddlesome busybody. Less than a week ago, when he'd waited outside her town house to watch Lady Beatrice, and then had begun following the Stratham carriage, he'd heard someone rap on the window of Lady Milford's town house. He had glanced up without thinking, to see only a twitch of the curtains. But it had been her, wanting a look at his face, no doubt about it.

Had she recognized him? He didn't know.

Miss Stratham took a swallow from the goblet and screwed up her face at the taste of the brandy. "Lady Milford only meant to be helpful. She came to Pennington House to invite Beatrice to make an afternoon call with her. That's why *I* kept the appointment with the modiste. Beatrice and I are the same height and it was the hems of her gowns that needed adjusting."

"A likely story."

Ellie Stratham stared disdainfully at him. "You're one to accuse me of lying. You, who snatched me off the street and brought me here against my will. Well, I've some questions for you, too, sir. Are you so inattentive that you couldn't distinguish me from my cousin?"

"Inattentive—!"

"Did you never stop to wonder why I had no carriage or footman awaiting me? Or why I would walk home alone at dusk, without the protection of a chaperone?"

Damien gripped his fingers into fists. At the time, he *had* wondered, then had convinced himself of Lady Beatrice's naïve nature. When fate had presented him with the perfect opportunity, there had been no time to dawdle. He had acted decisively and captured her.

Or rather, he had captured Miss Ellie Stratham.

He stomped back to the table and poured himself a glass of brandy, draining it in one swallow. Unfortunately, the burning heat failed to soothe his aggrieved pride. "Pennington House was nearby. It wasn't inconceivable that Lady Beatrice would proceed there on foot. And I presumed her to be a modest, unassuming girl who didn't wish to force servants to wait upon her."

Miss Stratham stared a moment, then let out a peal of laughter. The merry sound echoed through the great hall, bouncing off the stone walls and adding warmth to the chilly air. "Unassuming? You truly *don't* know my cousin, then."

Damien stood transfixed by the way her ordinary brown eyes now sparkled like topaz. Amusement illuminated her whole face, erasing the pinched hostility and lending her a younger, prettier look.

The reality of her identity struck him anew. How had he ever believed this woman to be two decades older than Lady Beatrice? Surely no more than a handful of years separated them in age.

Just how old *was* Ellie Stratham?

The answer didn't signify. Not when she was laughing at his expense. "Naturally, you've the advantage of me in knowing Lady Beatrice's character," he said stiffly. "I've never had occasion to meet her."

Miss Stratham leaned forward, her gaze intent on him. "But you were watching her. You were sitting in your carriage outside Lady Milford's house, and that's why you should know Beatrice is hardly the meek, retiring sort. Did you not notice the way she was flirting with Lord Roland?"

The memory was crystal clear. From his perspective, Lady Beatrice had behaved as any typical young girl just freed from the schoolroom.

But that wasn't the source of the unpleasant shock Damien felt now. "You saw me?"

"Quite. You looked rather sinister in your black coat and hat. And then you followed us home and stared at my cousin while she went up the walk." Miss Stratham narrowed her eyes at him over the rim of her goblet. "I suspected there was something wicked about you—and I was right."

So much for believing he'd been discreet. Damien cursed himself for discounting this woman, who had turned out to be a far greater danger to his plan than he could ever have imagined.

Brusquely, he said, "Then the very next day, you put on your cousin's clothes and went to the modiste without her. Were you posing as her because you thought she needed protection from me?"

Miss Stratham blinked, then gave a firm shake of her head. "No, I already explained why I attended the fitting. Though even if Beatrice hadn't had a change of plans, I'd been toying with the notion of taking her place anyway because . . ."

"Because?"

Her expression suddenly troubled, she glanced at the fire for a moment before returning her gaze to him. "The previous evening, Walt came to my chamber. He warned me to keep Beatrice at home for the time being. He claimed that my uncle—the earl—wanted her to be punished for calling on Lady Milford without his permission. But I had the impression that Walt was lying to me." Those dark eyes bored into Damien. "Now I understand why. He knew that *you* were a threat to his sister. He knew that *you* meant to do her harm."

"Not *harm*," Damien objected. "I merely wanted to hold her here until Walt brought the ransom. Then he could take Lady Beatrice back home and no one would be the wiser."

Miss Stratham gave an unladylike snort. "Did you think my grandmother and uncle wouldn't notice her absence? Or that the servants wouldn't gossip? The news of her disappearance would have been all over society within hours. Whether you'd seduced her or not, Beatrice would have been ruined before she'd even had a chance to make her debut!"

He ignored the tight coil of guilt in his chest. "Nonsense. The season hasn't yet begun, so no one in society would have missed her. And before leaving London, I sent instructions to Walt on how to protect her reputation. I told him to concoct a story about his sister being called out of town to nurse a sick friend. If he has a brain in his thick skull, he did exactly that—for you."

With a thump, Miss Stratham set down the goblet on the bench. "It's *you* who have the thick skull, not Walt. No one will believe such a preposterous tale. You'd risk the reputation of a young lady just to line your pockets with gold."

Damien resented being attacked when she didn't know the whole story. He felt provoked into saying, "I haven't asked for gold. I only want Walt to return something that he stole from me. I gave him the chance to do so last week. When he refused, he left me no other choice but to force his hand."

"Stole from you? What?"

He prowled back and forth through the shadows. The less she knew, the better. He didn't want this harpy poking and prying into his past. "Never mind. Just tell me this. How close are you and Walt? Surely he will feel an obligation to rescue you."

Her lips parted, then pressed into a thin line. She glanced down, and the firelight illuminated the anxiety on her face. That look eroded Damien's hope of salvaging victory from the jaws of defeat.

When she returned her gaze to him, her expression was as bleak as the winter sea. "Walt may be my cousin, but I wouldn't describe us as *close.* As to ransoming me, I don't know. It all depends upon the value of this item. Is it terribly costly?"

Damien had a sudden inkling of her lack of stature

in the Earl of Pennington's household. As a poor relation, she would be expected to serve the family members. But apparently her worth to them had a limit. And she knew it.

Damn Walt! The weasel might very well abandon his cousin to her fate. And what of the earl? If Walt hadn't done so already, he'd eventually have to tell his father what had happened. Given his reputation as a stickler for propriety, Pennington would very likely consider his niece ruined. He might cut off all association with Miss Stratham lest Lady Beatrice be tainted by the scandal.

Damien raked his fingers through his hair. What the devil was he to do with her if no one delivered the ransom? He needed time to figure that out. For now, though, maybe she deserved a version of the truth.

"It's a key," he admitted. "It has no value to Walt—but it's important to me."

Miss Stratham gawked at him. The fire snapped in the silence, while a fist of wind knocked at the door. Then she surged to her feet and uttered incredulously, "You abducted me for a *key*?"

"It isn't just any key. It was given to me as a child." Damien had no intention of explaining his complicated background, how he had been left as a baby to the care of Mrs. Mims, or that the key was his sole link to the parents he'd never known. No one else could possibly understand this hunger he felt to uncover his past—and not just for himself.

For Lily.

Softness pierced the armor of his antipathy. His daughter might only be six, but someday she would ask him about her missing grandparents and he wanted to be able to answer her questions. He was determined to give

Lily everything he himself had never had—including a knowledge of her ancestry.

Not that he would ever admit such a desire aloud, especially to Miss Ellie Stratham. *She* would only exploit his weakness.

He added aggressively, "I don't take well to people stealing what belongs to me."

"Yet you'd steal a woman away from her family."

"Yes. I'll do whatever is necessary to force Walt to return the key."

Frowning, she thinned her lips, looking remarkably like a strict governess. "What does it fit? A treasure vault? I can't think of any other reason why he would bother taking an old key."

"It was pure malice, that's why. He knew it was important to me." Damien took a step closer to her. "You've known Walt all your life. You must have some sense that he isn't the most honorable of gentlemen."

Miss Stratham's eyes widened slightly and a shadowy emotion flitted across her features. Then she snapped, "You're one to speak. You're hardly a bastion of honor yourself."

Damien barely noticed her jab. He was too busy wondering at the source of that brief distress on her face. An ugly thought struck him. Had Walt made untoward advances toward her? Had the scoundrel tried to force his own cousin? Had he taken advantage of an impoverished woman who was reduced to living on the charity of her relatives?

Damien told himself it was none of his concern. Her private life had nothing to do with his purpose . . . unless it could be used to his advantage.

"I wonder if perhaps *you* might have seen the key," he said smoothly. "It's quite distinctive. One end has three teeth and the other, a brass crown stamped into an iron circle. It's likely to be in Walt's chambers at Pennington House."

A flush crept up her cheeks. She crossed her arms and glared at him. "I assure you, sir, I've never set foot in his bedchamber. Let alone snooped through his belongings."

Damien didn't know if her prickly response verified his suspicions, or was simply an expression of her hostility toward him. "Forgive me, I meant no insult. I merely thought you might have gone to his room to speak to him for some reason. If he'd left the key lying about—"

"If he did, I never saw it. But perhaps you and I could make a bargain. If you'll take me back to London straightaway, I promise I'll look for it."

The determined glint in her eyes unexpectedly amused him, though he kept his face expressionless. As vexing as she was, he admired her pluck. Most women in her situation would have collapsed into tears by now.

He also knew that she might very well turn him in to the law. If she'd been Lady Beatrice, he'd have been safe, for the family would never have sought his arrest for fear of ruining her. But they might not be so willing to protect a poor relation.

"And why would I trust you to help me?" he asked.

"Because it's your only hope of getting what you want," she said tartly. "If I may be blunt, Walt isn't likely to remove himself from the pleasures of London simply to deliver a key. He'd have done so for his sister, but not for me. You'd be wise to recognize that now and avoid being stuck here for weeks, waiting for a ransom that will never arrive."

Damien saw her point, but he was too frustrated by the failure of his plan to acknowledge it aloud. Instead, he wanted to throw back his head and howl like the rising wind outside the keep.

He grabbed the oil lamp from the table and thrust it into her hand. "Go on back to the tower before this gale worsens. I'll let you know my answer in the morning."

Chapter 9

Ellie awakened to a dim-lit bedchamber and the rattling of raindrops on the windows. The air felt chilly, but the blankets swathed her in a cocoon of warmth. For a moment she was perplexed by the canopy overhead and the green velvet draperies on the tall bedposts. Why was she not in her narrow cot in the nursery?

Yawning, she pushed up onto an elbow and blinked at the curved stone walls. Her bleary gaze came to rest on the stout, mobcapped woman bending over the hearth to stir the fire. The events of the previous day and night came rushing back. How could she have forgotten that she was imprisoned in the castle of the Demon Prince?

"Mrs. MacNab! Good morning."

Glancing over her shoulder, the middle-aged maidservant gave a rusty chuckle. "'Tis nigh on noon, hinny. Ye must've had happy dreams to slumber so long."

"Noon!" The news swept the cobwebs from Ellie's mind. At home, she was accustomed to rising at dawn in order to get an early start on her daily duties. Although she had little to occupy herself here, there *was* one important task that must be accomplished.

She had to convince Damien Burke to release her.

Ellie threw off the heavy coverlet and scrambled out of bed, scarcely noticing as her bare feet met the icy floor. She hurried to the armoire, opened the double doors, and grabbed a gown at random.

Mrs. MacNab scurried to her side to take the watered blue silk from her. "Nay, milady. Ye'll need wool t' keep ye snug on such a cold day. Wot's yer hurry, anyhow?"

"I need to have a word with your master. We may be departing for London today."

The Demon Prince had made no such promise, though Ellie remained optimistic. When she had proposed the previous night that he release her, he had glared like an ogre without giving her a definitive answer. But he simply *had* to come around to her way of thinking. Now that he'd acknowledged his mistake in abducting her, there was no point in tarrying here at the castle.

The maidservant's broad face wore a skeptical look. "Depart fer London? Why, 'tis a proper gale a-blowin' out there. Only a daft fool would set sail in such foul weather."

As if to underscore her statement, the wind whistled down the chimney, making the flames dance on the hearth. Shivering, Ellie rubbed her arms over the fine lawn nightdress. Her teeth were beginning to chatter from the cold. She glanced up at the narrow window slit to see solid, charcoal-gray clouds through the drenched glass. "Surely it can't be all *that* bad."

"'Tis indeed, an' ye'll catch yer death, dearie. I brung ye a pitcher o' warm water, so run along whilst I find yer warmest petticoat."

Mrs. MacNab draped a soft fawn shawl over Ellie's

shoulders and gave her a gentle push in the direction of the washstand. Ellie gave in to the motherly advice. By the time she'd finished her ablutions, Mrs. MacNab had the garments laid out on the bed, and Ellie quickly arrayed herself in a fine gown of bottle-green merino.

Sitting down at the dressing table to fix her hair, she was startled to see a lady of fashion reflected in the oval mirror. How strange and wonderful it felt to wear such an elegant gown. Nevertheless, the low-cut bodice showed off too much bosom, so she draped the shawl around her shoulders to cover herself.

She did *not* wish to inspire lecherous thoughts in the Demon Prince. He'd been barred from society for seducing an innocent lady, and such a villain surely had preyed upon other vulnerable females as well—though, of course, he had exhibited no such inclination toward Ellie.

She did look much prettier from a distance . . .

Those had been the first words she'd heard from him upon awakening from a drug-induced stupor. Evidently, he preferred beautiful women, a fact that suited Ellie perfectly well. Nothing could be worse than having to fend off the amorous advances of a notorious scoundrel.

She had a sudden, vivid recollection of how large and strong his body had felt the previous night, when he had trapped her against the boulder in order to stop her furious attack on him. His chest had been like an iron plate pressed against her back, his legs like solid oak columns. Never in her life had she experienced anything so unsettling to her senses. Even now, the memory of his muscled form made her knees weak, for it was a reminder of how easily he could overpower her . . .

Mrs. MacNab's voice broke into her thoughts. "Sit ye down by the fire, hinny, an' break yer fast. I'll be awa' then, t' finish me chores." The woman wrapped herself in a shawl and vanished out the door.

After a meal of warm scones with gooseberry jam and a pot of bracing tea, Ellie felt restored and ready to do battle with the Demon Prince. She donned her cloak and boots, and as she stepped out of the tower bedchamber, she was surprised to see another door opposite hers.

The darkness must have been too thick for her to have noticed it the previous night. She opened the door in curiosity, only to be battered by a rush of frigid air. Poking her head outside, she found herself gazing upon the battlements atop the castle wall. A narrow walkway in between the ramparts led to another tower far in the distance.

The notion of looking out over the sea appealed to Ellie. But the furious gusts of wind and icy rain made her think better of it. It might be safer to wait until the storm had died down. Closing the door, she set forth down the winding stone steps.

The lighting was dim inside the stairwell, but thankfully she didn't need a candle today. Cold drafts of air swirled around her, and raindrops blew through the narrow slits that were set at regular intervals in the curved walls. Despite the thickness of the stones, she could hear the faint, muffled crash of the surf and the shriek of the wind.

The tempest *did* appear to have increased in intensity during the night, Ellie acknowledged uneasily. Yet she held out hope that her departure might yet be arranged. Storms had a way of petering out after a time. With luck, the sun would be breaking through the clouds within an hour or two.

Today marked the fourth day of her absence from London. The longer she was gone, the more dire her predicament became. Had Walt concocted a false story to cover up her disappearance? If he'd failed to do so, the consequences would be grim. She would be deemed an unfit companion for Beatrice and ejected from Pennington House.

Disquiet nipped at Ellie's composure. With her storybook far from complete, she wasn't yet ready to earn her own living. Where would she go? No one would hire a ruined woman, and her meager savings would sustain her only for a short while.

She drew a lungful of damp, cold air. Succumbing to panic would only make matters worse. Better she should focus her mind on escaping this island prison by persuading Damien Burke to release her.

For all his fearsome appearance and brusque manner, he had struck her as a rational man, well spoken and reasonably civil. During their conversation in the middle of the night, he had shown no propensity to do her bodily harm. Rather, he seemed to believe that he had a true grievance against Walt for stealing that key. A grievance powerful enough to justify the kidnapping of Walt's sister.

In spite of her predicament, Ellie found herself intrigued by his drastic scheme. Why on earth was that key so vitally important to the Demon Prince? What exactly did it mean to him? He'd said it had been given to him as a child, but mere sentiment didn't explain why he would go to such an extreme length to retrieve it.

According to him, Walt had swiped the key out of malice. Did that mean there was a long-standing feud between the two men? If so, what was the basis of it? Ellie knew little about her cousin's private life, aside from the fact that he often griped about his lack of funds, complaining that he couldn't even afford to move out of his father's house. Did the key perhaps fit a strongbox or a bank vault? Had Walt needed money to pay off a secret gambling debt before the earl found out?

Her mind swirling with questions, Ellie reached the door at the bottom of the stairs. She was struggling with the stubborn latch when the sturdy oak panel suddenly banged open, causing her to scuttle backward with a gasp.

The Demon Prince loomed in the doorway.

Her heart made a mad leap. Tall and broad-shouldered, Damien Burke looked larger than life in his black great-coat and gleaming knee boots. He wore no hat, and his dark hair was windblown and tumbled onto his brow. His strong-hewn features showed a hostile expression in the gloom of the stairwell.

Those extraordinary green-gray eyes gave her a quick scan from head to toe. "Another escape attempt, Miss Stratham?"

Ellie clutched the edges of her cloak together. It was in her best interests to be courteous, but his mocking tone grated on her nerves. "Actually, you've saved me the trouble of hunting you down," she said stiffly. "I was coming to see if you'd made arrangements to take me back to London."

"No. Nor did I ever agree to do so."

With that, he presented his back to her and bent down to peer at the door latch. Ellie clenched her teeth. What a rude, obstinate man! Maybe he had decided to wait and see if Walt would bring the ransom, after all. The Demon Prince must not know her cousin very well, she thought bitterly. Walt wasn't likely to leave the comforts of London for a long journey into the middle of nowhere, especially in foul weather. There was a chance that he might send the key by post, but Ellie had no desire to tarry here long enough to find out.

Just then, she noticed that Damien Burke held a

small can in his bare hand. He applied the spout to the latch, letting a small amount of liquid dribble out. Next, he used a rag to daub away the excess. She stared, riveted by the sight of him getting his hands dirty at a task more suited to a servant.

"What are you doing?" she asked.

"It's rusty, and I'm oiling it. Now, go back up to your chamber. It's too cold and damp for you to be roaming about." His manner dismissive, he turned his attention to the topmost hinge.

Ellie compressed her lips. Did he expect her to meekly obey his order? Apparently so. Yet as much as she wanted to rake him over the coals, she needed his help. For that reason, she had to avoid antagonizing him.

"You've had ample time to consider my predicament," she said evenly. "Since I'm not Lady Beatrice, it's extremely doubtful that Walt will deliver the ransom. So you must see the futility in holding me here."

A grunt emanated from Damien Burke. It was the only indication that he'd heard her.

She doggedly went on, "I suspect that you're angry about the way things have turned out. But what's done is done, and now we must be sensible. You won't get your key back so long as we remain on this island. However, I am willing to look for it—in exchange for you returning me to London straightaway."

He muttered something under his breath, a sound that conveyed skepticism, though the noise of the storm muffled his precise words.

"The sooner we leave, the better," Ellie persisted. "You said yesterday that a ship brought us here. Where is it now? Is it anchored nearby? If we could board it as soon as the storm clears—"

"The ship is gone," he growled over his shoulder. "I sent it to harbor."

"To harbor? Where is that?"

"Over a mile distant. In this weather, there's no way to signal it. So you see, Miss Jabbermouth Stratham, we won't be leaving here. At least not anytime soon. Good day."

Oil can in hand, Damien Burke strode back through the tower entry and shut the door in her face.

Ellie stood stunned. Not leaving? And what did he mean by "not anytime soon"? He couldn't hold her here indefinitely!

The newly oiled latch lifted easily, unlike the previous night when she'd had to wrestle with it. Clutching her skirts, she hurried after him. The Demon Prince was already far ahead of her down the long, narrow passage, and she half ran to catch up to him.

"Wait!" she called. "Haven't you a rowboat that could take us to the ship?"

He paused to flash her a scornful look through the gloom. "Even if I did, it would be suicide to set out in such a gale. The waves would drench you inside half a minute. In another half a minute, we'd capsize and drown."

"It's only a storm. Surely it will end soon."

"We're in the North Sea. Winter storms here can last for days."

Days! Her insides twisted into a knot. Was she truly going to be stuck here with him for heaven only knew how long?

She couldn't accept that fate. Not when she burned to find out how Walt had explained her abrupt absence. Her fear was that Uncle Basil wouldn't swallow a trumped-up tale of her being called out of town to care for a sick friend. Nor was her sharp-eyed grandmother likely to believe it. Subjected to their questioning, Walt might have to confess that Ellie had been abducted by a scoundrel who had been tossed out of society for seducing a young lady.

Some six or seven years earlier, Ellie had been present when Walt had gleefully related that gossip to their grandmother. The countess had condemned the Demon Prince in no uncertain terms. Now, Ellie felt sick to imagine her family learning that she was with that very man. Although she was innocent of any wrongdoing, her reputation would be tarnished irreparably. Her family might very well disown her.

Directly ahead, Damien Burke was striding toward the open archway that led to the castle yard. But he didn't go outside. Instead, he turned right and proceeded through another doorway that she hadn't noticed during her nighttime trek.

Ellie went flying after him. He wasn't going to brush her off so easily. If she had to be trapped with the ill-mannered brute, then the least he could do was to explain certain matters to her.

As she passed the open doorway, an icy gust from the courtyard nearly blew her off her feet. Shivering, she scurried behind him down a shadowy tunnel until they reached another heavy oak door. He pushed it open and she followed him into a high-ceilinged chamber.

While he stopped there to apply oil to the door hinges, Ellie found herself distracted by the surroundings. She walked slowly forward, her footsteps echoing off the stone walls. On either side of her lay double rows of stone benches. Directly in front of the aisle, the stained glass in two high windows cast a faint, reddish-gold light onto a stone altar. She bent down to run her gloved fingertips over the elaborate Celtic cross that was carved into the base.

"What a lovely room," she said over her shoulder. "This must be the chapel."

"How brilliant of you to notice."

Ellie had had enough of his boorishness. She went marching back down the aisle and stopped right in front of him, tilting her head up to glare at him. "No wonder you're called the Demon Prince. You're the rudest man I've ever had the misfortune to meet. And if I may point out, it isn't *my* fault that I'm trapped here with you. The least you could do to atone for ruining my life is to be civil."

He glared, his eyes as hard as gemstones in his harshly handsome features. Rain pelted the window glass, and she had a keen awareness of how isolated they were. He could attack her and no one would hear her screams over the noise of the storm . . .

His mouth uncurled ever so slightly from its disgruntled expression. "Pray accept my apologies, Miss Stratham. If you don't care for my manners, I've given you leave to return to your chamber."

"No. You owe me answers to my questions."

He gave her a hooded stare, then crouched down in front of the door to oil the bottom hinge. "What questions?"

Gazing down at his damp, tousled hair, Ellie had the peculiar impulse to reach out and comb it with her fingers. She gripped her gloved hands together. "Last night, you claimed that Walt took the key out of malice. But you never offered any further explanation. Tell me, why would my cousin feel such spite toward you?"

"It's a long, complicated story."

"Well, it appears that you may have several days in which to relate every last detail. So start at the beginning. Where did you two meet?"

He cast a wary glance up at her. "In my first year at Eton. I was a scrawny, half-grown lad and he was a bully."

Ellie compared the two men in her mind. "But you're much larger than him now."

"Yes, I sprouted up the summer after that first year." As if to lend substance to the statement, he rose to his full height. "And once I'd thrashed him a time or two, Walt learned his lesson. After that, he quit pestering me—and stealing my belongings."

On that, Damien Burke turned and stalked out of the chapel.

Ellie's eyes widened as she absorbed the startling revelation. Then she scurried to catch up to him. "Wait. Are you implying that Walt stole that key from you all the way back in your school days?"

"Yes."

"But that had to have been some fifteen years ago! How can you be sure that he still has it in his possession?"

"Because I could see the truth in his face when I questioned him. Walt never was a good liar."

As they headed down another dank corridor, Ellie struggled to wrap her mind around the notion that the inciting event had happened so far in the past. "For pity's sake, why did you wait so long to try to get the key back?"

"I *did* make several attempts while still in school. I searched his belongings, but the key was nowhere to be found. Walt taunted me that he'd hidden it where I'd never find it. So I decided to bide my time until I had the power to force his hand."

The ruthless look on his face sent a chill down her spine. If he would do anything to retrieve his precious key, then he wasn't likely to let her go very easily.

"You *don't* have the power," she said firmly, "because I'm not his sister. As I've told you already, Walt will feel no obligation to rescue me."

"Then perhaps your uncle or grandmother will do so. Now stop following me, lest you tempt me to lock you in the dungeon."

With that, the Demon Prince stalked through an arched doorway and plunged out into the storm-swept courtyard.

Chapter 10

This time, Ellie didn't go after him. Lashed by rain and wind, she stayed within the stone archway. The icy torrent appeared not to affect Damien Burke at all. He made no attempt to duck his head as protection from the downpour. His strides long and even, he proceeded across the yard to the tall keep with its high, barred windows.

Let the Demon Prince run off to his lair, she thought scornfully. He was like a grumpy child who needed time alone to cool his bad temper.

If indeed the storm kept them stranded here for the next day or two, she'd have other opportunities to question him. For one, she wanted to know what had turned him into such a cold, callous man. Being bullied as a youth? Or was it his ouster from polite society for his shameful behavior with that innocent young lady?

She also wondered about his family background and the source of his funds. How had he acquired this castle? By lease or by inheritance?

Gazing up at the high turrets and the crenellated walls, Ellie felt no inclination to return to the safety of her tower bedchamber. The prospect of reading all afternoon sounded far too dull. Despite the nasty weather, she had a keen desire to explore the castle. And why not? Fate had handed her this rare opportunity to gather details for the illustrations in her storybook.

She headed down a passageway that led away from the chapel. Immediately, she yearned for a sketchpad and pencil. How she would love to capture the atmospheric gloom of this corridor, the rough-hewn shape of the stones, the green moss that grew like a carpet on sections of the walls. Coming upon a closed door, she opened it to peek inside at a cluttered storeroom. The shadowy interior appeared to hold a cache of old weaponry, from crossbows to spears, pikestaffs to broadswords.

Ellie gingerly picked up a long sword and nearly staggered from its weight. For a moment she imagined herself using the blade to force Damien Burke to free her from this island prison. Just as swiftly, she acknowledged the futility of that scenario. They were both stuck here so long as the storm continued to rage.

But she *did* like the sense of power the sword gave to her. It made her feel brave and heroic. Gripping the hilt more firmly with both gloved hands, she hoisted the blade and made a few experimental swings in the air, the cloak swirling around her. She was Princess Arianna battling the evil rat prince who had invaded her chamber . . .

Prince?

No, the man-sized rat was merely the latest in a series of mythical creatures to be slain by the princess in her quest to find her way home. A rat could not be a prince . . . unless perhaps he was an *enchanted* rat.

The notion caught Ellie's fancy. Propping the sword against the wall, she mulled over the possibility of adding a new twist to her story. Suppose a witch had cast a spell over a cruel, hard-hearted prince as a punishment. Suppose again that the only way to break the spell was for him to prove himself worthy of love. Yet try as he might, he could never succeed because people either screamed at the sight of a gigantic rodent or tried to kill him. Nevertheless, he could not give up. Resolving to win Princess Arianna's heart, he entered her chamber to help her fight off an invading ogre . . .

A wry smile touched Ellie's lips as she closed the storeroom door and resumed her stroll down the passageway. Damien Burke could never know that *he* was the inspiration for this new character in her story. And she would take great pleasure in molding and shaping him exactly as she wished.

A pity she couldn't do the same to him in real life. Unfortunately, he would always be a surly scoundrel. Outside the pages of a book, rats simply had to remain rats.

Roaming onward, Ellie could see that the castle was laid out in a large square, with the occasional chamber here and there, mostly empty or scattered with rubble. There were open archways to the courtyard at regular intervals, and whenever she passed one, she hurried her steps to avoid being spattered by freezing raindrops.

Gaining entry to another of the towers, she called out to see if either of the servants might be nearby. Her voice echoed in the yawning emptiness of the stairwell. The winding stone steps had crumbled in places, so she decided against climbing to the top.

Had the tempest not been blowing so hard, she would have liked to have gone up to the parapet and gazed out over the sea. Damien Burke had said that a harbor lay only a mile distant, so perhaps she could have glimpsed land through the pouring rain.

Ellie pressed onward, hoping to view the dungeon he had mentioned. But though she searched everywhere, she could find no trapdoor in the stone flooring, no stairway leading down into the bedrock. Perhaps the entrance was located inside the keep. If such was the case, her exploration would have to wait, for she had no desire to venture into the den of the Demon Prince.

After what seemed like hours of wandering, she opened a door at the end of another long passage and discovered welcome signs of life. A torch sputtered and burned in a wall bracket. The delicious aroma of cooking drew her toward a partially opened door.

She peeked inside. An oil lamp glowed over a cozy kitchen with crockery on the shelves and provisions arranged in an open cabinet in the corner. A huge stone hearth filled one wall. There, Mrs. MacNab stood stirring the contents of a cast-iron pot that hung from a hook over the fire. The man named Finn sat eating from a bowl at a long, rustic table, the lamplight gleaming on his bald pate.

Spying Ellie, he quickly wiped his chin on his sleeve and jumped up from the bench to make an old-fashioned bow from the waist. "Yer ladyship! Was there somethin' ye need?"

Mrs. MacNab turned, a wooden spoon in her hand. "Why, bless me, come in, milady! I bin wonderin' what happened t' ye. I was about t' send Finn t' ask the laird if ye'd fallen into the sea."

The irresistible warmth of the fire drew Ellie forward. She felt half frozen, her fingers tingling and her toes like icicles inside her boots. She rubbed her hands together and held them over the flames. "Brrr. I've been exploring the castle, that's all. Until now, I hadn't realized just how cold I was."

"Poor, wee lamb," said Mrs. MacNab, clucking her

tongue. "Ye must be chilled t' the bone. Sit down an' I'll bring ye somethin' warm."

Within moments, Ellie found herself seated at the table with a blessedly hot cup of tea cradled in her palms. Seeing that Finn had removed his bowl and stood by the fire to eat, she said, "Please, do join me, sir. I didn't mean to usurp your place."

"Wouldn't be proper, me sittin' with a fine lady."

"Nonsense. There's a spot for you right across from me." As he came forward and seated himself, Ellie added, "By the by, I wonder if Mr. Burke has informed you that I'm *not* Lady Beatrice. I'm her cousin, Miss Eloise Stratham. I'm afraid your master has abducted the wrong woman."

Finn exchanged a glance with Mrs. MacNab. Then a great grin split his grizzled face with its bushy eyebrows. "We heard ye say so yesterday, but we dinna ken if 'twas true or not. 'Tis no wonder, then, the laird's been as snappish as a cornered badger today."

Mrs. MacNab sank down beside Finn on the bench and fanned her face with her apron. "Saint Andrew preserve us! Perhaps 'twill teach the laird a lesson. I warned him this wicked scheme would come t' naught! Didn't I, Finn?"

"Aye, ye did indeed, hinny," Finn said, placing a peck on her plump, rosy cheek. "There's no one better'n me to know what a scold ye can be."

It was Ellie's turn to be surprised. "Are you two married? But you've different names."

"Finn MacNab, I am," he declared. "'Tis no surprise the master dinna tell ye. He's ne'er been one t' babble, not even since he could scarce find a hair on his chin t' shave."

Her curiosity piqued, Ellie leaned forward with the

teacup clutched in her hands. "Did you work for his family, then?"

"Nay, miss, he has no family. 'Twas at Eton College where I met the master. I was a man-of-all-work there, an' he was but a poor wee lad in sore need of a friend."

No family or friends? Poor wee lad? Ellie's mind conjured up a picture of Damien Burke as a boy, all tousled black hair and sharp, sullen features. Even if he *had* been bullied by Walt, the Demon Prince had a prickly nature that might very well have contributed to his unpopularity with the other boys. "What was he like as a child? Was he as cruel and disagreeable as he is now?"

"The laird isna cruel," Mrs. MacNab protested. "Mayhap a harsh man at times, but he willna harm a soul."

"Now, now, hinny," Finn said. "The young miss only kens what she sees."

"I know that he dislikes my cousin Walt, Viscount Greaves. They attended Eton together as boys. Do you remember him?"

"Aye, that I do," Finn said with a sage nod. "A sturdy lad with gingery hair, always with his gang o' young lords."

"Gang?"

Finn hesitated, stirring the contents of the bowl with his pewter spoon. "I dinna wish t' speak ill o' yer cousin, miss. Yet I fear he an' his cronies had a reputation for tormentin' the smaller lads."

That corroborated what Damien Burke had told her. Ellie wanted to know more. "Your master mentioned that my cousin stole a key from him. I believe it happened in his first year?"

"Aye, 'twas also the first time I spoke t' the young laird."

"So you were a witness?" she said with a flash of eagerness. "If you wouldn't mind, I should like to hear the whole story."

He gave her a measuring look, then nodded. "As ye wish, then. One winter's eve, I spied that band o' miscreants comin' out from behind the cloisters, laughin' an' chatterin' an' lookin' far too pleased with themselves. Soon as they'd gone, I hurried back an' found the young master with his lip bloodied an' his robes torn." Finn gave a rusty chuckle. "He was none too happy fer anyone t' see him—too full up with pride t' ask fer help, even back then. I bade him come with me, but the little termagant was in no humor t' obey. He kicked an' wiggled, an' I had t' pull him by his ear into the kitchen."

Mrs. MacNab had arisen from the table to stir the pot. Now, she turned to exclaim, "Oh, he was a sight! I sewed up the rips in his robes whilst Finn scrubbed the wee lad's face an' tended his bruises. We couldna let the headmaster find out, lest the poor lamb be expelled."

Ellie resisted any softening in her heart. That long-ago event may have been a wretched experience for Damien Burke, but it didn't excuse his reprehensible behavior toward her in the present. "Since he'd been set upon by a band of boys, perhaps it would have been wise of him to report them—so they could be stopped from attacking anyone else."

Finn gave a vigorous shake of his bald head. "Nay, miss. The headmaster wouldna heed his word over those high-and-mighty sons o' lairds."

"Why not? Perhaps he wasn't heir to a title, but to be accepted at Eton he must have come from a respectable family."

He hesitated, trading a glance with Mrs. MacNab. "Go on, tell her, Finn," she said. "It willna harm naught."

Finn said, "The young master wasna so fortunate as his classmates. He attended on a charity scholarship."

Ellie was taken aback by the news. She hadn't known the exclusive school admitted destitute boys. But even so, Damien Burke must have had a blue-blooded background, for Eton would never welcome a common urchin. "You said he had no family, that he was an orphan. But he must have come from *somewhere*. Who brought him to the school?"

" 'Twas his guardian," said Mrs. MacNab. She laid two wooden trays on the table and arranged pewter cutlery on them. "What was her name, Finn?"

"Mrs. Mims, if memory serves. Not long after, she passed on t' the next life." Rising, Finn carried his empty bowl to the dry sink, adding over his shoulder, "Indeed, miss, the young master learned o' her death on the same day yer cousin stole that key from him. I reckon he'd gone behind the cloisters so the other lads wouldna see him weep."

This time, Ellie couldn't stop a rush of compassion for the little lost boy. She knew the tragedy of losing the one person dearest to her heart. She had been fourteen when her father had died, and although Papa had had his faults, she'd never doubted his love for her. At times, she still felt the keen ache of his loss. Never again would she laugh at his silly jests, smell the pungent aroma of his pipe, or feel his good-night kiss upon her brow . . .

Yet plenty of children experienced misfortunes and *they* didn't grow up to be wicked scoundrels who abducted women off the streets.

"I understand that the key was given to him as a child," she said. "Do you know by whom?"

Finn shrugged. " 'Twas tucked in his blankets when he was a babe. Perhaps his mam put it there."

"Who were his parents? Do you know their names?"

"I dunno, miss, nor does he," Finn said. "I suppose he's hopin' the key will help him find 'em."

If Damien Burke didn't know their identity, Ellie could only conclude that he'd been born on the wrong side of the blanket. She'd heard whispers of disgraced ladies who'd been forced to retreat to the country for an inconvenient birth, then left the newborn to be fostered with a wet nurse. How curious that he'd been given a key, though, and without any explanation.

Ellie told herself not to dwell on the mystery. But at least now she could understand why he was so keen to retrieve the key. It was his only link to the parents he'd never known.

Not, of course, that that made any difference to *her*. He was still a callous ne'er-do-well who had imprisoned her against her will. He hadn't spared a thought for the way he'd disrupted her life—and quite probably ruined her in the eyes of her family.

Mrs. MacNab ladled the fragrant stew into two bowls and placed them on the trays. She added slices of crusty bread and pats of butter and then covered each tray with a linen towel.

"Finn," she ordered, "take the laird his meal afore he starves. An' dinna forget to wear yer bonnet."

Obligingly, Finn jammed a bright red cap over his bald head before donning his coat. He fastened his gnarled fingers around one of the trays. "Wish me luck, hinny," he told his wife with a grin. "The master's like to bite my head off fer bein' late with his dinner."

As Ellie hurried to open the door for him, he gave her a broad wink and went out into the passageway. She turned to see Mrs. MacNab donning a fringed gray shawl over her ample form. "Ye must be famished, miss. I'll carry yer tray up t' the tower."

Ellie opened her mouth to say that she was perfectly happy to eat right here in the warm kitchen. Then another notion struck her, and she took the tray from the table before the maid could do so. "Thank you, but there's no need for you to wait on me. At home, I'm accustomed to fending for myself."

"But, miss, 'twouldn't be proper—"

"Nonsense. This isn't London, so we needn't follow decorum here." After reassuring the woman with a smile and a few more platitudes, Ellie finally escaped the kitchen with the tray in her hands.

She didn't turn to her tower bedchamber, however. Instead, she went down the corridor to the outer door. There, she bent her head against the driving rain and hurried toward the tall monolith of the Demon Prince's den.

Chapter 11

As Finn whisked the cloth off the tray, Damien caught a delicious whiff of beef stew from his seat at the other end of the table. His stomach gave a hollow rumble. Needing to keep himself busy in this godforsaken place, he had spent the past few hours diligently applying himself to one of the account books that he'd brought from London. Now, he gratefully closed the volume and slid down the bench to the place where Finn was arranging the meal.

"It took you long enough," Damien said, picking up the pewter spoon and dipping it into the bowl. "Did you send all the way to Edinburg for the ingredients?"

"Nay, 'twas only that yer prisoner paid us a visit."

Instantly suspicious, Damien paused with a spoonful of steaming stew halfway to his mouth. "She came to the kitchen? Why?"

"Starved fer company, I'll guess. We had a long, cozy chat, that we did. O' course, she wouldna have set a dainty foot in the servants' quarters if she was truly her ladyship."

Seeing the glee in Finn's squinty blue eyes, Damien

compressed his lips. The action wasn't conducive to eating, so he strove to relax his mouth. He had no intention of discussing Miss Ellie Stratham—or the stupid mistake that he'd made in abducting the wrong woman. "A chat about what, precisely?"

"Oh, this 'n' that. She was most interested in—"

The door banged open, thwarting Damien's need to find out just how much Finn had blabbered. A whoosh of icy air made the flames waver on the hearth. Then the object of his displeasure came scurrying into the great hall.

Miss Ellie Stratham looked like a half-drowned cat. The hood of her leaf-green cloak had tumbled back and her auburn hair glistened with raindrops. She was toting a tray, and as she attempted to nudge the door shut with her booted foot, Finn galloped bandy-legged to the rescue.

The manservant closed the heavy panel and took the tray from her hands. "Why, miss, I'd've brung that if ye'd asked."

"Thank you, Finn. But it's quite all right. I managed perfectly well."

Her appearance belied her words. The gale had yanked tendrils of hair from her bun to create a curly disarray around her face. Her damp cheeks were rosy from the cold. Advancing into the great hall, she stripped off her gloves and then undid the fastening of her cloak, draping the wet garment over a chair by the fire.

In the process, the shawl she wore beneath the cloak slipped off her shoulders. As she bent down to pick it up from the stone floor, Damien found his gaze dipping to her bodice. The plunging neckline revealed two mounds of creamy flesh that strained against the green fabric of her gown.

He sat riveted, his meal forgotten. Never had he

imagined while spying on Lady Beatrice that her companion's shapeless garb could hide such voluptuous perfection.

Miss Stratham's eyes narrowed as she caught him staring. The flush on her cheeks deepened. Turning away, she arranged the fawn-colored shawl around her shoulders, tying it in such a manner as to conceal her spectacular assets. She smoothed back her hair and then walked to the table, where Finn was arranging her dishes directly across from Damien.

Seating herself, she afforded Damien a gracious smile worthy of a London drawing room. "I trust you don't mind if I join you, Mr. Burke. It's rather dreary to dine alone in one's chamber."

Those brown eyes gleamed like topaz in the firelight. He felt her direct gaze like a punch to his gut. Her attempt to tidy her hair had done little to tame the reddish-brown curls. She had the look of a woman who had just arisen from bed, more like a mistress than a dried-up spinster.

Realizing that he still clutched the spoonful of uneaten stew, Damien muttered, "Do as you please."

He shoved the spoon in his mouth with the intention of conveying the message that he was interested in his food. Not in her.

Finn poured two goblets of wine, and placed the bottle on the table. "Just as ye ordered, master. The finest French burgundy. I'll wait by the fire in case ye'd like a refill."

Damien had no wish to be left alone with Miss Ellie Stratham. She had invaded his sanctuary, and the prospect of being forced to make polite conversation set his teeth on edge. But he wouldn't hide behind a servant—especially one who clearly intended to eavesdrop. "I'm sure we can manage on our own. The dishes can be collected later."

"'Tisn't proper fer ye an' the miss t' be alone."

"Then don't alert the London newspapers. Now go."

Finn made a disappointed face and trudged toward the door, looking back once as if hoping to be recalled. Damien glowered at the man until he vanished out into the storm. The moment the door banged shut, he focused his attention on eating. The stew was rich and hearty, the gravy thick with potatoes, carrots, and chunks of meat. Gradually, the warmth of food in his belly began to ease his ill humor.

Across from him, Miss Ellie Stratham also had applied herself to the meal. He noted that she didn't take dainty bites like most ladies who pretended to have the appetite of a canary pecking at a few crumbs. She ate with gusto, pausing only to slather butter on a slice of bread.

She didn't even speak until they were nearly finished. For blessed minutes, there was only the hissing of the fire, the clink of cutlery, and the muffled wailing of the wind.

She said abruptly, "I've been wondering about something."

He shot her a contentious glance, wondering again what the devil she and Finn had spoken about in the kitchen during their so-called cozy chat. "Yes?"

"It seems rather odd to place a castle on an island. If fortresses were built in medieval times as a means for a lord to secure his lands, then what could he have been defending on such a small island?"

"His wife."

"Pardon?"

Damien scraped the last of the stew from the bottom

of the bowl before washing it down with a swig of wine. "As legend has it, the local laird once had a young and beautiful wife who had been unfaithful. He caught her in bed with one of his men, and he slew the traitor on the spot. Then he constructed this castle and kept his wife imprisoned here until she died an old, toothless woman."

Ellie Stratham's face took on a wide-eyed look that made her appear much younger. Damien calculated her age, noting the lack of lines around her eyes or mouth. Mid-twenties, perhaps? She glanced up at the high, barred windows that let in the rain-washed gray light of late afternoon. She appeared to be imagining what it would be like to be locked away for a lifetime within these stone walls.

That enthralled expression caught at him in spite of his determination to remain aloof. He would never have taken her for a dreamer. Her manner was too direct, her outlook too sensible, her tongue too sharp.

She returned her gaze to him, her fingertips idly tracing the base of her goblet. "Is that a true story, do you think?"

He shrugged. "It's what I was told by the previous owner."

"Am I to conclude that *you* own the castle now?"

"Yes."

She cocked her head to one side. "But why would you purchase a place that's in such disrepair? Because you needed a remote locale in which to hide Beatrice?"

Damien picked up the bottle and refilled their goblets. "If you must know, I didn't buy it. I won the castle—and the island—in a game of chance several years ago."

A shuttered expression descended over her face. She sat back, her gaze turning cool and intolerant. "I see. I should have guessed that you were a gambler."

"Oh, it's much worse than that. I own the gaming establishment." Damien was glad to have erased the softness from her features. He felt more comfortable with Miss Stratham, the disapproving governess. "Perhaps you've heard of it. The Demon's Den."

Her eyes widened, and she surprised him with a small laugh. "Demon's Den? How odd, that's exactly how I've been thinking of this keep! Tell me, how did you acquire the name Demon Prince?"

He tensed. Did she know? Had Finn revealed that Mimsy had told Damien a fairy tale about him being a prince? Was Ellie Stratham fishing for a confirmation from him? She wouldn't get one. "It was back in school," he said brusquely. "Other than that, I really don't recall."

But he did recall. Far too clearly. When Walt and his cronies had attacked Damien all those years ago, Damien had been desperate and foolish.

In the throes of raw rage, he forgot all caution, shouting, "Let me go! I'm a prince! My father is a king, and he'll chop off your heads."

A moment of stunned silence reigned. Then derisive laughter burst from the trio of boys. "King?" one jeered. "You don't even have a father."

His nose bloody, Walt bared his teeth in a sneer. "You're a filthy bastard." He grabbed the key, snapping its gold chain. "Your sire must be the Devil. That's what we'll call you. The Demon Prince."

He realized that Miss Stratham was studying him with a frankly inquisitive air as if she didn't quite believe that he'd forgotten. In no humor for more of her probing questions, Damien resorted to rudeness. He pushed back the bench with a loud scraping noise. "I've work to do before all of the light is gone. It's been a pleasure, Miss Stratham, but I'm afraid I shall have to ask that you leave now."

Taking his goblet, he went to the other end of the table, sat down, and opened the ledger. He fixed his gaze on a long column of figures, though he didn't comprehend a single number. His full awareness remained on Ellie Stratham.

He could see her out of the corner of his eye as she took a drink of wine. Arising gracefully from the bench, she glanced down and dusted a few crumbs from her skirt. She started toward her cloak, which lay on a chair by the fire. Then she pivoted abruptly and marched toward him.

She stopped beside the table. Damien felt a childish urge to pretend she wasn't there. Instead, he grudgingly looked up at her. "What is it now?"

"Have you paper and pencil that I might borrow?" she asked. "A sketchpad would be ideal."

"Why?"

"It appears likely that I shall be stuck here for some time. Since you've brought me to this castle against my will, you should at least provide me with a pastime."

"Mrs. MacNab placed some books in your room."

"I don't care to read all day. I prefer to draw."

Damien fixed her with his best glower, not that it did him any good. Miss Ellie Stratham stood with her hands folded at her waist like a governess waiting for a naughty boy to repent. Judging by the resolute expression on her face, she looked prepared to stare at him for the next hour if necessary.

Worse, he was uncomfortably aware that she had a point. None of this was her fault. She hadn't asked to come here. He *was* holding her prisoner with little provision for her amusement.

Concluding that the best way to regain his solitude was to fulfill her request, he snapped, "Wait here."

Damien sprang up and stalked across the keep, his

footsteps echoing in the vast space. He mounted a narrow flight of steps in the corner and proceeded to the solar, which currently functioned as his bedchamber, returning downstairs a few moments later.

He handed over a pencil and a large, leather-bound notebook with blank pages in which he'd intended to work out his plans for a potential investment opportunity. But giving up the book was a small sacrifice to make in the name of peace and quiet. "Take this and run along now."

Then he sat down to resume work on the ledger.

Naturally, Ellie Stratham disregarded his wishes. She rounded the table and sat down on the very edge of the bench—much too close to him. As she did so, he caught a whiff of lilac soap. And he felt a mad urge to press his nose to her generous bosom and discover the source of that scent.

Thank God, she appeared not to have noticed his reaction.

Opening the notebook, she laid down the pencil on the first blank page. "Before I go, will you draw a picture of that stolen key? Perhaps seeing it will jog my memory."

He frowned. Why would she offer to help him? It had to be a ploy to convince him to return her to London in spite of the stormy seas. "My artistic talent is nonexistent."

"Then just sketch the rough form. Please, do give it a try."

Damien wanted her and that enticing feminine fragrance gone from the great hall so that he could concentrate again. He snatched up the pencil and made a few crude lines that showed the three teeth at one end. He laboriously added a circle at the other end with a crown enclosed within it. The crown was crooked, so he dampened his fingertip and tried to erase it, leaving a smudged mess that looked like something done by his six-year-old daughter.

"This is ridiculous," he muttered, slamming the book shut. When he tossed down the pencil, it rolled to the other side of the planked table.

Ellie Stratham hopped up to catch the implement, but it fell to the stone floor. Tut-tutting, she went chasing after it to the hearth. Then she returned to the table and seated herself across from him. "Let me have a look," she said, taking the notebook.

Her mouth quirked slightly as she surveyed his drawing, but he didn't care if she was amused by his inexpert attempt. He was too preoccupied by the sight of her.

The shawl had come loose again. It had slid down one shoulder and gave him a peek at the delectable mounds revealed by the low cut of her gown. Ellie Stratham seemed utterly unaware of her disarray. Her gaze focused on the notebook, she leaned over the table and employed the pencil on the page in front of her.

Meanwhile, Damien had a direct line of view to the shadowed valley between her perfect breasts. His body reacted to the sight with intolerable heat. And his mind concocted a fantasy that involved hauling her into his arms and kissing her senseless, coaxing her upstairs and undressing her, caressing her naked form and spending a passionate hour or two in bed with her. They were all alone here and no one need ever know if he seduced her . . .

Irked by the direction of his thoughts, he jumped up and strode to the hearth to hurl another log onto the fire. What the devil was he thinking? Ellie Stratham was a lady. She wasn't a harlot to be used for his pleasure and then discarded.

Hadn't he already learned his lesson about the dire consequences of seducing innocent ladies?

Taking the poker, he stirred savagely at the glowing embers until the flames shot up and engulfed the new log. He'd already damaged Ellie's reputation by abducting her. If truth be told, her situation was far more dire than Lady Beatrice's would have been. At least then, Walt would have felt obliged to protect his sister. He'd have delivered the key in exchange for Lady Beatrice and that would have been that.

Damien had strong doubts that the weasel would do the same for Ellie Stratham. Her face had revealed anxiety when she'd spoken of the matter. She clearly believed that Walt wouldn't bother to rescue her. Well, she didn't know it yet, but Damien could scarcely wait to return her to London and forget this farce had ever occurred. If it wasn't for the damned choppy seas . . .

"Are there any other decorative elements?"

At the sound of her voice, he spun around, the poker in hand, to stare blankly at her. "What?"

"On the key," she said, tapping her chin with the pencil as she glanced from him back to the drawing. "Is there only the crown and nothing else? It seems rather plain."

He cudgeled his brain to pull up the memory. "There's a swirly embellishment around the edges of the circle—open fretwork, I suppose you might call it. Like this." At a loss for how better to describe it, he traced the simple design in the air with his fingertip.

"Ah! Thank you."

She bent over the notebook again, and this time he caught himself admiring the smooth curve of her neck. A few loose curls gleamed reddish-brown in the firelight, and he wondered how she'd react if he pulled the pins out of that prim bun.

She'd jam her pencil into his groin, that's what.

Wincing at the thought, Damien propped the poker against the stones. Ellie Stratham had a blistering temper beneath all that ladylike decorum. He had an indelible memory of her attacking him on the seashore the previous night. In a fit of rage she had come at him with her fists flying, her fingers prepared to gouge out his eyes. He'd been forced to imprison her against the boulder, while she wriggled and squirmed against him . . .

"Is this accurate?" she asked.

She held out the notebook to him. Damien crossed to her in three steps and tilted the open page to the light of the fire. He stared in slack-jawed amazement.

Underneath his smudged, crude effort, she had redrawn a perfect rendition of his key. There were the three teeth at one end, and at the other end, a crown surrounded by a delicate design of open whorls. She had done something clever with shading to make the key appear three-dimensional. It looked so real, Damien felt as if he could reach down and pluck it off the page.

"You *have* seen it," he accused.

With a slight smile, she shook her head. "No, I'm afraid not. I merely followed your description."

She was telling the truth. He knew it by the way she met his eyes without hesitation. The discovery of her talent made him curious. "You're quite the gifted artist. What do you usually draw? People? Landscapes? Vases of flowers?"

She glanced away into the fire. "A bit of everything, I suppose. It's . . . a hobby of mine."

Then she stole a glance at him with a furtiveness that further piqued his interest. Ellie Stratham clearly felt discomfited by the mention of her artistic aptitude. Was she merely shy of praise? Or was she hiding something?

Taking back the notebook, she changed the topic. "About this key," she said, fingering the sketch. "Finn said that it was left with you when you were a baby. And that you have no knowledge whatsoever of your parents."

Damien stiffened. Blast that tattletale. "Finn talks too much. Don't pay him any heed."

"But you *did* go to Eton. When I enrolled my cousin Cedric there last year, it was plain to see the school only accepts boys from the best families. So, someone in admissions must have known that you come from a highborn background."

Damien had wrestled with the same supposition many times. Upon reaching his majority, he had returned to the school to make inquiries. He also had gone back to Southwark to question his old neighbors. He even had hired a private detective to track down anyone who might have known his late guardian, Mrs. Mims, or might have information as to the fate of her effects when she'd died, including the letter she'd mentioned that was supposedly related to his birth.

His efforts had been to no avail. Everything had vanished. It was as if he'd sprung from nothingness.

But he *did* have a past, dammit, even if it was obscured by shadows. A man had fathered him and a woman had birthed him. Then one or both of them had gone to great lengths to conceal their identity.

From him.

The thought stirred a frustration so bitter and raw that he feared Ellie might glimpse it on his face. It took all of his willpower to keep his voice cool. "I appreciate your help, Miss Stratham. But my private life is really none of your concern."

From her seat on the bench, she fixed her relentless gaze on him. "It became my concern when you abducted me in order to reclaim that key. Now, are you certain the headmaster knows nothing? There may be something in your file stating who paid for your schooling—"

"There's nothing," he bit out, pacing in front of the hearth. "Do you truly think I haven't looked into all this myself? The key is my last clue and I *will* have it back. No matter what the cost."

Pursing her lips, she ripped out the page from the notebook. "I'm afraid *this* is the only key that I can give to you at present."

Damien waved the paper away. "Keep it. Maybe it'll help you find the real one at Pennington House."

She sat up very straight. "Are you saying you'll take me back to London, then? You won't keep me locked in this castle like that laird did to his unfaithful wife?"

The sudden sparkle in her brown eyes had an unexpected effect on Damien, as did her fanciful assertion. His tension vanishing, he actually had to suppress a grin. He only just managed to keep his mouth from tilting up at the corners. "We'll depart as soon as the storm dies down."

She jumped to her feet. "I do hope you're a man of your word, Mr. Burke."

"Quite. Though I warn you, the gale may last for another day or two. You should have ample time to fill that notebook."

"Indeed, I shall."

Her smile took on a keen yet secretive quality that reignited his curiosity. "What will you draw?" he asked.

"Oh, this and that. Whatever strikes my fancy."

Turning her back, Ellie Stratham flung the leaf-green

cloak around her shoulders and fastened the clasp at her throat. She could not have made it more clear that their conversation was concluded. So why did he feel a compulsion to find out more about her life?

Damien watched moodily as she donned her gloves. She was evasive about her art, and he wondered why. Had her family denied her the time to draw? Did they require her to labor from dawn to dusk? Living in the Earl of Pennington's household, she ought to dress in fine garments as she did now, not dowdy sacks that added decades onto her age. And why had she never married? Had the Earl of Pennypincher not allowed her a season?

Damien clenched his teeth to keep those questions to himself. Poking into her private affairs would only invite her to poke into his.

As she scooped up the notebook and pencil, he went ahead of her to open the door. A spray of freezing raindrops blew inside to sting his face and whip at his clothing. Miss Stratham drew up her hood, murmured a distracted good-bye, and plunged out into the storm. As if she'd already forgotten him.

He stood in the doorway and watched her struggle against the heavy gusts. Dusk had spread deep shadows beneath the archways in the castle walls. The muffled crashing of the surf and the howling of the wind enhanced the gloomy atmosphere. Solitude surrounded him again, exactly as he preferred.

Yet a strange sense of loneliness plagued him.

It had nothing to do with Miss Ellie Stratham, Damien told himself. He missed his daughter, that was all. He could scarcely wait to leave this blasted island and return to his home in London. He yearned to sweep Lily up in his arms and find out what she'd been doing in his absence, to once again have tea with her upstairs in the sunny nursery.

Nevertheless, long after he'd shut the door and returned to his work, his thoughts kept returning to the mystery of Ellie Stratham.

Chapter 12

The next day, the tempest continued to blow unabated. The wind moaned like a banshee outside the tower, and the rain sounded to Ellie like sharp fingernails tapping on the narrow windows. Yet despite her imprisonment on the island, she felt remarkably cheerful. The fire in the hearth made a pleasant crackling sound, there had been delicious scones at breakfast, and most of all, she had a notebook full of blank pages just waiting to be filled.

Now that she had paper and pencil, Ellie was perfectly content to spend the day alone in her bedchamber. Clad in a lemon-yellow gown, a shawl draping her shoulders, she sat against a mound of pillows in the old four-poster with its green brocade hangings. She had her knees up, the notebook propped against her thighs, as she sketched by the light of the oil lamp on the bedside table.

She had been working all morning on preliminary drawings for the next chapter of her storybook. In his new role as the enchanted prince, the rat had acquired a flowing cape and a jaunty hat with a large ostrich feather. Ellie had decided to name him Prince Ratworth. In one paw, Prince Ratworth wielded a long broadsword while defending Princess Arianna against an attacking ogre.

Despite his ugly snout and twitching whiskers, Prince Ratworth had the most extraordinary green-gray eyes. Or at least he would once Ellie returned to London and had access to her watercolor paints.

Pensively, she nibbled on the end of the pencil. Thank goodness Damien Burke finally had conceded to the futility of waiting for a ransom that would never arrive. Walt wasn't likely to wrench himself from the comforts of civilization on her behalf. He had never been one to put much effort into anything other than his own idle amusements.

Besides, he probably didn't want to face her, anyway, after the reprehensible manner in which he had behaved that one night outside her bedchamber. The memory of him pawing at her bosom made Ellie shudder, and she quickly pushed it away.

And what of the rest of the family? Had the modiste delivered her cousin's new gowns? Who was taking Beatrice shopping for the rest of her accessories? Who was making sure Grandmamma remembered to drink her tisane before bedtime? Who was reading each morning to sweet Lady Anne as she did her embroidery?

Did they only miss having Ellie around to perform tasks for them? Or did they actually miss *her*? Well, perhaps Lady Anne did, but Ellie couldn't fool herself. No one else in the household would shed any tears over her disappearance.

She released a long sigh. Despite a twinge of nostalgia for her familiar old life, she also acknowledged a sense of guilty pleasure, too. In all her time at Pennington House, never had she enjoyed an entire day free of responsibilities. It was a rare indulgence to be able to sketch for hours on end. How peculiar to feel so happy here at this castle when she was a prisoner of the most notorious scoundrel in England.

The Demon Prince. How *had* he earned that name? He'd claimed not to remember, but Ellie suspected otherwise. He had thwarted her every attempt to learn anything about him. Truly, he was the most exasperating man she'd ever met.

With deft strokes of the pencil, she added black knee boots to Prince Ratworth, modeling them after the ones Damien Burke had worn the previous day. All the while, she pondered his cold, curt manner. He had to be furious with himself for abducting the wrong woman. Men didn't like to be made fools, and Ellie hoped he was flaying himself raw over the matter. That was the real reason why she had decided to join him for dinner the previous day. So that he would look at her and be reminded of his stupid blunder.

Of course, she'd also been very curious about his shadowy past, too. How disconcerting it must be to not know even the names of one's parents. Although her own family wasn't perfect, she had fond memories of her late father and the mother who'd died when Ellie was just a little girl. By contrast, Damien Burke had no roots, no relatives, no knowledge whatsoever of his ancestry.

His only clue was that stolen key.

Why had Walt refused to return it? Was it possible that Damien Burke was wrong, and Walt no longer had the key? Perhaps her cousin had tossed it into the rubbish years ago.

But if there was a chance that he hadn't . . .

Yes, she could understand why Damien Burke wanted it back. Nevertheless, he should not have resorted to such an extreme tactic. He'd had no right to disrupt *her* life in order to achieve his goal.

Looking down, Ellie saw that in the corner of the page, she had doodled a likeness of his face. In a few strokes, she'd captured his high cheekbones, the blade of a nose, the square jaw. A visceral reaction that had nothing to do with aversion stirred deep within her. As galling as it was to admit, Damien Burke fascinated her.

The attraction she felt made no sense. Not only had he snatched her off the street, drugged her, and held her imprisoned, he also owned a gambling club. That alone ought to repulse any proper lady.

Gripping the pencil, Ellie furiously blackened out his portrait until she'd dulled the lead tip. Men like him had taken advantage of her father's weakness for cards and dice. They didn't care how many lives they ruined. Without suffering a qualm, they would entice a hapless gentleman into wagering sums beyond his means . . .

A knock sounded on the door. Ellie tossed aside the notebook, jumped out of bed, and hurried on stocking feet to answer the summons. In a rush of cold air, Mrs. MacNab came bustling into the tower bedchamber. In her hand she carried a large covered basket, which she set on a table by the hearth.

The maidservant removed the shawl that was draped over her salt-and-pepper hair. "Oh, 'tis a nasty day outside, indeed! I see yer fire's died down. Poor wee lamb, ye'll catch yer death." Going to the fireplace, she used the poker to stir the embers before adding another log.

Ellie felt guilty to have neglected that duty; she had been too absorbed in her own thoughts. "I assure you, there's no harm done. I've been perfectly warm sitting in bed."

She lifted the cover of the basket. The delicious aromas of roasted chicken, fresh bread, and treacle tarts made her realize just how long ago breakfast had been. Spreading out the feast on the table, she poured herself a cup of steaming tea.

"Will you join me for luncheon?" she asked.

"Nay, 'twouldna be right, me sittin' with such a fine lady as ye. Besides, I must be awa' t' tend poor Finn. He slipped an' bumped his noggin whilst clearin' awa' the snow."

Ellie stared in surprise over her teacup. Snow? The window was too high for her to view more than the scudding dark clouds. "Is he all right?"

"Aye, though there's a lump like a hen's egg on his brow. The auld fool wanted t' stay outside, but the laird ordered him t' have a lie-down." The maidservant clucked her tongue. "'Tis a sheet o' ice out there. Ye're wise t' stay indoors today, miss." With that, she bobbed a curtsy and hurried out of the bedchamber.

Ellie had no intention of staying indoors. Not when there was a blizzard to be observed for future reference. Snow could be difficult to depict in a drawing, and she looked forward to the challenge of trying her hand at it. Perhaps she'd even create a chapter in her book wherein Prince Ratworth and Princess Arianna traveled through a frozen land . . .

After making swift work of her luncheon, Ellie threw on her boots and cloak, grabbed the notebook and pencil, and started down the winding stone steps. The air had a decidedly frosty bite. Reaching the base of the tower, she proceeded through the short passageway and to the yard. There, she stopped beneath the archway and gazed out in delight at the transformed scene.

Overnight, a mantle of snow had draped the gray stone of the castle, covering the crenellated walls and clinging to the roofs of the towers. Long icicles hung from every nook and cranny. The wild wind flung icy particles that stung like tiny needles against her face. With the sky dark and dreary, she fancied the scene as a fairy-tale setting, perhaps the home of an evil wizard.

How fitting, Ellie thought, that the Demon Prince lurked outside.

Near the keep, a hulking black figure labored with a spade, scraping away the snow and making a path across the yard toward the kitchen. Damien Burke must be finishing the task that Finn had been forced to abandon.

Heading in that direction, Ellie found the way treacherously slippery. Yesterday's rain had frozen beneath the coating of snow. She proceeded slowly, her stiff new boots sliding on the layers of ice, the precious notebook clutched beneath her cloak. If not for the fact that she needed something vital from him, she might have turned back.

Approaching from behind, she was almost upon Damien Burke before he noticed her. The howling wind and the metallic scrape of the shovel must have masked the sound of her footsteps. Turning to shake a load of snow off the spade, he stopped to glower at her.

"What are you—" he began.

Before he could finish, a strong gust struck Ellie just as the toe of her boot met a patch of ice. The combination thrust her off balance. Her right ankle gave way, and with a gasp, she felt herself plunging forward.

In the next instant, she was caught up against a solid form.

Damien Burke clamped his arm around her waist. She was splayed against the hard wall of his chest, her cheek resting on the fine black wool of his coat. Her heart hammered madly as she tilted her head back to look up at his stark features. Immediately, she found herself riveted by those extraordinary green-gray eyes.

Thick black lashes enhanced the unusual hue, and she marveled to see such beauty in a blatantly masculine face. A flake of snow landed on his cheek and melted at once. The fierce wind whipped his dark hair in a frenzy, and his ears looked deep red from the cold.

Without thinking, she reached up to cup one with her gloved hand. "You must be freezing," she said. "Why aren't you wearing a hat?"

"It kept getting blown off." His mouth thinned into a critical line. "What the devil are you doing out here, anyway? Don't you have the sense that God gave a peahen?"

Ellie yanked back her hand. "*You're* out here—and without adequate covering. So tell me again, which one of us is foolish?"

She stepped back, only to realize that although the notebook was still safely cradled in her arm, the pencil had dropped from her fingers. Simultaneously, she felt a spasm of pain in her ankle and clutched at his arm.

"What's wrong?" he asked in that gruff, demanding tone. "Did you hurt yourself?"

"No! I'm just looking for my pencil."

Pretending that she needed to hold on to his forearm for balance, she bent over to scan the drifts of snow. The slim cylinder was nowhere to be seen. Since it had flown out of her hand, it could have landed anywhere, even been blown by the wind . . .

"Here it is," he said, reaching down in between his black boots.

Ellie straightened up to accept the pencil from him. "Thank you," she said. "It needs sharpening. I was hoping that you might have a penknife that I could borrow."

Damien Burke gave her a keen stare, and the tingling flutter that swept through her had nothing to do with the cold. "Come inside, then."

He slid his arm around her as they slowly headed across the snowy yard to the keep. Ellie made a valiant effort not to limp. After the way he'd snapped at her, she didn't want him to notice that she was trying not to put weight on her right ankle. He would only use it as cause to criticize her.

Not that he needed any cause. The bad-tempered man seemed to have no end of insults at the ready. Maybe he lay awake at night, making lists of them in his mind.

Opening the door, he guided her inside. The air in the great hall felt only marginally warmer, but at least they were out of the snow and wind. She expected him to release her now that there was no more danger of slipping on the ice. But he remained at her side, his hand at the small of her back as he steered her toward the bench by the hearth.

As she sat down in relief, he turned away to add a few logs to the fire. Ellie set the notebook and pencil beside her on the bench. While he was absorbed in stirring up the blaze, she cautiously moved her ankle back and forth beneath her skirt, trying to assess the damage. Feeling a twinge of pain, she compressed her lips to keep from wincing.

The hollow echo of his footsteps approached. "You *did* hurt yourself," he accused. "Don't deny it. I noticed you were favoring your right foot."

"No! At least not much. It's nothing, really."

"I'll be the judge of that."

Before she could object, he sank down on one knee in front of her, thrust his hand beneath her skirts, and lifted her leg so that her booted foot was exposed. The warm pressure of his fingers cupping her stockinged calf struck Ellie speechless. She could only watch in stupefied silence as he carefully felt her ankle through the leather of her short boot.

"Does that hurt?" he asked.

"No. And that's quite enough. Have you no manners? You oughtn't be putting your hand under my gown like that."

She tried to wiggle away, but he held firmly to her calf. He aimed those luminous green-gray eyes at her, and a slight smile added a dangerous attractiveness to his chiseled features. "Rest assured, I've never forced my attentions on an injured lady. Even a scoundrel can have standards."

"I'm sure that's precisely what a scoundrel would say."

He chuckled. "Believe me, Ellie, if ever I decide to seduce you, you'll know it, and you'll want me to do it. But that moment is not now." Giving her no chance to respond to his outrageous statement, he added, "If you can manage to stifle your maidenly objections, I'll take a closer look at this foot."

His manner swift and efficient, he unlaced the leather ties and eased off the boot. Then he cradled her heel in one hand while using the other to gently press his fingers in various places along her white-stockinged foot.

Ellie gripped the edge of the bench with both hands. In spite of the coolness of the air, she felt flushed all over. The nerve of the man to make such an offensive remark! *Believe me, Ellie, if ever I decide to seduce you, you'll know it, and you'll want me to do it.*

An indignant tremor left her breathless. *Want* him to do it? What a conceited cad to think she would melt in his arms! Of course, a man like him must be accustomed to unchaste women fawning over him. But Ellie had no intention of allowing him anywhere near *her*.

Except at present, of course, while he knelt in front of her to examine her foot. His shoulders were broad beneath the greatcoat, the fine tailoring indicative of his ill-gained wealth. Gazing down at his tousled black hair, she muttered under her breath, "Arrogant, overconfident buffoon."

"Were you addressing me?" he asked.

He flicked an amused glance at her. It lent him a rakish quality that Ellie wanted to capture on paper. She must remember to give Prince Ratworth that faint crinkle of lines around the eyes, the slight quirk at one side of the mouth, the bold tilt of his head.

Seeing that he was expecting a reply, she said huffily, "Yes, I was. And by the by, I never gave you permission to use my first name."

He chuckled. "It's absurd to be formal when my hands are under your gown." Returning his attention to her foot, he added, "For that matter, you may address me as Damien if you like. I've never been one to care much for society's rules."

Was he trying to charm her? Maybe he believed he could seduce her as he'd done that other young lady. A fluttery warmth scurried over her skin, the sensation nestling deep within her body. She didn't understand how Damien could elicit such a response from her when she had every reason to despise him.

Damien? No, she didn't want to think of him in so familiar a manner. That was much too personal, as if they were friends instead of adversaries—

As he gently rotated her foot from one side to the other, a sharp pain wrested a gasp from her. "Demon! That's what I'll call you."

"You won't be the first." He rubbed his thumb over her ankle as if to soothe any lingering ache. "Well. There's some swelling, but it appears you're only suffering from a sprain. If a bone were broken, it would have swelled a good deal more."

"How do you know?"

The ghost of a grin lifted one corner of his mouth. "Because I fell out of a tree once and broke my ankle, that's why. Now, I'll need to wrap this securely to keep you from twisting it again."

He pulled off his cravat and began to wind the length of white linen around her ankle. Watching him, Ellie felt her animosity subside as swiftly as it had arisen. Damien. Maybe she *could* think of him that way when he smiled, for he looked so much more approachable. And if he was in a more agreeable frame of mind, perhaps he wouldn't care if she pressed him for some answers.

"How old were you when that happened?"

"Seven, I believe. It was summer, and I recall being confined to bed for weeks on end, looking out the window and envying the other lads at their play."

Ellie imagined him as a boy with a mop of rumpled dark hair, his bandaged foot propped on a pillow and a woebegone expression on his face. An innocent child who had never known his parents. "Finn said that you were raised by a woman named Mrs. Mims. I don't mean to pry, but . . . was she good to you? Did she treat you well?"

He glanced up from binding Ellie's ankle. "She was a fine woman, the only mother I ever knew. She fed me, clothed me, kept me out of trouble. We lived in Southwark, and it's because of Mimsy that I didn't end up on the streets."

Mimsy? It touched Ellie to learn that he'd had a pet

name for his guardian. Had she been a maidservant? Or a penniless lady hired to care for a noble baby born on the wrong side of the blanket?

"Was she your governess, too? Or did you attend another school before Eton?"

He carefully tied off the makeshift bandage. "Mimsy taught me at home. We may have lived in a garret, but she had quite a collection of books. As part of my instruction, she took me to museums and galleries and plays. My history lessons often involved visiting sites like the Tower and Westminster Abbey." Finished with his doctoring, Damien rose to his feet, standing over Ellie in an intimidating fashion. "Perhaps you'd deem it an unconventional education, but she was an excellent teacher and I learned everything I needed to know."

He spoke sharply as if expecting her to ridicule him. Gazing up at him, Ellie had a sudden understanding that the belligerent visage he showed the world had its roots in his childhood. He would allow no criticism of the woman who'd raised him, and his fierce loyalty caught at Ellie's heart. Until this moment, she had not thought him capable of love.

"She must have been a wonderful mother to you," she murmured. "Finn mentioned that she passed away shortly after you were admitted to Eton. Will you tell me what happened to her?"

Damien's mouth took on a grim twist. He picked up the notebook from the bench and thrust it into Ellie's hands. "She apparently fell ill of a fever. I wasn't permitted to attend her funeral. It was years later before I even found out where she was buried."

His voice was cold, controlled, yet a muscle clenched in his jaw. Mimsy's loss must have affected him deeply. Had there been a death record on file? Or had he been forced to walk through paupers' cemeteries searching for her gravesite? Ellie wanted to know, but he distracted her by slipping her pencil into an inner pocket of his coat.

"Why are you taking that—"

Before she could finish her question, he reached down and swung her up into his arms.

Chapter 13

Ellie instinctively looped her arms around his neck and clung for dear life. She clutched the notebook in one gloved hand against his back. Her cheek landed on his shoulder, and his face was so close that she could see the black stubble on his jaw. The shock of being carried by him made her heart drum so fast that she felt giddy.

She stiffened her body in resistance. "What do you think you're doing?"

Those stunning eyes gleamed down at her. "Isn't it obvious? You're injured and I'm taking you back to your chamber."

"Put me down at once! I don't need any help. I'm perfectly capable of managing on my own."

He carried her across the great hall. "Not on the ice. And not up those winding stairs, either. I won't have you breaking your pretty little neck on my watch."

He held her easily with one arm while he opened the door and stepped outside. The screeching of the wind precluded any further conversation, though his last comment already had silenced Ellie. Did he truly find her pretty? She immediately scolded herself for wondering. He was her captor, for pity's sake. Why should she care a whit for his good opinion of her?

Better he should think her a warty old witch. At least then she could be certain he didn't have designs on her.

Even with his arms full, Damien appeared to have no trouble navigating his way over the snow. The monstrous dark sky hurled handfuls of icy flakes at them. Ellie turned her face toward him for protection from the elements. Unfortunately, the action only made her more aware of him as a man: the hard muscles of his chest, the solid width of his shoulders, the iron strength of his arms around her. With every breath, she drew in his earthy masculine scent.

He felt threatening and thrilling all at the same time, and she had the scandalous desire to snuggle closer to him, to touch her mouth to the exposed skin of his throat and see if he tasted salty. Ellie pursed her lips to deny the thought. He was a rat, and not even an enchanted one at that. Damien Burke was tough and bad-mannered, and he couldn't ever magically transform into a prince.

Even if he *had* loved his Mimsy. Even if he *had* wrapped Ellie's foot with his own cravat and now gallantly transported her back to her chamber. None of that changed the fact that he'd abducted her without caring a fig for the damage to her reputation.

She knew the moment they'd left the castle yard. The gale ceased tugging at her cloak, and the dark afternoon grew even dimmer. Against her bosom, she could feel the steady rise and fall of his chest. He didn't seem winded in the least by the burden of carrying her. He carried her through the short passage and then up the circular tower stairs, his heavy footsteps echoing off the stone walls.

He shouldered open the door, kicked it shut behind them, and stopped in the middle of the bedchamber.

Tilting her head back, Ellie found him gazing down at her with a peculiar intensity. That look caused a lurch deep inside her that she didn't want to acknowledge as attraction. His hair was mussed by the wind, tumbling across his brow, and she clenched her fingers to keep from reaching up to straighten it.

No matter how much the Demon Prince captivated her, she must guard against him. She must never forget that he was a rogue and a gambler who used people for his own purposes.

"Pray, put me down," Ellie commanded. "I can do just fine on my own now."

He chuckled low in his throat, the sound reverberating against her breasts. "Why do I have a suspicion you won't be a very good patient? I shan't release you until I have your promise that you'll stay in bed and rest that foot."

"All right! I will! It's where I spent the morning, anyway."

He carried her to the four-poster and lowered her to the mattress. With great relief, she loosened her arms and let go of him. The notebook tumbled out of her grip and onto the coverlet.

Damien stood close, too close, for he didn't step back immediately. She was keenly aware of his nearness as he unfastened the clasp at her throat and helped her remove the cloak. Feeling awkward and discomfited to be lying beneath him, Ellie scrambled to push herself into a sitting position.

While she peeled off her gloves, he straightened the pillows behind her back. Then he proceeded to remove her boots, letting them thump to the floor.

"I presume you were sketching in bed today?" he asked, glancing curiously at her as he placed a spare pillow under her injured foot.

Ellie felt uncomfortable discussing her personal habits with him, especially when it involved her sleeping arrangements. "I . . . yes. It seemed a good day for such a pastime."

"I'm pleased to hear that it kept you occupied."

He stripped off his greatcoat, flung it over a chair, and then crossed to the hearth. The fire had burned low during her absence, though it still crackled and hissed. While he added another log, Ellie wondered in alarm if he meant to stay.

"It isn't necessary for you to sit with me," she said. "I'm sure you'll want to finish your shoveling. Or your ledgers. Or something."

"All in good time."

Damien turned toward her, thrusting his hand into an inner pocket of his dark blue coat. Despite the expensive tailoring of his coat and trousers, the waistcoat with its silver buttons, he didn't resemble any civilized gentleman she'd ever known. He seemed so much more powerful and dominant. He exuded a raw virility that made Ellie's pulse race.

He held her pencil in one hand and a penknife in the other. Standing close to the hearth, he proceeded to sharpen the pencil, letting the tiny wood shavings fall into the fire. The clean, controlled motion held her attention. She stared at his fingers and remembered how strong they had felt around her calf. What would it be like for him to touch her elsewhere on her body?

A warm throbbing stirred in her most secret depths. Ellie flushed and glanced away from him. How mortifying to harbor such lustful thoughts. Never in her life had she experienced so strong an attraction to any man. Being confined to the nursery as governess to her two younger cousins, she hadn't known many gentlemen outside the circle of her family. She had seen them at church on Sundays or during a rare walk in the park. Over the years, she'd occasionally encountered one or another who would engage her in polite conversation. But any interest on his part would end when he realized that although Ellie was niece to the Earl of Pennington, she had no marriage portion and no prospects of inheritance.

So she had poured her heart into writing and illustrating her fanciful stories. It gave her something to look forward to at the end of each day. No matter how many dreary tasks she had to perform, no matter how petulant Beatrice might be or how critical her uncle was, Ellie always had that one precious secret to brighten her spirits . . .

"Your pencil."

Startled out of her reverie, she saw that Damien had come to the bedside to place the sharpened pencil on the table. His nearness brought heat to her cheeks. She felt breathless, hardly able to bring herself to look up at him for fear that he could read her private thoughts. The sooner he left her alone, the better.

"Thank you," she forced out, pleased by the coolness of her tone. "I hope you don't mind if I ask you to leave now . . ."

Her words trailed off as he leaned over her and picked up the notebook where it lay forgotten on the coverlet. Perhaps it was the swiftness of his action or her own torpid state, but she didn't react until he'd seated himself on a nearby chair and had begun to leaf through the pages.

In a panic, Ellie sat up straight and swung her feet over the side of the bed. "Give that back to me!"

He glanced up to drill her with a stare. "Kindly keep your foot where it belongs."

"Only if you return my notebook at once!"

"Why? What could you possibly have to hide?"

Damien had the audacity to look back down at the book, flipping through the pages of sketches. A black eyebrow winged upward as he lingered over one of them.

Ignoring the pain in her ankle, Ellie hobbled over the rug to his side. She snatched the leather-bound notebook out of his hands and cradled it to her bosom. She felt violated and furious to have her imaginary world exposed to his view. Through gritted teeth, she said, "Beast! How dare you look at this without my permission."

"Pray forgive me, I should have asked you first," he said mildly. "I didn't realize your artwork was meant to be so private."

On that wholly inadequate apology, he jumped up and caught her by the waist, propelling her back to the canopied bed. Dictatorial as ever, he lifted her back onto the covers and rearranged the pillow under her ankle.

Then he stood at the bedside and stared down at her. "So tell me, why *are* you drawing flamboyant rats wielding swords?"

His sharp gaze pinned Ellie in place. She wanted to roll away, to escape the scrutiny of those vigilant eyes, but if she tried to climb off the other side of the bed he would be there to stop her. She couldn't run, anyway, not on this ankle. He had her well and truly trapped.

"I was merely doodling," she said tersely, averting her gaze to the green hangings on the bedpost. "Now, will you please just go away?"

The fire hissed into the silence. Snow tapped on the windowpanes like a visitor impatient to come inside. To her dismay, the Demon Prince didn't move from the bedside. He remained standing directly beside her, so close that Ellie could have touched him had she not been clutching the precious notebook to her bosom.

She braced herself for his ridicule. He was just the

sort of insensitive bully to laugh at her fantastical creations. If she refused to talk to him, maybe he'd give up and leave.

His fingers grasped her chin, turning her face back toward him. "You're telling a story through those pictures, aren't you?" he said slowly, his gaze intent on her. "The rat and that girl with a tiara—is she a princess? They're battling a hulking creature with a big head—a giant or some such."

"An ogre." Irked that he'd tempted her into speech, Ellie glued her lips shut and glowered at his chest.

Damien cocked his head to one side. "This rat character—I noticed in one of the drawings that his stance appeared somewhat unnatural. He wasn't handling his sword properly. Did you do that on purpose?"

"What? No!" Now he'd pulled another two words from her when she'd sworn not to speak to him. The last thing she wanted was to encourage conversation and give him a reason to stay.

Much to her relief, he walked away from the bed. But he didn't collect his greatcoat and head out the door. Instead, he picked up the fireplace poker and brandished it up like a sword. He struck a pose with one arm held stiffly at his side. "This is how he's standing in your sketch," Damien said.

Then he shifted position, placing a hand on his hip, his feet set apart as he thrust out with the poker at an imaginary foe. "And this is how he *should* be standing."

He looked so fluid and elegant that Ellie felt a thrill course through her body. She knew exactly which drawing he meant. It was one that she'd labored over with the sense that something wasn't quite accurate. Now, she could see precisely where she'd gone wrong.

Forgetting her anger, she picked up the pencil from the bedside table, opened the notebook to a fresh page, and did a quick preliminary sketch, the newly sharpened lead flying over the paper. As the figure took shape, she succumbed to curiosity and asked, "Where did you learn to use a sword?"

"Fencing lessons. An old-fashioned sport, to be sure, but quite popular at Eton." Damien executed several wickedly swift jabs, the poker making a swishing sound in the air. "By the by, does your rat have a name?"

Her pencil slowed on the paper. Remembering that she was still peeved at him, Ellie said tartly, "Prince Ratworth. And you may be interested to know, I modeled him after *you*."

The corner of Damien's mouth curled in that charming, heart-fluttering, almost-grin. He replaced the poker by the fireplace, then came over to the bed and reached for the notebook. "Let me see that again."

"No."

"Come, you can't make such a claim without letting me have another look."

Reluctantly, she surrendered the notebook, and he studied her latest drawing, then flipped through several other pages. "He *is* a rather dapper fellow, isn't he? Quite dashing, in fact." Damien handed the leather-bound book back to her. "I confess to being flattered. I can't say that anyone has ever put me in a story before. Dare I hope that Prince Ratworth is the hero of your tale?"

He was supposed to be insulted, Ellie thought sourly. She had no intention of telling him that the rat was under a magical spell. Or that once the prince redeemed himself and regained his human form, he and Princess Arianna would live happily ever after. "He's an arrogant, selfish, demonic rat, so of course he must be a villain."

"Yet he's fighting the evil ogre. That seems rather heroic to me." He eyed her for a moment, then added, "Did Prince Ratworth abduct the princess?"

"No!" Flustered, Ellie regretted revealing that he was her inspiration. He seemed to take it as carte blanche to critique her life's work. "Pardon me if I don't wish to explain the entire plot to you. It's none of your concern."

His expression grew pensive as he subjected her to a contemplative stare. She couldn't tell what he was thinking. His scrutiny made her uneasy, so she lowered her eyes to the page in her lap, distracting herself by adding a flowing cape to Prince Ratworth.

Damien pulled the chair closer and sat down. He propped one booted foot on the frame of the bed as if settling in for a long stay. "You needn't explain the particulars of the plot," he said, "but I'm curious about your plans for this story. Were you working on it back in London, too?"

The astute question increased Ellie's wariness. Her book had always been a closely guarded secret, and now she felt exposed and vulnerable. Why was the Demon Prince so interested, anyway? "It's just a little hobby of mine," she dissembled. "Something I do to amuse myself."

He wore a slight frown as if he were trying to figure her out. "Is there a text to go along with the drawings? Are you intending this project to be a book for children?"

Ellie attempted a cool laugh. "I can't imagine why it would matter to you," she said. "Or are you afraid that someone might spot your resemblance to Prince Ratworth?"

He leaned forward, his elbows on his knees. "Then you *do* intend to seek publication for your story."

Ellie's heart pitched in alarm as she realized how

shrewdly he'd interpreted her remark. She glanced away lest he read the truth in her eyes. "I needn't discuss my plans with you."

To her consternation, the mattress dipped under his weight as Damien seated himself on the edge of the bed. He took her hand in his and lightly rubbed the reddened indentation in her finger left by the pencil. "I know you don't trust me, Ellie. I can't say that I blame you. But please know that I bear you no ill intent. Quite the contrary. You're an exceptionally talented artist and I'd like to see you profit from your work."

Exceptionally talented?

Ellie absorbed his praise in the starving corners of her soul. For so long she had worked alone and kept her dreams to herself. Now, gazing into his eyes, she wanted to forget all the reasons why she should mistrust this man. The warmth of his hand on hers, the frank sincerity on his face, his nearness on the bed, all had a curious effect on her. She felt a bond of intimacy between them that went beyond the physical. It was as if they'd known each other for years instead of only two days.

She also felt an unladylike hunger to throw herself into his arms and lift her face for his kiss. That made no sense, for she had decided long ago that romance would have no place in her life. *Believe me, Ellie, if ever I decide to seduce you, you'll know it, and you'll want me to do it.*

Was that what he was doing now? Trying to seduce her with his charm? She couldn't think clearly when he sat so close to her.

Her cheeks flushed, she extracted her hand from his. "If you really want to hear more, I'll tell you. But first, you'll return to your chair."

Damien complied with a jaunty air just like Prince Ratworth. He settled down on the wooden seat and placed his hands behind his neck in a relaxed pose. "Go on, then."

Ellie drew a deep breath. "If you must know, I *am* hoping to find a publisher. I've been working on my storybook for a while now, and it's over halfway complete." She stopped, then added, "Although I've lost at least a week's worth of work, all because of you."

"Yet because of me, you've also gained a bold hero to defend your princess."

"Villain," she insisted.

He chuckled. "Perhaps Prince Ratworth is a bit of both, hmm? So, how many pages do you have done?"

She contemplated the thick stack hidden in the chest in her nursery bedchamber at Pennington House. "At last count, close to a hundred."

"A hundred? This book is meant for children, is it not?"

His sudden frown made Ellie defensive. "Yes, and what's wrong with that? You can't make a judgment about it when you've only seen a few sketches."

"It's not the content, but the length. Children—at least the younger ones—prefer shorter stories."

How peculiar to hear such a comment coming from a hardened scoundrel, she thought. The Demon Prince leaned back in the chair, one foot on the bed frame, his black hair attractively mussed by the wind. Was he always so confident about everything?

"What can *you* know about children?" she scoffed. "You, who spend your time playing cards and wagering on dice at your gambling den?"

His mouth curling wryly, Damien glanced away at the fire. There was a moodiness to his face that puzzled Ellie. But when he looked back at her again, a cool irony tinged his expression. "You're quite right. However, I *am* a businessman, and I merely thought to advise you . . ." He paused. "Never mind. I'm sure you've already determined the best way to attract the interest of a publisher."

Ellie found herself in a quandary. She had just spurned his opinion, yet she felt woefully ignorant when it came to matters of commerce. She far preferred to work on the story itself than to face the intimidating prospect of convincing a stranger at a publishing company to print the pages and bind them into a volume.

Dipping her chin and gazing at Damien through the screen of her lashes, she admitted, "If you must know, I haven't any notion how to find a publisher. I hadn't really thought that far ahead."

"It seems to me your first step would be to go to a bookstore or lending library and see who publishes this sort of book."

His answer was so logical that Ellie felt foolish for never having thought of it. "You're right, there should be an address for the publisher on the title page."

"Precisely." Damien leaned forward, his elbows on his knees. "Now, might I make a suggestion? Would it be possible to break your story into sections that could be sold as separate books?"

The notion stupefied her. "Why?"

"I'm assuming that illustrated books cost more to produce, so you might have an easier time convincing a publisher to invest in a shorter book. In addition, you'd likely earn more money by selling a series of works rather than just one."

"But at what cost to my story?" Ellie burst out. "For heaven's sake, that's a terrible idea. It would require extensive revisions."

Aghast, she turned her head to stare unseeing at the curved stone wall. Everything in her resisted committing the sacrilege of drastically altering the manuscript that she had worked on for so many months. She'd have to tinker with the plot, rewrite portions, and draw new illustrations in places so that each book could stand on its own. It might require weeks and weeks of additional work. And what if it didn't work? What if she destroyed her precious storybook in the process?

But maybe she would lose her chance of publication if she *didn't* do as he suggested. Then where would she be?

A flood of self-doubt inundated her. All of a sudden her dream of living in a cozy cottage in the country seemed farther away than ever. Ellie desperately needed to earn enough to support herself, and swiftly, too, because she had a horrible suspicion that her family wouldn't welcome her return to London after having spent more than a week in the company of a rogue. Her uncle might very well cast her out into the streets . . .

A loud knocking made her jump. She looked over to see that Damien was already striding forward to open the door.

Mrs. MacNab took a step inside the bedchamber, then stopped to gawk at him. "Why, 'tis the laird. An' what mischief are ye at, bein' in milady's bedchamber?"

"Miss Stratham twisted her ankle on the ice, so I carried her up here." He took the basket from the maidservant and placed it on the table. "Is it teatime already?"

Mrs. MacNab hurried to Ellie's side. "Oh, poor lamb. I brung only one cup, sir. Shall I run back down t' the kitchen t' fetch another?"

"No, I was about to depart. It appears I've overstayed my welcome here."

Grabbing his greatcoat, he flicked an enigmatic glance at Ellie. She glowered back at him. Did he expect her to beg him to stay? After the way he had shaken the foundation of her future?

Good riddance to him!

As he departed the chamber and closed the door, a sudden inspiration banished her gloom. Perhaps there *was* a simple way to solve her present dilemma. She mulled over the notion while Mrs. MacNab puttered by the table, pouring tea and arranging scones on a plate. By the time the maidservant bustled over to the bed with a steaming cup, Ellie could offer a cheerful smile of thanks.

No longer did her prospects appear so grim. Now, she knew exactly how to make the Demon Prince pay for ruining her life.

Chapter 14

The following morning, Damien ducked his head to avoid the low lintel as he entered the kitchen. Mrs. MacNab stood washing dishes at the dry sink, an apron tied around her stout waist. Finn sat at the rustic table, stuffing himself with jam-slathered scones. The angry red knob on his forehead didn't appear to have affected his appetite.

"Have you any linseed oil?" Damien asked.

His mouth full, Finn could only shrug and glance helplessly at his wife. Mrs. MacNab scurried to the corner cabinet and rummaged around for a moment, then produced a small brown jar. "'Tis lucky ye are that Finn rubs this on his achin' joints at times, else I wouldna have brung it here. Wot's that?"

She gazed askance at the wooden pole in Damien's hand. He had found half a broken pikestaff in the weaponry room and had spent the past hour sanding the rough end until it was smooth. "I thought Miss Stratham might use it as a cane until her ankle improves."

Finn waggled a bushy gray eyebrow. "'Tis good o'

ye t' think o' the wee miss. Mayhap she's lookin' a mite prettier now, huh?"

The old coot had a glint in his blue eyes, reminding Damien of what he himself had said upon their arrival at the castle. He had been standing beside the canopied bed, gazing down at the tangled hair and freckled face of the woman he'd abducted, and feeling surprised that the beauteous Lady Beatrice Stratham appeared rather plain at close view. He had remarked to Finn, *She did look much prettier from a distance.*

Damien had no intention of admitting that his opinion of Ellie Stratham had undergone a drastic change since then. He had acquired a decided preference for wavy auburn hair and warm brown eyes. Not to mention, a shapely figure and a charming bosom. "I'm responsible for her well-being," he said crisply. "Now, have you a rag that I might use?"

Mrs. MacNab obligingly provided a square of blue cotton cloth. "Dinna ye mind Finn. The auld fool likes t' poke his nose where it don't belong." She aimed a warning look at her husband on her way back to the dry sink.

Damien dribbled oil onto the cloth and sat down at the table to polish the staff. "The wind is beginning to die down a bit," he said, deliberately changing the topic. "Is there a chance we might depart on the morrow?"

"Could be aye, could be nay," Finn ruminated as he slurped tea from his brown mug. "Gales in these parts can last fer a week."

The old man had grown up on the Scottish coast, and he launched into a story about a legendary storm in his youth. Having successfully diverted him, Damien concentrated on rubbing the oil into the length of ash wood until it gleamed. He listened with only half an ear, offering a nod or a brief comment now and then. All the while, his mind was focused on the need to make atonement to Ellie.

The previous afternoon, she had summarily rejected his suggestion for her book. From the look of revulsion on her face, one would think he'd asked her to slaughter a litter of puppies. In retrospect, he couldn't blame her for being appalled. Who was he to tell her to reorganize a project so near and dear to her heart when he'd seen only a glimpse of the manuscript?

Granted, he had *meant* to be helpful. The discovery of her whimsical artistic talent had astounded him, and being a businessman, he immediately had begun to consider how best she might profit from it. But now Damien regretted speaking out. By disregarding her sensibilities, he'd damaged the fledgling closeness between them.

He hoped it could be repaired.

No longer could he deny that he felt a strong connection to Ellie Stratham. There was something about her that drew him, something more than mere physical allure. He had noticed it the moment she'd opened her eyes that first day and fearlessly challenged him instead of weeping or quavering. The tug of attraction had gained strength with their every encounter, although he had resisted it, fought it, denied it. How disturbing it was to acknowledge that he craved both her companionship and her esteem.

Finn's voice intruded. "Back in our courtin' days, I made an oak chest fer the missus. Spent many a long hour carvin' an' polishin' it."

Damien shot a suspicious scowl at the bald-headed servant. Finn had to be making a sly parallel to Damien fashioning the walking stick for Ellie.

However, Finn's attention was on his wife as she refilled his mug from the kettle. " 'Twas a labor o' love," Mrs. MacNab said with a fond smile.

"Love, bah! I wanted under yer skirts, hinny. Still do." He grabbed hold of her thick waist and pulled her down to plant a loud, smacking kiss on her lips.

"Daft auld goat!" She playfully slapped him with the edge of her apron. " 'Twas love at first sight, as well ye ken."

Watching them, Damien sensed a hollowness inside himself. He told himself it was nonsense; he didn't believe in love at first sight. The glorious state that poets praised and women romanticized was merely the fire of physical passion. Perhaps sometimes it became a devoted friendship, as it had with the MacNabs. But the comfortable intimacy shared by his servants was foreign to his own life. He had never known it, not even with Veronica.

Especially not with Veronica.

He hid a grimace by diligently rubbing at a rough spot in the wood. Their association had begun as a wager with his cronies to see if he could win the heart of the shy young lady who'd been forced to work as a companion to an old aunt. Her exquisite blond beauty had caused him to lose his head. Then later, there had been only quarrels and an oppressive sense of being trapped. Nevertheless, he could not regret his brief, tragic marriage.

Veronica had given him Lily.

He had amassed a fortune, he had built himself up from nothing, yet his daughter was undoubtedly his finest achievement. To protect her from gossip, he had kept Lily out of sight and away from society. Few even knew that she existed, only the MacNabs and a trusted staff of servants.

He had taken great pains to guard his privacy.

For Lily's sake, he'd kept his life divided into strict compartments. He never entertained friends or acquaintances at home. Business matters were handled at his club, and the occasional sexual liaison was conducted in a separate house he kept for that purpose.

Since Veronica's death, he'd never lacked for female company. There were always willing widows and improper ladies seeking the excitement of an affair with a notorious rogue. Yet he had never desired anything beyond a brief carnal indulgence.

Until Ellie Stratham.

Somehow, Ellie had stirred life into the dead realm of his emotions. She made him crave warmth and light after years of darkness. The novelty of it had thrust him into uncharted territory. He didn't know quite what to make of it.

Perhaps what he felt was merely a natural attraction to forbidden fruit. He'd wronged Ellie in order to retrieve that damned key, and her situation would be infinitely worse if he were to seduce her. Pennington would throw her out of his house, and then what would happen to her?

Maybe it was already too late. Maybe Walt hadn't bothered to concoct a story to cover his cousin's disappearance. Maybe Ellie would return home only to be refused entry to her uncle's house.

Brooding on the possibility, Damien corked the jar and handed it back to Mrs. MacNab. He ran his fingers over the cylindrical staff to make sure that all the oil had soaked into the wood and there was no trace of dampness left. Then he started toward the door.

Finn jumped up from the table and trotted after Damien, reaching out a gnarled hand for the walking stick. "Will ye be wantin' me t' take it up t' the wee miss?"

Damien kept a firm grip on the polished wood. "No, I'll do it."

"Are ye certain 'tis wise?" Finn asked with a shrewd expression on his weathered face. Lowering his voice, he rasped, "Mind, ye dinna make the same mistake as ye did with Miss Lily's mam."

Damien felt a rush of guilt so thick he could scarcely draw air into his lungs. Did Finn really think he'd be so stupid? Through clenched teeth, he muttered, "When I want your advice, old man, I'll ask for it."

Turning on his heel, Damien strode out of the kitchen. His footsteps echoed loudly in the corridor. Going outside, he welcomed the blast of chilly air. And immediately he wished he had not spoken so sharply. Finn was like a father to him. But Finn ought to know that Damien had put the past behind him, that he would never again commit such a colossal error of judgment.

Besides, Ellie was *not* Veronica. No two women could be more different.

Carrying the staff, he stomped down the path he'd shoveled through the drifts of snow. Icy gusts buffeted him, though not quite as fiercely as the previous two days. Only a few stray flakes fell from the cloudy sky. Beyond the castle walls, the rhythmic crashing of the waves served as a reminder that the storm was not yet over.

It was still too rough to set out on the open sea, and for that, Damien was glad. Though he had promised to take Ellie back to London, he wanted to prolong their stay here at the castle for at least another day or two. Maybe then they could regain the camaraderie that had developed between them the previous afternoon.

Finn was wrong, there was little danger in a brief flirtation with Ellie. Damien was no longer the reckless young daredevil who had made no distinction between innocent girls and experienced women. Now he possessed the self-discipline to keep his base urges in check.

Leaning on the polished stick to test its strength, he tramped through the arched entry and the short passageway, and then started up the winding stairs of the tower. All the while, his mind dwelled on Ellie. Would she accept his peace offering? Or would she give him that scornful look and send him away?

He wouldn't go. He'd use every ounce of his charm to win her over. And if that didn't work, well, then he'd find another way.

Reaching the small landing at the top of the stairs, he saw that the door to her bedchamber stood partly open. That surprised him, for she surely knew better than to allow the warmth of the fire to escape. He rapped lightly on the wooden panel, but no sound emanated from within.

"Ellie?" he called.

Receiving no answer, he cautiously peered inside. God help him if he made matters worse between them by intruding on her privacy. But a swift glance around revealed that the circular chamber was deserted.

The bedcovers were rumpled as if she'd just arisen. The leather notebook lay abandoned by the mound of pillows. Flames danced on the hearth, so she must have been here quite recently.

Where could she have gone? Had she hobbled down the stairs on her injured ankle? Had he just missed her? Perhaps she'd headed to the keep in search of him. Maybe her pencil needed sharpening again, and she would scold him for not leaving the penknife.

He would scold her in return for not remaining in bed. Then he would carry her back up here, only this time he wouldn't let go of her so quickly. This time, if he spied the same desire in her eyes that had been there the previous day, he might indulge her with a kiss.

The prospect stirred his blood. Yes, a soft and tender kiss, nothing lusty. Just a brush of the lips to heighten her interest in him . . .

Striding out of the bedchamber, he noticed the door at the other side of the staircase landing. He stopped dead. Ellie wouldn't have ventured out onto the parapet, would she? Surely she had too much sense to do so when the weather was still blustery.

Struck by unease, Damien propped the staff against the wall and opened the door. He stepped out into the cold. Snow covered the battlements atop the castle wall. The pulsing roar of the sea and the wuthering of the wind blended in a cacophony of wild sound. Then he spied a small, green-caped figure halfway down the narrow walk.

Ellie.

She was standing on tiptoes, leaning over one of the embrasures in the wall. Her cloaked head was barely visible between the stone teeth.

His heart gave a mighty jolt. In a moment she'd tumble over the verge. She'd plunge to her death on the rocks far below. She'd lie sprawled down there, bloody and mangled . . .

A vivid scene flashed in his mind.

The white-clad figure teetered on the edge of the moonlit roof. She spread her arms wide, a winged angel against the starry blackness. He cried out her name in horror. In the next instant, she stepped off the brink and was falling . . . falling as he sprinted madly through the garden . . .

"Ellie, no!"

Damien surged down the parapet. His boots slid on

the icy stones. The cold air burned his lungs. *Not again.* He'd never reach her in time. In another instant she'd be dead . . .

Ellie half turned at his approach. Her lips parted and her eyes widened quizzically in the pale oval of her face.

Damien yanked her away from danger and pulled her into the sheltering circle of his arms. His heart hammering, he buried his face in the tangle of her hair and breathed in her lilac scent. The feel of her warmth, her precious curves, unleashed a violent joy in him.

"Thank God, you're alive!" he muttered. "Thank God, you're safe!"

Without thought, he captured her mouth in a deep, drowning kiss. The need to revel in her life supplanted all logic and reason. There was only the driving compulsion in him to infuse her with his own strength and protection. He couldn't absorb enough of her to assuage the raw feelings inside him.

Ellie stood motionless, her hands resting on his shoulders, her face tilted up, his for the taking. All of a sudden, she uttered a small moan and lifted herself on tiptoe to return his kiss with matching fervor. Her arms slid around his neck, and her surrender magnified the wild elation that seared hot and hard through his body. For timeless moments, their mouths joined hungrily, taking sustenance from each other as if they were starving.

When it was no longer satisfying merely to kiss her, he parted her cloak to caress the ripe mounds of her bosom. Her skin felt like warm silk above the low-cut bodice. Exploring the valley between her breasts, he worked his fingers inside the tight corset until he found the sensitive nub. As he stroked her, a shudder ran through her body. She tucked her face into the crook of his shoulder, her breathing ragged against his throat.

A primitive desire throbbed in his blood. The desire to be one with her, to share the ultimate celebration of life, to hear her cry out his name in the throes of passion. Sliding his hands downward, he cupped her bottom and lifted her to him. He rubbed himself against her mound in a caress designed to give pleasure to both of them. Ellie gasped and for one fiery moment she melted in sweet surrender . . .

Abruptly she struck out hard with her fists, shoving him away. Damien staggered back a step, his feet sliding. As he reached out blindly to catch himself, his bare hand met cold stone. An icy blast of wind slapped him fully awake.

They were standing out on the parapet. The roar and crash of the surf came from below. A few snowflakes performed a frenzied dance in the air.

Ellie pressed her hands to her cheeks. The hood of her cloak had fallen back, and coils of auburn hair blew around her head. She stared aghast at him as if he were an ogre from her storybook. "What are you *doing*?"

The shock of reality sobered Damien. What *had* he just done? He had lost control of himself. He had forgotten his vow to woo her gently, to make up for his blunder of the previous day. Pinned by her accusing stare, he could only rasp, "I'm sorry."

Glancing away, he ran his fingers through his hair. He couldn't forget the sight of her leaning over the wall. Fear for her safety had triggered that terrible memory. But how could he tell her that? He didn't want to reveal the madness that had gripped him, or the panic that had wiped out all rational thought.

Because then Ellie would demand to know the source of it.

The last thing he needed was for her to learn about that long-ago tragedy. Nothing could be more guaranteed to make her view him with revulsion. A revulsion far worse than what she felt over a lusty kiss.

"You shouldn't be out here," he said gruffly.

"You shouldn't be kissing me. Especially not like *that*."

Never one to cower, Ellie stared straight at him. He had the uncanny feeling that those keen brown eyes could peer straight into his black soul. To ward off any probing, he said aggressively, "Why were you looking over that wall? You could have fallen to your death. Come back inside at once."

Sliding his arm around her waist, he guided her down the narrow wall-walk. Surprisingly, she didn't shun his assistance. Nor did she harangue him with recriminations. "I wasn't in any danger," she said rather mildly. "I was only hoping to see if I could spot the coastline."

"You're in the wrong place. This wall is on the seaward side of the castle."

"I'm aware of that. And I was gazing westward. Why else would I have needed to lean so far forward?"

Her green-cloaked form once again became a falling angel with outspread wings. Damien's arm tightened reflexively around her waist. He drew in a lungful of cold air to banish the queasiness in his gut.

Then he realized that Ellie was watching him closely. There was an intent look on her face as if she was puzzling over his odd behavior.

Better to distract her before she started asking questions.

Reaching the door, he thrust it open and ushered her into the tower. "You were supposed to stay in bed," he snapped. "It's dangerous to walk outside, especially on an injured ankle. You could have slipped on the ice again."

"Actually, my ankle is quite improved today." She

pulled herself free and took a few tentative steps across the landing. "See? I'm not limping so very much anymore."

Damien flicked a moody glance at her foot, though he could glimpse only the toe of her shoe peeking out beneath the hem. He felt frustrated by Ellie's cavalier disregard for her own safety on the parapet. She didn't seem to realize her error, and he feared that she'd blithely do it again when he wasn't watching. There was no lock, so short of nailing the door shut, he wouldn't be able to stop her.

Spying the staff propped against the wall, he thrust it at her. "I want you to lean on this when you walk. And I'll have your promise that you won't take any more foolish risks."

Ellie raised an eyebrow as she glanced at the stick, and then back at him. "If you insist."

"I *do* insist. You're my responsibility and, by God, I won't have you hurting yourself."

"Do stop shouting, Damien. If it really disturbs you so much, I won't go out again."

Turning away, she used the makeshift cane to hobble through the doorway and into her chamber. There, she proceeded to the foot of the bed and seated herself on a large chest. Laying the long stick across her lap, she lightly ran her fingertips over the polished ash wood.

Unsure of his welcome, Damien remained in the doorway with his hands planted on his hips. She didn't seem particularly angry at him and he couldn't fathom why. That in itself made him uneasy. She ought to be outraged over that kiss. He'd behaved like a lust-crazed beast. The aftereffects still burned in him like a banked fire.

And what about his criticism of her storybook the previous day? That alone ought to have earned the cold shoulder from her.

She glanced up at him. "Where did you find this?"

"What?" Then he realized she was still cradling the stick in her lap. "Oh. It's just a broken pikestaff from the weaponry room."

"It should be old and weathered, then. This one is beautiful. Did you polish it for me?"

Her praise made him relax a bit. "It's nothing," he said with a shrug. "I had little else to do this morning."

"Well, I appreciate it nonetheless."

Planting the stick, Ellie used it to lever herself to her feet. Then she unfastened the clasp at her throat and let the cloak fall onto the chest. Underneath, she wore a jade-green gown that enhanced the rich coppery highlights in her hair.

As she glided across the room to the dressing table, he watched her obsessively. The gown was a perfect fit, from the nipped curve of her waist to the generous globes of her bosom. Though he only had a side view, the silken softness of those breasts was burned into his memory. Ellie had responded beautifully when he'd caressed her. Her nipple had contracted to his touch, and he'd felt her tremble with desire . . .

She swung toward him, her skirts rustling. Their gazes met, and she frowned slightly as if guessing the direction of his thoughts. Judging by the flash of coolness in her eyes, he had not endeared himself to her. Then she draped a shawl around her shoulders, tying it over her bosom in the manner of a prim governess. She might as well have issued a verbal reprimand.

She sat down on a chair by the hearth, placing the cane within reach. Primping her skirts, she said politely, "You needn't stand out in the cold, Damien. Pray step inside and close the door."

He hesitated. Why did he sense he was being maneuvered by her? He ought to be thrilled to be alone with Ellie, to finally hear her speak his name. And in spite of his churlish behavior, she couldn't be seething with fury if she was willing to converse with him.

Maybe that lusty kiss hadn't been so ill-advised, after all. Maybe it had served to break down the barriers between them. Maybe now she'd be more amenable to his companionship. More than anything, he felt a compulsion to regain the camaraderie he'd felt with her the previous day.

He closed the door, shrugged out of his greatcoat, and slung it over the foot of the bed. Then he sauntered forward to stand by the stone fireplace. He leaned his elbow on the mantel in a pose more casual than he actually felt.

Ellie looked up at him. "Will you sit, please? We need to talk, and I don't care to have a crick in my neck."

Talk? If she meant to deliver a blistering lecture on proper behavior, he would gladly swallow his medicine and be done with it.

Obligingly, he took the opposite seat and gazed at her. His chest tightened in a soppy, unfamiliar manner. How lovely she was with those tendrils of hair framing the oval of her face. The dusting of freckles across the bridge of her nose enhanced the creamy hue of her skin, as did the rosiness of her lips.

How had he ever thought her plain?

He leaned forward with his hands clasped together. "Ellie, I must apologize for my behavior outside. I never meant to dishonor you. What I did was boorish and inexcusable, and I humbly beg your forgiveness."

She cocked her head to one side. "There can be no doubt that you *did* comport yourself as a scoundrel. However, I've a feeling that you didn't quite *mean* to do so."

Uneasiness churned in him. The intent look was on

her face again, full of questions. Maybe he could use charm as a diversion. All women were susceptible to eloquent accolades.

He cocked his mouth in a contrite smile. "You're right, I didn't go out there on the parapet with the intention of kissing you. But when I saw you standing there, I was captivated by your beauty. Perhaps it's difficult for an innocent lady to understand how a man's baser emotions can overrule his better judgment—"

"You're trying to deceive me," she said gently. "I heard the panic in your voice when you called out to me. I saw how you came running. Then you seized hold of me and said, 'Thank God, you're alive. Thank God, you're safe.' Why would you speak in such a manner if you were merely overcome by lust?"

Damien shifted in his chair. Now was the time to invent an excuse to flee the room, if only that wouldn't brand him the most craven of cowards. "As I said before, I thought you were about to fall and I feared for your safety . . ."

He lapsed into stunned silence when Ellie arose from her chair and came to kneel in front of him in a pool of jade-green skirts. She placed her hands on either arm of the chair, and those fine topaz eyes pinned him in place.

"No more prevaricating, Damien. You owe me the truth about what happened outside."

Chapter 15

Ellie had to restrain herself from reaching out and shaking him. Stubborn man! He was scowling in that domineering way of his, with his jaw clenched and his lips thinned. It was obvious that Damien thought he could fob her off with a lame explanation. He was entitled to his secrets, of course. But not when he'd dragged her into this one by his own extraordinary actions.

And not when he'd given her the most incredible kiss of her life.

Her insides still quivered from the impact of it. Never had she dreamed that a kiss could be so earth-shattering. Years ago, a would-be suitor had trapped her in a dark corner and pressed a dry, furtive peck to her lips. She had sent him packing with a blistering reprimand. The incident had fortified her belief that romance was for other women, and that she far preferred to devote herself to the make-believe world of Princess Arianna.

Now Ellie wondered if her decision had been premature. Nothing in her limited experience could have prepared her for Damien's mouth on hers. Or for the shockingly invasive way in which he had reached into her bodice. His caress on her bare skin had ignited a melting pleasure that had consumed her whole body. If that was lust, she would have to devote some thought as to whether or not she really *could* live without it.

But not now.

Now, she felt a pressing need to understand him. Gazing at his closed features, she remembered his petrified expression as he'd dashed toward her on the parapet. She had been in no danger, yet he had reacted with abject horror. Then his arms had crushed her close, and his voice had been fraught with raw emotion. *Thank God, you're alive. Thank God, you're safe.*

It was unsettling to wonder whether he'd been speaking to her—or to someone from his past. What experience of his had sparked such an unnatural fear in him? Maybe he would never tell her. Maybe it was too private, too personal, and she was wrong to probe for answers.

As the fire hissed into the silence, Ellie began to regret the impulse that had made her kneel in front of him. Her attempt at entreaty clearly meant nothing to him.

"Well," she said lightly, sitting on her heels and gazing up at him, "I don't suppose I can force you to speak, Damien. We're hardly friends, after all, and I've no real claim on your confidences."

A peculiar regret lurked in the depths of her heart. But she reminded herself that he was the Demon Prince, the villainous rat who had abducted her. As remarkable as his kiss had been, it mustn't be allowed to overshadow her plans for the future. For the past day, she had been pondering what to do when they departed the castle. Before Damien had come out onto the parapet, she'd been gazing at the stormy sea and considering how best to maneuver him into supporting the scheme that she had decided upon.

That was far more essential than exposing his secrets.

As she started to rise, Damien caught her by the shoulders. "Don't go, Ellie, please," he said gruffly. "I'll tell you what happened. You do deserve to know."

Ellie sank back, her full attention on his taut features. A thread of rough emotion in his voice belied his harsh, implacable expression. Very softly, she said, "I'm listening."

He glanced away for a moment before fixing her with those cool green-gray eyes. "You heard about the scandal with the young lady seven years ago. I can assure you, the gossip was true. I was caught in a bedchamber with Miss Veronica Higgins. The fault was not hers. It was entirely mine."

His gaze turned hazy as if he were peering into the past. "She was a delicate, blue-eyed blonde, shy and modest to a fault. From the moment I spied Veronica at a house party, I was determined to win her heart. She, of course, would have nothing to do with a notorious rake. So I laid wagers with a few cronies that I could make her fall in love with me."

His mouth formed an ironic twist. "However, I was foolish enough to take matters beyond a mere flirtation. When we were found together, it wasn't just me who was barred from society. Veronica, too, suffered the consequences. Not only did she lose her position as a companion to her aunt, she was shunned by her family. She had no recourse but to accept my offer of marriage."

A knell of shock struck Ellie. *"You're married?"*

He gave a sharp shake of his head. "Not any longer. I'm afraid it was not a happy union for either of us. I leased a house in the country as a means to escape the scandal. Even so, Veronica refused to show herself in public. She was weepy and disconsolate and . . . I cannot claim to have been a very considerate husband. To escape the endless melancholy, I began to stay away from home for much of the time."

Damien paused to draw a deep breath, shifting his moody gaze back to the fire. "Late one night, I returned from an evening spent drinking in a local tavern with friends. I was leaving the stables, walking toward the house, when I glanced up and saw her. She was wearing a white nightdress. And she was standing on the edge of the roof."

Ellie's throat tightened. Her skin prickled with apprehension. She suddenly dreaded to hear what he had to say. *"No."*

His voice flat and emotionless, he went on, "I realized later that it couldn't have been a coincidence that I was there to witness her actions. Veronica must have been waiting for me to come home. Perhaps she climbed out onto the roof when she heard my horse coming up the drive. All I know is that when I shouted her name, she stepped off the roof. I ran to catch her . . . But I was too late."

Aghast, Ellie reached out and covered his hands with hers. The look on his face was so bleak that she knew no words to offer as comfort. So she merely stroked his fingers, wishing there were some way to erase the grisly memory from his mind. His wife had taken her own life, and Damien clearly blamed himself. Ellie couldn't fathom the grief and guilt he must have borne all these years.

No wonder he'd reacted so strongly to seeing her lean over the parapet. He must have been transported back to the moment of seeing his wife perched on the edge of the roof. He had relived that horror through Ellie, only this time, he had reached her in time. He had pulled her close and uttered fervently, *Thank God, you're alive. Thank God, you're safe.*

Had he been thinking of his wife when he'd kissed Ellie? Had she been merely a substitute?

Ellie pushed the questions away. How selfish to dwell on her own needs at such a time. "I'm so sorry, Damien. I never knew—"

"No one knew. I concealed her suicide."

In an abrupt withdrawal, he surged up from the chair and paced across the circular chamber. He stood there with his back turned to Ellie. He combed his fingers through his hair, ruffling the black strands. He looked so tormented that her heart turned over in her breast. She ached to go to him, yet sensed he would reject any acknowledgment of his anguish. After giving him a moment to collect himself, she murmured, "How did you conceal it?"

He turned slowly. Once again, his features showed only a detached remoteness. "Finn had heard me shout her name. He came running. But Veronica had died instantly. There was nothing to be done for her. Finn said people would whisper that I'd killed her, pushed her off the roof myself. I'd be wrongfully imprisoned for murder. In my distraught state of mind, I agreed to let him arrange matters so that it would appear as though she'd been trampled by a horse."

His voice grew heavier. "I convinced myself that I was doing it to protect her character. There were still a few whispers that I'd murdered her, but I suppose that was only to be expected given the circumstances of our forced marriage. However, most people treated me with all the respect due a grieving widower. And as the weeks passed, I began to realize that *I* was the one being protected. I was never held accountable for causing the despair that made Veronica take her own life."

Ellie could see his point. From start to finish, his marriage had been a terrible disaster. It would never have happened if not for his disgraceful behavior. But he already knew that, so who was she to berate him more than he'd already done to himself?

And she couldn't help but wonder why Veronica had felt such extreme despondency. Even if she'd been as delicate and shy as Damien had described her, and had had difficulty adjusting to the forced marriage, that was no reason to give up all hope. Why had she not found a useful occupation to lend purpose to her life? Perhaps she could have done needlework for the poor or prepared baskets for the sick. In such a circumstance, Ellie herself would have taken solace in her drawing. And she would have *made* Damien behave himself.

Her ankle ached from the uncustomary position on the floor. As she prepared to rise by bracing her hand on the chair, Damien was there in an instant to help her to her feet. "Lean on me," he ordered. "I shouldn't have allowed you to kneel so long. You ought to be in bed with your foot up."

As he slid his arm around her waist and guided her across the room, Ellie glanced up at his sober features. No matter how much he painted himself the villain, she couldn't imagine him being purposely cruel to his wife. "I agree with Finn," she said. "I cannot see what good would have been accomplished by revealing the truth."

Damien scowled as they stopped beside the bed. "You don't understand. I should have been there that night. If only I'd stayed at home, perhaps—"

Ellie placed her finger over his lips. "Perhaps you've punished yourself enough, Damien. You can't change what happened. None of us can. We can only try to learn from our mistakes."

He gave her a grim look as he settled her on the bed.

"But I haven't learned. I ruined Veronica's life, and now I've ruined yours."

Watching him ease a pillow under her foot, Ellie felt the spark of a realization. This was her chance. The chance to present her scheme to him. She could not have planned it any better, for she had wanted to make him feel beholden to her so that he would comply with her wishes.

"Now that you mention it," she said, "you *have* ruined my life. I very much doubt that I'll be able to return home. My family isn't likely to welcome me back considering I will have been gone for over a week in the company of a notorious scoundrel."

Bending over her foot, Damien went very still. He cast a furious, incredulous look at her. "Are you angling for a marriage proposal?"

His mistaken assumption appalled Ellie. She had never anticipated him leaping to such a conclusion. When she had formulated her plan, she hadn't known about his forced marriage. "No! Absolutely *not*! I only meant that you owe me reparations for abducting me."

"Reparations." He gave her a hard stare. The mattress dipped as he seated himself at the foot of the bed. "Explain yourself."

She drew a fortifying breath, her fingers playing with the fringe on her shawl. It was time to reveal what she'd never told anyone else. "For a while now, I've been planning to leave my uncle's house. That's why I've been working on my storybook and hoping to sell it to a publisher. I need the income to live on my own rather than continue to stay there."

"Why? Is it Walt? Has he made illicit advances toward you?"

Once again, Ellie was taken aback. Damien couldn't

possibly know that she often felt uneasy around her eldest cousin. "Well, he *does* stare at me . . . in a certain way. And . . ." She paused, recalling that last night in the nursery when Walt had grabbed at her bosom.

"And?"

"There was one time—only one—that he touched me, but I burned him with the candle I was holding and that was the end of it."

Damien swore savagely under his breath. A muscle worked in his jaw as if he were struggling to master his anger. "And the others in the household? Have any of them mistreated you in any way?"

She hesitated. It felt disloyal to criticize her family. "Not really. I've always had a roof over my head and food on the table. When I was orphaned at fourteen, the earl was kind enough to take me in—"

"And he proceeded to treat you as an unpaid servant. Don't deny it, Ellie. I'm well aware of Pennington's reputation as a skinflint, and I saw how he garbed you in old sacks. I'm guessing he made you the household drudge and never paid you tuppence for your labor."

Ellie bit her lip. Had her situation been so obvious? "It's my duty to help the family. Anyway, I've always liked to stay busy. But I don't wish to spend the remainder of my life doing someone else's bidding."

"So tell me, how exactly *have* you spent your days there?"

He was gently massaging her stockinged foot, and Ellie had to concentrate to keep her mind on the conversation. "Mostly, I've been governess to my two younger cousins. Now that Cedric is off at Eton, I've been chaperoning Beatrice, helping prepare her for her upcoming season. I also read to Lady Anne every day and do errands for the countess."

"Ah, yes, old Lady Pennington," Damien said with a

cynical quirk of his mouth. "I recall that gorgon presiding over society parties. She's your grandmother, is she not?"

"Yes, my father was the earl's younger brother."

"Then by God, she ought to have provided you with a decent wardrobe as befitting your rank. Were you granted a season at least? A chance to marry?"

She shook her head. "Actually not. You see, my father had enormous gambling debts that my uncle was forced to pay off. He said there was nothing left to pay for my come-out."

"That miserly snake," Damien snapped. "Your father's debts were not your fault, Ellie. And Pennington is a wealthy man. He has more than enough to sponsor his own niece."

The vehemence in his tone warmed Ellie's heart. With a faint smile, she murmured, "You needn't rub my foot quite so hard, you know."

Looking instantly remorseful, he drew back his hands. "Forgive me. I was contemplating how I'd love to wring your uncle's neck."

She mustn't feel all aglow inside when Damien had just proposed violence. Or regret that he was no longer touching her. "Well, I don't suppose it matters anymore. I'm twenty-six now and quite content to be a spinster. Had I been given the opportunity to marry at eighteen, I might never have been inspired to compose my storybook."

He sat against the bedpost with one foot braced on the floor. The gleam in those green-gray eyes made her heart beat faster. "Continuing your logic," he said, "you also wouldn't be here right now. With me."

The glow settled deep in her core. It brought to mind that kiss . . . and the shocking pleasure of his hand stroking her bosom. Was he, too, remembering it? Ellie wouldn't allow herself to think about that now. If she became distracted, she might lose this opportunity.

"And I wouldn't be in such a pickle," she said. "But since you *did* bring me here against my will, it seems only fair that you should compensate me for the damage to my reputation."

His face sobered. "Are you certain the earl will throw you out on the street without any provision whatsoever? Is there no one in that blasted household who would care enough to help you?"

Thinking of her family, Ellie felt a pang. She had little faith in receiving any aid from her uncle, her grandmother, Beatrice, Walt . . . "Lady Anne would, I'm sure. But like me, she lives there on the earl's sufferance and has only a bit of pin money."

"Lady Anne?"

"The earl's spinster sister-in-law. She's no blood relation to me, but she's always been very kind and appreciative that I read to her each morning while she sews." Ellie stared defiantly at him. "I will *not* ask her for funds when she has so little herself."

"I should hope not. Tell me, what is it you wish from me?"

His cool masculine features provided no clue to his thoughts. He might have been a businessman negotiating a hard bargain. Yet she felt no hesitation at sharing her dream with him. "I want to live in a cottage in the country. Someplace cozy and bright, where I might gaze out upon the garden while I draw. A home where I can work alone all day without anyone handing me an overflowing basket of mending, or ordering me to write out a hundred invitations to a party."

He lifted a black eyebrow. "You want no one there with you? Not even a servant?"

"No one," she said firmly. "I am perfectly capable of

doing any necessary chores myself. You see, more than anything, I crave peace and quiet so that I might concentrate on my book."

"And I am to provide you with this cottage." He subjected her to a long scrutiny while she waited anxiously, her fingers twisting the fringe of her shawl. "All right, then," he said, "I'm sure it can be arranged. I'll direct my land agent to handle the matter upon our return to London."

Ellie felt as if a vast weight had been lifted from her shoulders. For so long she had been worried about the future. But she mustn't rejoice just yet. "You'll also provide me with a small stipend to cover my expenses for the coming year."

He chuckled. "Small? You need to learn lesson one in the art of negotiation—always ask for more than you really want."

"I won't play games, Damien. I only need enough to purchase food and other incidentals. Until I can sell my book."

"And if you cannot procure a publisher? What will you do then?"

"I'll take in students if need be. I'll find a way to support myself. But I do hope that won't be necessary." The leather-bound notebook lay beside her on the bed. Picking it up, Ellie riffled through her newest drawings, the ones she'd sketched since her dispute with him the previous afternoon. "By the way, I've been thinking about the suggestion you made to me yesterday . . ."

He leaned forward, his gaze intent. "Ellie, you must allow me to apologize for that. I should never have presumed to pass judgment on a manuscript that I haven't even seen."

"You're right, you shouldn't have," she said tartly. "However, I've decided it's a sound proposal, after all.

It'll take quite a bit of work, but it *is* possible to break the story into four or five separate books—perhaps more. I'll have the leisure to work on the revisions once I'm living on my own."

He raised an eyebrow. "Then you do see the advantage of it?"

"Yes. I'll know for certain once I can review the pages I've already done. I left them hidden in my bedchamber at Pennington House."

Would Uncle Basil even allow her through the front door? Perhaps he'd already instructed the servants to refuse her admittance . . .

"Hidden?" Damien asked with a frown. "So your family knows nothing about your book?"

She shook her head. "They'd be horrified at the prospect of me selling my work to a publisher. Ladies never engage in commerce, you see. I did my drawing late in the evenings, after Beatrice went to bed. In the hustle and bustle of the day, when everyone was making demands on me, it was always my little secret, something that belonged to me alone."

He regarded her with frank admiration. "The true secret is that you're a strong, accomplished woman, Ellie. I pity them for never realizing it."

That warm glow flared inside Ellie again. It made her skin tingle and her heartbeat quicken. Damien had awakened feelings in her that she hadn't known existed, and it was more than just that lusty kiss. A connection had formed between them, perhaps because they'd both suffered undeserved misfortune in their childhood, he being abandoned by his birth parents, and she as an orphan forced to live with relatives who did not love her. They knew each other's secrets now, too. She about his late wife, and he about her book.

But he was merely a charming rogue, Ellie reminded

herself, as he took the notebook from her, examined her latest drawings with interest, and proceeded to make a clever case for Prince Ratworth to be a hero rather than a villain. She couldn't help laughing at his inventive ideas to give his likeness a larger role in the story.

All the while, she found herself observing the economical movement of his hand as he turned the pages, the quirk of his lips whenever he told a jest, the way his expression softened sometimes when he looked at her. His every mannerism fascinated her, and the undeniable warmth she felt for him warred with her practical side.

It would be foolish to fall prey to his allure. The Demon Prince had committed the villainous act of abducting her, bringing her here against her will. Nothing could ever come of their unexpected friendship. Once they left the castle, they would part ways. Damien would return to his London gambling den and she would move into her cottage.

Yet the memory of that passionate kiss burned like a flame within her. In spite of all wisdom to the contrary, he had become a fire in her blood. She couldn't abide the thought of never again feeling his lips on her mouth, or his hands on her body. And the longer they sat talking and bantering on her bed, the more she found herself daring to ponder the unthinkable.

Chapter 16

Ellie took great care in readying herself for dinner that evening.

Using needle and thread, she spent the better part of an hour altering the bodice of a sapphire-blue gown to create a daringly deep décolletage that showcased her bosom. Then she sat in front of the speckled old mirror at the dressing table, combing and pinning until the artful cascade of curls finally pleased her. Lastly, she slipped her feet into the sparkly garnet slippers that Lady Milford had given to her.

How long ago that day seemed. Yet only a little more than a week had passed since she and Beatrice had come outside after paying their call, and Ellie had spied the menacing, black-clad stranger sitting in his carriage, watching her cousin. Never in her wildest dreams could she have imagined that less than ten days later, she'd be waiting in the tower of a faraway castle, hoping that same man would make passionate love to her.

No, she had done more than *hope*. She had set into motion a brazen scheme to lure him into her bed. A tremor of doubt and desire eddied through her. Did she truly dare to go through with it?

A rapping sounded on the door. Her heart fluttered, although a glance at the high window confirmed the time to be twilight, about half past five so late in February. That meant the visitor could only be Mrs. MacNab. Ellie had requested an early dinner on the excuse that she was weary and wished to retire for the night as soon as darkness fell.

She'd also sent Damien away in mid-afternoon, on the excuse that she was weary and needed a nap. Oh, and would he please be so kind as to return at six o'clock and bring pen and ink so that she could start on the final renditions of her preliminary sketches?

Leaning on the stick that he'd fashioned for her, she made her way across the bedchamber. Her insides felt like a tightly wound spring. She truly *was* a brazen hussy for fibbing to both of them—and for such a wicked cause. What if Mrs. MacNab suspected from Ellie's risqué gown the purpose she had in mind?

Good heavens. Why, oh, why hadn't she considered that before now? It would be mortifying if anyone else guessed how much she craved to indulge her sinful passions. She wanted it to be a secret known only to her and Damien.

The mere thought of the Demon Prince made her knees wobbly. Ever since that ardent episode on the parapet, she had been too distracted to work on her illustrations. Instead, she had existed in a dreamlike state, reliving his kiss again and again: the forceful hunger of his lips on hers, the rasp of his whiskered jaw against her cheek, the stimulating stroke of his finger across her bare nipple. Most thrilling of all had been the moment when he had cupped her bottom and lifted her against him, and she had felt the hard pressure of his loins against hers.

Tonight she wouldn't react like a shocked maiden and stop him. Tonight she would tempt Damien into another fervent embrace. And when he responded like the rogue he was, and hauled her into his arms, this time she fully intended to surrender to his seduction.

Taking a deep breath to steady herself, Ellie opened the door. Icy air rushed in from the dim-lit stairwell. But it wasn't the maidservant who waited out on the landing.

Damien himself stood there, gripping the handle of a large basket in one hand. He wore his greatcoat with the collar turned up, his black hair attractively mussed by the wind. One corner of his mouth was curled in a charming half-smile.

"I thought I'd save Mrs. MacNab a trip since I was coming up here anyway," he said in his deep baritone. "I assured her there was no reason for us both to climb those winding stairs . . ."

His voice trailed off as he took in Ellie's appearance at a glance, his gaze lingering on her cleavage. She felt a little shiver of pleasure. Was he remembering how he had put his hand inside her bodice? Despite the chill in the air, heat radiated through every part of her body. She basked in the realization that her plan to tempt him was already working. Or at least it would if she stopped gawking at him like a besotted ninny.

She stepped back to allow him entry. "Do come in, Damien. You must forgive me for being surprised. I wasn't expecting you just yet."

Those green-gray eyes subjected her to a penetrating stare. A controlled politeness replaced his smile. "I shan't stay more than a moment," he said. "I only wanted to deliver what you'd asked me to bring. I trust you had a good rest?"

As he spoke, Damien carried the basket to the table by the fire. The flames danced and crackled into the silence. He opened the lid and began to unload several covered dishes. As he did so, he glanced at her inquiringly.

Flustered by his statement that he wasn't staying, Ellie realized that he was waiting for her to reply. "Rest? Oh, yes, of course, the nap was splendid! I'm not weary in the *least*. Quite the contrary."

"That's odd," he said, arranging a plate and utensils for her. "Mrs. MacNab said that you intended to retire early tonight."

Ellie swallowed, her mouth suddenly dry. "Did she? Oh. I do recall saying something to that effect . . . but it must have been before my nap. I'm feeling perfectly wide awake now. I'm sure I won't want to sleep again for *hours*."

Standing by the door, her fingers still curled around the improvised cane, she watched as Damien finished laying out her dinner. Her heart skipped a beat when he straightened up and turned toward her. There was a remote quality to his expression that she didn't quite understand. He had not removed his coat, either, which could only mean that he'd failed to take her hint.

She tilted her mouth in a heartfelt smile. "I should very much like for you to join me for dinner, Damien. Will you, please?"

"There's only one plate and one fork, so I think not." His face somewhat somber, he stepped toward her. "I intend to have an early night myself. You'll be pleased to hear that Finn believes the storm will have abated enough for us to depart in the morning."

The news jolted Ellie. Just yesterday, she'd been counting the minutes until their departure. Now, she wanted desperately to prolong their time here at the castle. However, Damien was no longer the warm, relaxed man he'd been earlier in the day, when they'd sat and chatted for hours on her bed. What had happened to make him so indifferent toward her?

"Are you quite certain?" she asked. "Perhaps the seas will still be choppy."

"Finn is an excellent judge of the weather since he grew up in these parts." Stopping directly in front of her, Damien reached into the pocket of his greatcoat and drew forth a feathered quill and a corked inkpot. "You requested these earlier," he said, holding the items out to her. "I trust you'll have an enjoyable evening working on your storybook."

Ellie couldn't bring herself to take the implements from him. He would leave then, and that was the very last thing she wanted.

Oh, why was he not smiling? Would he make no attempt to seduce her, despite the low-cut gown and the care she'd taken with her appearance? Had she been mistaken to believe that he'd enjoyed her company? Mistaken to conclude that he felt as attracted to her as she was to him?

Maybe he really *had* been thinking of his late wife during that impassioned episode on the parapet. Maybe Ellie had just been a convenient substitute for the outpouring of his emotions.

Her heart endured a painful shriveling. Upon their arrival here at the castle, she'd overheard him comment that she was much prettier from a distance. Perhaps he preferred his women to be dainty and blond, the way he'd described his late wife. And yet . . . Ellie had seen heat in his eyes when he'd looked at her, too.

She couldn't bear his return to coldness. He had reverted to being the stranger again, as if the warmth, the laughter, the friendship they'd shared only a few hours ago had never happened.

But it *had* happened; their closeness had not been a figment of her imagination. And if this was to be their last night at the castle, she couldn't let him just go away now. Not when this might be her only chance to learn the mysteries of being fully a woman.

Not when she felt full to bursting with desire for him.

She propped the polished stick against a chair and then took the quill and inkpot from him. The brief touch of their hands ignited sparks of pleasure over her skin. Emboldened, she cast a guileless glance up at him from beneath her lashes. "I'm afraid I can't manage the cane with my hands full, and I really shouldn't put weight on my ankle. Would you mind helping me over to the bed? I'd like to put these things on the table there."

He gave her a keen stare. She half expected him to snatch back the pen and ink and take them over to the bed himself. But he didn't, much to her satisfaction. Instead, he slid his arm around her waist and walked her across the room.

She made sure to lean heavily on him, to let her bosom brush the side of his chest and to bump her hip against his as if by accident. By the time they reached the bed, her legs felt weak as jelly and she truly did need his assistance in standing.

An oil lamp burned low on the bedside table, casting a soft glow over the plumped pillows and the feather quilt. Ellie craved to be lying there in his embrace, happily subject to his ardent kisses and skilled caresses. But her knowledge of how to achieve that goal was woefully inadequate. In all of her illicit imaginings of this moment, she had never thought to be the one to direct the seduction.

He was the scoundrel, after all. Oughtn't he seize her in his arms and have his wicked way with her?

She quickly set down the items atop the notebook. Before Damien could remove his supporting arm, she turned to face him. Her hands came to rest on the lapels of his coat, and by design, her breasts met the hard wall of his chest. His earthy masculinity made her aware of an insistent pulse beating deep in her core.

She gazed up at him imploringly. "Are you quite certain you won't stay with me for a time?"

His chest expanded as he took in a lungful of air. "No. No, that wouldn't be wise. Not at all."

It sounded as if he was trying to convince himself. His large hands encircled her waist as if to set her away from him. Yet he did no such thing. He only stared ferociously at her as if wrestling with an inner demon.

Sensing her chance, Ellie reached up to cradle his cheek in her hand. His skin felt wonderfully rough from the day's growth of his beard, and she ached for him to touch her in return. "Don't leave, Damien, please don't. I want you right here with me. I want you to kiss me again as you did before."

His jaw clenched beneath her hand. He stared at her with grim concentration, his fingers flexing around her waist. "You can't know what you're asking, Ellie. It won't be just a kiss this time. Give me half a chance, and I'll strip you naked and ravish you in that bed."

The vehemence in his tone only made her melt, though it was clear he meant to frighten her away with his plain speaking. She smiled up at him. "I *do* know what I'm saying. And that *is* what I want."

But not even that brazen declaration had the desired effect on him.

He stood rigid, motionless, a fiercely luminous quality to his green-gray eyes. "For God's sake! I can't do this, not to you of all women."

You of all women. What did he mean? That she was

special to him? Or simply that he didn't wish to compound the wrong he'd already done by abducting her?

In a flash, she comprehended the source of his resistance. It all made sense to her now. Damien didn't want her to be forced into marriage as his first wife had been. He still carried a terrible burden of guilt from the past, and he feared to repeat his mistake. Despite his sordid reputation, he was determined to treat Ellie with respect.

But she didn't want him to coddle her, not now. Now, she simply wanted *him*. The only way to accomplish that was to break down the wall of his stubborn scruples.

With one finger, she traced the shape of his mouth. "I'm afraid you've no choice in the matter," she murmured. "You see, Damien, it's part of my compensation. You owe me one night of pleasure."

Chapter 17

As always, Ellie had surprised him.

In the midst of a self-inflicted battle between honor and lust, Damien felt the mad urge to laugh. Here he was, determined to do one decent act in his misbegotten life, and she was offering herself to him on a silver platter. He ought to vacate her bedchamber at once, never to return. He absolutely ought *not* to be eyeing her lavish bosom and wondering if a tug on her bodice would allow those beautiful breasts to spring free.

The light touch of her fingertip on his lips was far too provocative, so he caught hold of her wrist to stop her. Didn't she realize how difficult this was for him? Or maybe the little minx *did* know.

"I've already promised you a cottage and a stipend," he growled. "We made an agreement, and you can't add anything more to it."

"Why not? I don't recall signing any legal papers." As if the matter were settled, Ellie began to undo the buttons of his greatcoat. "Besides, in the eyes of society, I'm already ruined. Since people will whisper that I've lain with you, why not do so in fact? At least then

I will have gained the benefit of *experiencing* the sin that I am believed to have committed."

He should step away from those deft fingers. But he was roasting hot. He needed to shed the heavy coat and then bury himself deep inside her body. No, he'd be wiser to take a plunge into the icy depths of the sea. "You're supposed to save yourself for the man that you marry."

"Then pray be assured, I have no intention of ever marrying."

Her calm statement caught him off guard. Why would she say such a thing? Even Veronica had wanted to get married—just not to a bastard rogue like him.

Ellie pushed the greatcoat off his shoulders. As he shrugged out of the sleeves and let the garment fall to the floor, he snarled, "What the devil do you mean, never marry? All women want to marry."

"I can't speak for all women, only for myself. And *I* don't care to have a husband." She reached up to work at the knot of his cravat. "After twelve years in my uncle's house, I've had my fill of tending to the demands of other people. I want to live on my own without any entanglements. Why would I trade one form of servitude for another?"

Her frank assessment made him glower down at her in unaccountable ire. He didn't want to marry again, either. Didn't that make them a perfect match? She was every scoundrel's dream, lovely and willing, requiring no commitment from him except to fulfill her sexual desires. Yet perversely, Damien wanted to shake sense into her.

He pulled her fingers away from his neck cloth and imprisoned them beneath his, flat against his chest. "If you truly wish to live alone, that's precisely why we *shouldn't* do this. I could impregnate you, Ellie. You may very well conceive my child."

She glanced away for a moment, biting her lip. Then she returned her gaze to him, those big brown eyes as direct as ever. "I accept that risk. And if perchance I should find myself in a delicate condition, I'll raise the child on my own. Never fear, I absolve you of any and all obligation."

Absolve him! Her assumption of his irresponsibility lit a powder keg in Damien. He wanted to explode in fury that he would never, ever abandon his own child. Why in *hell* would she assume that he would?

It was his unsavory reputation, of course. That, and the fact that no one knew about Lily. He had taken great pains to keep his daughter's existence hidden from the world, to protect her from society gossips who might whisper of her father's ill-repute. He would not speak of her now, either, not even to exonerate himself in Ellie's eyes.

She was staring up at him, a faintly quizzical expression on her face as if she sensed his powerful reaction and sought to understand it. He wouldn't allow her to fathom his thoughts. His private life belonged to him alone. The only knowledge she would elicit from him tonight would be carnal.

If Ellie thought him a rake, then by God, he would be one.

He thrust his fingers into her elegant coiffure, dislodging the pins so that her rich auburn curls cascaded over her shoulders. Bringing his mouth close to hers, he murmured silkily, "Then you shall have what you wish, Ellie. How could any man resist such beauty and fire?"

Ellie had been perplexed by the tautness of anger on his face. Everything she'd said had been designed to clarify that she was *not* like his late wife, that she would *not* trap him into marriage, not under any circumstances. Wasn't that what men of his ilk wanted? An easy liaison without commitments? Yet she had sensed the rise of ire in him, his eyes taking on a shuttered look that concealed his thoughts.

Then, like a slate wiped clean, the harshness had altered into a look of seductive charm. In one swift move he made a tangle of her carefully arranged curls—and she could not be happier. Now, his fingers were doing delicious things to the sensitive skin of her scalp and neck, while his mouth trailed soft kisses over her face.

Did he truly think of her in terms of beauty and fire?

A sublime longing seared through Ellie and melted her knees. She clung to his broad shoulders and closed her eyes, the better to enjoy the sensations he aroused in her. This was not the same as the mad, impassioned embrace on the parapet, but she liked it just as much. Perhaps even more, she amended, as his lips brushed over hers, his tongue taking provocative sips at her mouth.

Believe me, Ellie, if ever I decide to seduce you, you'll know it and you'll want me to do it.

He'd said that to her only the previous day, when she had sprained her ankle. At the time she had scoffed, but not anymore. How very right he had been. She could think of nowhere else she wanted to be than in his arms, every part of her alive with anticipation. More than anything in the world, she wanted him to seduce her just like this.

His hands moved down her back, opening the row of pearl buttons that she'd struggled with for ten minutes to fasten by herself. Damien made much shorter work of them. In a matter of moments, he'd loosened her gown and tugged off the sleeves, letting the silk of her bodice drop to her waist. Cool air caressed her skin. She had purposely left off her corset tonight, so that now only a simple chemise preserved her modesty.

One arm looped around her waist, he turned his attention downward to her bosom. Her overly large breasts jutted against the white linen, the darker nipples visible through the fine fabric. His eyelids were lowered somewhat, and he wore a look of such sober concentration that shyness crept over her.

Was he comparing her to his delicately beautiful wife?

Her arm moved of its own volition in a feeble attempt to shield herself. Haltingly, she murmured, "I'm sorry I'm not . . . dainty. As a lady ought to be."

He looked up sharply. One corner of his mouth quirked in amusement. "Sorry? Good God, Ellie. You *are* an innocent."

Placing his hand on the outside of her chemise, he cupped one voluptuous globe in his palm, his thumb rubbing idly over the linen-draped tip. "You're exquisite exactly as you are. See? We're a perfect fit." Continuing to stroke her in that exciting manner, he added, "I've no doubt we shall fit just as perfectly elsewhere, too."

A quiver of anticipation suffused her from head to toe. He was referring to the intimate act they would share, Ellie knew. She had only a general idea of how it was accomplished, and his implication made her eager to lift the veil on the mysteries of lovemaking. He teased her again with those small, stirring kisses over her face and throat. Her skin had become acutely sensitive to his touch, and the caress of his fingers on her breasts created a river of heat that flowed downward to enrich the ache between her legs.

"Damien." Sighing his name, she wreathed her arms around his neck, as much for support as to encourage his kisses. He obliged her with a playful skirmish of their open mouths that left her wanting more. How could he be so controlled? She herself felt possessed by a wild yearning that she knew not how to assuage. When he drew back abruptly, she made a small mewl of protest.

He rubbed his knuckles soothingly down her cheek. "You oughtn't be standing on that injured ankle."

"Mmm," she said, rising on tiptoes to invite another kiss, "it isn't hurting me at all right now."

"Nevertheless, I'd prefer to make love to you in bed—without the impediment of clothing."

With a flick of his fingers, he untied the strings of her petticoat, sending it and her gown slithering to the floor. He swept her up against him and half carried her to the large four-poster, where he drew back the covers and laid her down against the pillows.

Reclining on the cool sheets, she wore only the gossamer chemise, silk stockings, the garnet slippers. Should she remove them? The fleeting thought vanished as Damien straightened up beside the bed.

He peeled off his coat and waistcoat, letting them fall where they might. As he reached up his arms to strip the white linen shirt over his head, Ellie rolled onto her side and watched in utter enthrallment. She had always wondered if the marble statues of Greek gods had been exaggerated by the sculptor; surely the subject had been carved to appear larger than life. But Damien could have been a model for a masterpiece of classical art. He had a powerful torso, his arms and shoulders were defined by taut muscles, his chest was a broad expanse with a scattering of black hair that disappeared into his waistband.

The mattress dipped as he sat down to tug off his boots, dropping each with a thud onto the carpet. Clad in only his breeches, he turned to brace one arm on either side of her. Their gazes held for an eloquent moment. The only sounds were the snapping of the fire and the beating of her heart in her ears. His green-gray eyes revealed a concentrated ardor, along with something else, something she couldn't define.

A muscle tightened in his jaw. "Ellie," he said gruffly. "You can still change your mind."

He was granting her a choice. Even now, he was being considerate of her sensibilities. He didn't want her to make a mistake that she might regret for the rest of her life. Reaching up, she lightly touched the rigid set of his jaw. "I want this, Damien. I want *you*. So very much."

He searched her eyes for another moment, and whatever he was seeking must have satisfied him. The tension in his expression eased and he gave her a scoundrel's smile that promised exciting things to come. Then he joined their mouths in a deep, meltingly intimate kiss.

Succumbing to temptation, she explored the hard planes and angles of his upper body. His skin was hot, smooth in places and rough with hair in others. She loved the solidity of his muscles, the firmness of his chest abrading her breasts. All of her senses felt alive and vibrant. Never had she known that a man's taste could be so delicious, or that his scent could stimulate her passion.

How incredible to reflect that a week ago, she hadn't even met him. Damien seemed a part of her now, an extension of her own body, as if they were bound by some inexplicable force. She could no more send him away than she could stop the swift thrum of her pulse beat.

He kissed a scorching path down over her chemise, then proceeded to remove her shoes and garters, lingering over the task of rolling down her silk stockings, one at a time. The brush of his fingers on her thighs and calves was exquisite torture. In her naïveté, Ellie had not known that lovemaking could be unhurried and prolonged, with every action savored. It was fulfilling—and it was tormenting, too, a splendid frustration that honed her desire for him. At last, when her legs were bare and he had finished worshiping them, he tugged up the hem of her chemise.

Ellie shifted position to help him draw it over her head. Then she sank back against the pillows as he gazed over her nakedness. She felt no shame, only a sense of rightness in letting him look upon her. The keen appreciation in his eyes made her feel beautiful, admired, womanly in a way she'd never before known.

He ran his fingertips over the hills of her breasts, then down over the plain of her belly and around the curve of her hips. "I'm glad now that you wore those shapeless sacks," he said, his voice deep and raspy. "No other man has ever seen you like this."

The look he gave her was fierce and profound. His chest rose and fell with quick, shallow breaths, and she sensed that he was keeping his own passions under strict control. But she didn't want him to be disciplined. She wanted him to give free rein to the madness that he'd displayed out on the parapet.

"Make love to me, Damien. *Please.*"

He still wore his breeches, and when she fumbled to unfasten them, he caught hold of her hands. A strained chuckle came from deep in his chest. "Patience. Else this will be over too swiftly."

He lay down alongside Ellie and idly stroked her, his fingers gliding down her arm, then over her hips and breasts, while skirting the one place that burned the most for him. Was it wicked to wish that he would touch her there? She wanted to ask him, but couldn't quite formulate the words. Surely such a request was far too indecorous for a lady . . .

Lowering his mouth to her breasts, he suckled each one in turn, his teeth lightly nipping while she sighed with pleasure. She combed her fingers through the tumbled strands of his hair. How novel to gaze down at his dark head ministering to her bare bosom. The lust he provoked in her transcended all rules of propriety.

No wonder young ladies were warned to avoid ne'er-do-wells. What woman could resist the allure of such an accomplished lover?

The thought aroused a forbidden thrill in her. The Demon Prince was *her* lover now. Her sinfully perfect lover.

Then Ellie forgot all else when at last he moved his hand lower and delved into her private folds with small, teasing strokes. She caught a ragged gasp at the unfamiliarity of a man's touch where none had ever been. He took the time to kiss her face, to whisper her name, to tell her how beautiful she was, while he continued to play with her.

As his exploration grew bolder, she felt so overcome by desire that she hid her face in the lee of his neck. The enticing caress of his fingers absorbed all of her awareness. Awash in wanton delight, she could hear the rhythmic wet sounds of his stroking and her own shuddery breaths. He pressed ever deeper, and she parted her legs, her hips moving fluidly, without conscious directive. She simply *had* to assuage this torturous hunger inside her, and she strained against his hand, panting, moaning for surcease. It came in a startling rush of blissful waves that coursed through her body, leaving her limp and spent and marvelously gratified.

She had a vague awareness of Damien leaving her for a moment as he stripped off his breeches. As he lay back down to gather her into his arms, Ellie clung weakly to him. It felt utterly decadent to lie flesh to flesh with him. Against her thigh lay his male member, thick and long and hot. She was still stunned by the climactic intensity that he had wrought in her—and aware that he had not yet derived the same enjoyment for himself.

He placed his hand between her legs again, his finger sliding up inside her, stroking deeply and causing another small echo of paradise almost as an afterthought. Laying his brow against hers, he whispered, "Ellie . . . this is where I want to be."

She quivered with readiness. *"Yes."*

Immediately, he brought himself over her and began to press into her body. She knew intuitively to tilt up her hips and spread her legs to accommodate his entry. Then a sharp inner pinch caught her unawares, and she hissed out a breath even as Damien fully sheathed himself within her.

He went still, his fingers tenderly lifting a lock of hair from her face, his gaze searching hers. His voice deep and husky, he said, "Darling, I've hurt you. Forgive me?"

Darling. A soft outpouring of emotion flowed from her heart. Ellie was too enthralled to examine it closely. No doubt he'd whispered sweet nothings into the ears of scores of women. Yet that was in the past. Right here and now, his green-gray eyes shone with a fierce fire—all for her. How had she ever thought him cold and cruel?

A tremulous smile curved her lips. "Oh, Damien . . . you feel perfect." She realized it was true; a radiant sense of fullness had replaced the momentary discomfort. Moving sinuously beneath him, she yearned to satisfy him as much as he'd done her. "Tell me, how may I please *you*?"

As she swirled her hips, he groaned, his face taut with sensual gratification. "*That,*" he muttered. "That's how."

The outside world faded away as they kissed and caressed. There was only the two of them, wrapped in each other's arms. He moved inside her with an unhurried friction that reawakened her desires. She relished the heaviness of his weight over her, the way he filled her completely. Bracing his hands on either side of her, he rode her slowly at first, then with ever-increasing vigor. Passion surged in her again, and she closed her eyes, the better to savor it. Her hands flitted over him, sliding down his back, feeling the slickness of his skin.

Now that Ellie knew the joy that lay just beyond her reach, she strained to achieve it, arching herself up to meet his rhythmic thrusts. He responded by driving harder and deeper into her, and when the tension finally broke in a deluge of ecstasy, she cried out from the beauty of it. A moment later, he gave a long groan, his muscles rigid as a series of shudders convulsed his entire body.

He settled heavily atop her, his swift breaths fanning her hair. Against her breasts, she could feel his thundering heartbeat begin to slow. With the easing of her own excitement, a lovely lassitude spread through every part of Ellie's body and she drifted in a state of perfect contentment. So this was lovemaking. It was indescribably wonderful, amazingly blissful.

How had she ever thought to live without it?

A measure of lucidity returned to her at once. She would *have* to live without it, Ellie reminded herself. There was only this one night to savor. Tomorrow, they would start the journey back to London. Damien would return to his gambling club, and she would finally have her cottage in the country, her haven from the demands of others, where she could work in peace and quiet on her book.

But she didn't want to think about the future just yet. Not while she lay in the arms of the Demon Prince.

With a muffled thump, a log settled on the hearth. She opened her eyes to see the familiar canopy overhead, the green hangings on the bedposts, the curving stone walls of the tower. The high windows showed darkness, though it could not be much beyond twilight. The entire evening lay ahead like a gift from the heavens.

Would they do it again? Oh, she did hope so. But perhaps not quite yet. She had been raised a lady, after all, and she did not want him to think her *too* debauched.

Damien shifted his weight from her, and she turned her head on the pillow to see him gazing at her. The lamp on the bedside table cast a warm glow over his tousled black hair and the harshly masculine angles of his face. His expression held a cocky satisfaction that she knew he richly deserved.

That giddy softness spilled from her heart again. Ellie was surprised to feel somewhat shy, considering the intimacy they'd just shared. How foolish of her. She had loved every transcendent moment of lovemaking. Nothing in her life had ever felt better than being with Damien like this.

She tenderly brushed back a lock of hair that had fallen onto his brow. "I fear, sir, that you've made a very wicked woman of me."

He grinned at her, then stretched lazily like a powerful jungle cat, one of his hands resting possessively at her waist. "As you'll recall, I was merely fulfilling the parameters of your . . . compensation."

"And quite satisfactorily, too." He made her so happy that she could not help bantering. "I have been thoroughly ravished. You have earned your reputation as a rake extraordinaire. It's no wonder you're known as the Demon Prince."

At that, his eyes narrowed ever so slightly in a secretive look. His smile acquired a sardonic twist. And as he glanced away, Ellie was left to wonder what exactly she'd said to wreak the change in his mood.

Chapter 18

Her words struck Damien with an unpleasant jolt. The ease of sexual satisfaction began to subside with the intrusion of reality. Ellie was smiling at him, having no notion of her mistaken belief. One corner of his mouth twisting, he glanced away for a moment. She couldn't begin to guess the true reason why he was called the Demon Prince.

Nor would he would tell her.

He felt the light touch of her hand slide upward over his chest to cup his jaw. Returning his gaze to her, he saw that her face had taken on a somewhat pensive look. At the same time, he had a keen appreciation of the erotic picture she made. She lay beneath him, a wealth of auburn hair spilling over the pillows and curling around those fine breasts. She had the rosy glow of a woman who'd been well satisfied. How incredible to recall that he'd believed her to be a dried-up spinster when, in truth, she possessed an abundance of natural sensuality.

Ellie was studying him earnestly, as if she'd noticed the shift in his temperament and sought to understand it. Those warm brown eyes held a note of query that boded ill for his privacy.

That was his cue to depart. They'd had their pleasure—and it had been very gratifying. Spectacular, in fact. But he had never cared much for a woman's prattling in the aftermath. There was no point to it. The purpose of their sharing a bed already had been accomplished.

He would give Ellie a farewell kiss, throw on his clothing, and return to his own chamber in the keep. He should sleep well after enjoying so powerful a release. Useless conversation would only irk him. Especially if it involved questions that he didn't wish to answer.

Damien pulled her close and nuzzled her hair, savoring her lilac scent. God help him, those breasts felt soft against his chest. "I really should go now. We'll be departing in the morning—"

"Oh, but you cannot leave." Ellie placed her hands firmly on his shoulders and looked him square in the eyes. "You promised me one *night* of pleasure. So you are bound by our agreement to stay until dawn."

Damien chuckled. He couldn't help himself. She had the manner of a stern governess, which was absurd in light of her nudity—and her erotic demands. He lightly slapped her bare bottom. "You'll have me thinking you're insatiable."

With a faint smile, Ellie shifted position, reminding him of the movements of her body during their rutting. "Then people *do* make love more than once in a night?"

His blood stirred. It was much too soon, but lust for her already simmered in him again. "Yes. They do. We can . . ." Ah, hell, he couldn't even speak coherently when she looked at him like that. Of course he was staying. How could he not? "But you've wrung me dry for the moment. You'll have to allow me a few minutes to recover."

Ellie wriggled into a sitting position against the pillows. She drew up the covers against the chill in the air. "Then in the meantime, you may tell me why you're called the Demon Prince. It isn't to do with your wild reputation at all, is it?"

Devil take it! She was far too perceptive.

Damien rolled off the bed and paced buck naked across the room to toss another log on the fire. "It was a long while ago," he said over his shoulder. "I scarcely remember."

He took his time jabbing with the poker until the flames shot up to consume the new fuel. Maybe she'd take the hint and quit probing into his private affairs. Ever since his ill-fated marriage, he'd kept his relationships with women superficial, and that wouldn't change now.

He went to the table to glance over the now-cold dinner of chicken, medallion potatoes, and crusty bread. With his fingers, he popped one of the potatoes in his mouth, then uncorked the bottle of burgundy and filled the single goblet. He washed down the morsel with a long swallow before strolling back to the bed with cup and bottle.

Wrapped in the quilt, she sat watching him. It pleased him to see that her gaze swept covertly over his nude form, lingering a moment on his groin. A faint flush had crept into her cheeks. If she was flustered by his lack of clothing, perhaps that would serve to deter her from any meddlesome questions.

He sat down on the bed and held the goblet to her lips. "Take a sip. It seems we'll have to share tonight."

She drank from the pewter goblet, her topaz eyes studying him over the rim. Sitting back again, she ran the tip of her tongue over her reddened lips. The charmingly provocative action fanned the embers of his passion.

He was glad he'd decided to stay. Very glad, indeed.

Ellie Stratham had a fresh, alluring sensuality so unlike the practiced jades of his other dalliances. He would relish making love to her again. With the night still young, they could take their time indulging themselves.

He refilled the goblet, then placed the bottle on the bedside table. There, on the leather notebook, lay the quill pen and ink that she'd asked him to bring to her. He was struck by the suspicion that had flitted through his mind when he'd first spied her in that extremely low-cut gown. "You planned this liaison from the start," he said in amusement. "It wasn't mere happenstance, was it? Earlier this afternoon, when you asked me to return here, you fully intended to seduce me."

Ellie gave him an artful look from beneath her lashes. "Perhaps."

"Minx. There's no 'perhaps' about it. You duped me. You set the bait and reeled me in."

He found that he didn't mind one whit. At least not anymore. Odd that, for as a matter of rote, he resented being manipulated by scheming women. He preferred to keep females pigeonholed until his physical needs drove him to seek them out on his own terms.

Little did Ellie realize, though, she could be maneuvered in turn. Only look at how easily he had diverted her attention away from his past.

As he drank again from the goblet, she said, "Enough with the distractions, Damien. I still wish to know why you're called the Demon Prince."

He almost choked on a swallow of wine. "What?"

"You heard me. It's time you told me the truth. In fact, you really have no choice in the matter." Tilting her head, she gave him a shrewd smile. "I am making it part of my compensation."

He ought to be annoyed, but found himself chuckling instead. "Is that so? And how many more ways must I compensate you, Miss Stratham? Best to lay them all out on the table right now."

"I promise to be satisfied with the truth about this one matter." Her hand came from beneath the covers to press lightly to his knee in a gesture that was both sensual and sweet. "Will you tell me, please, Damien?"

The warmth of her smile thoroughly disarmed him. A mawkish sentiment crept into his chest, and he felt a vast desire to make her happy. When she looked at him like that, he couldn't form a single coherent rebuttal. Oh, hell, what did it really matter if she knew?

Besides, she might ask Walt upon her return to London, and maybe it was best that she hear it from himself.

"If you insist, then."

He placed the goblet on the bedside table and climbed back into bed with her. Ellie cuddled up against him, settling her head in the crook of his shoulder and draping her arm across his chest. She felt far too perfect in his arms. As if she belonged there. Yet he only wanted sex with her, not confidences that might draw them closer in their minds.

He blew out a breath and decided the best place to start was at the beginning. "You'll remember that I mentioned Mrs. Mims, the woman who raised me. When I was a little boy, she would relate stories to me at bedtime each night. Sometimes, they were true historical events about the kings of England, the emperors of Rome, even the czars of Russia. But at other times, she spun tales of fictional princes slaying dragons. She talked of strong heroes who battled monsters and rescued princesses from the clutches of evil witches."

Ellie lifted her head, her eyes shining. "Really? That must be why you didn't mock *my* book. Because you'd grown up hearing such fairy tales."

There was truth in her observation, Damien realized. Perhaps her illustrations of fantastical creatures *had* spoken to a place deep inside his past. He smoothed his hand over her tousled hair. "Yes, well, just like you, Mimsy had quite a knack for storytelling. She often advised me to be as gallant and brave as a storybook prince . . . because I, too, had royal blood."

Ellie gave him a startled stare. "What? She *told* you that you were related to the royal family?"

He shook his head emphatically. This was why he'd been reluctant to reveal his past to her. He disliked anyone knowing that he'd once been naïve enough to believe such a Banbury tale. "No. Absolutely not. It was just a morality tale, her way of convincing me to comport myself as a prince. You see, I was a rather rambunctious lad, always getting into scrapes, and since I had no father, she thought to encourage me to model my behavior after heroic figures."

"But what about the crown on the missing key? Doesn't that prove—"

"It proves nothing. It's far more likely to be the other way around, that Mimsy was inspired to tell me such a tale *because* of the crown on the key. She must have known that a child would be gullible enough to believe her."

From the slight puckering of her brow, Ellie didn't appear convinced. "Mad King George had more than a dozen children. Perhaps one of them sired an illegitimate son—*you*."

"And then arranged for me to be spirited away to be raised in poverty?" Damien shook his head again. In his youth, he'd entertained such a fantasy, but no more. "Royal bastards have a certain standing in society. So I'm sure my story is far more prosaic. I was likely an inconvenient surprise for an unmarried lady and needed to be hidden from sight. When I retrieve the key, it may provide a clue to her identity. I intend to find her if I can, and to learn the truth . . ."

He stared at the flames on the hearth. Because of Lily, he thought fiercely. Someday, Lily would ask him about her grandparents, and he wanted to have answers to her questions. But he could not—would not—reveal that part to anyone, not even to Ellie.

She gently stroked his cheek, drawing his attention back to her. "You haven't yet explained how you came to be called the Demon Prince."

"It was a slur invented by your cousin Walt during my first semester at Eton. One afternoon, he and his cronies ganged up on me behind the cloisters. I fought back and bloodied a few noses. But they were bigger and there were three of them."

"Finn told me about that incident. It happened the same day you'd learned that Mrs. Mims had died. You went there to be alone, only to be set upon by those boys. He said that you were roughed up, your robes torn."

"Yes, they pinned me down on the ground so that I was helpless. I struggled, but I couldn't free myself. That's when I made the mistake of shouting that my father was a king and he would chop off their heads. You can only imagine their mirth."

He gave her a cynical smile, but Ellie didn't smile back. Instead, she had a suspicious sheen in her eyes. "So my cousin started calling you the Demon Prince." Before Damien could make a jest of it, she circled her arms around his neck and kissed him gently on the cheek. "Walt should never have mocked you that way. Boys can be very cruel sometimes."

Damien folded his arms around her, too. He held her tightly, quilt and all. Not that he needed comforting. No. It would be ridiculous for a grown man to want consoling over an event that had happened in the distant past. Nevertheless, he couldn't deny feeling somehow relieved for having shared the story.

"I despised the name at first," he said, "but in time I came to embrace it. I used it to finagle my way into a group of dissolute young bucks at Eton. I fleeced them at cards, won enough to open my own club, and called it Demon's Den." He grinned at her. "And of course, my scandalous reputation as the Demon Prince has also made me quite popular with women."

Ellie gave him a severe look. "Most gentlemen try to live up to their principles. You, I think, have tried to live *down* to yours."

He laughed. "So now you will be the strict governess again. Perhaps you will punish me for my sins, hmm?"

His hands delved beneath the covers to play with her breasts. They were soft and abundant, and the tips puckered to his touch. The warm silk of her skin made him keen to have her again.

She melted against him, her fingertips trailing down his chest. "Punish? Oh, no, my prince. I was thinking more in terms of a reward. You see, I have become as sinful as you are."

At the impish sparkle in her eyes, Damien felt his potency return in a mad rush of heat. He untangled her from the quilt and then reclined against the pillows, bringing her down to sprawl on top of him, his very own goddess of love. Her hair spilled around them in a fiery curtain. She smiled in delight at the new position and suggestively swiveled her hips.

They began to kiss and caress at a leisurely pace, taking pleasure in each other, murmuring and sighing. Time ceased to exist. Damien could not remember when he had enjoyed himself more—perhaps never. Again, he felt possessed by an irresistible affection for her, the desire to make her happy. When at last he pressed deeply into her body, he derived a fierce satisfaction from her cries of bliss before allowing his own completion.

In the aftermath, he blew out the lamp and then settled back down in the bed. Ellie lay hugging a pillow, already half asleep. He drew the covers over them, tucked her into the cradle of his body, and dropped a light kiss into the fragrant tangle of her hair.

His arms enfolding her, he gazed into the semidarkness that was lit only by the glowing remains of the fire. A mental restlessness kept him from joining her in slumber. With any other woman, he would be making his departure. He never actually *slept* with his partner once his physical needs had been slaked. But with Ellie, he wanted to stay. He didn't want to let her go.

It wasn't like him to be so irrational. They had only this one night, after all. She had been very explicit about that. And no matter how much he might crave it, he could not bring himself to dishonor her by offering the position of his mistress. He had already abducted her, ruined her reputation, and claimed her innocence.

He couldn't rob her of her ambitions, too.

Ellie had a plan for her life, an admirable determination to live alone and work on her storybooks. He had no right to interfere with that. Nor would he. Once they returned to London, this obsession for her surely would vanish.

He concentrated on that thought. It had to be merely their enforced isolation here at the castle that had fostered his attachment to her. Once he resumed his business dealings and the routine of his daily life, he would forget about Ellie Stratham. She would join the legions of other women that he'd enjoyed and then barred from his private life.

Satisfied by the logical conclusion, he closed his

eyes and succumbed to a postcoital lethargy. For tonight, there could be no harm in indulging his wish to remain with her. But he must be away before first light. Finn would have Damien's head on a pike if he was unwise enough to be caught in Ellie's bed.

Thankfully, he had an internal clock that never failed to awaken him at dawn. His last thought before drifting into slumber was a hazy resolve to bestir himself early enough to make love to her one last time.

Chapter 19

A thumping sound summoned Ellie from the depths of a deep sleep. Every part of her resisted swimming to the surface of awareness. She felt too contented in mind and body, too happy in her dreams. Then the noise intruded again, and in her groggy state, she identified it as an insistent rapping.

She opened her eyes to the watery sunlight streaming through the high, narrow windows of her bedchamber. At the same instant, she realized that her back rested in the heated cradle of a man's body. His heavy arm lay draped over her waist. *Damien.*

All at once, the events of the previous evening flooded her mind, the hours of sensual enjoyment, the heady rapture of release. They had made love twice, then again sometime during the dark of night. She had asked him to stay just until dawn. But he hadn't departed, he had fallen asleep in her bed. And now . . .

A realization struck away the last cobwebs of sleep. Dear God, someone was at the door. They were about to be discovered!

She rolled over, intending to shake him awake, only

to find Damien already blinking drowsily at her, his black hair in attractive disarray. His green-gray eyes widened on her, then cut over to the brightly lit windows. He thrust himself up on one elbow as the knocking rattled the door again, louder this time.

"What the devil—" He sprang out of bed and snatched up his breeches, hopping on one leg and then the other as he yanked on the garment.

Ellie frantically searched the tangle of covers for her missing chemise. He had stripped it from her in the midst of their lovemaking. Where had it fallen?

Spying a white heap on the carpet beside the bed, she caught it up in her hand just as the door was flung open and Mrs. MacNab came marching into the bedchamber.

The maidservant's eyes goggled. She let out a screech. "Ahhh! 'Tis just as Finn feared, ye was in milady's bed! Oh, laird! How could ye treat her so ill?"

Mortified, Ellie clutched the chemise to her bare bosom and tried to cover her nakedness. Despite the chill in the air, her face felt blazing hot. She wanted to dive beneath the covers and not come out again until next week. No, next *year.*

Damien had his breeches only half buttoned. "Devil take it, woman, turn around! Better yet, step outside for a moment."

Mrs. MacNab remained standing in the doorway, glowering, her hands parked on her ample hips. "Mind yer tongue, young man. 'Tis *ye* who's at fault here! Dinna ye have no shame?"

Ellie drew a shaky breath. No matter how embarrassed she was, she couldn't let the servant go on thinking that Damien was responsible. Not when it had been Ellie who had coerced him into sharing her bed. "Mrs. MacNab, it isn't quite as it seems. You see—"

"It is precisely as it seems," Damien cut in, his voice cold and hard as he yanked on his black boots. "Last night, I seduced Miss Stratham. I took advantage of her innocence. It was not the act of a gentleman, and I am entirely to blame."

He flicked a stern glance at Ellie as if warning her to be silent. Or perhaps he'd realized that making love to her had been a mistake to be repented in the harsh light of day. That second thought made her heart wither. *Did* he regret it? She remembered how he had resisted her at first. *For God's sake! I can't do this, not to you of all women.*

After the tragedy of his first marriage, he had not wanted to entangle himself with a virginal lady. Yet Ellie had enticed him, tempted him, convinced him. And now he appeared to be having second thoughts about their intimacy. Except for that one stony glance, he took no notice of her at all. He merely donned his shirt and turned to gather up the rest of his garments where they lay in a trail over the floor.

"'Tis best ye make haste, laird," Mrs. MacNab said stiffly. "Finn sent me t' tell ye there's a rowboat a-comin' an' ye're soon t' have guests."

Damien turned sharply on his heel. "What? Who?"

"Dinna ask *me*." She shook her stubby finger at him. "'Tis *ye* who should've been keepin' watch, instead o' plantin' yer seed in virtuous young ladies."

During their short exchange, Ellie managed to surreptitiously pull the chemise over her head to cover her nakedness. A rowboat! Someone was heading to the island. Who? Had Walt brought the stolen key, after all? Did he intend to ransom her?

The thought shook her to the core. She had been so certain that her cousin would never leave the pleasures of London on her behalf . . .

Then a worse fear struck her. Perhaps the Earl of Pennington had come, too. Perhaps he had coerced the story from Walt and now intended to rescue his niece from the clutches of a notorious scoundrel.

Her stomach churned. If indeed it was Uncle Basil, he would be in a rage to avenge the family honor. He might very well have brought an officer of the law with him.

The more she considered it, the more plausible that possibility seemed. Damien would be arrested on the spot.

She opened her mouth to warn him, but he was already pulling on his coat and striding toward the door. As he brushed past Mrs. MacNab, he snapped, "Keep Miss Stratham here. I'll send for her if necessary."

Blast his orders! Ellie had no intention of being confined to the tower room. Not when he could be walking into a trap.

She scrambled out of bed and grabbed her petticoat from the floor. The fire on the hearth had long since died, and her teeth chattered from both the cold air and an attack of nerves. She had to get down to the beach as swiftly as possible in order to avert a disaster.

Damien mustn't be thrown behind bars—even if he *had* committed the crime of abducting her. It wasn't just because she now knew him to be a worthy man who'd only wanted the return of that stolen key. Nor was it because they'd shared a wonderful night together, one that she would remember for the rest of her life, one that had left her body pleasantly tender in places from their unaccustomed activities.

She swallowed a lump in her throat. No, he mustn't be imprisoned because he was vital to her own independence. Damien had agreed to give her the cottage in the country where she could be alone to work on her storybook. He also would provide her with a small stipend to tide her over until she could sell her book to a publisher.

It was a dream come true.

But how could she explain all that to her uncle—and to Walt? They would say only that Damien had dishonored her. They would seek his punishment.

Her trembling fingers made a tangle of the ties of her petticoat. She would *not* permit her family to interfere in her plans for her life. If Walt or the earl made a misguided attempt to avenge the stain on the family honor, then she would lose everything. Damien could hardly fulfill his promise to her if he was confined to a dank cell.

Locked in prison—perhaps for the rest of his life.

Her vision blurred suddenly. Now she couldn't see the ties at all. Tears burned down her cheeks—tears of frustration, surely, because she had never been a weepy watering pot of a female. And she certainly would *never* cry over a *man*.

She felt herself drawn into a pillowy embrace. Mrs. MacNab patted Ellie on the back, comforting her like a child. "Poor wee lamb. The laird charmed ye, did he? Never ye mind, he'll do right by ye in the end. Finn'll see to that. Now, come, dry yer eyes an' ready yerself."

Ellie didn't bother to correct the woman's misapprehension about Damien's guilt. There would be time for that later. It was far more important to gird herself to do battle with Walt or her uncle—or both.

In short order, she had washed and dressed. While Mrs. MacNab buttoned the back of the jade-green gown, Ellie quickly tamed her wild curls into a severe knot and secured it with pins. Then she snatched up her cloak and went dashing from the bedchamber, ignoring the maid's caution to wait for the laird's summons.

Ellie made haste down the winding stairs and through the short passage. Emerging from the stone arch of the doorway, she found the courtyard of the castle empty. The tall square keep appeared forbidding even in the brightness of sunshine. The snow was melting, causing mud puddles everywhere, and the icicles on the walls dripped water.

It was a thoroughly depressing scene after the wondrous fairy-tale whiteness of the blizzard when she had wrenched her ankle and Damien had carried her up to her bedchamber. Only a slight twinge remained, a pain that was far overshadowed by the ache in her heart.

If truth be told, she didn't want her stay here at the castle to come to an end. Ellie wanted it to be yesterday when she'd been full of dreamy hope. In her naïveté, she had never imagined that in the morning Damien would revert to being a hostile stranger. Had her demand for intimacy ruined their friendship?

How foolish. They had agreed to share one night together. There could be no enduring ties between them. They were destined to part once they returned to London. Or perhaps sooner if her uncle or Walt had their way.

To her surprise, the iron gate of the portcullis had been drawn up. How much time had passed since Damien had left? Ten minutes? Fifteen? Was it long enough for the newcomers to have arrived?

There was only one way to find out.

Ellie hurriedly picked a path through the slush, lifting her skirts to keep her hem dry. Upon reaching the gate, she proceeded through the opening to the outside of the castle. She paused there to shade her eyes against the morning sunshine. Her gaze followed the rutted path that meandered through the rocky landscape and down to the shore.

There was the gigantic boulder where she had encountered Damien after escaping on her first night at the castle. He had frightened her half to death by appearing from out of nowhere. When she had lashed out at him in a rage, he had trapped her in between himself and the granite . . .

He was at the water's edge now, a tall figure in his black greatcoat, his hair ruffled by the brisk breeze. He and Finn were dragging the bow of a large rowboat partway onto the beach. There were three people in the boat. One was the oarsman, who hopped out, splashing through the water to help land the vessel.

Then Damien reached into the boat to assist one of the two passengers in disembarking. She was a slender woman in bonnet and gown, and he lifted her onto the shore. The other passenger managed on his own, a stoop-shouldered man clad in a dark coat and hat.

Ellie blinked in astonishment. Neither of them was Walt nor her uncle. All of her worries had been for naught.

But who on earth *were* these people? Locals from the mainland? Neighbors who had come to call? She could think of no other explanation for their presence on the island.

Now that the storm had cleared, she could see in the distance the dark line of a landmass across the choppy sea. A cluster of buildings formed a small town or village. There must be a dock, too, for she spied the white sails of several ships.

How unusual that these neighbors would make a journey across the water when Damien had not been expecting them.

Intensely curious, Ellie decided to wait at the castle entry. There was no point in muddying her half-boots on a trek down to the beach. The newcomers stood talking to Damien for a few moments. Then the small party started up the path. Damien led the way with the woman, who had tucked her hand into the crook of his arm.

She appeared to be a lady. And she was no rustic frump, either. Her royal-blue mantle with its white fur collar would have been stylish even on the streets of Mayfair. The wide brim of an elegant bonnet shaded her face from view.

Damien's frowning attention was on the woman, and they appeared to be deep in conversation. Ellie noted the stiffness to his bearing. One thing was certain, he didn't seem terribly happy to be entertaining unexpected guests. Perhaps because he had wanted to depart for London this morning.

Belatedly, she wondered if she ought to have stayed out of sight. How would he explain the presence of a young, unmarried woman at the castle with only two old servants as chaperones? The situation would be awkward, indeed.

But it was too late to retreat. The small party was almost to the gate, and they had spied her. The woman turned her head from saying something to Damien and looked straight at Ellie.

Her feet grew roots into the muddy ground. Ellie couldn't have moved in that moment if her life had depended upon it. Her mind struggled to deny the reality of who she was seeing. She knew those patrician features inside the brim of that blue bonnet, the large violet eyes in a face of exquisite, timeless beauty.

"Lady Milford! Whatever are *you* doing here?"

On that blurted comment, Ellie remembered her manners and dipped a curtsy, heedless of the puddles that soaked her hem. She arose to find herself being kissed on the cheek in a waft of rose perfume.

"My dear Miss Stratham, how very good it is to see

you again." Lady Milford spoke as if they were in a London ballroom instead of a castle on a remote island off the Scottish coast. "May I say, you're looking quite well in light of your ordeal. I understand from Mr. Burke that you've been trapped here by a terrible storm these past few days."

"Miss Stratham slipped on the ice and twisted her ankle two days ago," Damien said before Ellie could reply. "She was supposed to remain in her chamber with her foot propped up."

He aimed a glower at Ellie, and while she understood the necessity of concealing their passionate affair, she nevertheless felt goaded by the coldness of his manner. "You'll be happy to know that I'm much recovered today. I retired early yesterday evening and enjoyed a most excellent and restorative night's sleep."

For the barest moment, his green-gray eyes revealed a heated intensity. As if he, too, was remembering exactly how they had spent the previous night—the kissing and caressing, the intimate touches, the wild pleasure of coupling their bodies.

Then Ellie noticed Lady Milford was observing both of them with keen interest. Stepping forward, she looped her arm through Ellie's. "I believe that you'll be interested to learn what has happened in London since your disappearance. Is there somewhere that we all might talk?"

They proceeded to the great hall inside the keep. Damien escorted Lady Milford to the best chair, a heavy wooden piece with a tall back and wide arms. Then he threw a few more logs on the dying fire. He had already dispatched Finn to the kitchen to fetch a tray of refreshments.

Ellie glanced curiously at the stoop-shouldered man

who had settled himself on a stool in the shadows. He held his hat in his gnarled hands, and his pale scalp shone through the feathery white hairs on his head. His dark garb was plain and sober rather than fashionable. She wondered who he was. No one had bothered to introduce her, and she surmised that he must be an inconsequential gentleman who had come along as Lady Milford's escort.

Ellie sank onto the bench near the fire and tried not to fidget. What news had the woman brought? Had she met with the Earl of Pennington? Had he sent her here to negotiate the return of his niece? And where did Walt fit into the story? Did she know that Damien only wanted that stolen key as ransom?

Ellie barely restrained a barrage of questions as Lady Milford removed her bonnet and placed it beside her on a table. Her raven-black hair was styled in an elegant chignon. Because of the chill in the vast room, she had not removed her royal-blue cloak with the fur collar. In the tall chair, she appeared rather intimidatingly like a queen on her throne.

Ellie's acquaintance with the woman was slight. They had met only twice, first when her cousin had insisted on paying that ill-advised call, and then when Lady Milford had come to take Beatrice to visit the Duke of Aylwin. She also had given Ellie the pair of beautiful garnet dancing slippers. But a generous nature couldn't begin to explain her presence at the castle. Why would a pillar of society travel so far from London on behalf of a nobody like Ellie?

She could no longer bide her tongue. "May I ask why you've come here, my lady? And how did you even know where to find me?"

Lady Milford smiled rather enigmatically. "You'll understand everything in due course. But first, let me confess to feeling somewhat responsible for your fate. Had I not urged you to take your cousin's place at the modiste's, you would not have been mistaken for Lady Beatrice." She glanced rather sternly at Damien. "And Mr. Burke would not have abducted you in her stead."

His arms crossed, Damien stood by the fireplace. He had reverted to being the cold stranger, as he had been on the first day Ellie had sparred with him in the tower bedchamber.

If he wouldn't speak, then she would. "Has there been gossip already?" she asked. "About my disappearance?"

Lady Milford nodded. "I'm afraid so. Your family tried to hush it up, but servants will talk and the rumors began to fly rather quickly. You are, after all, Pennington's niece. When I called on your family, they were in quite a state of agitation. Lady Beatrice cried out that you'd never returned from your appointment the previous afternoon. Your uncle said that you had dishonored the family by running off with a scoundrel." She paused to gaze at Ellie with some sympathy. "I shall not mince words, my dear. The earl was in quite a disagreeable state over the matter, as was your grandmother."

Ellie could imagine the scene: Beatrice bursting to share the news, Uncle Basil blustering in anger, the countess making her usual acid remarks. Yet surely Lady Milford had misunderstood. "Are you saying they had no notion that I'd been abducted? They believed I'd gone *willingly* with—with Mr. Burke?"

Lady Milford inclined her head in a nod. "Yes. It seems your eldest cousin, Viscount Greaves, had already told them that he had reason to believe you'd run off with the Demon Prince. And that you must have been carrying on an illicit affair because on several occasions, he'd spied you creeping out of the house late at night."

Ellie gasped. "That's a lie! I did no such thing!"

"The devil!" Damien stood in front of the fire, his fists clenched at his sides, fury blazing in his eyes. "I'll kill him when I return to London. By God, I will!"

"You most certainly will not," Lady Milford said sternly. "You've caused enough trouble already without adding murder to your list of sins."

Ellie tried to make sense of it all. Walt must have seized the opportunity to weasel out of returning the stolen key. He knew how much his father despised gambling, and he wouldn't have wanted Pennington to know about the debt. So her spineless cousin had smeared her good name in order to save his own skin.

She felt sick inside. Not just because Walt would tell such an outrageous falsehood, or that her uncle and grandmother would believe it of her. No, she cringed to think that both Damien and Lady Milford now knew precisely how little regard her family had for her.

Lifting her chin, she forced her lips into a wooden smile. "I can only wonder how they thought I'd ever met the owner of a gambling club. Or why such a notorious rogue would have had any interest whatsoever in a drab spinster."

Her gaze met Damien's. His jaw was set tightly, his lips thinned, his eyes narrowed. He looked nothing like the lover of the previous night who had held her in his arms and made her feel infinitely desirable by his words and actions. *How could any man resist such beauty and fire?*

She swallowed past the constriction in her throat. Their brief liaison was over now. He wouldn't ever say such passionate things to her again. There would only ever be that one night. And that was exactly as she wanted it.

"Well," said Lady Milford, "I saw through your cousin's story at once. You struck me as a sensible woman, Miss Stratham, not someone who would carry on an affair under the very noses of your family. So I requested a private audience with Viscount Greaves and wrested the sordid truth from him, that he'd incurred a gaming debt to you, Mr. Burke. And that you'd resolved to kidnap Lady Beatrice as a means to collect your payment."

"Except that I abducted the wrong girl," Damien said in a clipped tone. "So Walt never saw fit to protect her. And he never delivered the ransom."

"A stolen key, I believe?" Lady Milford said. "He showed me your letter—though only under duress, I might add."

One eyebrow arched, she aimed a strict stare up at Damien, and Ellie had an inkling of why Walt had caved to her demands. Lady Milford exuded an air of regal authority and steely resolve. But if she was seeking an explanation as to the significance of the key, Damien didn't offer one. He merely folded his arms and gazed stoically back at her.

After a moment, she returned her attention to Ellie. "It may be of some comfort to you to learn that I convinced your cousin to confess the whole of it to his father. At least now Pennington knows the truth about what happened. Though I fear to say, the earl is quite adamant that you are not to be permitted to return to his house."

Ellie wasn't surprised. The truth would matter little to her uncle. In his critical eyes, it wouldn't change the fact that she'd spent more than a week in the company of the Demon Prince. Nevertheless, she felt pained to know that her family had cut her off while knowing that the circumstances had not been her fault.

Had her uncle even offered to provide her funds on which to live? It didn't matter.

She met Lady Milford's gaze. "It's quite all right, since I hadn't planned to return there, anyway. Mr. Burke has agreed to compensate me for the damage to my reputation. He's promised me a cottage in the country and a stipend on which to live. I need nothing more."

And she would be happy to embark on a new life as an independent woman, Ellie told herself. Once she was settled in, and she could concentrate on her illustrations, then this awful tension in her bosom would vanish. She would be content and cheerful again, and not feel as if she had lost everything.

Lady Milford rose from her chair and came to sit on the bench, her kid-gloved hands taking hold of Ellie's. "My dear, I don't believe you *do* understand. All of society is convinced that you ran off with the Demon Prince and are now living in sin with him. Even if the truth comes out, that you were abducted against your will, it won't matter to the gossips. You will still be branded a fallen woman in their eyes."

"Then I'll live somewhere far away from London. I assure you, their ill opinion matters nothing to me."

"But it *does* matter to your family. They, too, have been tainted by this scandal."

"Walt is to blame for that," Damien snapped. "He lied about Ellie—Miss Stratham. He ought to have done as I told him. He should have said that she'd been called out of town to care for a sick friend. Then no one would have questioned her absence."

"May I remind you, sir," Lady Milford said sternly, "that it was *your* dastardly plot that started this unfortunate chain of events. Now, not only has Miss Stratham's good name been ruined, but other innocent parties have been harmed as well."

Damien made no reply. He stared in disgruntled silence at her.

Lady Milford turned her attention back to Ellie. "Fair or not, the ton believes that you, Pennington's niece, are now living in wicked debauchery with a scoundrel. Because of all the gossip, the earl has spoken of postponing Lady Beatrice's debut until next year."

Ellie felt a twinge of sympathy to imagine how desolate her cousin would be. Beatrice's entire existence revolved around preparing for her first ball, purchasing a new wardrobe, and plotting how to attract a titled husband. But how was that Ellie's concern anymore? "I'm sorry, my lady. I know how very much she was looking forward to her first season. Yet I cannot see how it can be helped."

"Ah, but there *is* a way to salvage matters," Lady Milford said sagely. "Perhaps the *only* way."

She rose to her feet and beckoned to the stoop-shouldered old gentleman. He left his stool and shuffled forward, stopping in front of Ellie and giving her a respectful nod.

Lady Milford introduced him. "Miss Stratham, I should like you to meet the Reverend Mr. Ferguson. He will officiate over your marriage to Mr. Burke."

Chapter 20

From her seat on the bench, Ellie stared up at the weathered features of the elderly gentleman. His pale blue eyes held a kindly look. He extended his knobby fingers to her in greeting.

But she could not lift her own hand to shake his. A paralysis held her body in place as if she were trapped in a nightmare. She desperately wanted to run, yet her limbs refused to move. Her heart thudded so hard against her rib cage that she felt light-headed.

She must have misheard. *Reverend Mr. Ferguson . . . to officiate over your marriage . . .*

She glanced up at Damien. His hard-edged face was forbidding, his mouth a thin slash. There was no surprise in his expression. He must have already been told of the minister's purpose in being here. And his displeasure could not have been clearer.

Yet he offered no protest.

Her gaze shifted to Lady Milford, who stood beside her, and then back at the minister. He had reached inside his dark coat and brought forth a small black prayer book. To perform the marriage service.

A second shock reverberated through Ellie. This was Scotland. There were no banns to be read, no special license to be procured, no waiting period in which to talk sense into Lady Milford.

The ceremony could be conducted at once. Right now.

Fright energized her. Ellie jumped up from the bench, swaying slightly as she caught her balance. "No," she whispered, then much louder, *"No!"*

The word echoed off the stone walls of the great hall.

With sharp footfalls, Damien closed the distance between himself and Lady Milford. He glared down into her patrician face. "There is your answer, my lady. Your interference is entirely unnecessary. Miss Stratham will not be harmed by this scandal so long as she moves far away from London gossips. As to her family, perhaps they deserve to suffer for their ill treatment of her."

"And what of *your* family?" Lady Milford murmured. "What of Lily? Does *she* deserve to suffer?"

Damien went very still. His face looked like granite. In a tautly soft voice, he stated, "You will leave her out of this. She is none of your concern."

The exchange bewildered Ellie. It was as if she'd fallen asleep at a play and then awakened in the middle of another scene. "Who is Lily?"

The two of them paid her no heed. They continued to stare at each other, Lady Milford in that regal manner of a queen, Damien tense and grim-faced.

"Lily *is* involved whether you like it or not," Lady Milford told him. "She will be tainted by your actions. It is one thing to own a gaming club frequented by gentlemen, to carry on discreet affairs, even to seduce an impoverished lady before deigning to wed her. But it is quite another matter entirely for people to whisper that you've lured a *second* innocent lady into sin—this time, without offering her the benefits of marriage."

He made a sharp move of his hand. "Nonsense. It'll all blow over eventually. There will be no permanent harm done."

"Can you be so certain of that? Are you willing to risk your daughter's future on a prideful whim?"

Ellie could not believe what she was hearing. She tried to put their words together in different ways. But they all came out to the same, inescapable conclusion. "Damien . . . you have a *daughter*?"

His steely gaze cut over to her. "Yes. But she's merely six years of age. So it's ludicrous to suggest that this incident will *taint* her."

Feeling an odd detachment, Ellie studied the boldly sculpted angles of his face. She had thought—believed—that she'd come to know him well in the space of a few days together. They had laughed and talked and traded details about their lives. They had lain naked together and had shared intimate caresses. But all the while, he had kept a secret from her. He had not told her that he had a *daughter.*

What else didn't she know about him?

He was suddenly a stranger to her again. A cold, aloof man that she had never truly known. The Demon Prince.

Lady Milford turned to place her hand on Ellie's arm. "My dear, I know all of this has come as a shock. But you must consider what is best for all parties. The scandal can be greatly diminished by portraying your disappearance with Mr. Burke as an elopement. Then society will come to view it in a romantic light, and people will be more forgiving. That is why the only sensible solution for both of you is marriage—"

Damien and Ellie both interrupted at once.

"No, you're wrong," he began.

"I'd sooner wed a . . . a filthy *rat*."

Picking up her skirts, Ellie took off at a dash. She couldn't remain in the great hall for a single moment longer. She refused to let herself be coerced into bondage to Damien Burke. The lump in her throat grew larger. She would never surrender her independence, especially not to a man of his ilk, a gambler and a rogue.

Yanking open the door, Ellie nearly collided with someone. It was Finn, carrying a large wooden tray. The cups and cutlery rattled as he quickly straightened his load to keep it steady. She smelled a whiff of freshly baked scones and fruit jam.

The servant's blue eyes twinkled at her. They seemed to say that he knew in whose bed the master had spent the night. "I've brung tea, milady. But why are ye leavin' . . . ?"

Ellie didn't stay to hear the rest. Pushing past him, she hurried out into the cold sunshine, her quick steps swiftly carrying her through the large courtyard of the castle. Her half-boots splashed in the puddles. The icy water and snow splattered her stockinged legs as she ran toward the stone archway that led to her tower bedroom.

No sooner had she entered the shadowed passage than she paused, her thoughts awhirl. The last place she wanted to go was her own chamber, where the sight of the tumbled bedsheets would bring back vivid memories of Damien and their activities of the previous night. Nothing could be more abhorrent. She felt sickened by her own naïveté in thinking they were close friends. And she was aghast at the notion of being obliged to speak her vows to such a man.

She turned blindly down another passage. There had to be somewhere to hide. To stay out of sight until they all went away, Lady Milford, the minister, Damien, even the MacNabs. It would be preferable to starve to death, or die of cold, than to give up her dreams in order to become the wife of a scoundrel.

And a stepmother. Damien had a daughter. Lily. A little girl whom he hadn't bothered to mention. Granted, maybe the opportunity had not arisen . . .

Or maybe it had.

On the day he'd learned about her illustrated book, he had made the comment that young children liked shorter stories. *What can you know about children?* she'd scoffed. *You, who spend your time playing cards and wagering on dice at your gambling den?*

Damien had glanced away, his expression brooding. He'd had the chance right then and there to tell her . . . but he hadn't done so.

And why should he have? He was merely her abductor. Nothing more. She had been utterly imprudent to forget that.

Ellie took a ragged breath as the knot in her chest pulled tighter. The castle felt like a prison, and she longed to be gone from here, never to think of him again. She wanted to be off this island without delay.

The rowboat.

Belatedly, she realized that the beach should have been her destination. She could tell the oarsman that Lady Milford had dispatched her on important business in town and that he must take her there straightaway. Yes. By the time everyone finished their tea, she could be disembarking at the dock and seeking a way back to London . . .

Intent on the new scheme, Ellie spun around. But an alarming sight met her eyes. Damien strode toward her down the passageway, the greatcoat flapping around his long legs. The sound of his booted footsteps had failed to penetrate her stupor until this moment. His face was an austere mask, cruelly handsome and sternly resolute.

In a panic, she ran in the opposite direction. It was a foolish act, for he easily chased her down and caught hold of her arm to bring her to an enforced halt. "Ellie, wait."

She whirled toward him. With both hands, she shoved hard at the wall of his chest. "Go away! I won't marry you!"

He took a step backward, his palms up. "Good God, I should hope not. I would make a terrible husband. Do you think I'm here to persuade you otherwise? You may rest your mind on the matter."

"Then why did you follow me?"

"Because I had no wish to remain in Lady Milford's company, either. The woman is a blasted busybody, just as she's always been."

"Always been?"

"This isn't the first time she's meddled in my life. A long time ago, she warned me to stay away from Veronica."

Ellie was intrigued in spite of herself. He looked moody and livid—exactly the way she felt, too. "Are you saying that Lady Milford forced you to marry back then, as well?"

"No. Her warning came *before* I seduced Veronica." He gave Ellie a belligerent stare. "But just so you know, I'm not sorry I didn't listen to Lady Milford that time. I have no regrets. If not for my misdeeds, I wouldn't have Lily."

Ellie matched his glare. "Ah, yes. Your daughter. The one you've abandoned for more than a week while you carried out your abduction of me."

His scowl turned thunderous. "Are you accusing me

of neglect? I left Lily in the excellent care of her governess and nursemaid, along with a full staff of loyal servants."

"And what if it had been my uncle in that rowboat—with an officer of the law? What if you'd been arrested for kidnapping me? Who would have watched over Lily if her father had been imprisoned?"

Damien glanced away. Combing his fingers through his hair, he gave her a surly look. "If I'd captured Lady Beatrice according to plan, Pennington would have moved heaven and earth to hide the scandal. There would never have been the slightest danger of involving the police. But . . . your point is taken. I should have considered all possibilities."

Ellie refused to be mollified. "Doesn't Lily have relatives on her mother's side? Surely she would be better off in the care of family."

"They disapproved of Veronica's marriage and wanted nothing to do with her daughter, either. I'm afraid that Lily has only me." He gave Ellie a piercing stare, then began pacing back and forth in the narrow corridor, the click of his heels echoing off the stone walls. "I'm sorry I didn't tell you about her. It's just . . . habit, I suppose. I've done my best to protect Lily, to safeguard her from gossip. She lives in my house in Kensington, and I've a strict rule about never inviting any guests there. Most people don't even know she exists."

"Yet Lady Milford knew."

"Devil take that woman! She's the sort who always has her ear to the ground for tittle-tattle. But I will *not* allow her to interfere in my life. Nor will I permit her to use my daughter as a weapon to control me."

At the fierceness in his voice, the zealousness of his manner, Ellie felt a reluctant softening in her heart. There could be no doubt that he truly loved Lily.

Or at least as much as a wicked scoundrel was capable of love.

She fell into step beside him. "Lady Milford is a harbinger of doom, I should say. She's someone who paints the most dismal picture possible in order to manipulate one's thoughts and actions. Imagine, trying to make me feel guilty about the effects of the scandal on my family!"

"It was Walt who told a barefaced lie about your character. The dastard deserves to be horsewhipped." Damien uttered a self-deprecating chuckle. "And myself, too, for involving you in this tangled web. Believe me, I rue the day that I conceived the harebrained scheme of kidnapping his sister."

From out of nowhere came the memory of Damien spying on Beatrice from his carriage as she'd flirted with Lord Roland outside of Lady Milford's house. The girl would enjoy no more encounters with handsome young gentlemen, Ellie realized with a pang. At least not in the near future.

Irked with herself, she suppressed any sympathy for her cousin. "Well, it isn't my fault that Beatrice will have to wait another year to be launched. Or that she shall likely be forced to retire with the family to the country until this blows over."

"Quite so, you must *not* blame yourself for any of that." They reached an archway and, by tacit agreement, turned in unison to pace back down the corridor. He went on in a clipped voice, "And if it takes only one year for the scandal to die down for your cousin, then I can't see why it would be any different for Lily. She's only six, for pity's sake. There'll be more than a decade before I need to think of *her* season."

Matching his steps, Ellie looked up at him in surprise. "You wish for her to join society someday? To marry into the gentry?"

Damien slid a cautious glance at her before nodding. "I've been cultivating friendships with several gentlemen who are members of my club. Already, there have been a few invitations here and there to card parties and the like. I hope to regain a measure of acceptance eventually. Not for my own sake, but for Lily's." He paused, then added darkly, "If that's even possible anymore."

Would he find acceptance after despoiling the Earl of Pennington's niece? Ellie wondered uneasily. Or would her uncle see to it that Damien was reviled for the rest of his life—and Lily by association?

She shook off the disquieting questions. "Surely this scandal will be long forgotten ten years from now," she said lightly. "By then, no one will even remember the name of the governess you lured into sin."

Damien stopped pacing, so she did, too. He was frowning at the wall as if stricken by an unpleasant thought. He brought his troubled gaze back to her. "But if you're forgotten . . . that means you won't be a famous author."

She attempted a laugh. "Well, perhaps I won't be *famous,* though I certainly hope my books will enjoy a modest success."

"Will they?" His hands came down heavily onto her shoulders. "Something just struck me, Ellie. I've made you notorious in the eyes of all society. What if no publisher of children's literature is willing to purchase manuscripts from a woman who dallied with a rogue?"

A chill slid down her spine. She shook her head in denial. "Then I'll write under a *nom de plume.* No one need know who I am."

"But you can't hide your real name from the publisher. He would have to know your identity for the purposes of correspondence and record-keeping, contracts and the issuance of bank payments." He gave her a look of intense worry. "I know how businessmen think, Ellie. There won't be a publisher in all of England who will invest money in a project if he thinks people may boycott it. And what decent parent would purchase a book written and illustrated by a fallen woman?"

Queasiness assailed the pit of her stomach. "It can't be that bad. It just can't be. As we both said, it'll all blow over eventually."

"And if it doesn't? What then?" His green-gray eyes bored into hers. Abruptly turning away from her, he raked his fingers through his hair again. "Good God, Ellie. I've not only ruined your reputation, I've ruined your life's work. And quite possibly, Lily's future, as well."

Ellie tilted her head back against the wall of the corridor and tried to resist the intrusion of harsh reality. Yet a bone-deep shiver shook her. Everything he'd said was frighteningly possible—if not probable. All of her toil, her dreams, her hopes . . . gone. Oh, she could still draw, but her illustrations would only be for herself. She wouldn't ever have the chance to see her books in print, to take pride in earning her own way, or to know that children everywhere were enjoying her stories.

She flattened her palms on the wall behind her. The stones felt icy against her bare hands, as bleak as her prospects. If only life was like her book, she could rip out the offending pages and reconstruct the events to her liking. She could throw away the day when she had taken her cousin's appointment at the modiste's shop. She could toss the whole mistaken abduction into a rubbish bin, and none of this would have happened. She would not be facing the stark choice of ruin . . . or wedlock.

But it *had* happened. Reality could not be changed. And there was no denying that fate had backed her into a corner.

She returned her gaze to Damien and found him watching her. Though his jaw had a rigid set, his green-gray eyes held a certain stoic awareness. He knew, as she did, what had to be done.

She gave him a fierce stare. "I do *not* want a husband."

He matched her glare. "I swore never again to take a wife."

They both fell silent, looking at each other. The drip-drip of water echoed hollowly somewhere down the passageway. Now more than ever, he appeared intimidating, overwhelming, larger than life. How much did she really know about him? He was a gambler just as her father had been. Would Damien, too, end up beggaring himself, turning to drink in order to escape his failings? The very thought stirred panic inside her.

She couldn't allow herself to become too entangled in his life. Nor could she let herself be smothered by the demands of being his wife, of having no time for herself or her artwork. If circumstances forced her to wed him, Ellie thought in desperation, then it must be on her terms.

She crossed her arms and lifted her chin. "This marriage will be in name only. I will have my independence. *And* my cottage in the country, exactly as we'd agreed."

He cocked an eyebrow. "You want us to lead separate lives? Fine. That will suit me perfectly well. But we *will* share a bed on occasion. That is *my* stipulation."

In the midst of her turmoil, Ellie felt a traitorous softening in her body. A deep throb of heat assailed her womb. She had a keen awareness of all the places he had touched her the previous night, including a pleasant ache between her legs. Three times he had ridden her—and the bliss had been glorious.

He stood watching her now with a hint of conceit in the set of his mouth, as if he knew that she still desired him. It angered and frightened her to be so tempted by him. This was not how she had planned her life. Ellie feared that if she gave in to his demand, it would be harder to leave him. How could she continue to share such intimacy with him and not risk losing her heart?

Yet she couldn't bring herself to voice an outright refusal.

"You will not claim the rights of a husband without my consent," she stated coldly. "And at the moment, I am not of a mind to grant it."

He frowned slightly. His hooded gaze studied her for another moment before he gave a nod of acquiescence. "As you wish, then. We have a bargain."

Chapter 21

As Ellie accepted Damien's assistance in stepping out of the hansom cab, she lifted her gaze to the stone mansion. For a moment she could only gawk in surprise. The impressively large house had a pleasing symmetry of design with tall windows and a columned portico. The afternoon sunlight glinted off the many chimneys in the tiled roof. Her new home—her *temporary* home—was situated on a sizable plot of land and surrounded by a stone fence. White and yellow crocuses filled the front beds. The trees were just beginning to set their leaf buds so early in March, but she could imagine the tranquil beauty of the landscape filled with the greenery of spring and summer.

The property was located in the borough of Kensington, on the far side of Hyde Park. Ellie found that she preferred this quiet area with its separate homes to the crowded town houses of Mayfair. Here, there was the illusion of living in a rural setting, yet they were only a short carriage ride from the myriad entertainments of London, the shopping and plays and museums.

Not that Ellie had any plans to be gadding about

town. No. She intended to dedicate her time to working on the illustrations for her book until Damien could procure for her the promised cottage in the country. He had assured her that the household servants were extremely efficient and would not require any supervision. She would be free to do as she pleased.

Yet Ellie didn't feel free. She felt edgy and anxious about her brief stay here. How would Lily react to her father bringing home a new wife? Would the little girl want Ellie to be a mother? Damien had said that his daughter spent most of her time in the nursery under the care of a well-trained staff. And he had specifically instructed Ellie not to interfere.

Well, then, she wouldn't. It would be better that way. She had her own interests to pursue.

She waited while he paid the driver of the hansom. They had come straight from the docks, and she felt windblown and sticky from the salt air. By contrast, her husband looked elegantly groomed in a tailored gray coat, his crisp white cravat a perfect foil for his strikingly masculine features and coal-black hair.

Her husband. Thinking of Damien that way still caused a quake inside her. Four days ago, they had been wed in the chapel of the castle, with sunlight pouring through the ancient, stained-glass windows on either side of the stone altar. The minister had read the service with Lady Milford and the MacNabs in attendance. Reciting her vows, Ellie had felt rather like an actress in a play. There had been a sense of unreality about it all, as if it were happening to someone else.

When Damien had brushed a chaste kiss over her lips, she had been too numb to react. She had feared he might ignore their agreement and press his attentions on her that night. But he had not kissed her since then. He had made no advances at all toward her during the voyage back to London. Each night, she had slept alone in the single bunk, the motion of the waves rocking her to sleep. By day, she'd wrapped herself in a warm cloak and sat on deck, sometimes sketching, sometimes observing the activities of the seamen or staring out at the endless blue water. Often, she'd had lively conversations with the MacNabs, who had accompanied them back to London.

Damien had been cool and polite. He had kept himself busy at his account books or directing the sailors at various tasks. And he'd patiently answered her many questions about the ship. Believing him to be merely a gambler, she'd been surprised to learn that he owned a small fleet of vessels that were used for shipping goods to England from various ports in the Mediterranean and elsewhere.

Now, as the hansom cab drove away, he strolled back to her side. His mouth curved in a smile that didn't quite reach his green-gray eyes. Ever since their wedding, his face had become an impassive mask again, shuttering his thoughts. Nevertheless, Ellie felt a lurch of attraction. There was an ache deep inside her, a desire to be held by him, to hear him whisper words of love in her ear. How very rash it would be to indulge herself. She had insisted on a marriage of convenience. And it had to be that way if ever she hoped to live as an independent woman.

She suddenly longed for a familiar face. "Where are the MacNabs?"

"The baggage cart will drive around back to the mews." He offered her his arm. "Shall we go inside?"

Striving for composure, she curled her fingers around the crook of his arm. A footman stood at attention on the porch, holding open the front door. They proceeded up a set of wide steps and entered the house. Ellie had a quick impression of an airy, two-story entrance hall with cream-painted walls and a gracefully curving staircase to one side. A crystal chandelier sparkled in the sunlight that came through the tall windows on either side of the door.

A dignified butler with neatly combed brown hair stood waiting, along with a wiry, middle-aged woman who must be the housekeeper. The ring of keys at her waist jangled slightly as she bobbed a curtsy.

Their gazes flitted to Ellie. The servants' grapevine must be buzzing with rumors of the master's latest misdeed, she realized with a faint flush. Did they even know that it had been an abduction? Or did they believe the gossip that the Earl of Pennington's niece had run off with the Demon Prince to live in sin? Perhaps they were wondering why the master had brought his new paramour home rather than discreetly setting her up in a separate house somewhere else.

It was too soon for anyone to have learned of the nuptials. Lady Milford, who had traveled to Scotland in her coach, had intended to stop to visit friends on her way back to London. She could not yet have begun her campaign to dispel the rumors that must be titillating all of society.

The manservant bowed. "Welcome home, sir," he said, accepting Damien's coat while the housekeeper took Ellie's cloak and bonnet. "I trust you had a pleasant journey?"

"Indeed so," Damien said. "More than pleasant, in fact, since I've brought back a new wife."

He kept his hand at the base of Ellie's back while he made the introductions, and she found the possessive gesture somehow comforting. The butler was Kemble, and the housekeeper Mrs. Tompkins. Though both had impeccable manners, it was plain by their smiles and words of felicitations that they were genuinely delighted by the news.

Ellie felt like something of a fraud smiling and accepting their congratulations. Little did they realize this marriage was a sham. Their new mistress wouldn't be staying here for long. As soon as the cottage could be procured, she would be moving out of this grand house for good. What would they think of that? What excuse would Damien tell them? That his wife had wearied of him already? And what would society have to say about the unusual situation?

Perhaps it would revive the rumors about his first wife's untimely death. Perhaps people would whisper that no true lady could abide marriage to the Demon Prince.

As troubling as the prospect might be, Ellie pushed it from her mind. Damien had freely made the agreement with her. If there was any awkwardness, it would only be his just due for creating the scandal in the first place.

While he was inquiring with the butler about any messages that had arrived during his absence, a commotion on the upper landing drew Ellie's attention.

A small figure clad in a powder-blue gown and white pinafore came flying down the staircase. "Papa, Papa, I saw you from the nursery window! You're home!"

Damien's face lit up with a genuine smile. He strode to the bottom of the stairs and caught the little blond girl up in his arms. "Who is this wild urchin running through my house without any manners at all?"

She giggled, patting his cheeks with two small hands. "It's me, Papa. Lily! Don't you remember me?"

He pulled back to scrutinize her face. "Ah, so it is, indeed! You've grown so tall in my absence that I almost didn't recognize you."

"Don't be silly. Miss Applegate says that I've grown only this much since last month." Lily held up her forefinger and thumb to indicate a fraction of an inch.

"Well, I'm sure that Miss Applegate must be correct. Perhaps it is my eyesight that needs checking. Now, I have someone that I would like for you to meet."

Carrying Lily in his arms, he came toward Ellie. The warm smile on his face diminished somewhat as he approached. She was sorry that it did. She had only seen him smile in so relaxed a manner a few times back at the castle, mostly when they'd laughed over his inventive efforts to turn Prince Ratworth into the hero of her story.

And when they had made love.

Now, however, he looked wary, guarded. As if he would have preferred to avoid this introduction entirely.

"Lily, may I present my wife. She is . . ." He paused, giving Ellie a penetrating look. "Your new stepmother."

The sprightly girl took one startled glance at Ellie and promptly hid her face in the side of Damien's neck. She peeked out shyly, her eyes big and blue. A tumble of golden hair framed the exquisite features of a china doll, though with a smudge of jam at the corner of her mouth.

Ellie's heart melted. It was clear the girl seldom encountered strangers. Damien had said that he kept his daughter out of sight as protection from the gossips. How confusing it must be for her to be presented to someone new without any warning. Having never known her own mother, Lily very likely had no notion what a stepmother even was.

"I'm very pleased to meet you, Lily. I do hope that we might be friends. Do you mind if I fix your ribbon? It's come undone."

The girl gave a little shake of her head. She was

clinging to Damien's neck for dear life. Ellie pulled out the loosened white ribbon in the girl's hair. Using her fingers, she gently combed the golden tresses into a smooth waterfall, then retied the bow to keep the girl's long locks down her back. "There, you're right as rain."

A tiny burble of laughter came from Lily. "Right as rain. What does that mean, Papa?"

"It means that you look presentable again, and not like an unruly scamp," Damien said, as he used his thumb to wipe the jam from the corner of her mouth. "It's just a silly saying."

Lily thought for a moment. "Like when Miss Applegate says that I must be neat as a pin?"

"Yes, like that. And speaking of your governess, I had better take you back upstairs right now before she discovers you've escaped."

As if on cue, an older woman with a lace cap over her graying hair appeared at the top of the stairs. Beginning the descent, she apologized profusely. "Good gracious, sir! I'm ever so sorry. I left the dear child at her reading while I went to fetch a book from the library. One moment she was there, the next gone!"

"Never mind, Miss Applegate. I'll bring her up to you at once."

Damien started toward the stairs with his precious cargo still nestled in his arm. Almost as an afterthought, he turned back. "Mrs. Tomkins, perhaps you'd be so good as to show Mrs. Burke to her chambers. I'm sure she'll wish to freshen up and have her tea."

Then he mounted the stairs, leaving Ellie feeling oddly bereft. She would have liked to have gone with them to the nursery. Damien probably wished to see the progress of Lily's lessons during his absence, and to catch up on all the happenings of the past fortnight.

Ellie was curious to view the schoolroom for herself.

Having been a governess for many years to her two younger cousins, she felt a keen interest in Lily's schooling, too. And she could admit to feeling an affection for the girl already. Who wouldn't fall instantly in love with such a delightful child?

But Damien had not invited Ellie upstairs to the nursery. Clearly, he wanted to discourage any closeness between her and his daughter. He'd said that protecting Lily was his primary concern. So perhaps it was only natural that he would want to prevent his little girl from being hurt when her new stepmama moved away forever.

The housekeeper led Ellie along an upstairs corridor, the thick carpet muffling their footsteps. Near the end of the passage, Mrs. Tomkins opened a door. "Here we are, Mrs. Burke. I do hope you'll find the accommodations to your liking. Though we were not warned of your arrival, never fear, everything will soon be put to rights."

"You mustn't fuss," Ellie said quickly. "I'm sure it will be perfect."

She stepped into a dimly lit bedchamber that was larger than any of the bedchambers at Pennington House, including her uncle's. The shadowed furnishings appeared to be dainty, with a four-poster bed, a writing desk against one wall, and chairs draped with dust covers. The housekeeper headed straight to a bank of windows and drew back the tall draperies. As the afternoon sunshine poured into the room, it was like adding watercolor paints to a pen-and-ink drawing.

Awash in delight, Ellie turned slowly around to survey the décor. The palette of leaf green and buttery yellow made her feel as if the outdoors had been brought inside. She admired everything from the cozy armchairs by the white marble fireplace to the luxurious carpet with its subtle pattern of yellow roses to the high ceiling with its decorative moldings. She had never thought to be given such a lovely room.

What *had* she expected? On the journey here, she had devoted no more than a passing thought to Damien's house. But to her chagrin, Ellie realized now that at the back of her mind, she had pictured a gaudy bordello filled with heavy dark furnishings and crimson hangings with ornate gold fringe.

How wrong she had been. Based on what she'd seen of the rooms on the way upstairs, the entire house appeared to be done in a tasteful style that was both comfortable and inviting.

"You'll find there's a grand view of the gardens from here," Mrs. Tomkins was saying as she adjusted the green silk curtains. "The tulips and daffodils will be blooming soon. It's always such a pretty sight."

Ellie knew that she was likely to be gone before the spring flowers opened. Nevertheless, she went to the windows to peer outside. "Oh! It *is* lovely."

Instead of a more traditional geometric design, the landscaping gave the impression of a woodlands setting, with stone pathways meandering past beds where spikes of greenery already pushed through the soil. Benches had been placed here and there, where one might sit and sketch on a quiet summer afternoon.

A wistful longing came over her, but Ellie swiftly quashed it. She would have her own garden by summer, outside her very own cottage, where she could be alone to concentrate on her storybook. And that was exactly the way she wanted it.

The housekeeper bustled around the chamber, twitching off the dust covers from the chaise longue by the window and then from the bed. "If you'll permit me, Mrs. Burke, may I say that it's such a pleasure to finally have someone occupying this chamber." She clucked her tongue. "I feared—well, we *all* feared—that after suffering such a tragedy, the master would never again see fit to marry."

Struck by an uncomfortable thought, Ellie turned to look at the woman with her plain features and friendly brown eyes. "Was this *her* bedchamber? His first wife?"

"Oh, nay, ma'am. It was shortly after her sad passing that the master purchased this house and had it refurbished from top to bottom." A fond smile touched her mouth. "Miss Lily was just a babe in arms back then, and he wanted the dear child to have a happy home in which to live."

It *was* a happy home, Ellie realized. There was a sense of tranquility here that she had never noticed in her uncle's house. Of course, there she had been relegated to her tiny chamber up in the nursery, with no fire to warm her in the winter and a stuffy closeness in the summer. And there, she had been little better than a servant, always at the beck and call of Beatrice and their grandmother . . .

A young housemaid in a white mobcap entered with an armload of linens. Seeing Ellie, the girl bobbed a curtsy. Then she immediately set to work making up the bed with its feather pillows and embroidered silk counterpane.

"This is Harriet," the housekeeper said. "She will assist you until a proper lady's maid can be hired."

Ellie was appalled to think of acquiring a personal servant who would have to be let go again in a matter of weeks. "I won't need much help. I'm sure Harriet will do just fine."

Mrs. Tomkins gave her a strange look before carrying the towels into the dressing room. Coming out again, she said, "I daresay you'll be wanting to freshen up after your voyage, ma'am. I've taken the liberty of ordering a bath drawn for you. It should be ready in a few moments. Unless you'd care for your tea first?"

"A bath would be lovely," Ellie said.

How peculiar it felt to be waited upon. At home, she would have gone down to the kitchen herself to fetch the tea. But in this house, she occupied a high status. Why did she feel that she didn't deserve it?

Restless, she wandered through the bedchamber, looking at the china figurines on a side table, the ormolu clock on the mantel, the elegant writing desk with its cubbyholes empty of pens and paper. She couldn't shake a vague sense of being an interloper. These were not really *her* belongings. They had been selected by a decorator and meant for the lady of the house. Damien's wife.

She was Damien's wife, Ellie reminded herself.

But was she truly?

They had married for the sake of expediency, to silence the gossips by placing a veneer of respectability over his abduction of her. By mutual agreement, they would lead separate lives—except for her short stay here. They had never intended to remain together as husband and wife.

A true marriage to Damien would require a commitment of the heart. She didn't see how that could ever be possible. He was a gambler, a scoundrel, a womanizer. He had earned his notorious reputation as the Demon Prince.

Yet he loved his daughter to distraction. His servants held him in high esteem. And the one night Ellie had spent in his arms had felt right and good, so perfect it seemed now like an impossible dream.

Desire for him simmered inside her. She wanted Damien to hold her close, to caress her body, to share her bed. Yet he had not come to her in the four days since their wedding. Was he merely abiding by the rules she had set for him?

You will not claim the rights of a husband without my consent. And at the moment, I am not of a mind to grant it.

There had been nothing welcoming in her words. He had probably decided it was easier just to stay away from her. And perhaps it *was* better that way. Allowing herself to grow accustomed to his nightly lovemaking would only soften her heart and make it more difficult for her to leave here.

Would he seek his pleasure elsewhere, then? In a discreet affair with another woman? The very thought set her teeth on edge. Ellie had to draw in several deep breaths to calm herself. And she had to remind herself that she had no real claim on his fidelity.

Resolutely, she marched into the dressing room to take her bath. He had every right to lead his life as he pleased—and so did she. They had made their devil's bargain. It served no purpose to pine for what could never be.

Damien could hear someone splashing in the bath next door.

Stripped to the waist, he stood before the washstand and mixed his shaving soap. Having assured himself of Lily's happiness, he intended to go to his club for the evening. There undoubtedly had been business problems that had arisen during his long absence. And he wanted to look over the account books to see that everything looked satisfactory.

Yet his gaze kept straying to the door reflected in the oval mirror.

The door that connected his dressing room to Ellie's.

The splashing sounds set fire to his blood. He imagined her sitting naked in the brass tub, perhaps drawing a sponge over those magnificent breasts. Her hair would be loose and wet, her lips moist, her face damp and rosy. She would soap her hands and reach beneath the water to give herself a thorough washing between the legs . . .

Muttering a curse, Damien snatched up the shaving brush and spread the foamy lather over his face. Then he took the long razor and drew it carefully over one cheek. Watching himself in the mirror, he tried to block out the enticing noises coming from next door.

It was an impossible task. He wasn't used to hearing someone in that dressing room. No, not just someone. Ellie. His wife.

His very reluctant wife. She had made it clear that she did not want a husband. Like him, she'd felt compelled to marry, she to avoid a scandal that would destroy her dream of having her books published, and he to protect Lily's future. They had come to a mutual agreement.

You will not claim the rights of a husband without my consent. And at the moment, I am not of a mind to grant it.

The sound of humming joined the watery splashing. She sounded relaxed and happy, a fact that made him all the more disgruntled. Ellie, apparently, didn't mind that they weren't enjoying the privileges of being husband and wife. He should never have allowed her to dictate the boundaries of their sexual relationship. She was too damned determined to be independent.

Their one night together had magnified his hunger for her. It was more than just physical gratification that he wanted. He craved the closeness that they had shared, the sense of intimacy that had bound them when he'd shared his inmost secrets with her. He wanted Ellie to love him in spite of the darkness in his past.

Ah, hell. All he needed was an outlet for his carnal appetites. A vigorous bout of bed sport would clear his mind of these mawkish sentiments. The trouble was, no other woman appealed to him but Ellie.

What would she do if he threw open the door right now? If he took the soap and began to wash every inch of her lovely body? Would she respond with fire and passion? Would she abandon her opposition to being his wife and invite him into her bed?

"A wee bit o' spit an' polish can work wonders."

Damien felt a sharp sting as he nicked himself. He scowled at the bandy-legged servant who was walking in from the bedchamber. Finn displayed a pair of shiny black boots for his master's inspection.

"Blast it!" Damien growled, tilting his head to examine his jaw in the mirror. "You startled me."

Finn handed him a linen towel. "If ye'd have a seat, I'd be happy t' finish up fer ye."

Damien blotted a droplet of blood. "The day I can't shave myself is the day you lower me into my grave."

Chuckling, Finn set down the boots and went to the wardrobe to lay out a set of evening clothes. Damien finished shaving and then used the towel to wipe a few stray bits of soap from his face.

He could no longer detect any splashing next door. Had Ellie heard them talking? Surely she must have. It occurred to him that maybe she hadn't realized until now that their dressing rooms were adjoining. He grinned at the thought. Maybe she was sitting in the cooling water of the tub in a state of alarm, staring at the door and wondering if he might walk in on her at any moment.

His theory was corroborated when he perceived a few slight noises through the closed door, as if Ellie was trying to make a quiet escape. There was the faint squeak of wet bare flesh on the tub, the slither of water, the muffled thump of one foot, then the other on the floor.

He imagined her reaching for a towel, wrapping it around that damp, lush, womanly form. His groin tightened painfully, and he had to discipline himself to keep from going to her. If Finn wasn't here . . .

Now he could hear two voices in the next room. Ellie must be conversing with her maid. Damn! He couldn't woo his own wife when they were surrounded by an army of servants. But one thing was certain, he'd had enough of this marriage of convenience.

To hell with celibacy.

Ellie had not given him an outright refusal to allow a physical relationship. She'd merely said that it would be *her* decision when it happened. Well, then, he was going to seduce his wife. He was going to make Ellie beg him to join her in bed.

Not tonight, for he would be gone late at his club. But soon. Very soon.

Chapter 22

The following morning, Ellie set out on an important errand that could not be postponed. It was a rare luxury to have a carriage and coachman at her disposal. Several trunks of clothing had been brought from the castle, and with Harriet's aid, she had arrayed herself in a gown of royal-blue taffeta with a lace fichu, a wide-brimmed bonnet, and a pelisse of dark gold merino. The maid also had transformed Ellie's unruly auburn hair into a stylish chignon.

She had been pleased by her fashionable appearance in the pier glass. After years of wearing hand-me-downs, she liked having a new wardrobe. Today, in particular, she wanted to look her best.

Because she was going to do battle with her family.

Gazing out the carriage window at the barren trees of Hyde Park, Ellie felt a knot of tension in her stomach. What would Damien say if he knew that her destination was Pennington House? Would he have insisted upon accompanying her? But she hadn't seen him since he'd gone up to the nursery with his daughter directly upon their arrival the previous day.

She *had* heard him, however.

A flush came over her at the memory. She had been lounging in a tub of warm water, enjoying the indulgence of a bath after the long sea voyage, when the muffled sound of male voices had come from the next room. Nothing could have been more startling. She had gone perfectly still, the cake of lilac-scented soap dripping in her hand, her eyes glued to the closed door that she'd assumed led to a servants' staircase.

How remiss of her not to have realized that her dressing room was connected to Damien's. In many grand houses, the master and mistress occupied a suite of adjoining rooms so that nighttime visits could be accomplished discreetly without having to venture out into a corridor. But in the newness of her situation, she hadn't had time to consider the bedroom arrangements.

And then she'd had the embarrassing realization that Damien must have heard her loud splashing. That had been followed by the alarming thought that he might open the door and walk into her dressing room. Ellie had crept out of the tub at once and wrapped herself in a towel. Grabbing her undergarments, she'd escaped into the bedchamber, only to encounter Harriet bringing in the tea tray.

Ellie had felt rather awkward voicing a polite thanks to the maid while she stood dripping on the fine carpet. She had been obliged to retreat to the dressing room again while the bright-eyed maid had come to help Ellie with her gown. All the while, she had not been able to shake her awareness of Damien's proximity. In the coming days, he could enter her bedchamber whenever he liked.

Would he? The thought had left her breathless. She didn't know if she could resist his seduction. Or if she even *wanted* to resist him. Oh, why was her mind so muddled on the matter?

Later, Mrs. Tomkins had come to say that the master had been called away to his club and would not be joining her for dinner in the dining room. So Ellie had requested a tray in her room and had settled down to work on the drawings in her notebook.

As darkness fell, she had stayed awake late by lamplight. Eventually she'd curled up in the feather bed, listening for his footsteps, hoping to hear the door opening. It was useless to fool herself anymore; she *did* want him with her. But he had not come to her during the night. Evidently, he had taken her cold stipulation to heart. She had made her views on their marriage quite clear.

And wasn't that for the best, anyway? Being together as man and wife would only complicate their eventual parting. Nevertheless, she yearned to be swept away by his passionate kisses, to feel his strong body against hers again . . .

The carriage came to a gentle rocking halt, and a footman opened the door. As she stepped out in front of Pennington House in Hanover Square, Ellie struggled to reorient her thoughts to the confrontation that lay ahead. Was her uncle at home?

She glanced up at the brick façade of the town house with its tall windows. On the floor above, the blue draperies of the drawing room stood open. So the house hadn't been closed up. Since the beginning of the season was still a few weeks away, perhaps the scandal had not yet sent her family scurrying to the earl's country seat in Lincolnshire.

The temptation to climb back into the carriage overwhelmed Ellie. Then she wouldn't have to face censure from any of them. But she also wouldn't be able to retrieve the packet of illustrations from her old bedchamber, which was one of the purposes of her visit.

She took a deep breath and marched toward the portico with its maroon door and the polished brass fittings. On countless occasions, she had gone in and out the front entry, accompanying Beatrice to the shops or running errands for the countess. How strange to think that now she would enter as a guest.

An unwanted guest, she feared.

Lifting the brass knocker, she rapped hard. After a moment, the door swung open and a young footman stood gaping at her. His cheeks flushed red beneath his white wig, an indication that the gossip of her running off with a scoundrel must have been the subject of much discussion in the servants' hall this past fortnight. "Miss Stratham!"

"Hello, Joseph." She stepped past him and into the foyer with its black-and-white tiled floor and the mustard-brown walls displaying age-darkened scenic paintings. "Is my uncle at home? I would like an audience with him and with my grandmother, too, if she's here."

He gulped, then glanced furtively up the stairs. "I don't . . . don't know if they're available, miss."

Ellie pursed her lips. Well, at least now she knew for certain that they were in residence. Had the staff been ordered not to admit her? She felt insulted and angered and unsettled all at the same time. But her family *would* receive her whether they wished to or not.

She removed her bonnet and pelisse and thrust them at the footman. "Never mind announcing me," she said. "I shall go and find them for myself. You may tell everyone that I pushed straight past you in a most unladylike manner!"

With that, Ellie clasped her skirts and hurried up the

wide marble staircase in the center of the entry hall. She had timed her visit for eleven o'clock on purpose. In late morning each day, Lady Anne and the countess had a habit of doing needlework in the sitting room that overlooked the tiny garden. The earl often sat chatting with them for a time before going off to take luncheon at his club. Beatrice would likely still be in her bedchamber, which was all for the best, since Ellie didn't want any bids for attention to distract from her purpose.

At the top of the stairs, she proceeded along an ornate corridor that seemed suffocating in comparison to the airy freshness of Damien's house. Or perhaps the oppressive sensation she felt arose from her dread of this interview. She had never been one to defy the edicts of her uncle or grandmother. It had always been easier for her to avoid trouble by being obedient and agreeable, while escaping to the fairy-tale world of her imagination.

Nearing the back of the house, Ellie slowed her steps. This would be an unpleasant encounter, she knew. But it had to be done. The air must be cleared. There were points that needed to be spoken.

She reached the morning room with its faded green draperies and the clutter of outdated furnishings that the earl was too tightfisted to replace. For a moment, no one noticed her standing in the doorway.

Ellie's grandmother and uncle sat conversing on the chaise near the fire. Her stout form encased in puce silk, the countess was working at her tambour frame, moving her needle in and out, embroidering a cover for one of the ugly cushions that she liked to give away as Christmas gifts. The Earl of Pennington tapped a folded newspaper against his leg in an irritated gesture. Across from them, Lady Anne was making herself invisible as she always did during quarrels, her slender form hunched over the basket of embroidery threads in her lap.

"I refuse to withdraw to Lincolnshire," the earl was expounding to his mother. "As if *I* am at fault for this shameful scandal! There are my duties in Parliament to consider . . ."

Ellie stepped forward. "There is no need to leave London, uncle. You'll be pleased to hear that my abduction has come to an end."

As one, everyone turned to gape at her in shock. Lady Anne was the first to move. She half rose from her chair, the basket tumbling from her lap and spilling its contents over the shabby floral rug. "Ellie, my dear girl! Thank heavens you're safe!"

Ellie had time for only a quick, gratified smile in the woman's direction before her uncle surged to his feet. A look of aversion twisted his florid features and his nostrils flared with anger. "What is the meaning of this, Eloise? I gave strict orders that you were not to be admitted to this house!"

His cold manner cut her to the quick. With effort, she forced herself to curtsy. "I must beg you not to chastise the footman, my lord. I came upstairs before he could stop me. I should like to speak to you—to all of you, if I may."

"Your request is impertinent," the countess said, without rising from the chaise. Her eyes like sunken raisins in her wrinkled face, she looked Ellie up and down. "I see that the Demon Prince is garbing you in expensive gowns. It is plain that you have become his mistress. Well, it only proves that bad blood will tell. You are just as wicked as your father was!"

Ellie held tight to her temper. Nothing would be served by engaging in a shouting match. "The proper name for the Demon Prince is Mr. Damien Burke, and he is now my husband. It has been several days since we spoke our vows in front of a minister."

Once again, she had succeeded in shocking all of them. She allowed herself a moment of satisfaction as the countess and her son exchanged a disbelieving glance.

"Oh, my gracious!" said Lady Anne, one dainty hand fluttering to the cameo necklace at her throat. "That is wonderful news!"

"Rubbish," Pennington snapped at his sister-in-law. "I cannot think of a more disastrous match." When she shrank under his sharp words and bent down to collect the fallen bundles of thread, he added, "Leave that be and run along from here. This conversation has nothing to do with you."

Lady Anne stammered an apology and hurried out the door, her head down, the white spinster's cap on her silvering dark hair hiding her face. Ellie compressed her lips at the boorishness of her uncle's decree. Yet perhaps it was for the best. What she had to say was bound to cause a squabble that would only upset the gentle woman.

The earl watched Lady Anne go, then turned on Ellie. His face was flushed with displeasure. "Did you think I would welcome such an unfortunate connection? Burke is a gamester and a ruffian. You should never have wed him without my permission."

"I quite agree," her grandmother said. "Who is he but a baseborn rogue? He may have attended Eton on scholarship, yet he is a mere commoner without a drop of blue blood."

That wasn't true, Ellie wanted to say. Damien had very likely been born of the gentry—perhaps even a royal. Though *he* was skeptical, she believed there could be truth to the claim made by his late guardian, Mrs. Mims, that he was a prince. But no proof existed. The only clue was that missing key.

Slapping the folded newspaper against his palm, Pennington paced back and forth in front of the fireplace. "I suppose, Eloise, that he has sent you here to apply to me for a settlement. He must be too cowardly to face me, man to man. Well, you may tell him I will not give him tuppence! He has wed you for naught."

"That isn't why I'm here," Ellie objected. "He doesn't even know that I came to Pennington House today."

"Then he married you in the hopes of finagling his way back into society. He will gain no sponsorship from me. Rather, I will see to it that he is not admitted to any of the best homes!"

"How do we even know this is a real marriage?" the countess asked as she fixed a sly stare on Ellie. "The scoundrel may have tricked her."

Despite her determination to be polite, Ellie took great pleasure in saying, "Oh, it was no sham. Lady Milford was there as witness. In fact, you may thank *her* for making all the arrangements."

The countess dropped her needle and thread onto the tambour frame. "Lady Milford!" she uttered in astonishment. "Do you mean to say that she traveled all the way to Scotland on your behalf?"

"I do indeed, Grandmamma."

Let the bitter old woman stew on *that,* Ellie thought. Her grandmother knew that Ellie had been in Scotland because Walt had been forced to confess everything to his family, including showing them the letter from Damien that had contained instructions on where to bring the stolen key. Yet no one in her family had bothered to fetch her home. They ought to be ashamed to learn that a pillar of society had felt compelled to involve herself in the affair—all because *they* would not rescue Ellie.

Her uncle and grandmother were frowning at each

other as if in silent communication. The earl looked about to explode. Ellie had only a moment to savor her victory before he turned sharply and flung his newspaper onto the coal fire, making the flames flare bright.

"Blasted woman! How dare she interfere without my permission. I've a good mind to—"

"Basil! Pray, do not say anything you might regret." Rising to her feet, the countess patted her son on the sleeve of his dark brown coat. "We must think of how to make the best of this situation. Remember, Lady Milford is an influential woman. Her intervention may be beneficial to Beatrice. Since Eloise is now safely married, the scandal is not quite so damaging as we feared it to be."

"Nevertheless, *I* am the head of this family and these matters are *mine* to decide," Pennington said testily. "But I don't suppose I should be surprised at her effrontery after the way she came here, asking all those prying questions, forcing Walt to—" He pinched his lips shut, his surly gaze focused on Ellie.

"Lady Milford told me that she made Walt retract the vicious lie that he'd told about my character," Ellie said. "Is that what you were about to reference, Uncle?"

The scowl on his broad features spoke volumes. Walt had made the outrageous claim that he'd seen Ellie sneak out of the house at night, ostensibly to meet the Demon Prince. Walt had wanted it to appear as if she had run away voluntarily so that his father wouldn't learn of the gambling debt that had triggered Damien's plan to abduct Beatrice. How mortified Pennington must have been to discover his eldest son's dishonorable actions, both in gambling and lying.

"I have dealt with Walter in my own way," he said stiffly. "And Lady Milford ought to have kept her nose out of our affairs."

Her gloved fingers gripped at her sides, Ellie took a step toward him. "Well, I am glad that she did not. You had left me to fend for myself. And if not for Lady Milford, you'd still believe that I'd gone off with Mr. Burke of my own volition."

He had the good grace to flush. "I must beg your pardon for that."

"Thank you, but the true apology should come from Walt." Ellie wondered suddenly if she might discover what had happened to the stolen key. "Is he upstairs? Perhaps a footman should be sent to fetch him."

"My, you have become quite strident under the influence of the Demon Prince," the countess declared, her wrinkles shifting as she arched an eyebrow. "If you must know, Walter isn't here. He has been sent away for a time."

"Sent away? Where?"

"To rusticate in the country," the earl said. "I will not permit him to be lured into losing his quarterly allowance to men like your husband."

Ellie felt the impulse to defend Damien—but how could she? There was no denying that he owned a gambling club. And for all she knew, he *had* lured Walt into that game. "Damien cares nothing for Walt's money. He merely wants the return of a key that was stolen from him. Do *you* know what Walt did with it?"

The earl narrowed his eyes to slits. Turning away, he began to pace again, throwing a scornful glance her way. "Ah, yes, the mythical key. If it ever existed, it was tossed into the rubbish years ago."

Ellie had had enough of his condescending manner. Damien seemed certain that Walt still had the key, and she would sooner believe her husband than her uncle or her cousin. "The key does indeed exist. If Walt claims that it does not, then he is fibbing. This is no small matter, either. After all, your own daughter was very nearly kidnapped in order to force Walt's hand."

Pennington said nothing. He merely gave her a stony stare.

"Eloise does bring up a salient point," the countess said. "Beatrice might have been ruined. Only think what a tragedy it would have been if *she* had been abducted and forced into marriage to such a man."

She and the earl exchanged another long glance. Again, Ellie had the impression of a silent message being passed between the two of them.

"Quite so," he said crisply, before looking at Ellie again. "I'm sorry, Eloise, I would not have wished this fate upon you. However, what is done is done, and I'm afraid there is nothing I can do to rectify your unfortunate situation."

So that was the end of it, Ellie thought, her throat tight with bitterness. To them, it would have been a calamity if Beatrice had been the one whose reputation was sullied. But not the unwanted daughter of the prodigal second son. They had shunned Ellie's father and now they shunned her. It had been foolish of her to hope they might offer her a scrap of affection, or show even a smidgen of joy over her safe return.

She had a sudden longing for the sunny tranquility of her bedchamber at Damien's house. The oppressive atmosphere here was weighing on her spirits. She wanted to be curled up on the chaise longue with her sketchpad and escape into the world of her imagination . . .

"If you'll excuse me," she said stiffly, "I shall go upstairs now to pack my belongings. You may rest assured that I shan't bother you—any of you—ever again."

With that, Ellie turned on her heel and departed the sitting room. She wanted to be out of this house as swiftly as possible. But as she headed down the corridor to the staircase that led up to the nursery and schoolroom, a slim girl in a lemon-yellow gown came rushing around the corner and nearly collided with her.

They both stopped to stare at each other.

Lady Beatrice's lips parted in shock, her blue eyes rounded against pretty features that were framed by strawberry-gold curls. "Ellie!" she squealed. "My maid told me you were back. I was afraid I might miss you!"

Ellie found herself enveloped in a perfumed embrace. Her heart squeezed and she blinked back tears. It was gratifying to know that at least someone besides Lady Anne was happy to see her. Ellie had always felt an exasperated affection for her headstrong, self-absorbed cousin, even though the girl had been spoiled by her father and grandmother.

She stepped back. "I'm afraid I can't stay long, Beatrice. I've only come to fetch my trunk from the nursery."

Her cousin's gaze held an avid interest. "Papa said that you couldn't live here anymore now that you have been ruined. And by that wicked scoundrel, the Demon Prince! Tell me, is he as handsome as people say?"

"Damien Burke is indeed handsome, yes, but more importantly, he is . . ." How could she describe him? Despite his ill-planned abduction of her and his reputation as a gambler, Damien had depths of character that she was only just beginning to see. "He is a kind man, a true gentleman. And he is now my husband."

Beatrice gasped, her fingers fluttering to her bosom. "You're *married*? To the very rogue who abducted you?" She scanned Ellie from head to toe. "Why, no wonder you're dressed so finely. He's a very wealthy man, I've heard. Oh, how did it happen? Did you fall in love at first sight? Or did you scold him into doing right by you?"

"It was a mutual decision." Ellie didn't care to go into all the details, so she threw out a distraction. "And how have you been faring without me? Did you manage to charm the Duke of Aylwin?"

"Oh, the duke!" Beatrice wrinkled her pert nose. "I have quite changed my mind about marrying His Grace. Lofty title or not, he is far too uncouth for my tastes. His house was cluttered with Egyptian artifacts, and when I suggested that he clear them out so that the rooms might be seen to a better advantage, he very rudely ordered Lady Milford to take me away at once. Can you *imagine* how humiliating that was?"

Ellie bit back a smile. "Then I presume you will not be decorating your come-out ball with an Egyptian theme, after all?"

A mournful look drew down that bow-shaped mouth. "There will be no ball for me, I fear. Papa means to cancel it because of the scandal . . ." She paused, her face brightening again. "But now you have returned a married woman. Oh! Do you suppose that means the scandal will go away? That I might still have my season, after all?"

"You may wish to ask your papa. I spoke to him just a few moments ago in the sitting room."

Beatrice clutched Ellie's hand. "Oh, thank you! You will pardon me if I say good-bye now, won't you? I must see him at once if the invitations are to be sent out in time!"

With that, she turned and hastened down the corridor.

Ellie stood watching until that yellow-garbed figure vanished around the corner. In spite of everything that had happened, she felt a certain wistful sadness that she would not be present to witness her cousin's debut into society. Perhaps the feeling was only natural. She had spent the past twelve years of her life as governess to Beatrice. She had taught the girl her letters, bandaged her scrapes, kissed her at bedtime each night.

Now Ellie was leaving Pennington House forever. She might never again cross paths with Beatrice or any other members of this household. As trying as they could be, they had been an important part of her past. There were no relatives left on her mother's side, either.

Her sense of melancholy deepened. She had no family anymore. And she was only staying with Damien for a short while. Soon, she would be utterly alone in the world. But that, she reminded herself, was exactly what she wanted. Wasn't it?

Chapter 23

That afternoon, Ellie was standing beside her bed, looking over the many pages of illustrations spread out on the coverlet, when a tapping came from the door.

The sound startled her. She had given instructions that no one was to disturb her. To boost her spirits, she had resolved to focus her mind on her storybook. She wanted to determine how to break it into separate books as Damien had suggested. To that purpose, she had retrieved the finished pages from her uncle's house and had laid some of them out so that it would be easier to view the overall progress of the plot.

Now, however, Ellie felt a flash of alarm. She reached out to snatch up the papers and hide them. Then she stopped herself. She needn't conceal her work anymore. No longer was she the poor relation who would face punishment for shirking her duties.

She was the mistress of this house. The liberating thought eased her mind. If she chose to litter the entire room with sheets of paper, then no one could gainsay her.

Nevertheless, she had asked to be left alone. She

wanted to concentrate on the project without interruption. Perhaps Harriet had neglected to relay the message to Mrs. Tomkins . . .

As Ellie started across the bedroom, the door opened a crack and a tiny blond head poked inside. A darling little face peered up at her. "Please, ma'am, may I come in?"

Ellie's heart softened. "Why, Lily! Of course you may."

The girl slipped into the bedchamber, but hovered by the open door, her big blue eyes trained on Ellie. Today she wore a ruffled pinafore over a pale pink dress with a matching pink ribbon in her golden hair. She looked so precious that Ellie yearned to draw her close for a kiss.

But Damien would frown on that. He didn't want his daughter to become attached to the stepmother who would be leaving soon. So Ellie reluctantly kept her distance. "Does Miss Applegate know where you are?"

"She went out on her afternoon off, and Nurse fell asleep in the rocking chair. And I *did* finish writing out my spelling list."

Lily looked anxious to please, so Ellie reassured her. "That's excellent, darling. Perhaps we should go up to the schoolroom so that you may show me your work. Have you learned to read, then?"

"Yes, ma'am. I can read lots and lots of words. Even *sentences*." Curiosity lighting her face, Lily ventured a few steps toward the bed. "Why do you have so many papers scattered about?"

"I'm an artist, and those are my drawings. I was just looking at all of them."

Lily went to stand at the foot of the four-poster. She clasped her hands behind her back as if she'd been taught not to touch things that didn't belong to her. She stared in wide-eyed silence at the illustrations of Princess Arianna encountering fantastical forest creatures, curling up to sleep in a hut, awaking to find an old crone attempting to cast a spell on her, and using her wits to escape the wicked witch.

Lily craned her neck to see the other drawings. Then she glanced up at Ellie in confusion. "But . . . these are pages from a book!"

"Yes, I *am* making a book," Ellie said. "I'm drawing the pictures and writing the story."

Lily looked up at her in openmouthed amazement, as if it had never before occurred to her that books didn't appear magically in a store or library, that an actual person *wrote* them.

"Would you like for me to read you a little of it?" Ellie asked on impulse. "Just the beginning, so that you can know what the story is about?"

"Oh! Oh, yes, please."

Ellie collected the pages into an orderly stack, then seated herself in one of the pale green armchairs by the fireside. She was intending to instruct the girl to sit on the rug to listen, as Beatrice and Cedric had always done as children. But without warning, Lily climbed onto Ellie's lap and snuggled into a comfortable position.

It seemed the most natural thing in the world for Ellie to put her arm around the girl. Lily tucked her head in the crook of Ellie's shoulder, released a contented sigh, and then gazed down at the pile of papers, clearly waiting for the story to begin.

Ellie couldn't find her voice. She needed a moment to absorb the joy of cuddling a child on her lap, to relish having that small form curled up against her. It felt lovely and humbling to be the recipient of such trust. But in light of her plan to depart soon, should she even be encouraging this closeness?

She drew in a shaky breath. It would be wiser to send the girl straight back to the nursery. Wiser to maintain a distance between them. Yet Ellie *had* offered to read the story, and now she couldn't bring herself to disappoint the little girl.

She picked up the first page. Completed in watercolors, it depicted an adolescent girl in a fancy blue gown with a tiara nestled in her flowing, coppery hair. Behind her, a king and queen beamed proudly at their daughter.

"'Once upon a time, there lived a princess named Arianna. She was an only child and rather naughty, for she was greatly indulged by her parents. On the occasion of her fifteenth birthday, the king and queen invited everyone in the land to a huge celebration. There was dancing and feasting and games. But then something dreadful happened. While playing hide-and-seek, Princess Arianna tried to trick the other children by hiding where no one would find her. She ventured too far into the Forbidden Forest and soon lost her way among the thick, dark trees . . .'"

While turning the pages, Ellie glanced down to see Lily's reaction. It was a delight to view the rapt attention on her face. Never before had Ellie had the opportunity to read her book aloud to a child. By the time she'd conceived the idea for it, Beatrice and Cedric had been too old for fairy tales. So Ellie had kept the book her own precious secret, working late at night in the privacy of her tiny bedchamber at Pennington House. Damien had looked at bits and pieces of scenes from later in the saga. But not even he had heard the story from the very beginning.

Reading the short script at the bottom of the pages, she gave Lily a few moments to study each illustration. And she allowed herself the pleasure of watching the little girl. She could see something of Damien in Lily's smile and in her cheekbones, though her face was much more delicate. Her fair coloring must have come from her mother. Damien had mentioned that his previous wife had been a dainty blonde.

What a sad circumstance for the girl to grow up without ever having known her mother. Ellie's own mother had died when Ellie had been about the same age as Lily. Ellie had clear memories of a dark-haired woman, of a lovely voice singing, a soft hand on her brow, a warm smile and comforting hugs.

Lily had only ever known Miss Applegate, the nursery maids, and Mrs. Tomkins. From her own experience, Ellie knew that no matter how kind and caring servants were, it was not the same as having one's own mother. Lily deserved to know that special love. Yet who else could fulfill that need but her father's wife?

And Ellie would be moving away from this house very soon. She would finally achieve her cherished dream of having a cottage where she could be free to pursue her art. To that end, she and Damien had made a mutual agreement to live apart. The marriage had been arranged so swiftly that there had been no time to consider the effect of it on his daughter.

Guilt nibbled at her, but she pushed it away. At least Lily *did* have an attentive father. Damien adored her—as Lily did him. What would he say if he were to see Ellie and Lily nestled together in this chair? He would be angry, and justifiably so. He wanted Ellie to stay out of his daughter's life, and she couldn't blame him. He was only trying to shield Lily from being hurt.

Ellie reached the final page in the stack, wherein Princess Arianna escapes from the clutches of a wicked witch only to become lost again in the vastness of the Forbidden Forest. With a hint of regret, she placed the paper with the others on the table beside the chair.

Lily tilted a worried expression up at her. "Will the princess ever find her mama and papa again?"

Smiling, Ellie brushed back a lock of hair from the girl's cheek. "Yes, she will, I promise you that. But first, Arianna will have many more adventures. She will learn to be brave and strong, and not to be quite so naughty anymore. Only then will she find her way back to her mother and father."

Lily had a solemn look on her face. Anticipating a plea for another installment of the story, Ellie dropped a kiss on the top of that golden head. "I believe it's time for you to return to the nursery. We wouldn't want Nurse to become alarmed by your absence. Up you go, now."

Instead of arising, Lily threw her arms around Ellie's neck. "Nurse said that you're my new mother. May I call you mama? *Please?*"

A flood of affection caught Ellie unawares. How marvelous it was to feel such a close connection to this sweet child. Awash in the euphoria of unguarded emotion, she hugged Lily close. "Of course you may . . ."

Even as the impulsive words left her lips, Ellie realized her mistake. Oh, no. She oughtn't encourage any familiarity. She was supposed to remain aloof and detached. But she couldn't bring herself to retract the permission, especially not when Lily beamed at her in delight before scrambling off her lap.

As Ellie arose from the chair, she tried to think of what to do. Damien would be furious if he heard Lily addressing her as "mama." Yet how could she explain that to the little girl? Perhaps there was a tactful way to instruct Lily to remain in the nursery henceforth, and never to come back here for any more visits . . .

"Papa, you're home!"

It took a moment for Lily's glad cry to register. Then

Ellie looked over her shoulder to realize two things in quick succession. Lily had never closed the door. And Damien stood behind them in the doorway, his shoulder propped against the frame and his arms crossed.

He was not smiling.

Dear God. How long had he been standing there?

Lily started toward him, then came back to grab Ellie's hand and drag her forward on resisting feet. "Papa, guess what? Mama has been reading me a story."

"Indeed?"

His voice had a cold undercurrent. He directed a piercing stare at Ellie, and she strove not to quail under the force of it. Yet she felt lower than a worm slithering through the bowels of the earth. He had every right to condemn her.

As he bent down to greet his daughter, a smile banished the fierceness from his face. He ruffled her hair, saying, "Nurse has been looking for you, princess. She was certain that you'd run away into the Forbidden Forest, never to be seen again."

Ellie's mouth went dry. Oh, no. He must have been standing there for a *long* time.

Lily giggled. "How silly. I've been right here with Mama."

"So you have," he said, one black eyebrow lifted in clear rebuke of Ellie. He looked back at Lily. "It's time to go upstairs now. Our tea is growing cold. Cook has sent your favorite jam tarts."

"Can Mama come, too? Please, Papa?"

Ellie's gaze met his. He looked exceedingly handsome today in a dark green coat that enhanced the color of his cool, critical eyes. In spite of his obvious displeasure, she felt a shiver of attraction scurry over her skin. How could she feel so enticed by him even in the face of his anger?

"I'm afraid I'm rather busy with my work today," she told Lily. "It takes quite a lot of time to sketch all the pictures for my story."

Lily gave her a woebegone look. "But it will only be for a little while."

Ellie was about to voice another firm refusal when Damien stepped forward to place his hand at the small of her back. "If it pleases you, Lily, I'm sure that *Mama* can spare the time. Shall we go?"

Ellie found herself directed out the door and down to the end of the corridor, where a small staircase led up to the upper floor. It was painfully clear from Damien's harsh expression that he didn't desire her company. He merely had a soft spot when it came to his daughter's happiness.

Lily skipped ahead of them, bounding up the steps with all the enthusiasm of youth. Ellie was keenly aware of her husband's hand burning into her lower back. He must think that she would balk if he didn't force her to accompany them. His nearness made her all the more conscious of her dreadful blunder.

As they mounted the stairs, she cast him a sideways glance. "Damien . . . I must explain—"

"Explain what?" His voice was clipped, his gaze furious. "For God's sake, Ellie. You knew how I felt on this matter. It will make things so much more difficult for Lily when you leave here."

Feeling the prick of tears, Ellie glanced at him before turning her head down. "I *am* sorry," she murmured, biting her lip. "I didn't mean for her to call me Mama . . . but she *asked* me . . . and she looked so darling . . . well, I just didn't *think* . . ."

His silence only contributed to her misery. Her throat felt taut, her stomach sick with tension. She couldn't blame him for being livid. They both knew that Lily would feel betrayed by Ellie's inevitable departure. And that Damien would be left with the task of consoling the grieving little girl.

Then, as they reached the top of the stairs, he surprised Ellie by rubbing his palm over the middle of her back in a comforting gesture. Bending his head close, he said in her ear, "I will admit, the little scamp *is* hard to resist. Only look at her now."

Lily stood waiting in a doorway up ahead. With her hands on her hips and a stern expression on her face, she resembled a miniature governess. "Do hurry, Papa, you are walking far too slowly."

"Some people prefer not to gallop through the house like wild horses on the loose," he said dryly.

As they strolled forward, Ellie cast a cautious glance at him. His expression no longer looked quite so forbidding. Had he decided to forgive her? No, it was more likely that he'd just temporarily set aside their quarrel for Lily's sake.

A pudgy, gray-haired woman in aproned gown and mobcap hovered just inside the door. She bobbed a curtsy. "Bless you, sir, for finding the little miss! Why, I'd only rested my eyes for half a minute and she was gone."

"She was safely visiting with Mrs. Burke." Once he had introduced Ellie to the kind-faced nursemaid, and had dispatched the servant to the kitchen to fetch another teacup, Lily slipped her small hand into Ellie's.

"I have a hobby horse, Mama," she said, apparently inspired by her father's remark about wild horses. "Come and see."

Ellie found herself being drawn across a schoolroom with several small tables and matching chairs, and tall windows that let in the afternoon sunshine. There were low shelves filled with many books, a world globe on a pedestal, and framed prints of alphabet animals on the walls. Nostalgia filled her as she breathed in the familiar scents of chalk dust and book bindings. Having spent most of her life as a pupil and then a governess, she had always felt at home in a classroom.

Lily hopped onto a rocking horse in the corner and began to ride back and forth with great enthusiasm. "Look, Mama. I'm practicing for when Papa buys me a real pony. I *hope* when I am seven."

"Ten," Damien said firmly, coming up behind Ellie. "And that's only if you're a good girl and learn proper behavior."

Stepping forward, he plucked Lily off the rocking horse and set her standing on the floor. Then he crouched down in front of her, placing his hands on her small shoulders. "I am sorry to end your fun, Lily. But I must have a word with you. Two days in a row, you've left the schoolroom without permission. You have caused Nurse *and* Miss Applegate to worry needlessly about you."

Lily tucked her chin down, her lower lip suddenly wobbling. "I'm sorry, Papa. I know . . . I know it was wrong."

"I will have your promise that it won't happen ever again."

In a very small voice, she said, "I promise."

"Excellent. And I shall be watching to make sure that you *do* obey."

He cupped her chin in his large hand, running his thumb over her cheek in a loving caress designed to take the sting out of his reprimand. He had done a similar thing to *her,* Ellie realized, when he had glided his hand over her back out in the corridor. That small touch had been a balm to ease her wretchedness.

But it was too much to hope that he had forgiven her. Not when she was guilty of the deplorable act of setting his daughter up for heartache. Though at least now, he had made certain that Lily wouldn't be paying her any more unexpected calls. Perhaps that had been part of his purpose, to keep the two of them separated.

Ellie told herself to be glad. Yet she couldn't deny she would miss visiting with the little girl. Being with Lily helped to fill the empty place in her heart left by the loss of her family.

Rising to his feet, Damien smiled down at his daughter. "I believe I'm hungry for a tart now," he said. "I presume Dora will be joining us for tea today?"

Dora?

As Lily dashed out of the schoolroom, he cast a guarded glance at Ellie. "I hope I wasn't too easy on her. I know many fathers would have taken a willow switch to her backside."

Ellie searched his face. Was he seeking her advice? "You mustn't doubt yourself. You handled the matter exactly right."

"I don't want her to grow up too spoiled." His mouth crooked into a faint, worried smile. "I never had a father to show me how to behave. And at times I fear that I don't know the first thing about being one."

How difficult it must be for him to face parenthood alone, Ellie thought, with only servants to help him out. Yet he had professed not to want a wife. He had been just as reluctant to marry as she had been.

Stepping to his side, she placed her hand on his forearm, feeling the smoothness of his sleeve beneath her fingers, the strength of his muscles. "You've done very well with her, Damien. She's a happy, precious, perfect child. Well, nearly perfect, anyway."

They shared a laugh, and Ellie was glad that the tension between them had eased. His eyes were warmer now and he was looking at her in a way that caused a thrill down her spine. *Had* he forgiven her? Perhaps he'd only decided that since Lily wouldn't be sneaking out of the nursery anymore, he had resolved the issue of her forming an attachment to Ellie.

The notion was somehow disheartening.

Lily came running back, clutching a shabby, homemade doll with yellow yarn hair, black button eyes, and a sewn-on smile. "This is Dora," she told Ellie. "She has tea with Papa and me every day."

Every day?

Ellie shook the doll's mittenlike hand. "It's a pleasure to meet you, Dora."

Lily giggled in delight. Skipping toward one of the schoolroom tables, where the silver tea tray sat waiting, the little girl haphazardly piled some books onto a chair and perched Dora on top of the stack. Nurse delivered the extra cup and then departed the room again.

As the three of them took their places around the table, Ellie bit her lip to keep from smiling at the sight of Damien settling his large frame onto one of the child-sized chairs. He seemed matter-of-fact about the whole process, plucking off the knitted cozy from the blue china pot and pouring the tea as if he'd done it a hundred times before.

Perhaps he had. Sipping from her cup, Ellie marveled to realize that the notorious Demon Prince really did have tea with his young daughter every day. The harpies of society would never believe it.

She would have never believed it a fortnight ago. He had allowed very few people to see the real man behind the cynical mask.

Lily was on her best behavior. She sat up straight in her chair and took dainty sips from the milky tea in her porcelain cup. Every now and then, she leaned toward Dora, pretending to feed bits of raspberry jam tart to the doll. And she directed the conversation as if holding court in a drawing room.

"Mama is an artist," Lily informed her father. "She is making a book about a princess who is lost in the forest."

"So I heard." One corner of his mouth curled upward as he eyed Ellie across the table. "You should know, Lily, that later in the story, Princess Arianna meets a dashing hero named Prince Ratworth."

"Villain," Ellie corrected.

"Hero, for he's a master swordsman who saves the princess from an ogre. And he *is* a prince, after all."

"A princess has to marry a prince," Lily said, as if that settled the matter.

Ellie laughed. "Well, the book is not yet finished. So we shall see how it all turns out in the end."

"Yes," Damien said. "We shall."

She fancied there was a note in his voice that held a deeper meaning. His inscrutable gaze rested on her for a moment before he returned his attention to his daughter. But that brief, intense look had fanned the embers of longing in Ellie. What did it mean? Did he, too, desire a closer relationship with her? Did he want them to have a real marriage?

A bone-deep quiver shook her. She mustn't let herself even *think* of staying with him. She had set into motion a plan to live on her own, to dedicate herself to the long-held dream of writing and illustrating her books. Nothing must come in the way of that. Besides, Damien had said that he'd never wanted to marry again. He didn't want a wife any more than she'd wanted a husband.

They had made a pact with each other. They had wed for the sake of propriety while agreeing to lead separate lives. And she had insisted upon a chaste marriage.

You will not claim the rights of a husband without my consent. And at the moment, I am not of a mind to grant it.

Those cold words had arisen out of her anger and fear. She had felt trapped, forced by circumstances to speak her vows to the man who had abducted her. But somehow, in the space of a few days, all of those distressful feelings had vanished. Now she could think of nowhere else she wanted to be at the moment but right here with Damien and Lily.

A bittersweet joy filled her bosom. She felt privileged to be allowed into the little circle of their family—even if it could only be for this one afternoon. Yet surely it was imprudent to wish for more from a man who made his living from gambling. She mustn't forget the hard lesson she'd learned from the downfall of her father.

Nevertheless, while watching Damien laughing with his daughter, Ellie realized that something perilous was happening to her. She was in grave danger of falling in love with her own husband.

Chapter 24

Damien had resolved upon a scheme to stop Ellie from leaving him. It was a dastardly objective, considering that he'd already abducted her, ruined her good name, and compelled her into a marriage that she didn't want. He knew exactly what she had always envisioned for her future. Before the first time they had made love at the castle, she had stated her wishes in no uncertain terms: *After twelve years in my uncle's house, I've had my fill of tending to the demands of other people. I want to live on my own without any entanglements.*

He yanked off his cravat and threw it onto a chair in the semidarkness of his bedchamber. How could he even think of thwarting her dream of living alone in some blasted cottage? Yet he couldn't just let her go, either. He was not a gentleman who could politely stand by while the love of his life made plans to move out of his house forever.

Frowning into the gloom, he shrugged out of his coat. *Was* it love? Was that the appropriate term for the mawkish, heart-melting sentiment that she stirred in him? He felt cast adrift in uncharted waters. Never before had he known such a strong desire to protect a woman, to hold her close, to talk and laugh with her.

And to make love to her. Which was what he intended to do tonight. *If* Ellie would allow him.

The waistcoat came off next. As he tossed it onto the chair, it slid onto the floor along with his other discarded garments. Finn would have a conniption tomorrow when he found the crumpled heap of clothing. No doubt the old man also would make a ribald comment or two about why Damien had been so quick to dismiss him for the night.

On second thought, he grabbed the clothes and went to hang them on hooks in the dressing room. Here, the light of a single candle cast his elongated shadow over the connecting door. He couldn't discern any sounds coming from the adjoining chamber. According to his pocket watch, it was a minute shy of ten o'clock, and he wasn't sure Ellie was even still awake.

He had meant to return home sooner from Demon's Den, but there had been several issues that had required his attention, a dispute to be tactfully settled between two gentlemen who'd been about to come to blows over who had rights to a certain chair, and a complaint to resolve with the finicky French chef who threatened to quit at least once a week. Then there had been the usual invitations from club members to partake in a shot of brandy or a glass of port, to join in a debate over who owned the finest horseflesh or which Covent Garden actress might be amenable to a tryst.

On any other night, he'd have made it his business to move among the smoky throngs of aristocrats, playing a few hands of vingt-et-un, tossing the dice in a game of hazard, building friendships and camaraderie. By now, everyone knew that he'd married Pennington's niece. Most had accepted his word that it had been a secret elopement due to the earl's disapproval of the match. Only a few malcontents had dared to reference the sordid story being bandied about by the gossips, that his intention had been to dishonor Ellie.

Those Damien had silenced with a cold stare. He had made it clear he would kill any man who dared to cast a slur upon his wife. No one, thank God, realized that it had been an abduction gone awry, a mistake that had turned out to be the luckiest move of his misbegotten life.

Other than begetting Lily, of course.

Sitting down on a stool, Damien tugged off his boots. He debated whether or not to strip down to the buff and don a dressing gown, then decided that that would make his intentions too obvious. Ellie needed to be wooed and enticed. He would have to employ all of his charm to coax her into making love.

Especially given the way he'd chastised her earlier in the day.

He could still feel a blow of shock at hearing Lily's voice in Ellie's chambers. He had stepped silently into the doorway to see his daughter cuddled in Ellie's lap on the chair, their two heads bent together, one golden, the other red. He had stood there, frozen in place, listening to Ellie read her story.

They were not supposed to look so perfect together. They were not supposed to intermingle at all. He had warned Ellie to stay away from his daughter. He had believed her to be perceptive enough to see the harm in seeking out any association with the motherless girl. Then had come their short conversation.

May I call you mama?

Of course you may.

A cold fury had gripped him. Ellie should have known to refuse the request. She should have recognized the danger of it at once. Instead, she had embraced his vulnerable daughter and *encouraged* Lily to believe that she finally had a real mother. And all the while, Ellie was intending to walk out of the girl's life in a matter of weeks.

He'd had difficulty containing his rage in front of Lily. And he had spoken sharply to Ellie on the stairs, when Lily had run ahead of them. Ellie's remorse had hit him hard. There had been tears in her eyes before she'd turned her head away. From her halting words, he gathered that she had granted his daughter's request out of an impulsive desire to make Lily happy.

She, too, had fallen under Lily's spell. He knew exactly what that was like because he battled it all the time, the urge to indulge Lily simply because she was so adorable. How could he remain angry at Ellie when she clearly felt a strong affection for his daughter?

Yet there was still the problem of Lily referring to Ellie as "mama," which Lily had proudly done at every opportunity. He'd known that his daughter would only be confused and unhappy if he'd tried to correct her. And then, while they had been drinking tea around that miniature table, he had been struck by the obvious solution.

The three of them together made a real family, the family that he had always craved in the deepest part of himself. Ellie blended in perfectly with them. She had contributed to their silly, child-centered conversation as if she belonged with them.

And in that moment, he had vowed to do everything in his power to win her heart. So that she would never leave him. No, *them*. He was doing this as much for Lily as himself.

Rising from the stool, he blew out the candle. He had contrived an excellent reason to pay a private visit to Ellie in her bedchamber. He needed to speak to her on an important matter that had occurred to him belatedly in regard to hearing her read that storybook aloud.

Once they had that issue settled, he would find a way to turn things in an erotic direction. He would have to proceed carefully in order to overcome her resistance to the marriage. But he hoped to succeed in the end. Ellie was an incredibly sensual woman. God help him, he wanted to spend the rest of his life making love to her.

He went to the connecting door and quietly turned the handle. And if she was already asleep in her bed? So much the better. Then there would be no need for talking at all.

Ellie made another aimless circuit of her shadowed bedchamber. The air was chilly despite the fire burning on the hearth, and she wore a sapphire-blue shawl over her white lawn nightdress. Her feet were bare on the plush carpet, but she scarcely noticed the cold. She was too caught up in her own thoughts.

There had been no sound from next door all evening. Damien was away at his club and wouldn't return home until late into the night. She had discerned his habits by asking casual questions of her maid about the household schedule. Like clockwork, she'd learned, he went out in the morning each day, returning home in late afternoon to take tea with his daughter in the nursery; then he left again for his club, staying out until the wee hours.

The ormolu clock on the mantel quietly dinged the hour of ten. Ellie had resolved to stay awake until her husband came home. But now the endless evening stretched out, and she was feeling bored and drowsy. She had given up on sketching a while ago, unable to keep her distracted mind on her work. If she sat in her bed to read by candlelight, she feared to nod off to sleep and not awaken until morning.

Glancing at the darkened dressing room, she smothered a yawn. Did she dare to venture into Damien's chambers? Perhaps she should slip into *his* bed to await his return. Yes! That was the perfect solution. Then it wouldn't matter if she dozed off. He would find her snuggled beneath his covers at whatever time he came home.

And that was the whole point, anyway. To be with him in bed. To let him know that she regretted all that coldhearted nonsense about not allowing him the rights of a husband. To tell him there was no reason for them *not* to enjoy the benefits of marriage during the few weeks that she would be here.

And then he would draw her into his arms and do all those wonderful things to her again. He would kiss her and caress her and press himself inside of her. The very thought of it caused a ripple of excitement to flow through her body.

Ellie picked up the candlestick from the bedside table. Cupping her hand around the tiny flame, she started toward her dressing room and the connecting door that led to his bedchamber. She was almost there when she discerned a movement in the black rectangle of the doorway.

Her heart jumped. Her breath caught in a startled gasp. In the next instant, the tall figure of a man stepped into her bedchamber.

Her hand went to her bosom to clutch at the folds of her shawl. "Damien! Why are you here? Why aren't you still at your club?"

She noticed at once that he had shed his coat and cravat. He wore only a loose white shirt and dark breeches. Like hers, his feet were bare. His proximity made her keenly aware of the intimate, shadowed bedchamber and her own state of undress.

Her pulse beat quickened. Was it possible that . . . he had come here in the hopes of charming her into bed?

"I returned home early so that we could have a private talk," he said smoothly. "I trust you won't mind if we do?"

Taking her by the arm, he led Ellie over to one of the chairs by the hearth and bade her sit. He plucked the candlestick from her nerveless fingers and placed it on the mantel. The fire hissed gently on the grate as he settled himself into the chair opposite hers.

His formal manner was daunting. He wouldn't have seated them apart if he'd had seduction on his mind. The sight of his austere features in the firelight brought back the memory of her dreadful gaffe. He must mean to rebuke her more thoroughly now that they were alone and he could speak freely.

Gripping the edges of her shawl, she leaned forward to convince him of her sincerity. "Damien, please know that I'm very sorry about what happened this afternoon. You're right, I should never have allowed Lily to call me mama. I don't know what came over me—"

"Lily came over you, that's what. She has a way of winding a person around her little finger." His mouth curled into a slight smile. "But never mind that. It isn't why I'm here."

"No?"

"No, although I will allow that the topic *is* related." His green-gray eyes took on a narrowed intensity. "When I first spied Lily sitting in that chair with you, I was angry. So angry that I didn't stop to consider something. You were reading to her from your storybook. Which means that you must have gone to Pennington House today to fetch the manuscript."

Ellie nodded cautiously. "You're right, I did. This morning I paid a call on my uncle and grandmother. I thought they should know straightaway that I was safe. And that you and I had been married."

He raised a stern eyebrow. "And did you never stop to think that *I* should have been with you? That perhaps you ought not to have faced them alone? That you might have asked *me* to accompany you?"

"You weren't at home," she countered. "And you'd expressed no desire to meet my family, anyway. Besides, I just wanted to get the interview over with and done."

She stared defiantly at him, and after a moment, his taut expression relaxed into a wry smile. "All right, I concede your point. I wasn't here, and there's nothing to be done about it now, anyway. So tell me about this visit. What did Pennington have to say?" Damien must have seen the hesitation in her face, for he added, "I want to know every last syllable. And that pertains to your grandmother, too. Don't leave anything out."

Ellie supposed he had a right to hear it all—or at least most of it—so she related her uncle's unwelcoming manner, his scorn of her marriage, and his belief that Damien had only wed her to further his ambitions. She said that the earl and her grandmother had both been shocked to learn that Lady Milford had traveled all the way to Scotland on Ellie's behalf. The only details she left out were the peculiar silent exchanges she'd noticed between her uncle and his mother. She had a suspicion that there had been conversations in private in which harsh, unfair criticisms had been leveled against her. It was dispiriting even to think about their biased opinion of her.

Damien watched her closely, a tight-lipped look on his face. "And Walt? Did you speak to him, too?"

"No, apparently he's left London. My uncle has banished him to the country for a time. He was furious to find out that Walt had been gambling at your club, that he'd incurred a debt to you."

"Indeed? One would think he'd be *more* furious that Walt had told lies about your character."

Warmed by Damien's heated defense of her, Ellie managed a wan smile. "Speaking of Walt, I asked the earl about the stolen key. But my uncle denies that it even exists. So my cousin must have lied to him about that, as well."

"Never mind. Walt will return to London eventually—perhaps sometime during the season. I'll confront him about it then."

"If I hadn't been so distressed by the interview, I should have thought to sneak into his bedchamber and search for the key right then and there. Perhaps I can return sometime and—"

"No," Damien said sharply. "You will do no such thing, Ellie. I forbid you to enter that house ever again without me at your side. You're my wife now, and I won't allow you to be subjected to any more of their deplorable insults."

His dictatorial manner ought to have irked her, but she found herself pleased instead. It felt good to have someone on her side for once. She confessed, "Grandmamma *did* say that it would have been a tragedy if Beatrice had been the one who was abducted and forced into marriage to a scoundrel. But she doesn't realize how happy I am to be gone from there, or that I'd been planning to leave, anyway."

He leaned forward, his elbows on his knees, his fierce gaze focused on her. "My God! I wish I could fathom how that woman can venerate one granddaughter while scorning the other. Especially you, Ellie. What could she not love about you?"

Ellie couldn't speak for a moment. Her throat felt too tangled with emotions . . . hope and longing . . . and apprehension, too. Did Damien really think so highly of her? Could *he* ever love her? Did she even *want* him to love her?

Restless, she jumped up from the chair and began to pace back and forth. "I suppose it all goes back to my father," she murmured. "As I told you, he was a gambler. My uncle and grandmother have always referred to Papa as the black sheep of the family. He couldn't keep himself away from the gaming tables. I was only a child at the time, but I remember him being gone for days at a time."

Damien sat watching her. "Where was your mother?"

"She died when I was six—Lily's age." Ellie pulled the shawl tighter around her shoulders. "I spent most of my time in the care of servants. I suppose that's when I developed a love of stories. No matter what happened, I could always escape into my own world of make-believe."

"Did you and your father ever live at Pennington House?"

She shook her head. "Oh, no, he wasn't welcome there—neither of us were. We moved from place to place, each one more ramshackle than the last. By then, Papa had turned to drink to drown his sorrows. One night, he stepped into a busy thoroughfare outside a Covent Garden theater and . . . a carriage ran him down. He died right there on the street." Shivering, she rubbed her arms and took a deep breath before continuing. "Since I was only fourteen, I was sent to live with my uncle. I was expected to help with my younger cousins in the nursery. I . . . always felt obliged to the earl for settling Papa's extensive debts."

As she walked past his chair, Damien caught hold of

her hand to bring her to a halt. "And Pennington never let you hear the end of it. Like father, like daughter. Is that what he led you to believe?"

"Yes. Grandmamma always said I had bad blood." Her chest tight, Ellie gazed down at their clasped hands. "But Papa wasn't a wicked man. He was very charming and he *did* love me. He often told me so. Whenever he came home, we would read books together, talk for hours, go out for long walks in the park. It's just that . . . he was weak. He could never give me the one thing I needed most. He couldn't stop destroying himself at the gaming tables."

Aghast when a tear rolled down her cheek, Ellie tugged at his grip to free herself. She had locked away those painful memories and it hurt to let them out. Now she just wanted to curl up in a ball and make the world go away.

Damien, however, grasped her waist with both of his hands. As he swung her down into his lap, the shawl slipped from her shoulders and fell onto the floor. But she wasn't cold anymore, not when he placed his arms around her and cradled her close to the heat of his body.

Ellie found herself leaning against him, the way his daughter had been nestled against *her* that afternoon. She rested her head on his shoulder and let herself absorb his warm strength, while she breathed in his clean, spicy scent. Perhaps she *was* like her father in a way; she was very weak-willed when it came to Damien.

He gently thumbed a tear from her cheek. "That's twice today that I've driven you to tears."

"No, it's just that . . . my spirits have been a bit low today after visiting my family. It isn't *your* fault."

"No?" He tilted up her chin so that she could see the ruefulness in his expression. "You're married to the owner of a gaming club. Perhaps you think I take advantage of men like your father. Or worse, that I'll be caught up in the madness of gambling and destroy myself, and Lily will end up orphaned like you were. You do fear that may happen, don't you?"

Ellie opened her mouth to deny it. But he was right. The dreadful prospect *had* lurked at the back of her mind. "Yes, I suppose so."

"Then it may help for you to know that I'm very scrupulous about the membership at my club. If a gentleman is unable to pay his debts, he isn't allowed to play at my tables. That is one of the house rules at Demon's Den. No man may come to ruin under my roof. As to my own predilections, I no longer gamble as deeply as I once did. Now, I play only as necessary to be sociable with the club members." He cupped her cheek in his hand. "Ellie, I want you to heed me well. I could never be tempted into losing my fortune on a roll of the dice or a turn of a card. It won't happen. That's a sickness in some men, but not in me."

He sounded so firm that Ellie was tempted to believe him. Yet her father had always made promises, too. "Well," she said lightly, "I don't suppose I can complain too much since I'm to benefit from the fruits of your success."

He gave her a speculative look. "Ah, yes, the cottage. I've been meaning to speak to you about that."

Ellie didn't want to think about leaving him. Not at present when she felt so deliciously warm and comfortable nestled in his lap. But she was the one who had alluded to the cottage. "Has your land agent begun looking for a place, then?"

"Not yet. First, I need to find out precisely where it is you wish to live. Hampshire? Cornwall? The Lake District? Be forewarned, finding the perfect house for you may take a month or even longer if he has to go far afield."

Damien had moved his hand to her back, and his fingers idly rubbed up and down over her nightdress, making it difficult for her to concentrate. She tried to fathom why none of those locations appealed to her. Out of the haze of her thoughts, an idea sprang into her mind, a prospect so risky that she feared he would reject it outright.

But she had to voice it. "I would rather stay close to London, I think. So that I might perhaps . . . come and visit Lily sometimes." Realizing that her future happiness was dependent upon his answer, she touched his cheek in supplication. "May I, Damien? I know how protective you are of her, but . . . would you ever allow me to do so?"

He was silent a moment, his expression inscrutable. But his eyes took on a certain gleam in the firelight. "I believe I could permit you under certain circumstances."

"What do you mean?"

"You would have to visit me, as well."

Just like that, the air between them became charged with sensuality. His fingers began to play with her unbound breasts through the thin fabric of her nightdress. As he stroked his thumb over her nipple, a rush of heat made her shiver. The pleasure of it was so intense that she sucked in a breath and closed her eyes, the better to savor the sensation.

He brought his mouth close to hers. "Have I made myself clear?"

"Very," she whispered. Her impulse was to accept his condition with alacrity. But was that wise? Did she wish to continue an intimate relationship with him even after she had moved out of his house? It would certainly increase the chances of her conceiving his child.

A baby. A sister or brother for Lily. The prospect filled Ellie with the softness of yearning. But having children would make it more difficult for them to live apart. Already, she could feel the silken bonds that tied them together. And she feared to become inextricably bound to a man who made his income from the pastime that had ruined her father's life.

"Are you agreeable, then?" Damien continued to lightly run his fingers over her breasts. "Your visits would include being with me, sharing my bed."

"Oh, Damien, I don't know if I can make such a promise," she said in a rush. "I'm sorry. I can only say that I . . . I *will* consider it."

His disappointment was revealed by a slight quirk of his lips, a brief lowering of his eyes. He brought his hand up to cup her neck while he pressed a kiss to her forehead. "Well. You did make your views on our marriage clear from the start."

Nonplussed, Ellie gazed at him, wishing that he had not ceased to be seductive. Heaven help her, she hadn't meant for him to take her words as an utter rejection. He had to understand that it was one thing to contemplate an interlude of a few blissful weeks together, and quite another to agree to continue their intimacy once she had established a new life for herself elsewhere.

"Please, you misunderstand me." Catching hold of his hand, she brought it back to her bosom, shaped it around her breast, and held it there. "Until I move out of this house, I *do* wish to be with you—as your wife. In fact, I was heading into your bedchamber tonight when you walked into mine. I thought you were gone, and I'd intended to slip into your bed and await your return."

His gaze sharpened on her. His mouth curled into a slow, rakish grin. "Oh? You might have said so from the start. I wouldn't have wasted all this time talking."

She laughed, and all the worry and fear and confusion vanished in an instant, leaving only the bliss of being free to satisfy her craving for him. Their mouths met in a long, deep, delicious kiss that felt so much more arousing than memory served. They had not made love since that last night at the castle, when she had naïvely believed that his initiation of her would be sufficient to sate her passions forever.

Would she always feel such an all-consuming desire for Damien? She wouldn't let herself think of the future just yet. There was only the here and now, the taste of his skin, the scent of his body, the strength of his muscles. He was all hers, and she loved the way his lips skimmed over her throat and breasts, while his hand delved beneath her nightdress to tease her in the most wickedly wonderful way. What a pleasure it was to enjoy each other without any constraints whatsoever.

After a timeless interlude of petting and kissing by the fire, they shed their scant clothing and lay down in her bed, their naked bodies entwined. Ellie indulged herself by touching the width of his shoulders, the sculpture of his back and chest, the thickness of his hair. And she loved being touched by Damien in return. He had a maddening skill for prolonging the act, for knowing exactly how to bring her to the brink without allowing her over the edge.

She enjoyed torturing him, too, reaching between them to stroke the hard length of his manhood until he groaned deeply, trembling with the effort to hold himself in control. Only when the fire in both of them burned at a fever pitch did he press her back against the pillows and slowly enter her. He gazed into her eyes, murmuring her name, making her feel beautiful and very, very desired.

It was truly a transcendent experience. Somehow, the act of lovemaking felt so much richer and deeper than ever before. She felt one with Damien, in perfect accord, body and soul. Then the irresistible pull of passion banished all coherent thought. Ellie surrendered to the urgent need building inside of her, lifting her hips to take him more fully inside herself, striving toward completion and the waves of ultimate bliss.

In the aftermath, as they lay cuddled together beneath the covers, the bedchamber dim from the dying fire, she had one last hazy thought before drifting into slumber. Tonight had been a consecration of their wedding vows. They were truly husband and wife now.

Chapter 25

In the days that followed, Ellie found herself fitting seamlessly into the fabric of the household. Damien was gone much of the time at his club, and she had the leisure to do as she wished. It seemed peculiar at first not to have every moment regimented by the demands of her cousin and grandmother. After all those years of servitude, she felt an almost guilty pleasure to be pursuing her own interests.

A large parcel arrived for her the next afternoon, and to her amazement, it contained art supplies, from paper to pens to watercolors, all of the finest quality. There was a note from Damien saying that Ellie was to order whatever else she deemed necessary and have the bill sent to him. She felt a clutch of her heart. Never in her life had anyone given her a more perfect, thoughtful gift.

Armed with her new equipment, she devoted a great deal of effort to the project of dividing her long fairy tale into a collection of shorter books. It took considerable thought to concoct plot twists and to find ways in which to create plausible endings to each section.

For hours, she would sit at the desk in her bedchamber or on the chaise longue by the windows and apply herself to the task of writing and illustrating the revised pages.

As much as Ellie loved her work, however, there were occasions during the course of each day when she needed a break. So she went exploring through every nook and cranny of Damien's house. She felt rather like an interloper, peeking into rooms and antechambers, going up and down the several staircases, wandering from one floor to the next, and marveling at the tranquil beauty of the décor.

This was her home. And yet it wasn't. How strange to think that she was the mistress of this fine mansion, albeit temporarily.

One of her favorite places was a large conservatory with a glass roof. Here, the air was moist and tropical with lush vegetation, and there were benches where she sometimes sat with her sketchpad. She also loved the library, a high-ceilinged chamber with groupings of chairs where one might sit in the hushed silence and read or draw. The shelves were half empty, though, and she wondered if Damien meant to fill them slowly over the coming years. How lovely it would be to visit bookstores with him, to make new selections and carry them home to unwrap . . .

Then Ellie would remember she wouldn't be here for much longer.

Sometimes she would venture belowstairs. She had discovered that Mrs. MacNab was Damien's cook. Perhaps it wasn't quite dignified for her elevated station, but Ellie enjoyed sitting at the long table in the kitchen, chatting with the woman about household gossip or menus. On a number of occasions, she'd had to stop herself from reminiscing about certain incidents at the island castle. There were always other servants nearby, and no one on staff other than Finn and his wife knew that the master had abducted Ellie.

Strange, how she could feel such wistful nostalgia about that interlude at the castle, when the raging winter storm had trapped her in the company of the Demon Prince. She remembered how gruff Damien had been at first, how his manner had gradually thawed, how he had carried her up to her tower bedchamber when she'd sprained her ankle, how he had brandished the fireplace poker as a sword while posing as Prince Ratworth. And she remembered that first wild kiss on the parapet and their magical night together when she had coaxed him into her bed.

Damien needed no coaxing anymore. They slept together every night, although work often required him to stay late at his club. How she relished being awakened with kisses, feeling the warmth of his body beside her in bed. And always there was the intense pleasure of his lovemaking, the intimate touches, the sense of being one with him. When she allowed herself to consider it, Ellie feared a strengthening of the silken bonds that tied them together. But she had resolved to savor each moment of this interlude and not fret about the future.

Each afternoon, her heart leaped when he came into her bedchamber to give her a lingering kiss before they went upstairs to take tea with Lily in the nursery. On Sundays, they would attend church and then take a walk in Hyde Park so that Lily could look for ducklings to feed. While the girl skipped ahead of them on the path, they strolled arm in arm and talked about many topics, from the progress of her book to household matters to Lily's schooling—but never Ellie's departure.

Ellie didn't want to spoil their easy camaraderie by

inquiring about the cottage. Damien had said that the task of finding the perfect place might take a while, and surely he would tell her when he had news of a good prospect. In the interim, she let herself drift along in a glow of happiness, never looking further ahead than the next scene in her book.

One day, she had an unexpected caller. Summoned to a sunny yellow sitting room, she found Lady Anne perched nervously on a chair. The earl's sister-in-law wore a nondescript gray gown that turned her eyes more gray than blue, and a lace spinster's cap that covered her silvering dark hair. A shy smile lit her delicate features.

Ellie gave her a warm hug. "Does my uncle know you're here?"

"Heavens, no! He said we are to cut off all ties. But . . . my dear girl, I could not rest easy without assuring myself of your happiness."

Ellie was touched to the depths of her heart. Lady Anne had been the only one in the Pennington household who had ever shown her kindness. Not wanting the woman to worry, Ellie portrayed herself as perfectly serene in her marriage, with Lily a lovely stepdaughter and Damien a kind husband.

"Might I . . . meet him?" Lady Anne asked rather hopefully.

"Oh, my lady, I'm sorry, he's away at his club. Perhaps . . ."

Ellie stopped herself before inviting Lady Anne to dinner one evening. How could she make future plans when she didn't know the timing of her exodus from London? And anyway, it seemed unfair to encourage more family visits when she would be gone soon. As she hugged the woman good-bye, she felt the wrenching pain of knowing they would likely never again meet.

Ellie didn't know how she would bear saying farewell to Lily and Damien. Perhaps it was best not to let herself even think of it . . .

The following day brought matters to a head. Ellie awakened with a familiar low ache in her back. And she soon discovered that her monthly courses had commenced.

The realization left her feeling somehow bereft. She'd last had her monthlies onboard the ship after they'd left the island castle to return to London. That meant that four weeks had passed since her arrival here at this house. It seemed impossible that the time had flown by so swiftly.

Glancing out her bedroom window, she saw that the yellow daffodils and red tulips were in full bloom. She had meant to be gone by now. A haze of green covered the trees and the earthen beds between the pathways. Spring had arrived, and the garden was full of new life.

Yet she was not.

Was that the source of her sudden bout of melancholy? Had she secretly yearned to conceive Damien's child? Common sense told her it was best that she hadn't. A baby would only bind her to Damien, making their parting all the more difficult. They had not wed with the intention of staying together. And as fulfilling as their time together had been, he had never spoken of love. For a brief idyllic interval, she had let herself forget that they both had been forced by circumstances into a marriage that neither of them had wanted.

All day, Ellie mulled over those troubling thoughts while she tried to concentrate on her sketching. At the edge of her mind lurked an awareness that she had dallied here with him long enough. The honeymoon had to come to an end sometime . . .

In late afternoon, Damien strolled into her bedchamber to find her sitting on the window seat, gazing outside, the sketchbook lying forgotten in her lap. She turned her face up for his kiss as had become their custom every day. The brush of his lips filled her with bittersweet longing and she arose quickly, giving him a wan smile and avoiding his eyes.

He slipped his arm around her waist, his gaze questioning. "You look pale, Ellie. Is there something amiss?"

"No . . . yes. I don't feel well today, that's all."

"I'm sorry. Are you ill, then? Perhaps you ought to be in bed."

Ellie didn't want to see that look of solicitous concern on his face. Nor did she wish to feel this weak-willed urge to bury her face against the folds of his cravat, to seek comfort in his warm embrace.

"I'm not *ill*. It's perfectly natural." Despite their intimacy, she felt herself blush to explain, "It's . . . my monthly time, that's all."

His expression cleared. "Ah. Then you must stay here and rest. Lily won't miss you this once. Well, she *will* miss you, but I'll find a way to keep her entertained." Catching hold of her arm, he walked Ellie toward the bed and drew back the covers. "I'll have Mrs. Tomkins send up a hot water bottle to help with any pains you might be suffering. In a day or two, you'll feel much better, I'm sure."

His masterful management of the situation grated on Ellie. She resented being handled like a business problem at his club. Especially when an unresolved issue weighed heavily on her mind—as it should on his, too.

Stepping away from him, she crossed her arms. The thoughts and emotions churning inside her came out in a rush. "I won't lie down, I'm not an invalid. And I should like to know the status of my cottage, for it is an excellent time for me to leave here!"

The faint ticking of the mantel clock filled the silence. He gave her that inscrutable stare. "Because you are not with child, you mean."

"Yes. You must allow, this would be the ideal circumstance for my departure. So what is being done? Have you found any prospects?"

He glanced away for a moment. Then he stepped closer and his green-gray eyes burned into hers. "Ellie," he said urgently, gripping her hands. "Why move away at all? Stay right here with me—with Lily. She loves you, she regards you as her mother. And you've all the supplies you need to illustrate your books, do you not? I've ordered the servants to leave you be so that you may work in peace. Surely there is nothing that you could gain from a cottage that you can't find right here with us."

His invitation shook her to the core. It was so very tempting to contemplate staying here with him forever. But he had only spoken of Lily's need for a mother. What of *his* love? Or was he too much the scoundrel ever to give his heart?

Ellie realized in that moment the truth she had been avoiding. She was madly, passionately, head-over-heels in love with the Demon Prince. Perhaps she had been for a long time, since even before they had left the castle. Yet he was a gambler, a rogue, a flirt. They had married for all the wrong reasons. And if she was merely a convenience to him, as a mother to his daughter and as a readily available lover, then eventually he would tire of Ellie and stray to other women.

He would disillusion her as her father had done.

She withdrew her hands from his. "There is my independence to be gained," she forced out. "You *know* that I've always desired to live on my own, Damien. We made an agreement in that regard. So where is my cottage?"

Again, he averted his gaze for a moment. "There have been several possibilities that I've rejected as inappropriate. It will likely take a few weeks longer."

A horrified thought struck Ellie. She didn't want to believe it. "Are you *lying* to me? Have you even assigned your land agent to the task?"

"Yes. I swear I did. But . . ."

"But what?"

Damien combed his fingers through his hair, mussing the black strands. His mouth formed a sheepish half-smile. "He's been working on some other projects for me, and I . . . told him that your cottage was not a particularly urgent matter. I'm sorry. I can see now that it is, so I'll meet with him tomorrow. I'll make it his top priority. You have my word on that."

Every part of her body felt rigid. She'd been right to fear his betrayal. Already, he had let her down when she'd been counting on him. Tears stung her eyes, and she whirled around to face the windows. "How can I trust your word, Damien? I can't believe your promises anymore."

"Ellie . . ."

Sensing his close presence behind her and fearing that he might touch her, she snapped, "Go! Get out. You'll be late to tea with Lily."

She stood there stiffly, hugging her aching middle, until the sound of his footsteps disappeared out the door. Only then did she do what she hadn't done since the death of her father. She curled up on her bed and wept copiously into her pillow.

By the next afternoon, Ellie was feeling clearheaded again and, after much thought, had settled upon a plan to force Damien's hand.

For that purpose, she had ordered the carriage and now she followed a white-wigged footman up the elegant staircase of a town house. To bolster her spirits, she had donned a fine gown of marine-blue silk and a dark gold pelisse. In her hands, she carried a blue velvet bag, which was the superficial excuse for her visit today to Lady Milford.

Although Ellie wasn't feeling at all cheerful, she *was* resolved, and besides, there was only so much wallowing in misery that a person could do. She had resigned herself to the cold, hard truth. Damien had come to view their marriage as quite comfortable—presumably on the day when he had witnessed Lily's instant devotion to her new mama, and then later that evening, when Ellie had invited him into her bed. Why *should* he be in any rush to secure a cottage for her? From his perspective, he had acquired a mother for his child and a convenient lover as a bonus. So why not simply delay until he had her so charmed by her new life that she forgot all about leaving him?

It was a dishonest, diabolical scheme, and . . . perhaps if he had done it out of desperate love for her, she might have forgiven him. But he had not. He had merely used her for his own purposes. And now she didn't dare trust him to honor their agreement. For that reason, Ellie had decided that she needed leverage to push him into acquiring the cottage. That leverage would be information about his mysterious past.

The footman stopped just inside a doorway and announced her.

As he bowed and went out, Ellie entered a sitting room decorated in pleasing shades of pastel yellow and rose. It was the same room where she had come with Beatrice all those weeks ago, on the day that Ellie had first spied Damien bundled in his black coat and hat, watching her cousin from his phaeton outside on the street.

Lady Milford was seated at a dainty desk in the corner of the sitting room, and she put down her quill and rose to her feet. An elegant gown of amethyst silk complemented her fine features and upswept black hair. As she glided forward, there was an ageless quality about her, as well as a lovely feline grace.

Curtsying, Ellie hid a smile. Little did the woman know, she had been the inspiration for the Furry Godmother, a sleek and beautiful cat in Ellie's storybook. Ellie had been working on an illustration of the character that very morning when the inspiration to come here had struck her. If anyone in society would know the answers to Ellie's questions, this woman would.

Lady Milford greeted her with a smile. "Ellie, my dear! You don't mind if I call you that, do you? It does seem that we are old friends now. May I say, I'm so very glad that you've come to call. We've much catching up to do."

They sat together on a chaise by the fire, and in response to Lady Milford's polite queries, Ellie made a dogged effort to avert any suspicion of her difficulties with Damien by dwelling upon the beauty of his house and her happiness at being a mother to his daughter. If Lady Milford gave her a searching stare, at least she was too well bred to ask any probing questions. Instead, she relayed that the nasty gossip about the abduction had been successfully eradicated. With the season now in full swing, everyone accepted that Ellie had eloped with Damien because her uncle had disapproved of the match. The Earl of Pennington had confirmed the story to any naysayers in order to protect his daughter from the taint of scandal. And Lady Beatrice herself had benefited by acquiring a whole string of eligible suitors.

Ellie managed a smile. "I'm pleased to hear that my cousin is so popular with the gentlemen. She must be keeping her new chaperone quite busy at all those balls and parties. Oh, and since I am no longer required to attend her in society, I shan't be needing these." She handed over the blue velvet bag containing the garnet dancing slippers. "I do hope you're not offended to have them returned, but I . . . I had a notion that you might perhaps wish to give them to someone else."

It had been the oddest thing, Ellie recalled. When she had gone into her dressing room just before departing, the sparkly garnet shoes had been sitting on top of her clothes press, as if the maid had placed them there and then forgotten to put them away again. And Ellie had felt an inexplicable compulsion to bring them here.

Lady Milford's lips curved in a mysterious smile. "I'm not offended in the least. Indeed, I shall pass them on to another deserving lady very soon, I'm sure. Now, I sense that there is something else troubling you. Might I ask what it is?"

Ellie realized this was her opening. "Yes, my lady. It has to do with my husband being called the Demon Prince. I've learned that he came by the name not so much for being a rogue and a gambler, but because of something peculiar from his childhood."

She gave a quick summary of what Damien had told her, that he had no knowledge of his parents and had been raised by a gentlewoman named Mrs. Mims, who had spun bedtime stories about him being a prince. When he had been admitted to Eton on scholarship, he had made the mistake of blurting out his royal heritage to Walt, who had promptly dubbed him the Demon Prince.

"Damien no longer credits the story told to him by

his guardian," Ellie said. "He believes Mrs. Mims was only trying to encourage him to behave by giving him an heroic figure to emulate. But I'm not so certain." She took a breath for courage. "My lady, pray pardon my frankness, but I've heard rumors that you were once mistress to one of Mad King George's sons. You must have been in the inner circles of royalty at one time. Have *you* ever heard that one of the princes sired a baseborn son and then arranged for the baby to be fostered?"

During Ellie's speech, Lady Milford's fine features had taken on a guarded quality. It was evident in the slight thinning of her lips and the hint of a frown in her brow. Those lovely violet eyes regarded Ellie with a trace of hauteur. "If Damien Burke was related to our royal family, I would indeed know. But he is not. I can, without question, assure you of that."

"But someone must have paid for his schooling at Eton. Being without any family connections to recommend him, how was he even granted admittance to such an exclusive school? My lady, I am convinced that a very influential benefactor pulled strings on his behalf."

"My dear, I truly wish that I could be of assistance to you in this matter. But there is nothing more to tell. If ever I should hear anything to the contrary, I shall be sure to contact you."

Lady Milford spoke with such finality that Ellie realized to her disappointment there was no more information to be had here. But the woman knew *something*. That strong suspicion nagged at Ellie.

As she took her leave and went back downstairs, her mind dwelled on the nebulous theory that had brought her here in the first place. Lady Milford had carried on a love affair with a prince many years ago. Could Damien's mother possibly be Lady Milford herself?

Wouldn't *that* better explain why she had come all

the way to Scotland to see about the marriage? It hadn't been to safeguard Ellie's reputation, but rather, Damien's. And he had mentioned that Lady Milford had attempted to interfere in his life another time, when he had been pursuing his first wife . . .

Ellie needed to prove her hunch. But now the stolen key was the only clue to Damien's past. And if ever she was to have the necessary leverage to force his hand, she must go straight to Pennington House and search for that key.

Chapter 26

Damien was riding his chestnut mare past Hyde Park Corner when he spied a familiar face in the crowd.

It was late afternoon on a gorgeous spring day, and a crush of vehicles and horses proceeded through the wide gate for a drive along Rotten Row, the long sandy thoroughfare through the park where the ton went to see and be seen. Damien, however, had just left his club after a hard day's work and was heading home for tea with Lily. Consequently, he skirted the edge of the throng, guiding the mare along Knightsbridge Road, his mind preoccupied with thoughts of Ellie and their quarrel.

A sudden commotion in the stream of carriages drew his attention. He glanced over to see a stray dog run barking across the pathway, in hot pursuit of a gray cat. Horses stomped their hooves, coachmen reined in their teams, and ladies squealed in alarm. The disturbance was over in a moment with no harm done. But it called Damien's attention to a gentleman astride a large bay horse.

Walt Stratham, Viscount Greaves.

Nattily clad in a forest-green coat and tan breeches,

Walt was riding alongside an open landau, in which his family sat. There was the Earl of Pennington in a black top hat and dark blue coat, the earl's stout mother squashed into a gown of a putrid olive green, and Lady Beatrice, the classic debutante in pale blue with a broad-brimmed straw bonnet. A frail-looking older woman in dove-gray also sat with them. Damien presumed her to be Lady Anne, the earl's sister-in-law, who, according to Ellie, had been the only family member who'd been kind to her.

No one in the party noticed Damien. The landau, driven by a coachman in livery, was caught in traffic as it proceeded slowly toward the gate. Likely, they were heading back toward Hanover Square after completing a circuit of the park.

Damien thinned his lips. Walt's banishment to the country had lasted no more than a month. After the vile lies he'd told about Ellie, the bounder deserved to be sent into exile for the remainder of his sorry life. How satisfying it would be to confront Walt, to yank him off his horse and knock out a few of his teeth.

But Ellie wouldn't appreciate Damien creating a dustup in full view of the ton. People would clamor with questions about the source of the dispute. The titillating scandal of their marriage would rekindle. Once again, she would be an object of vicious gossip.

And he was already in dire straits with her.

Reluctantly, he turned his mount homeward, deciding there would be an opportunity in the coming days to confront his nemesis. He needed to formulate a new strategy to retrieve that key. Besides, he felt a desperate need to see Ellie again.

He had not spoken to her since their quarrel the previous afternoon. During the night, lying alone in his bed, he had been sorely tempted to visit her chambers.

How swiftly he had grown accustomed to holding his wife, to sleeping beside her, their bodies melded together.

But his campaign to win her heart had failed miserably. He had tried to give her everything she wanted, ample time to work on her book, all the necessary art supplies, a staff of servants to perform the mundane tasks of everyday life so that she would be free to do as she pleased. And he had kept her enthralled in bed each night, too. Yet still she had clung tenaciously to her plan for their separation.

I should like to know the status of my cottage, for it is an excellent time for me to leave here!

He could still feel those words like the twist of a knife in his gut. It had been a great disappointment to learn that they had not conceived a child together. But even worse had been seeing the horror on her face when she'd realized that he'd been dragging his heels on the cottage.

How can I trust your word, Damien? I can't believe your promises anymore.

His throat tight, he turned the chestnut mare down the street leading toward his house. He wanted to tell Ellie that he would make it all up to her—not that she would have the slightest confidence in him. He would have to prove it to her. His first act that morning had been to instruct his land agent to immediately secure a suitable cottage close to London. If an occasional visit was all that Damien could hope for, then he would take whatever crumbs she was willing to give him.

Perhaps, too, it was time for him to give voice to his love for her. He had been a coward, afraid to admit aloud that he had placed his heart into her keeping. The demons of his past had caused him to fear exposing himself to pain. Yet she had rejected him regardless, so what good had reticence gained him?

Nearing the mews that led to the stables behind his house, he was startled to see his carriage approaching from the north side of the park. Was Ellie inside? She must be. There was no one else in the household with the authority to take the carriage. On the rare occasions when Miss Applegate took Lily out to the shops or to the park, the governess always requested his permission in advance.

Peering at the windows, he hailed the coachman. The stout fellow drew the team to a halt and tipped his hat. "Afternoon, sir."

The carriage appeared empty, and Damien glowered at the man. "Have you taken Mrs. Burke somewhere?"

"Aye, she bade me leave her in Hanover Square and return in two hours' time."

Hanover Square? Ellie could only be going to her uncle's house. Why? Was she so distraught that she intended to throw herself on Pennington's mercy? Did she really despise Damien so much that she couldn't bear to spend another night under his roof?

The grim thought sent him into a panic. He reminded himself that she likely hadn't yet had a chance to speak to her family. They had been out on a drive in the park. In the slow landau and with all the traffic, they might not have reached home by now.

Gazing at him, the coachman looked somewhat alarmed. "I hope I ain't done wrong, sir."

Damien collected his wits. "No, of course not. But pray send word to the nursery that I won't be taking tea today."

He snapped the reins and the chestnut set off at a smart trot. Blast Ellie's independence. He would go to Pennington House, talk sense into her, stop her rash plan to live there again. But more than that, by God, he didn't want her to face that nest of vipers alone.

* * *

Ellie had no trouble gaining entry to Pennington House.

Fortuitously, the family had gone out on a drive to Hyde Park. Joseph, the young footman, had regarded her warily at first, clearly fearing she might demand to wait for her uncle when she'd been barred from the house. He had looked relieved when she'd claimed to have forgotten a few of her belongings in the nursery, and that she would let herself out once she'd collected them.

But instead of going to her old quarters, Ellie proceeded up to Walt's suite of rooms on the second floor.

She cautiously opened the door, stepped inside, and then closed it behind her. To her surprise, the draperies were open to the late afternoon light. With Walt banished to the country, the curtains ought to have been drawn shut. Perhaps a maid had come in here today to dust and had forgotten to close them.

Having never before had occasion to enter the bedchamber of her eldest cousin, Ellie took a moment to orient herself. The large room held a mahogany four-poster bed, various tables and chairs, and a chaise covered in green chintz in front of the fireplace. Despite the sunshine, the maroon walls and dark oriental carpet created an oppressive air.

Or perhaps that was merely her own disconsolate mood. The dreadful quarrel with Damien lurked at the edge of her mind. If she let herself remember it, she might end up weeping again.

Concentrate, she told herself. Where would Walt hide a key?

She went to his writing desk, opening the drawers to find stationery and quills, sealing wax and inkpots, a penknife and a packet of fine sand. Reaching all the way back into each drawer, she came up with nothing but a length of string and a few loose pins. Crouching down, she felt around on the underside of the desk for a hidden compartment. There, to her surprise, she found a key tucked on a tiny shelf.

In triumph, she brought it out, only to realize that it looked nothing like Damien's key with the crown and three teeth. This one was plain, and it fit perfectly into the keyhole in the top drawer of the desk.

Discouraged, Ellie stood up and dusted off her hands. Might Walt have a safe or a strongbox somewhere? She peeked behind each one of the numerous pictures of hunting scenes, but found nothing. Next, she poked futilely through a collection of miscellany in his bedside table.

Hoping to improve her luck, she ventured through an open doorway and into his dressing room. Here, light streamed through a high window onto a masculine preserve of boot racks and clothespresses, a shaving stand with a white porcelain bowl, and gilt-framed paintings of horses on the walls. The air smelled faintly of her cousin's cologne, raising a prickle over her skin. He wasn't in London, Ellie reminded herself, yet she couldn't shake a nagging uneasiness as she rifled through a tall mahogany chest of drawers.

She felt like a thief—or worse, a voyeur. With a sense of revulsion, she touched the articles that her cousin had worn: the kid gloves, the starched linen cravats, the smallclothes and nightshirts, looking underneath those items for the key. It was surprising that he'd left so much behind while on a long sojourn in the country.

While searching in a drawer full of silk stockings, she was startled by the click of the bedroom door opening. Ellie froze, her heart pounding. It must be a servant. How could she explain her presence?

Heavy footsteps approached. In a panic, she quietly

tried to shove the drawer shut, but it stuck at one end. She gave up and jumped to her feet, looking for somewhere to hide. Too late.

A ginger-haired gentleman in riding clothes entered the dressing room. He was looking down while unbuttoning his green coat.

Ellie gasped in recognition. "Walt!"

Jerking up his head, her cousin gaped at her in slack-jawed shock. "You! What the devil are *you* doing here?"

Ellie thought fast. Perhaps she could salvage something from this utter disaster. "I believed you were gone. And I came to see if I could find that key you stole from my husband."

"Your husband, eh? A pity you were compelled to marry the bastard. I see he's sent you to do his dirty work."

"He most certainly did not! Damien doesn't even know I'm here."

A predatory smile spread slowly over Walt's face. He took a menacing step closer. "Indeed? Then we are quite alone here."

Ellie's heart jumped. She couldn't forget that one awful night in the nursery when he had crudely pawed her bosom.

Nevertheless, she held her chin high. He didn't dare harm her, not in daytime when there were servants within earshot. "You don't frighten me, Walt. I want that key. Tell me where you've hidden it."

His mouth twisted into a crafty leer. "Do you really wish to know, dear cuz? Then first, you shall have to make it worth my while."

As quick as a striking cobra, he lunged toward her.

Without invitation, Damien strode past the footman who answered the door and stepped into a dreary entrance hall with mustard-brown walls. "I've come to see Mrs. Burke."

"Sir? If you would be so kind as to give me your name—"

"I am Mr. Burke. The earl's niece is my wife. You will show me to her at once."

The young servant eyed him warily, no doubt having heard hair-raising tales of the Demon Prince. "I—I'm afraid she isn't here." Subjected to Damien's coldest stare, he amended, "Er . . . rather, she *was* here. To fetch an item from the nursery perhaps half an hour ago. She promised to let herself out."

Odd, Damien thought. Perhaps, knowing she wasn't welcome, Ellie had hidden herself there to await the return of her uncle. "Did you actually see her depart?"

"N-no, sir. But I'm sure—"

"Then you may show me the way up to the nursery." Seeing the footman about to raise a protest, Damien added, "Or perhaps you would rather I wander about the house at will. On my own."

The footman's face turned chalky beneath his white wig. Apparently realizing the validity of the threat, he stuttered, "As—as you wish, sir. If—if you'll come with me, then."

He led the way up a wide marble staircase. Damien followed close behind, his mind focused on what he would say to Ellie. How could he convince her not to leave him? It was daunting to think that she despised him so much that she would prefer to return to the house where she had been treated as an unpaid servant.

At least there was one bright note. He'd ridden fast and arrived before her family. It was possible they'd made a stop on the way home. That gave Damien the chance that he needed to beg her to reconsider . . .

But as they reached the next floor, the front door

opened in the hall below. Glancing down the stairs, he saw Lady Beatrice and her grandmother sweep inside, followed by Lady Anne and then Ellie's uncle.

Removing his top hat, the Earl of Pennington looked up and spied Damien on the upper landing. There was a moment of utter silence as the two men stared at each other. Then his lordship's broad features flushed red with displeasure. "You!" he said, stomping toward the staircase. "What the devil are you doing in my house?"

Damien clenched his teeth. Dammit, another few minutes and he'd have had his opportunity to speak to Ellie alone. Now he would be forced to placate her uncle first.

But fate intervened.

A muffled scream make Damien pivot sharply, his blood turning to ice. The sound had emanated from somewhere on an upper floor. Ellie? He took off up the stairs at a run.

Ellie shoved hard at her cousin's chest. His arms were like snakes, coiling around her as he attempted to press a loathsome kiss to her lips. He had her trapped against a wardrobe, the knob digging into her back. She couldn't even move her hands high enough to scratch his face.

"Don't deny me any longer," he said, his lips slobbering over her cheek. "You've lifted your skirts for that lowborn bastard. Now you can share a little taste with me, too."

As he attempted to grope her breasts, Ellie opened her mouth and screamed loudly. At the same time, she stomped her heel down hard on his instep, and Walt yelped in pain. But his riding boots must have provided some protection, for he didn't release his cruel hold. His face screwed up in a grimace, he clamped his sweaty hand over her mouth and nose to cut off her air. "Hush, you little tart."

Ellie struggled to breathe. Twisting and fighting, she couldn't wrest herself free of his vile touch. She tried to scream again, but only muffled sounds emerged. Black spots began to swim before her eyes.

Walt rubbed his loins against her. "D'you like it rough, then? Be happy to give it to you. And don't think to tattle to the earl. He'll never take your word over mine—"

"But *I* shall," a deep voice said from behind Walt.

It happened in the blink of an eye. One instant, his hot breath seared her cheek, and the next, he was yanked away from her. Gasping, Ellie sagged against the wardrobe, trying to draw air into her starved lungs. In a haze of shock, she saw who had come to her rescue.

Damien?

He spun her cousin around and, in a flash of movement, landed his fist to Walt's jaw. The sickening smack of flesh on flesh resounded in the dressing room. Walt staggered backward against the washstand. The porcelain bowl tipped and crashed to the floor. His hands came up ineffectually to ward off the next blow. Damien yanked Walt upright and hit him a second time. Blood began to pour from her cousin's nose.

"Enough!" roared the earl from the doorway.

Coming to her senses, Ellie rushed forward to step in between the two combatants. She caught hold of Damien's arm, knowing that a fight would only make matters worse. "Don't, oh, please, don't!"

The fury hardening Damien's face eased slightly as he looked at her. He caught her by the waist and pulled her close. His green-gray eyes scoured her face. "Are you all right?" he asked. "Did he harm you?"

"I'm fine, truly I am." She touched his reddened knuckles. "But . . . what brought *you* here?"

His jaw tightened. "Ellie, I had to come, I had to tell you that—"

"Only a bastard like you would have the effrontery to invade my home," the earl broke in furiously. He tossed a folded handkerchief to Walt, who tilted his head back and tried to stanch the flow of blood. "And to attack my son! I've a good mind to send for the police!"

"You wouldn't dare," Ellie said, wheeling toward the earl. "Because if you do, I will tell all of society how your son tried to force his unwanted attentions on me just now."

Walt made a muffled protest from behind the blood-stained handkerchief. "Ain't true, Papa. She's a thief! Caught her poking through my things." He pointed at the tall dresser. "See, the drawer there is standing open!"

Damien aimed a questioning frown from Walt to her. Ellie paid no mind to either of them. She folded her arms and coolly addressed her uncle. "I was looking for the key that Walt stole from my husband. It's high time that it was returned to its rightful owner."

"What key?" Beatrice asked from the doorway.

"Never mind, it's all drivel," her grandmother proclaimed from beside her. "Basil, shall I ring for a pair of footmen to toss both of these interlopers out on their ears?"

"An excellent notion, Mama," the earl said.

"And entirely unnecessary," Damien snapped. "I shall be quite happy to remove my wife from this den of vipers."

He placed his hand at the small of Ellie's spine and urged her toward the door of the dressing room. Beatrice, her blue eyes wide beneath a pretty straw bonnet, stepped back to let them out. So did the countess, along with Lady Anne, who hovered in the background like a slim gray wraith, fingering the cameo at her throat as she stared intently at Damien.

Ellie let herself be walked into Walt's bedchamber before she dug in her heels and came to a stop in the middle of the room. She glowered at her uncle. "We most certainly will *not* leave," she said firmly. "I will *not* be cast out until I have in my possession what I came here to fetch."

"Ellie," Damien said warningly, "you will leave this matter to me. It is no concern of yours."

"Oh?" She gave him scornful look. "You abducted me in order to retrieve that key. I would say that gives me a vested interest in it!"

"You're on a fool's mission," the earl said bluntly. "My son does not have this key in his possession anymore—nor has he since his school days. Tell them, Walter."

Walt, who had trailed them into the bedchamber, sank onto a chair and gingerly dabbed at his nose. "I don't have it, and that's God's truth!"

"There, you see?" Pennington said triumphantly. "You are wasting your time—and ours. There is no purloined key to be found here!"

Ellie looked from her uncle to her cousin and felt a sinking in the pit of her stomach. Perhaps they really *were* telling the truth. And even if they weren't, how was she ever to prove it? She had wanted leverage to force Damien to procure the cottage for her. But all of her efforts had been for naught.

"Come," Damien murmured, sliding his arm around her again. "You needn't suffer any more of their insults."

Ellie took one last look at the sneer on her uncle's florid face, the hauteur in her grandmother's manner. Beatrice watched with avid fascination, while Lady Anne appeared distraught almost to the point of tears, her hand over her mouth. Walt sat slumped on the chair, preoccupied with his injured nose.

Ellie nodded in acquiescence to Damien. She felt too dispirited even to voice a good-bye as they started toward the door.

"Wait," Lady Anne said in an agonized voice. "Oh, please do wait. Damien—Mr. Burke—*I* have your key."

Stunned, Ellie turned back to see Lady Anne gliding toward them, fingering her cameo on its delicate gold chain. Even as Ellie and Damien exchanged a startled glance, Pennington stepped swiftly toward his sister-in-law.

"What is this farcical tale?" he demanded. "You should not be here at all, Anne! You are poking your nose where it is not wanted!"

She faltered. "But I *do* have the key. I found it in your study."

Ellie stood riveted. Her *uncle* had had the key? Why?

The earl caught Lady Anne by the arm and began to tow her across the room. "Enough of these wild fancies. I've dozens of household keys in my drawers. You picked up one by mistake."

"But it's the one with the brass crown on it," Lady Anne said quietly. "I would know that key anywhere."

"Hush your mouth! And how dare you search my possessions. Such shameful ingratitude after all I have done for you!"

He was steering her toward the doorway when Damien stepped out to block their passage. "She's staying here."

The earl's face turned a mottled shade of red. "Bastard! Move out of my way at once!"

His eyes narrowing, Damien tightened his fingers into fists. For an instant, Ellie feared the two men would come to blows. Then a movement in the doorway caught her attention.

Lady Milford stood there, resplendent in amethyst silk, a stylish bonnet with ostrich feathers framing her fine features. She raised an eyebrow at the earl. "This charade has gone on long enough. You may have sworn me to secrecy long ago, Pennington, but it is past time for the truth to be told."

Chapter 27

Silence cloaked the sunlit bedchamber. Ellie tried to fathom how Lady Milford fit into the puzzle. *Was* she Damien's mother? But that could hardly have anything to do with Ellie's family. She felt as if she were trying to solve a puzzle while only viewing a few small pieces.

Beatrice was the first to speak. "Truth?" she asked in a perky voice. "Why, what truth is that, my lady?"

"It is ancient history and of no interest to you," her grandmother said. "Walt, you and your sister will leave this room at once."

Walt removed the handkerchief from his face long enough to say in an offended tone, "But it's *my* bedchamber."

"Papa, do tell Grandmamma to let me stay," Beatrice wheedled.

"Go," Pennington snapped. "Both of you. *Now.*"

Shooed by the countess in her olive-green gown, brother and sister trooped out of the bedchamber, Walt scowling and Beatrice pouting. Their grandmother shut the door. Displeasure on her wrinkled face, she pivoted toward Lady Milford. "You are meddling in our affairs again, Clarissa. Have you not done enough damage already?"

Lady Milford's eyebrow arched higher. "I daresay I should be thanked for sweeping up the damage done by your family!"

She stared imperiously until the countess harrumphed and went to plop her bulk into a chair by the door.

"I would like some answers," Damien said in a grim tone. "Starting with the key that Lady Anne apparently has in her possession."

All eyes turned to the slender woman in dove gray who stood beside the Earl of Pennington. Seeing Lady Anne tremble under all the attention, Ellie hastened forward and guided her to the green chintz chaise in front of the fireplace. "Come, my lady, there's nothing to fear. I shall sit right here beside you." She took the woman's cold hands in hers and gently rubbed them. "You said that you'd found the key. The one with the crown on it. Pray tell, how did you even know about it?"

"The earl sent me out of the room the last time Lady Milford was here, when you'd been abducted. But I—I heard them quarreling. They were speaking of—of the Demon Prince. And the key." She cast a distressed glance up at Damien, who stood frowning at her. "It was the first time that I realized . . . that I even *suspected* . . . and even so, I still wasn't quite *certain* . . ."

"Eavesdropping!" the earl muttered. "If I had known you would repay all my benevolence with such treachery—"

"It would behoove you to remain silent, Pennington," Lady Milford said, seating herself on the other side of Lady Anne. "This is not *your* story, though I will allow that you do figure into it."

"Will someone kindly tell me what is going on here?" Damien said in exasperation. He stood by the fireplace, his hands on his hips.

"It may be best if *I* relate the course of events," Lady Milford said. "Nearly thirty years ago, a young lady of sixteen was permitted by her indulgent older sister to attend a house party at which members of the royal family were present. The occasion was in honor of a visiting delegation of Russian diplomats. Among them was Prince Rupert, a cousin to the czar." Lady Milford glanced at Lady Anne, who had dropped her gaze to her lap. "Prince Rupert was a very handsome man of one-and-twenty and quite dashing to a girl still in the schoolroom. He swept her off her feet, and it was shortly after the delegation left England that she discovered she was in a delicate condition."

Lady Anne lifted her head. "Rupert loved me," she murmured, looking up at Damien. "He *did*."

Still holding the woman's hands, Ellie felt a tremor that shook the foundations of her world. She didn't want to believe what she was hearing. She *couldn't* believe it. She glanced up at Damien to see him standing stock-still, his expression taut, his gaze focused on Lady Anne.

"Love, bah," the earl snapped as he paced back and forth. "The prince was a bounder, that's what."

"We've no need of such commentary!" Lady Milford reprimanded before returning her attention to Damien. "When I discovered that Pennington had threatened to cast his own wife's sister out on the street, I placed Lady Anne into the care of a trusted friend, the widow of a vicar. And when Anne's son was born, the earl insisted the child be fostered under a false name, never to be seen or heard from again. Having no real authority in the matter, I could do nothing but entrust the boy to Mrs. Mims and pray for the best."

Granite-faced, Damien stared at Lady Anne. Yet still he said nothing. Ellie's heart went out to him. How utterly shocked he must be. She herself could hardly wrap her own mind around the revelation.

Lady Anne . . . Damien's *mother.* It just didn't seem possible.

"But you *did* continue to interfere, Clarissa," Ellie's grandmother said resentfully from her chair against the wall. "You arranged for the boy to be admitted to Eton. You should have left well enough alone!"

"What?" Damien snapped, his eyes shifting to Lady Milford. "*You* paid for my tuition? I was told it was charity."

She turned a kind smile up at him. "I stipulated to the provost that you were to believe so. You see, I could hardly allow a boy of high birth—indeed, *royal* birth—to be denied a proper education."

He fell silent again, his jaw tight, his gaze brooding.

Ellie was trying to fit all the pieces together, as much for his sake as her own. "Uncle Basil, did you *know* that Damien was at Eton? Did you *tell* Walt to steal that key from him?"

The earl gave a start of surprise. "No! I knew nothing about any blasted key until Walter brought it home. Didn't even know Anne's brat was at Eton until Walter told me there was a bastard there claiming to be a prince. When I found out his name, you can be sure that I confiscated the key at once!"

Lady Anne drew a shaky breath. "You never knew that I'd slipped the key into my baby's blanket, along with a letter."

As if seeing her for the first time, Ellie clutched the woman's slender fingers. She had always viewed Lady Anne as a dear aunt, even though they were not blood relations. To think that the tenderhearted woman had hidden such a secret all these years. And now, she had to relive the terrible memory of her newborn son being taken from her.

"Mrs. Mims told me there was a letter," Damien said in a clipped tone. "She'd promised to give it to me upon reaching my majority. Yet I never saw it." He swung toward the earl. "My guardian died shortly before you found out about the key. And all of her effects mysteriously vanished. Did *you* steal them?"

Pennington glared back at him. "The woman disobeyed my strict order not to speak of anything that you might use to trace your family and make demands on us someday. Naturally, when I learned that she'd blabbered about you being a prince, I had to see if she'd left any written proof as well. So, yes, I found the letter and I burned it."

"What did it say?" Damien demanded. "And what does it have to do with the key?"

"Anne wanted to present you with the deed to an old hunting box in Berkshire," Pennington said dismissively. "A ramshackle place on a small piece of acreage, nothing of significance."

"It was an inheritance from my grandfather," Lady Anne said, her voice vibrating with emotion. "And it was all I had to give to my son. But you're wrong to think the key fits that door."

Withdrawing her hands from Ellie's, Lady Anne reached up to the cameo on its gold chain around her neck. Opening the back, she plucked out a key and reverently cradled it in her palm.

"When I overheard Basil speaking of a key belonging to the Demon Prince," she went on, "I knew that I had to find it, to see if it was the same one. I searched for weeks. It was only three days ago that I discovered it tucked inside a box on a high shelf in the earl's study."

"Three days ago!" Ellie exclaimed. "That's when you came to call on me. You must have been hoping to catch a glimpse of your son."

"Yes." Lady Anne lifted her yearning gaze to Damien. "I had to be *certain*. And now I am, finally. He looks ever so much like Rupert—especially his beautiful eyes."

Damien took a step toward her. His expression intent, he said, "Where is this old roué now? Did you ever write to him about me?"

"I did, but . . . my letter was returned with a note from his secretary." She glanced away, biting her lip. "Rupert succumbed to a fever onboard ship. He died before ever reaching his home."

Damien prowled in front of the hearth. "So this knave was my sire? He seduced an underage girl. By God, I would like to have confronted him for abandoning you."

"But Rupert did *not* abandon me," she said earnestly. "He was returning to Russia to seek the blessing of his parents on our wedding. You see, before he left, we were married in secret."

"Bosh!" the earl broke in. "The marriage was invalid. I was your guardian and you did not have *my* permission."

"Perhaps I did not, Basil," Lady Anne said with uncustomary passion. "But Rupert *did* persuade the archbishop to issue a special license and a vicar *did* perform the ceremony. I secured our marriage papers at the hunting box. This key fits a small coffer hidden inside the chimneypiece there." She held out the key to Damien. "I wanted you to have proof that you are indeed the son of a prince."

Damien stood unmoving for a moment. Then he came slowly forward and took the key from her. He held it up to the light, and Ellie could see the crown stamped into one end, just as he'd described to her.

He gripped his fingers around it. "I'd always hoped the key would lead me to my parents," he said, gazing down in wonderment at his mother. "I dreamed about that for so long, it's difficult for me to believe it has actually happened."

Tears shimmered in her eyes. "Damien," she whispered. "I am so very sorry that I was not a mother to you. They took you away shortly after you were born. Not a day has gone by that I haven't thought of you, pondered where you might be, and what you were doing. I should have been there for you in your childhood. Can you ever forgive me?"

The harsh mask left his face and Damien graced her with a smile. Sinking to one knee, he drew her into his arms and held her close, his hand moving over her slender back. A sheen of tears lit his green-gray eyes before he closed them momentarily and kissed his mother's cheek. "There is nothing to forgive . . . Mother. You've done nothing wrong. The wrong was done *to* you."

Watching them, Ellie felt tears spring to her own eyes. All those years he'd been searching for his parents. He'd been so determined to retrieve the key that he'd even abducted her out of desperation. Now, at long last, he had solved the mystery of his past. And she could not imagine a more perfect mother for him than kind, gentle Lady Anne.

Lady Milford sat watching with a gratified smile. "Well! This reunion has been long overdue. I finally realized that, Pennington, when Damien's wife came to call on me today. I was coming here to tell you that I intended to break my vow to keep your dreadful secret."

"I hope you're satisfied," the earl said bitterly. "No doubt, he'll spread our family dirt hither and yon."

Sitting back on his heels, Damien looked at Pennington. "You hid my connection to this family because you feared I'd extort money from you. Well, I shall indeed demand my just due. I'm taking my mother away from here to live in *my* house." He kissed Lady Anne's hands. "*If* the arrangement is acceptable to you, Mother."

Her delicate features glowed. "Oh! Why, I would be honored—"

"This is intolerable!" declared the countess, rising from the chair. "Anne must stay here to chaperone Beatrice. How are we to find a replacement in the height of the season?"

Ellie had put up with her family's selfishness for many years. But they would *not* stand in the way of Damien's happiness. She surged to her feet to glare at her grandmother. "*Pay* someone," she said tartly. "For it appears you have finally run out of poor relations to misuse."

Chapter 28

Two days later, Damien drove Ellie and his mother in his open phaeton into the rolling green countryside of Berkshire. Birdsong blended with the clopping of the horses' hooves and the jingling of the harness. It was the perfect day for a drive. The air was balmy for April, and the breeze felt soft and fresh against Ellie's face. All around them, an artist's palette of spring flowers bloomed in the wooded valleys, beside the hedgerows, and along the edges of the fields.

Although Ellie tried to enjoy the ride, the memory of that quarrel still loomed like an insurmountable wall between her and Damien. She yearned to beg his forgiveness, yet she had been hesitant to intrude on his reunion with his mother. Even now they couldn't speak of the matter, though from time to time, his enigmatic gaze lingered on Ellie.

Lady Anne sat in between them. Her blue-gray eyes sparkled as she and Damien chatted freely, having nearly thirty years of catching up to do. Ellie was pleased to see that the shy woman had blossomed with the happy disclosure of her long-held secret. It was obvious how much Lady Anne adored her son and her granddaughter. Lily, in turn, had been ecstatic to discover she had a grandmamma.

Sitting with them at tea in the nursery the previous afternoon, watching them laugh and talk, Ellie had felt awash with yearning. Damien had his happy family at last, and she could think of no one more deserving than him. She wanted so badly to belong with them, too.

It was dismaying to realize that she had willingly cast herself out. Caught up in her own foolish fears of being hurt, she had clung to her dream of independence. But now Ellie knew that all she really wanted was to stay with the three people that she loved most in the world.

How had she ever imagined that living alone would be preferable?

"There is where you turn," Lady Anne said, pointing to the road ahead. "Between the two stone columns."

Damien guided the horses around the bend and down a narrow track. Thickets of beeches and oaks formed a cool tunnel surrounding the drive. As the carriage emerged into a clearing, a lovely stone house appeared on a slight rise, surrounded by a riot of wildflowers.

Ellie was transfixed by the sight. It was not at all what she had imagined a hunting box to look like. In her mind, she had pictured a rugged masculine lodge built of dark wood, perhaps with a deer head nailed above the door. Not this charming, two-story cottage with a thatched roof and a white-painted door.

Her husband drew the pair of grays to a halt, and the groom jumped down from the rear seat to hold the horses. Damien carefully lifted his mother down first, and then Ellie. The feel of his strong hands clasping her waist rendered Ellie quite breathless. How she longed to slide her arms around him, to lift her face for his kiss . . .

But he was already turning toward the spacious cottage, offering each woman an arm. As they proceeded up the walk, the door opened and Ellie was startled to see the MacNabs step out, Finn holding a paint brush and his wife drying her hands on the apron tied around her stout middle.

Sunshine gleamed on Finn's bald pate as he grinned at Damien. "'Tis spit-spot, just as ye ordered, laird."

Ellie and Lady Anne both looked questioningly at Damien. He patted his mother's hand. "I sent them ahead yesterday morning to clear away thirty years of dust and cobwebs."

They all proceeded into a sunny chamber with gleaming windows open to the spring breeze, and a faint smell of paint and beeswax, overlaid by the delicious aroma of Mrs. MacNab's scones. The servants vanished through a back doorway, presumably leading to the kitchen.

What a cozy room, Ellie thought, as she untied her bonnet and let it fall onto a writing desk by the door. She turned around slowly to view the sapphire-blue chairs by the fireplace, the glass-fronted cabinet of books, the table by the window where one could drink tea and gaze out over the valley. She had dreamed of a place just like this . . .

"The house looks exactly as it did all those years ago," Lady Anne marveled. "Rupert and I spent our wedding night here, you know." So saying, she went to the mortared mantelpiece and grasped a loose stone with her kid-gloved hands.

"Allow me," Damien said.

She stepped aside to let him wiggle the stone free. Reaching into the space behind it, he pulled out a small coffer enameled in jewel tones, which he brought to the table by the window. Then he found the crown-topped key in a pocket of his charcoal-gray coat. Fitting it into the keyhole, he opened the box.

"Rupert gave me this coffer as a wedding gift," Lady Anne said. Misty-eyed, she took out an old document, the penmanship spidery and somewhat faded. "There is his signature, Damien. Your father, Prince Rupert of St. Petersburg. Oh, I do wish you could have met him."

"I'm glad that he made you happy. True love is all too rare."

As he spoke, Damien's gaze flitted to Ellie, and her heart catapulted in her breast. It no longer mattered if he considered her merely a convenient wife. She loved him enough for both of them. More than anything, she wanted to be a permanent part of his life.

But that was assuming he would grant her another chance. What if it was already too late to repair the damage she had wrought with her cold rejection of him? The thought was so very daunting . . .

Lady Anne smiled at them. "Would you mind leaving me in here for a bit? I should like to look around by myself and remember."

With Damien at her side, Ellie walked back out into the sunshine. She was very conscious of his hand pressed warmly at the base of her back. Though wanting desperately to talk to him, she felt tongue-tied and anxious. The groom was tending the horses on the grass alongside the front drive, and Damien steered her away up a pathway on a slight rise through the trees. They walked in silence, surrounded by birdsong, until reaching a place overlooking the valley with its squares of farmland.

Ellie glanced back to see the stone cottage some distance behind them, like a lovely painting in a frame of green leaves. She released a sigh. "For so long I dreamed of a place like this. But—"

"It's yours," Damien broke in. He turned to her, his hands on her shoulders, his green-gray eyes intent on her face. "My mother has given it to me, and in turn, I'm giving it to you."

"Pardon?"

"When she described the place to me, Ellie, I knew it would be the perfect cottage for you. And it's close enough to London that perhaps you might come and visit us at times. Lily will miss you . . ."

She hardly dared to move. "And you, Damien? Will *you* miss me?"

The dappled shade played over his handsome features as he gently caressed her cheek. "I'll miss you every moment. I love you, Ellie. Abducting you by mistake was the best stroke of luck ever in my life."

He loved her? A thrill of joy induced her to take a step and close the small distance between them. "Oh, Damien, I—"

He placed his finger lightly over her lips. "I know I don't deserve your trust, darling, so let me prove myself to you. I'm selling my club. I've already found a buyer, and you have my word that I'll never again set foot in any gaming establishment."

He would do that just for her? Amazed, she moved his finger from her mouth. "But . . . I never meant to stop you from earning a living!"

"I have my fleet of ships, and I'll use the money from the sale to invest in property, as well. London is growing, and there's a demand for more homes to be built in the city." A smile quirked one corner of his mouth. "Perhaps in time you'll see that I've reformed my wicked ways."

She smiled giddily back at him. "Speaking of reformed scoundrels, have I told you that Prince Ratworth is now the hero of my storybook?"

"What? No." His grin deepened in the rakish manner that she adored. "But I always knew he would be."

"He has been under an enchantment, you see, and he needed to earn the true love of the princess in order to transform back into a handsome prince."

"And did he? Earn her love, I mean."

The hint of vulnerability on his face arrowed straight into Ellie's heart. She slipped her arms around his waist and gazed tenderly at him. "Oh, most assuredly. And I love you, too, Damien. You're *my* prince. Can you ever forgive me for wanting us to be separated—"

He stopped her words with his mouth, kissing her deeply and hungrily, his arms holding her as if never to let her go. She poured all of her love into returning his kiss, and when he finally drew back slightly, they were both dazed and breathless and happy.

He cupped her face in his hands. "Ellie, darling, I meant what I said. This place is yours. I know it's the key to your happiness."

She glanced back at the cozy stone house, then smiled up at him. "It *is* my dream cottage. But we'll come here together, my love. You see, now my dreams will always include you."